The Blesser and the Curse of Damascus

The Blesser, Volume 2

A.L. Schank

Published by A.L. Schank, 2024.

This is a work of fiction. Similarities to real people, places, or events are entirely coincidental.

THE BLESSER AND THE CURSE OF DAMASCUS

First edition. February 12, 2024.

Copyright © 2024 A.L. Schank.

ISBN: 979-8224531356

Written by A.L. Schank.

Table of Contents

Dedicated to my Lord and Savior

Nations of Lykos

Vaska:

Population 2.mil

Dire Saulder- platinum blond hair, silver eyes
Dire of Vaska.
Son of Zastar and Lore
Alias: The Dreaded Dire Saulder
Zastar- black hair, silver eyes
Ex-dire of Vaska
Husband of Lore. Father of Saulder and Sova
Lore- white hair, blue eyes
Ex-queen of Vaska. Seavallian
Wife to Zastar. Mother of Saulder and Sova
Sova- platinum blond hair, silver eyes
Prince of Vaska
Son of Zastar and Lore
Alias: The Royal Traitor
Casavore- brown hair, blue eyes
Blesser of Vaska. Eradusk Mind Melder
Husband to Fala. Father of Feran
Feran- brown hair, brown eyes
Mind Melder
Alias: The Dire's Damsel

The Mosharick Plains:

Population 500.k

Oland- bald, hazel eyes
Leader of the Blind Seers. Dormant Hyde Howler
Husband of Saphelle. Father of Roeseph
Alias: The Blind Hound
Roeseph- light brown hair, blue eyes
Blind Seer
Son of Oland
Alias: The Last Soldier

Elling- black hair, green eyes
Shepherdess
Daughter of Chemon and Sulia
Alias: The Feral Shepherd

Seavale

Population 100.k

Kyce- dark brown hair, amber eyes
Mysterious tavern fighter
Alias: The Eradite Exile

Eradawn:

Population 40.k

Lanton: silver hair, brown eyes
Elderly chief of Eradawn
Uncle of Vohwe
Vohwe: red haired, yellow eyes
Standing Eradawn Chief

Eradusk:

Population 35.k

Jerah- dark brown hair, amber eyes
Eradusk Royal
Brother of Willowreed

Prologue: Ten Years Ago

"*You can't do this!*" Casavore hissed, his voice blasting off the walls of the throne room. "Zastar would never stand for this!"

Queen Lore sat drumming her finely polished nails on the arm of her husband's throne, her blue eyes piercing the woman on trial. General Hylan stood before the platform with her head bowed, her wavy dark hair willowing a dark, stunning face tense with shame.

General Hylan was a soldier in every aspect; a decorated protector of Vaska exalted to the highest extent. Only, she'd failed her one task—protect the Dire of Vaska.

Now, after a month of Dire Zastar lying in his bed, more dead than alive, Zastar's queen, Lore, had taken it upon herself to deal out the general's punishment; a day she so eagerly awaited.

"This is madness, Lore!" Casavore snarled, clutching his medallion as he marched up the platform. "You have no right to do this!"

"On the contrary Blesser Casavore," Lore smiled, her finely trimmed brow drawn in an arch. "I have been given full authority by the dire to deal out this trial."

"Dire Zastar hasn't awakened since the Venom Tongue attack," Casavore snapped. "It's impossible for him to have granted you authority."

"Of course, he hasn't," Lore shrugged. "But Dire Saulder has. Have you forgotten, Casavore? My son has been crowned Dire in my husband's absence."

"You're lying," the Blesser seethed. "Saulder would never allow you this kind of authority."

"Dire Saulder is too heartbroken to deal with silly trials. So, he has burdened me with dealing out the general's punishment. Perhaps you should take some time for yourself as well, Casavore. Only a day has passed since our patrol returned with the devastating news regarding your daughter's disappearance."

A tear befell Casavore's scowl.

"You can't do this," he sneered. "Hylan is Vaska's general. She has served and protected this kingdom since she was old enough to pick up a sword. She has stood loyally by Zastar every day of her life!"

"And yet, she failed to save my husband," Lore said, her glare burning past Casavore. "Or have you forgotten it's because of her negligence your wife and daughter rot in the earth?"

Casavore grabbed the arms of the throne, making Lore gasp and press herself to the backrest.

"That's enough, Casavore," Hylan said as she reached for her sword. "Please step away from the queen."

Casavore looked back at the general, hesitating before he drew from the throne. "She can't do this to you, Hylan. Zastar won't stand for this—"

"Zastar isn't here," Hylan managed past the bobbing of her throat. "My relationship with the Dire doesn't pardon me from a trial. I couldn't save him from the Venom Tongues. Lore is right. A punishment must be dealt out."

"Hylan. You can't be serious. She—"

"Is Dire Zastar's queen," Hylan's gaze dipped to the medallion hanging from Casavore's neck. "...Thanks to you."

Casavore gulped, his jaw clenching under his beard as remorse flooded his blue eyes. "It could've been you. I came to you first, Hylan. You refused."

"I would never betray my dire, Casavore." Hylan raised her chin, revealing striking amethyst eyes. "What is done is done. So, please. Step away from the queen."

Casavore hesitated and then stepped back from the queen. Lore grinned, pleased by his surrender.

"General Hylan," she began all too eagerly. "For your failure to protect the Dire and his kingdom, I hereby exile you from the Valley of Lykos."

"No," Casavore whispered.

"You have twenty days to find a way out of this valley," Lore continued. "Should anyone see you after, you'll be killed on sight."

"That won't be necessary," Hylan uttered. "I'll be out of Lykos by the end of the week. I do have one request."

Lore rolled her eyes and exhaled. "Fine. Out with it."

"My son, Arison. Let him stay. He's shown great promise in training, and will one day be a great soldier for Vaska."

"Fine. The brat can stay," Lore looked to the throne room doors as a malicious grin spread her lips. "Speak of the devil."

Hylan lashed around to find a young man, no older than fourteen, standing in the doorway. His skin was dark, his face dappled in freckles, and he had fluffy dark-brown hair. He stared at his general, his amethyst eyes wide and tear-speckled.

"Ma?" he said, trying not to shake. "What's the verdict? What did they say?"

Hylan's stoic visage broke like glass, and she rushed to her son, stealing him into greedy arms. Arison stood frozen in his mother's embrace as she sobbed into his shoulder.

"Arison," she pulled away. "Arison, I have to go."

"No," Arison shook his head. "That's not fair. This—This wasn't your fault. What happened to Dire Zastar wasn't your fault. They can't do this."

"I've been ordered to leave Lykos," Hylan continued, her callused hands wiping his tears as they fell. "Lieutenant Afti and Casavore will look after you while I'm away."

"You can't," Arison stepped back, his chest pulsing rapidly as he looked to the Blesser with desperation. "C—Casavore. Casavore, do something." The Blesser looked away. "Blesser Casavore, please!"

Hylan cupped both sides of Arison's face, forcing his gaze to meet hers. "This isn't something he can change, Sweetheart," she pulled his chin down to kiss his brow. "I'm leaving. There isn't anything you or I can do to change that."

"Then I'll go with you—"

"No. No, you can't."

"Why not? You've been training me since the day I could walk. I can defend us out there. I can—"

"Arison," Hylan croaked, a tear tracing her quivering jaw. "You can't come with me. I can't explain it to you now, but you just can't. But, I do need to ask something of you..."

Arison swallowed, his voice just a crack away from shattering. "What?"

Hylan shuddered and brushed a tuft of dark hair out of his face. "You mustn't anger Dire Saulder or Queen Lore," she whispered. "Keep your head down. Be a good soldier. Do as they say. No matter the horrible things they ask of you, you do as they say."

Two Vaskan soldiers walked into the throne room, their eyes weighing to the polished floor.

"General Hylan," one said, his voice dripping with guilt. "It's time."

Hylan nodded and looked back to her son. Grinning through trembling lips, she cupped his face and said, "I love you. I'm sorry I failed you."

Accompanied by the other two soldiers, she left Arison between the throne room doors. Sobbing, Arison looked to the platform. Lore smiled smugly while the Blesser stared back at him with guilt-ridden eyes. Arison stepped back, tears flooding down his cheeks before he fled out of the room.

Casavore sighed, his chin raising to the dome ceiling as he prayed, "God, be with her... she is not at fault for this."

"Well, someone has to be," Lore grumbled, patting down her dress as she stood from her husband's throne. "Now the wrong has been righted, and Vaska can move on."

"A wrong has been righted?" Casavore repeated. "You just banished an innocent woman."

Lore laughed. "Innocent? Please. A religious man like yourself knows Hylan was no saint. How do you think that purple-eyed brat came to be?"

As Lore turned her back, Casavore's eyes narrowed into murderous slits, and he reached for his medallion. Before he could do something he wasn't sure he'd regret, a guard stepped into the throne room.

"Queen Lore. Blesser Casavore," the guard bowed. "We found him."

CASAVORE HURTLED UP the twisting staircase of the tallest tower. At the top, a young boy with platinum blond hair sat against a lonesome door, his face hidden against his knees.

Casavore stopped, his medallion swinging forward and slapping back against his chest. "Prince Sova," he huffed. "Have you seen your brother? He wasn't in his chamber."

Sova looked up, his big, silver eyes glistening with sorrow. "In there," he nodded to the door. "He won't let me in. 'Said he wanted to be alone with him."

Casavore sighed, his heart weighing like an anchor in his chest. "Move over a little, will you kiddo? Thanks."

The Blesser slipped through the door and into a cobblestone room drenched in sunlight flooding in through a single window. In the center of the room, a man lay buried under the sheets of a canopy bed. His skin was bruised, and his hair was stark-black and grey on the sides. A wheezing breath brushed past the man's lips, followed by the violent crash of his ribcage—the only indication of life.

Casavore looked away. He hated seeing his best friend, brother, and dire in such a broken state, as did the boy kneeling at his bedside. The boy wore the dire's black armor, much too big for his small frame, and he looked like Prince Sova in every way, only, his hair was long and braided. Pressing his face to the edge of the mattress, he clutched his father's hand.

"Dire Saulder," Casavore whispered. "You weren't in your chamber."

"It's not my chamber," Saulder growled. "It's my father's chamber."

Casavore nodded, his jaw clenching. "Saulder, I have to speak with you—"

"What was the verdict?" Saulder asked. The coldness of his tone cast ice into Casavore's soul. "What did Lore decide to do with Hylan?"

Casavore swallowed. Not a month ago, the future dire was filled with joy and light. He was the type of boy all fathers wanted their sons to be, the boy Prince Sova modeled himself after, the boy Casavore was thrilled his daughter would one day marry. Now he seemed empty, like a soulless body forced to live.

"She's gone," Casavore answered. Saulder didn't so much as flinch at the news. "Saulder, why did you appoint Lore to her trial? You must have known she would do something like this."

"I was busy," Saulder growled, his grip tightening around his father's hand.

"You're the dire now, Saulder. You can't just hand power off to someone else because you don't feel like taking responsibility. Especially not to Lore."

"She was supposed to be ok."

"Well she isn't. Arison is without a mother now, and Hylan's been banished off to God knows where—"

"I'm not talking about General Hylan."

Casavore stopped. He could see it now. The sheet the boy pressed his face against was soaked, the fingerprints of tears long shed. "You said she would be ok," the young dire croaked. "You said Feran would be ok. You said we would find her."

Casavore looked away, the agony he tried so hard to suppress surfacing like a geyser of boiling water. He looked away to hide a silent tear.

Saulder gasped, "I sent a thousand men after her. They were supposed to bring her back. You said they'd bring her back."

"I wanted them to," Casavore whispered through gritted teeth. "I needed them to."

"Instead, they came back with bones. Meatless bones. Those dirty pirates didn't even have the decency to bury her. 'Just let the buzzards have her."

"Stop it," Casavore begged. "Please. Stop it."

"I hate them," Saulder whispered. "I hate the Venom Tongues. I want them dead. All of them."

Drawing a deep breath, Casavore touched the young dire's shoulder. "That's why I came for you, Dire Saulder. The Hyde Howlers we sent out... They found him. The Viper of Seavale is here."

DRESSED IN HIS FATHER'S oversized armor, Saulder struggled into the throne room and settled in his father's throne, Casavore and Sova on either side while Lore hid behind a curtain on the west wall, her smug eyes now wide with terror. Two guards burst through the throne room doors, dragging in a Seavallian pirate bound at the hands.

"Let me go, you filthy dogs!" the pirate snarled, his black hair lashing over his blazing blue eyes. "Let me go, or I'll gut you in your sleep!"

The guards threw the pirate before the platform. He struggled to sit upright, freezing when he met the gaze of the dreaded dire.

"Dire Zastar?" he gasped. "I thought you were dead."

"You're mistaken, Viper," Saulder growled and removed his father's helmet, his long white hair spilling down his shoulders.

"Tsk," the Viper scoffed. "A boy? They've given the dire's crown to a boy?"

"They have," Saulder glared. "A crown you forced me to carry when you crippled Dire Zastar to his bed."

"You're the one who sent the Hyde Howlers to my home," the Viper snarled. "I'll kill you for what you did!"

Saulder tilted his head. "Why so angry, Viper? All I've done is even the score. An eye for an eye. Or rather... an eye for a leg."

"She was a child!"

"So was Feran."

"I wasn't responsible for that. I never gave the command to harm the Blesser's wife. Nor his daughter. What those men did they did on their own accord."

"Nonetheless, they were your men. I'll kill them in due time. After I've finished their captain."

The Viper threw back his head as a monstrous laugh split open his throat. "Don't make me laugh, pup. You're but a child. Who are you to threaten the most powerful gang in all of Seavale?"

Saulder gripped the arms of his throne, his silver eyes blazing. "Casavore," he motioned for his Blesser. "Help the Viper understand who I am."

Casavore dipped his head and stepped down the platform before the Viper, his eyes dark with a lust for revenge.

"What would you have me do, Dire Saulder?" he asked.

"Not what you'll do, Casavore," Saulder corrected. "What he'll do."

"Understood, my dire."

The Viper looked anxiously from Saulder to Casavore, his arrogance dissipating in an instant. "What? What does he mean by that? What is he doing?"

Casavore raised his medallion before the Viper. The gangster stilled—his mind stolen by the mind melder's weapon. With the Venom Tongue captain subdued, the Blesser looked back at the dire.

"Eyes first," Saulder instructed.

"Yes, my dire," Casavore obeyed, looking back at his victim. "Oh, loathed Viper. Killer of innocents. Lover of evil. Just as the holy teachings tell us, abstain from your wicked temptations, and pluck out your soul's betrayer."

With a shaking hand, the Viper reached for his eye.

The sound of squelching flesh and blood-curdling cries echoed through the throne room. Prince Sova turned away, the hand over his mouth trapping vomit against his palm.

"Is it over?" he whimpered.

The sound of tearing flesh ended as the Viper fell to the floor, his hands open on the stone, holding little white masses covered in red sludge. Casavore turned to the dire.

"I'll have him taken to the dungeons," he said as he placed his medallion around his neck. "We can discuss his execution after—"

"No," Saulder said coldly.

Casavore looked up. "Pardon, Dire Saulder?"

"No," Saulder stood from his throne. "He won't be staying in the dungeon."

"Where would you have me put him then?"

Saulder stepped down from platform to loom over the sobbing pirate. "In the pig pens. Those beasts are always good at disposing of corpses."

The young dire grabbed the Viper by his hair, forcing the gangster's hollow sockets to meet his eyes. This time, Sova couldn't stop himself from getting sick. Lore gasped. And Casavore was stricken dumb.

Saulder glared at his enemy, his grip tightening in the man's ebony locks. "You took everything from me. I was happy. My family... my father. My brother. Fala, Casavore. They were all proud of me. Feran was proud of me. And you took her from me. You killed my best friend."

The Viper gasped, scarlet waterfalls raining from his sockets and down his cheeks and neck.

"Everyone said I was a good person. I was proud of that." Saulder shook his head. "But I don't care about that anymore. I don't care about being fair or making people proud. I just don't care. Come morning, I'll send out as many as a thousand Hyde Howlers to Seavale. And I won't stop sending them until the shores of Seavale are red with Venom Tongue blood. I won't stop until every single one of them is dead."

The Viper chuckled through the blinding pain. Had he still had his eyes, he would've looked at Lore cowering behind the violet curtain across the room.

"He takes after you."

Saulder grabbed the Viper's throat, making him gasp as his hollow sockets widened like two gaping holes into the abyss.

"Saulder, that's enough," Casavore ordered and reached for the young dire.

Saulder's gaze lashed onto the Blesser, his eyes glistening with murderous intent and frightening Casavore back. Saulder looked back to the Viper as the man's bloody tears seeped over his hands.

"You know. I wish I hadn't made my Blesser gouge out your eyes," he said as the Viper grew blue. "I would've loved to look into them as you died."

The Viper's squirming ceased. His skin turned white, and his mouth unhinged. The dire released the corpse and it fell to the stone.

Prince Sova slipped from the platform and up to his brother, his silver eyes wide with fright.

"You killed him," he whispered. "My Lykos, Saulder, you killed him."

Saulder ran his bloodied hand under his nose, smearing his cheek in crimson.

"Make haste, Casavore," the young tyrant growled and placed the dire's helmet over his head. "The Venom Tongues are sure to make a break for the Adder's Isle once they find out their captain is dead."

Casavore and Lore followed Dire Saulder out of the throne room, both too speechless to speak.

Sova stood before the Viper's corpse, his boots drenched in blood. He didn't know then, but that wouldn't be the last murder he ever saw Dire Saulder commit. No. There would be more. Much, much more...

Chapter One: Ten Years Later

The island was quiet. A full moon shone through the treetops, turning the jungle a sleepy shade of blue. The tumbling of tired waves could be heard in the distance, barely even a noise to those who inhabited the wretched sanctuary. And the place smelled of rain; fresh, musky rain.

Suddenly, from the rare quiet, a cloaked figure shot through the undergrow, their sword catching the moonlight as they passed by. With each lunge, something metal creaked beneath their cloak, the result of a past injury sustained back in the Valley of Lykos across the sea. The figure ran until they came to the edge of the jungle. A great, blue bay lay before them, home to a rickety old dock where stolen ships waded in the shallows, tethered to the posts. The cloaked figure lingered in the undergrow, their obsidian-black eyes lashing from side to side in search of foes.

Slowly, they slipped out across the moon-lit beaches toward the dock. Something rustled within the jungled. The cloaked figure stopped. They drew back their hood, revealing the face of a woman with pale skin, and hair as dark as the midnight above. Out from the jungle seven sailors emerged, their arms coated in black skulls and snakes. They surrounded the woman, glaring at her with as dark as the night.

The woman straightened and smirked, not the slightest bit bothered. "Beautiful night for a stroll, isn't it boys," she said, drumming her fingers on the handle of her sword.

"Don't even think about it, pup," snarled a large Venom Tongue with a massive scar over his eye. "What do you think you're doing out here this late at night?"

"Like I said," the woman taunted, "it's a beautiful night. Perfect for a midnight sail."

"You aren't permitted to leave the island, Taige," spat another Venom Tongue. "Captain Rayze would have our heads if she knew we let you leave the isle."

"Captain Rayze is not my mother, so she has no need to act as such," Taige replied with a voice bitter like the salt of the sea. "And I don't need permission from anyone. You forget I was the Viper's daughter before she was his wife."

"Daughter of the Viper or not, Captain Rayze is your captain no. And your guardian. Her word is law."

Taige looked from the goons to the ships wading in the bay. She smirked, a playful gleam sparking her eyes. "You can tell Captain Rayze that my business is my business alone. If I wish to sail my father's ships, then I may do so as I please." One of the Venom Tongues, a man with serpent-like eyes and a barnacle smile, cackled at Taige. "Is there a problem, Mr. Fidi?" she asked, glancing over her shoulder.

"You know full well a cripple like you can't sail these seas," the Venom Tongue, Fidi, cackled. "The coral fields will tear you apart before you even make it past the shallows."

"Cripple?" Taige repeated. The Venom Tongues traded a fearful glance. "Cripple..." Taige shook her head, chuckling. "Oh, Mr. Fidi, how your stupidity amuses me. Go ahead. Say it again."

Fidi looked at his comrades, unsure why they all looked so afraid. He seethed, "Cripple."

The Venom Tongues clutched their holstered swords as Taige drew a deep breath and pushed back a lock of ebony hair. "Oh, Mr. Fidi," she sighed, almost pitying the foolish sailor. "You should've never left Seavale."

Taige drew her curved sword, its metallic whisper ringing through the air as she slashed through Fidi's knee. He fell to the sand, screaming, while the others rushed to pacify the Viper's Heir. She lashed her sword across the chest of the first pirate and then turned and slammed her metal leg into his gut of another. One by one, they fell, for she was like a ruthless tide—lethal and unending.

Taige slammed her forehead into the last pirate, and he whipped against the sand, knocked out cold.

"Ouch," Taige winced, rubbing the bruise forming on her forehead. "That really hurt." All seven Venom Tongues lay at her feet, their faces covered in the blood pouring out their noses and lips. "Boys," she curtseyed before making her way to Fidi trembling against the sand. She looked on him with disappointment, annoyed by the tears. "Come on, Fidi, you're a Venom Tongue for Lykos sake."

"You're a monster," Fidi sniveled as a snot bubble expanded from his nostril.

"Sticks and stones, Fidi," Taige muttered before she turned and stalked onto the docks. "Sticks and stones."

She sliced a tether tied to a small barnacle-infested ship, setting the wooden beast free.

"Wait," Fidi pleaded as Taige snuck aboard the ship, stationing herself at the wheel. "Wait, stop. Taige, please. Captain Rayze will—"

"Tell your captain I'll be back in two weeks," Taige licked her finger, lifting it to the wind. "Three weeks tops."

"Why are you doing this? There is nothing for you in Lykos that isn't here on the Adder's Isle."

"That's where your wrong, Fidi," Taige called as the ship drifted towards the mouth of the bay. She looked back at the beach, her ebony eyes shining like polished coals. "There is something in Lykos I want. Something I need."

"What is it?"

Taige looked back, a dark grin crossing her lips. "Revenge, Fidi."

Taige navigated the ship out of the bay and into the midnight-painted sea, looking back as her home disappeared over the horizon.

I am sorry, Rayze, she thought, her heart growing heavy. This is my only chance to make the dire feel what I felt when he took my father. He'll pay for what he did. I'll make sure of it...

Chapter Two: Recruit

S eavale...

The sun rose from the cliffs of Eradawn, hovering over the sea as drunken roars shook the town of Seavale carved into the side of a cliff. Even in the early day, the Sinner's Sanctuary knew no rest.

Just beyond the beaches, in the shadows of the Vaskan forest, a white soaring wolf treaded the dense green undergrowth, trampling the autumn leaves under his paws. He stopped short of the beach, his coal-black nose poking just beyond the shadows to inhale the scent of the salty waves.

"We're here," Roeseph said as he slid from Saber's back, followed by Kyce and Feran.

Elling maneuvered her legs to one side and cautiously pushed herself off, falling right into Roeseph's awaiting arms. She moved away bashfully.

"Thank you," she mumbled, averting her emerald-green gaze.

Roeseph smirked fondly, "Any time."

"Hey, lover boy," a rather obnoxious voice snapped. "Me next."

Roeseph exhaled and looked up to see a man with white-blond hair and silver eyes sitting atop Saber, staring down at him.

"You're a grown man, Sova," Roeseph scolded. "I'm not helping you down."

"I can't get down by myself," Sova griped. "Saber throws me every time I try."

Feran rolled her eyes.

"Stop complaining and get down, Sova," she snapped as she slipped her father's medallion beneath her shirt. "We can't afford to waste any time."

"But he'll throw me!" Sova whined. "The last time he did, I walked with a limp for a week. It made running from Vaskan soldiers very difficult."

Feran sighed, and pinched the bridge of her nose.

"Tell you what, Sova. I'll make sure he won't throw you. He's bonded to me. He'll listen."

"Promise?"

Feran drew an x over her chest, "Cross my heart."

Sova looked nervously from Feran to the leaf-covered ground, his stomach tying into a million knots as he shakily drew his legs to one side and lowered himself down. Without warning, Saber lunged into the sky. The Dire Wolves watched blankly as Sova screamed and fell to the forest floor, sending up a flurry of mummified leaves in his wake.

Feran chuckled as Saber ascended to his side, his snout flexed in a snarl.

"Ah, that never gets old."

"I forgot," Sova wheezed, his lungs flat from the fall. "You need to have a heart before you can cross it."

Roeseph offered his hand to Sova and lifted him to his feet.

"Did your gauze come loose?" he asked.

"I don't think so," Sova mumbled as he inspected the gauze wrapping his left shoulder. "I should probably change it soon, though. Aren't you proud that I learned how to dress it myself, Roe?"

"You close your eyes when you do it," Roeseph sighed.

"Aha, that makes it all the more fun."

"You're a child."

"No, I'm traumatized."

Kyce walked towards the sunlight beyond the forest, stretching his sculpted arms as he looked down the beach to the mountainside cave.

He sighed with contentment.

"Home sweet home. It feels good to be somewhere a little livelier after being stuck all summer surrounded by those Mosharick Plain stiffs."

"Hey," Elling snapped. "Roeseph and I were born in the Mosharick Plains you know."

"My point exactly."

"We're not here to relive old times, Kyce," Roeseph reminded as he took his place beside the Eradite Exile. "We're here to recruit soldiers to fight against the dire."

"What makes you think anyone in there will want to join us?" Feran asked as she stroked Saber's ears. "We spent all summer in the Mosharick Plains looking for recruits. No one's willing to join as long as Oland and the Blind Seers are locked up in Saulder's dungeon."

"Hey, you never know," Sova piped in. "After all, Seavallians are a little tougher than Mosharick folk. Roeseph and I actually came here a while back to recruit soldiers at the beginning of our exile... But then someone stole Casavore's medallion, and we had to cut our visit short."

Kyce smirked, a proud chuckle rumbling in his throat. "Good times."

"Thieving mutt," Sova grumbled.

"Alright, everyone," Roeseph sighed as he beckoned everyone to gather. "That place is crawling with bounty hunters, so we need to get in and get out as quick as possible before anyone recognizes us."

"That means no stopping for Odin's Slayer, Sova," Elling scolded.

Sova pouted and hung his head.

"Hoods up," Roeseph ordered. Everyone drew their hoods and lifted black scarves over their faces.

Sova grumbled and griped as he adjusted his bandana, his silver eyes flashing with vivid frustration.

"What's the problem, Sova?" Feran sighed as she watched the Royal Traitor toy with his covering.

"It's itchy," Sova complained.

"You're kidding me."

"No, it's really itchy."

"Stop messing with it, Sova."

"Do I have to wear it?"

"Yes."

"What if I—"

"Sova, wear the stupid scarf right, or I'll hypnotize you," Feran lifted the Blesser's gold medallion around her neck.

While Sova and Feran argued, Roeseph walked to Elling, who had yet to draw her hood. She looked up from tying her raven hair out of her face, her heart somersaulting in her chest when she saw him approach.

"Try and stay close to me," Roeseph cautioned as he pulled her hood over her head. "We're not looking to pick fights with anyone, but that doesn't change the fact there are still some hostile characters in there."

"Says you," Kyce snapped. "I'm looking to relive old times."

"No fighting anyone, Kyce," Roeseph scolded as Elling adjusted her scarf over blushing cheeks.

Feran stroked Saber's snout, causing his wings to flutter.

"Stay hidden, boy," she ordered before planting a kiss on his nose which he immediately licked. "We'll be back in an hour."

Sova gagged.

"She just kissed a dog."

"Could be worse," Feran shrugged as she stalked past Sova and stuffed the Blesser's medallion down her cloak. "I could be kissing you."

Elling sputtered and looked away just as Sova turned to face her.

"Something funny, El?" he grumbled.

"No," Elling sniffled as she tried to suppress a smile. "Not at all."

"Come on, you hoodlums," Roeseph called as he marched out of the shadows and onto the scorching hot sand. "Let's get this over with."

"Aye—aye, Captain," Feran joked as she and the others trailed after their leader toward Seavale.

THE DIRE WOLVES WALKED through the stalagmite jaws at the cave entrance and into the dreary streets of Seavale. Moss-polished cobblestone streets glittered in the torchlight as drunken belches filled the miserable town, rising over the rooftops.

As the legends navigated the liquor-influenced sanctuary, Kyce stopped at a familiar tavern. The very one he had fought in so many times before. He drew a deep breath, the stench of bourbon stinging the back of his throat.

"Hey guys," he called, making the Dire Wolves turn. "I think we found our first stop."

Roeseph led the four exiles into the tavern. A wave of bourbon-soaked cries met them at the entrance, accompanied by the stench of liquor and sweat. Ruffians wrestled one another into tables while the gruff melody of sailor shanties filled the room.

Roeseph exhaled, already overwhelmed.

"Ok, everyone," he began tiredly, "let's be discrete. And if someone gives you trouble, step away from the situation. That means you, Kyce."

"No promises," Kyce smirked as he looked around.

"And remember, everyone, we're on an important mission," Roeseph recited. "So please stay focused—"

Before Roeseph could finish, Sova whisked towards the bar, followed by Feran and Kyce. Roeseph sighed. Getting the Dire Wolves to comply was like playing shepherd to a pack of hyenas. Before he could slip further into silent frustration, Elling gently clasped his callused hand.

"I'm sorry," she said through a pouted smile. "They just want to enjoy themselves."

"What's there to enjoy?" Roeseph grumbled. "The last time we were here, Sova got blackout drunk. Kyce beat him up—robbed us. And then we got attacked by a bunch of Seavallian thugs—"

"And then we found each other," Elling added. "We'll have plenty of time to search for recruits. Try not to stress out too much."

"Fine," Roeseph exhaled as Elling led him towards their friends perched on rickety old barstools.

Sova leaned over the counter.

"One serving of Odin Slayer, please," he asked with a scarf-covered smile. The white-bearded bartender on the other side turned away with a scowl to fix Sova's poison. Sova looked up and down the table, his eyes twinkling. "What are you guys drinking?"

"None for me, thank you," Elling said.

"None of us are drinking, Sova," Roeseph growled as he drummed his fingers on the countertop. "And you shouldn't be either."

"Fine," Sova shrugged as he turned forward. "I'll drink on all of your behalf."

"Sova—"

"It's a sacrifice I'm willing to make."

Roeseph exhaled and sunk in his seat, his face flexed in a deep scowl.

Elling patted his back. "There—there."

As the gang eagerly awaited the death sentence of Sova's kidneys, Feran looked behind the bar at an assortment of wanted posters hanging on the wall. Her stomach.

"Sova," she whispered, elbowing the Royal Traitor in the arm. "Look."

Sova looked up. His comrades' solemn faces printed across the wanted posters stared back at him, each priced at a bounty of one hundred thousand coins—enough money to buy out all of Seavale.

"They really captured your eyes, Kyce," said Sova.

Kyce glared at him, his eyes shining with amber-colored blood-lust.

"Yep," Sova nodded. "Identical."

Elling pressed closer to Roeseph. The woman in the poster looked nothing like her. Her usual gentle green eyes were cold and lifeless as stone. Her smiling lips were curved in a subtle snarl. And she had a sort of darkness about herself the others didn't have. That was because the woman in the poster wasn't Elling at all, but the Feral Shepherd. A Hyde Howler.

"Quite a bounty on those five," mumbled the bartender as he fixed Sova's drink. "Just one of those traitors, and I could open as many as seven taverns."

"I take it you're not too fond of the Dire Wolves," Feran asked cautiously.

"Not fond of?" the bartender spat as he lashed around with a mug of Odin Slayer in hand. "Those bunch of sorry saps are my heroes."

"Heroes?" Roeseph tested, suspicious.

"Of course," the bartender cheered as he slammed the Odin Slayer in front of Sova. "Every sailor, thug, low life, and runaway in Seavale can't help but admire the Dire Wolves. Bout' time someone stuck it to the dire."

"You don't say," Sova smirked as he took a bold gulp of the Odin Slayer. His throat coiled and his stomach rolled. "Good Lykos that's ripe."

"Baby sips, Sova," Feran warned out the corner of her mouth. "Baby sips."

Sova suppressed a belch. "Worry about your own self."

Kyce leaned back in his stool, scanning the bartender's grey face with distrusting amber eyes.

"And why such interest in those bunch of exiles?" he tested.

"Well, for one, the Eradite Exile is one of our own," the bartender praised. Kyce straightened ever so slightly. "He used to be a fighter in this very tavern. Would bring in customers by the handfuls. I miss that cash cow. Though, I would've never guessed he was an Eradite."

"Yeah," Sova elbowed Kyce in the side, "I guess you never really know a person, huh."

"I'll say," the bartender grumbled. "But I have to admit, the brute surprised me. All of those Lykos forsaken outcasts did. I mean, a Hyde Howler turning against her own commander? Tremendous!"

Elling shrunk in her seat as the bartender rambled.

"And don't get me started on the Last Soldier. The man is a legend born from a legend. Before all this, people were already talking about his skill and leadership. And the Dire's Damsel—"

"The Dire's Curse," Feran corrected, her eyes narrow with spite.

"Yes, her—well, she's something else entirely. I mean, the dire's betrothed, the daughter of his Blesser, betraying him and hypnotizing his entire army in the battle on Era? Stupendous! Not to mention she's rumored to have a power so great, her abilities surpass her own father's. I mean, truly, she's just amazing. And don't get me started on the Royal Traitor."

Sova perked in his seat.

"Oh no," Feran muttered.

"What about the Royal Traitor?" Sova asked.

"He's a hero! A victor for all of Lykos," the bartender claimed. "The man literally brought the Blind Seers into his own home and then singlehandedly fought the dire. Though he lost, that Lykos forsaken traitor wouldn't give up, and brought together the Dire Wolves so that together they could thwart the dire and all his ambitions."

"Sounds like quite a guy," Sova smirked.

"I'm telling ya, sailor, that Royal Traitor is going to change things for the better. He's going to change Lykos—if not the world!"

"You don't say."

Feran's shoulders slumped forward in a groan. "This is my worst nightmare."

"If there was anyone who could destroy that Lykos forsaken dire, it's him," the bartender said, his eyes starting to mist. "And by the waves of Seavale, if I could ask the God of Era for one thing, it would be that I could shake the hand of that man and tell him how grateful I am for his bravery and service... But I'm just a rambling old fool. I don't deserve the kindness of a man so noble."

Sova snapped upright, his barstool crashing to the floor.

"Uh oh," Kyce grumbled.

"Sir, I don't think you're a rambling old fool," Sova said valiantly. "In fact, I believe you'll meet your hero someday soon."

Roeseph coughed into his sleeve, his eyes boggling with dread. "Sit down," he ordered between ragged breaths. "Sit down, now."

"That's kind of you to say, sailor," the bartender sighed sadly. "But you've got a better chance of a righteous man in Seavale than for the likes of the Royal Traitor showing up here."

Sova puffed out his chest, intoxicated on arrogance and Odin Slayer.

"Then call it a miracle, good sir."

Sova ripped off his scarf and drew back his hood.

"For I am your Royal Traitor, Prince Sova, brother to the dire and son of Zastar. And the good people that stand before you are, in fact, my devoted Dire Wolves. The Last Soldier, the Eradite Exile, the Dire's Curse, and the Feral Shepherd."

"Hello," Elling said meekly as she twiddled her fingers at the bartender.

"My comrades and I have come seeking soldiers to aid our cause," Sova recited. "And sir, I would be honored if you would shake my hand."

Sova stuck out his hand to the awestruck bartender.

The bartender pointed a trembling finger at Sova and roared, "It's him! It's the Royal Traitor! It's the Dire Wolves!"

Sova's proud smirk tightened into a mortified grin, and his hand coiled into a fist.

"Pardon?"

Like a back of hounds called by the dinner bell, the entire tavern lashed around to face the Dire Wolves. Slowly, the thugs and criminals stalked towards the bar, their hard faces scrunched in greedy scowls.

"That bounty is mine," one of the Seavallians growled.

Feran ripped her scarf off her face to reveal her scowl.

"Sova!"

"I admit, mistakes were made," Sova nodded.

Kyce grabbed Sova by the hood of his cloak and dragged him away as he and the Dire Wolves tore towards the exit. They pushed open the doors. An angry mob of Seavallian thugs surrounded the tavern, their swords drawn, and knives sharpened.

"Wow," Sova pierced his lips. "Word travels fast around here."

Rolling her eyes, Feran pulled out the Blesser's medallion. The crowd scrambled to hide their faces, lest they inherit a fate like the Vaskan troops in the battle on Era.

"What do we do?" Elling shrieked, clinging to Roeseph's arm.

Clasping Elling's hand on his bicep, Roeseph shouted "Scatter!" and whisked her away down the street with Kyce at their heels.

Sova watched as they fled, annoyed they'd leave him so hastily.

"I guess it's just you and me, Feran."

When he looked to the side, Feran was gone, having scaled the wall. He caught a glimpse of her disappearing over the roof shingles. With the medallion out of sight, the Seavallians unsheathed their eyes and scowled at the Royal Traitor.

"So..." Sova smiled awkwardly. "Would any of you gentlemen be interested in joining a noble cause?"

The Seavallians roared and charged the Royal Traitor. Squeaking like a frightened mouse, Sova ran through the moss-covered streets of Seavale.

WHILE SOVA ENGAGED in a game of cat and mouse, him being the mouse, Roeseph, Kyce, and Elling tore through the maze of Seavale's sewage-flooded alleys.

"Where's Sova?" Elling yelled.

"Who cares?" Kyce snapped, drawing his sword. "He brought this on himself."

The three looked up, digging their heels into the sewage-polished stone as they stopped. A large bear of a man stood at the end of the alley, a rusty ax in hand, and his bottom canines skimming his nostril as he smiled a crooked smile.

"Oh great," Kyce grumbled, "It's Olive. You still owe me ten gold coins, you cheat!"

The grisly man lifted his ax and roared, making the walls and sewage puddles tremble.

"What a sore loser," Kyce sneered with a smirk.

"Kyce, don't!" Roeseph warned as Kyce charged.

The Seavallian beast heaved his ax back and plunged it at Kyce. The Eradite Exile ducked as the ax cut straight through his sword. Straightening, he glared at his broken blade.

"Hey!" Kyce snapped just as a fist hurtled towards him. Roeseph and Elling flinched as Kyce soared into a wall and splashed into a green puddle.

"That's gotta hurt," Roeseph winced.

"Roeseph!" Elling cried as the beast charged toward them like a bull seeing red.

Roeseph shoved Elling out of harm's way and drew his sword. Evading the ax, he vaulted off the wall and landed on the Seavallian man's back. The beast gave a ghastly roar, grabbed Roeseph by the neck, making him gasp, and threw him into Kyce across the alleyway.

"You know that guy?" Roeseph coughed through bruised lungs.

"Kind of," Kyce groaned. "He's a cheat at cards."

The beast stalked towards the Eradite Exile and the Last Soldier, his ax skimming the cobblestone floor. Before he could lay waste to the two defeated Dire Wolves, something broke across his back. He straightened, completely unaffected, and turned to find Elling holding a piece of splintered driftwood.

Trembling, she tried to strike him again. He grabbed and crushed the weapon in his fist. Elling stumbled back into a wall as the beast stalked toward her, the cold mossy brick sending shivers up her spine.

"You are the Feral Shepherd?" the Seavallian grumbled with a voice like raspy thunder. He laughed, humored. "You're nothing but a frightened little Mosharick girl."

The sound of squelching flesh and a shattered bone rang through the air, and the man opened his bulging arms to the ceiling and screamed. A sword plunged into the bend of his knee, straight through the cap. Roeseph darted out from behind the Seavallian beast and struck his jaw. The man fell like Goliath.

Roeseph exhaled, his rage-fueled eyes softening when he turned to Elling.

"Are you ok?" he asked, grabbing her by the arms.

Elling nodded as the words of the Seavallian beast rang in her head like a gong.

...Nothing but a frightened little Mosharick Girl...

Roeseph sighed with relief and hung his head, "Oh thank Lykos."

Kyce prodded his foot into the unconscious Seavallian. When the beast didn't wake, he turned to Roeseph and Elling.

"We need to get out of here. Word that we're here has probably spread through all of Seavale by now."

"Head to the beach," Roeseph ordered. "Sova and Feran will just have to meet us there."

As Roeseph and Elling started out of the alley, Kyce knelt to the unconscious Seavallian and rummaged his fur-stitched pockets.

"Kyce," Elling began, "what are you doing?"

"Like I said, he owes me ten coins."

FERAN WATCHED FROM the rooftops as Sova ran up and down the streets of Seavale, the angry mob growing larger with each lunge. Eyes narrow, she tore across the rusted shingles, determined not to let him out of her sight.

Sova turned into an alley and wove his way through the Seavallian maze. He lost most of the mob, except for two large Seavallian thugs who managed to stay at his heels. Sova turned down another alley, only to meet an unforgiving dead end.

"Forsake Lykos," he hissed.

"The Royal Traitor," a voice hissed. Sova turned. Two rabid thugs loomed over him, their eyes flickering with lethal greed. "It's a true honor to be in your presence."

Sova gulped and looked around. "The honor is mine. I don't suppose you two are after me to join the fight against the dire?"

"Sorry, my prince," the second thug growled as he drew his blade. "It's nothing personal. Your bounty is just too great."

"I guess everyone's got to make a living," Sova shrugged as he reached for his sword. He charged. The thugs intercepted his blade against theirs and shoved him violently into the wall. Scraping down the brick, Sova fell to the cobblestone floor. He rubbed a sore spot on the back of his head as the two thugs stalked towards them.

Laughing sheepishly, he asked, "Two out of three?"

A figure darted between the rooftops overhead, snagging Sova by the corner of his eye. He smirked, suddenly no longer afraid.

"I take it neither of you read the Bible much, do you?" he asked smugly.

"Save your breath, boy."

"No? Ever hear the verse Luke ten—eighteen?"

Like lightning from the sky, Feran leaped from the rooftops and came down on the two thugs, crushing them beneath her feet. She drew back her hood, her eyes narrowed on the Royal Traitor.

"Did you just compare me to Satan?"

"Of course not," Sova snickered.

Rolling her eyes, Feran offered her hand. "You had to tell him who you were," she said, hauling Sova to his feet.

"Everyone has their weaknesses," Sova shrugged. "Mine is praise. So, how do you suppose we get out of here?"

Feran looked at the thugs dozing beneath her boots. A fiendish smirk crossed her lips.

"I have an idea."

BEYOND THE ALLEYS, a hoard of Seavallian thugs and criminals patrolled the moss-covered streets of Seavale. As they searched, two cloaked individuals darted out of an alley.

"It's the Dire's Curse and the Royal Traitor," they cried and gave chase. With the entirety of the town after the imposters, Feran and Sova peeled out of the alleyway and into the empty street to watch as the two Seavallians they disguised in their cloaks ran for dear life.

"I have to say," Sova smirked. "That medallion of yours does come in handy from time to time."

"Shut your trap and start running," Feran warned as she grabbed Sova by the wrist and whisked towards Seavale's exit. Not a moment after Sova and Feran reached the stalagmites, Roeseph, Elling, and Kyce appeared, their faces red from the run.

"I—" Roeseph gasped between breaths, "—hate... Seavale..."

Kyce smirked, "It grows on you after a while."

Roeseph stood upright. "Look, we're clearly not going to find any allies here, so let's cut our losses and make ourselves scarce."

Before anyone could agree, what sounded like a pride of roaring lions bloomed through the washed-up town, causing the cave to tremble. The Dire Wolves looked up. A tidal wave of Seavallians charged them, their eyes dark with a lust for blood and bounty.

Sova looked to Feran, "I guess our imposters aren't that fast."

"Clearly," she replied bitterly.

Taking Elling by the hand, Roeseph led the Dire Wolves out of Seavale and onto the scorching beach.

"Get the dog, Feran!" Sova shouted. "Get the dog!"

"Saber!" Feran called. "Saber, help us!"

Like an ivory angel breaking through the tree line, Saber ascended the sky and hurtled towards the Dire Wolves. Stirring clusters of sand under his wings, the Dire Wolves scrambled onto the monster's back.

"Fly! Fly! Mush! Go!" Sova ordered. Saber snarled in response.

"Don't yell at him!" Feran snapped.

"We are being chased by the entirety of Seavale!" Sova roared. "Make the Lykos forsaken dog fly!"

Feran kicked Saber in his rib, and he leaped into the air, lost somewhere in the eye of the sun. Sova looked over his shoulder as they soared, their roaring mob becoming mere ants against the golden beach. He exhaled, relieved.

"That was a close one," he sighed. Everyone glared back at him, their eyes drawn in odious slits. Sova shrugged. "What?"

Chapter Three: The General's Boy

The Kingdom of Vaska...

Beneath the great Palace of Vaska, in the dark dungeons where hymns of skittering rat feet and clanking shackles harmonize, the once-great Blesser of Vaska sat alone in his cell. His bare back pressed against the cold wall, he stared at the ceiling to watch condensation drip into a puddle at the center of the floor. Dim torches lit the unbearable prison, casting shadows of guards and rats across the walls.

"Casavore," croaked the tired voice of Oland through the wall he and the Blesser shared. "Casavore, are you awake?"

"Yes, Oland," Casavore muttered tiredly. "I'm awake."

"I had a dream," Oland said wistfully. "A dream about Roeseph when he was just a boy. My Saphelle was there too. She wasn't scared to be there with me. It was like she never left. Like I never became a Hyde Howler. I was watching them from a hill while they played with the sharick fawns. Roeseph was laughing... he used to be so little..."

"It sounds like a wonderful dream, Oland."

"Suppose—" Oland coughed through a chuckle. "Suppose Roeseph and Feran fall in love... Perhaps they plan to wed and come break us out of here for the wedding."

"I think you're still dreaming, Oland."

"Why do you say that my friend? Roeseph is a good man and a noble soldier. Not to mention a handsome one. He takes after Saphelle, after all. And Feran—if the legends are true, she is as powerful as Fala was beautiful."

"...Feran is betrothed to someone else, Oland. Has been since she was born."

"Don't make me laugh, Casavore. You don't actually consider Feran and Dire Saulder betrothed anymore, do you? He tried to kill her in Era. If she hadn't hypnotized the Vaskan army, who knows what might—"

"Not everything is as it seems, Oland. The tyrant that keeps us locked away in here is indeed a monster. But the Saulder I know is—"

The clomp of metal boots over the cold dungeon floor bloomed through the prison cells as approaching torchlight made its way toward the Blind Hound and the Blesser's cells.

"Who goes there," Oland spat defensively.

"Easy there, tiger," came a friendly voice. A Vaskan soldier peeled around the corner to stand before the bars of the Blesser's cell. His skin was dark with freckles aplenty, his eyes were of amethyst, and he bore a gentle smile unfamiliar to the likes of Vaskan soldiers.

"Ah, Arison," Casavore sighed contently. "What brings you to our humble prison?"

"Oh Casavore, you know I can't go a day without our talks," the guard, Arison, smiled. "I actually have something to give you."

"Is it another flogging?" Oland grumbled. "God knows we get our fair share of those."

"No," Arison assured as he reached into his back pocket and drew a charred, golden medallion. Casavore sat up from the wall he leaned against, his tired, blue eyes wide with awe.

"Arison, is that—"

"It is. I was sent to guard the dire's chamber the other day. I got bored and went snooping around, and well—" Arison looked to the medallion, "I found this stuffed in the back of his drawer."

Oland chuckled and shook his head at the young soldier, "Arison, my boy, if you aren't careful, you'll wind up down here with us."

"I have committed no treason," Arison said through a smirk. "Casavore, while a prisoner, is still the Blesser after all. And what is a Blesser without a medallion?"

Casavore crawled to the bars of his and stuck his face through the gaps.

"Arison, are you mad?" he scolded. "You'll be executed for this."

"Relax, Blesser Casavore," Arison shrugged. "Many soldiers guard the dire's chamber every day. He won't even know it's gone as long as you promise not to use it. You'll gain more trouble than good should anyone know you have it."

"I won't. I promise," Casavore blubbered as he stuck out his hand to the benevolent soldier. "Please. My daughter's medallion?"

Looking left to right, Arison laid the charred medallion in Casavore's palm. The Blesser drew from the cell bars to stare at the forbidden treasure—the last remnant of his sweet daughter.

"I've heard legends of the Dire's Curse, but never would've dreamed she was Feran," Arison began curiously. "Is this really her medallion?"

"Yes," Casavore gulped. "I made it for her when she was just a child." Casavore paused, allowing mournful silence to fill the dungeon. "I thought she was dead for over ten years. She was alone out there. All that time she was alone—" he stopped, his voice quivering as he held down a sob.

"She's not alone anymore, Casavore," Oland assured. "And you'll see her again. Someday soon, you'll see her."

Yes, Casavore thought as he reclined against the wall to stare at his daughter's medallion. Someday...

The squeal of the dungeon doors opening sounded through the dungeon. Casavore tucked his daughter's medallion into his shirt, lest whoever entered take it from him.

"Who goes there?" Arison snapped as he reached for his sword.

The light clap of pointed heels over cold stone echoed through the dungeon as a dark shadow peeled around the corner. The prisoners pressed themselves to their cells, curious to see who had come to visit. Lore, the ex-queen of Vaska and mother to Dire Saulder, strolled through the Vaskan dungeon. She wore a violet dress with long sleeves and a train, her ivory hair was in a tight bun on top of her head, and silver crystals hanging from each ear scathed bare shoulders.

"Lady Lore," Arison gasped, surprised. "I am sorry, your highness, I didn't know it was you."

"At ease, soldier," Lore replied with a voice like honey. "Leave me to speak with my prisoner."

"Of course, m'lady," Arison bowed before retreating out of the dungeon. Lore watched as he went, suspicious of the kindhearted guard.

"Friend of yours, Casavore?" she taunted. "I should surely hope not. You have a track record of getting your friends into unfortunate situations."

"Go jump off the Cliffs of Era, wench," Oland spat.

"Ah, the Blind Hound," Lore greeted. "Always a pleasure."

Oland grunted.

Glaring through the bars of his cell, Casavore grumbled, "What are you doing here, Lore?"

"Is that any way to speak to the mother of your dire, Casavore? You know, my son would be very displeased if he heard you speaking to me in such a way—"

"Out with it, Lore."

Lore exhaled, displeased with Casavore's lack of respect. "Very well. The dire sent me here to—"

"Did he?" Casavore arched his brow.

"Let me finish, you miscreant. The dire sent me with some rather unsettling news. Upon hearing his decree, I asked if I could deliver his message personally."

"And why would you do that, Lore?"

"Because I wanted to see the look on your face," Lore smirked. "In ten sunrises, you and all of your conspirators are to be executed before Vaska."

The Blind Seers simultaneously gasped with alarm while Casavore didn't bat an eye.

"Is that all?" he asked.

Lore's smug grin faded. "No," she said. "Until the day of the execution, you will be held in a private dungeon under the dire's watchful eye. Say goodbye to your friends, Casavore. This is the last you'll be seeing of them."

Before Casavore could protest, two guards stalked into the dungeon and pulled him from his cell.

"This is madness!" Oland shouted, rattling the bars of his cell as the guards dragged Casavore away. "He is your Blesser! You can't treat him this way!"

"I'll be fine, Oland," Casavore called. "Everything will be ok."

As Casavore was led through the dungeon, he passed by the Vaskan Guard, Arison.

"Casavore?" Arison muttered before calling to his comrades. "Where are you taking him?"

"The Blesser is to be held in a remote jail cell until the day of his execution," Lore answered as she glided by.

"Execution?" Arison gawked. "W—When?"

"In ten sunrises," Lore looked back at the amethyst-eyed soldier, perplexed by the familiarity of his face. "You look familiar. Have we met before?"

"Yes, ma'am," Arison gulped nervously and straightened. "I believe you knew my mother. She served under your husband as his general."

"Ah yes," Lore replied. "You're Hylan's boy... I was never fond of her. I'd hope that you'd learn not to make the same mistakes as she did."

"No, ma'am," Arison shook his head, the muscle around his jaw flexed and quivering with fury.

"Good. Send out as many messengers as you can to all of Lykos and have them know of the Blesser's execution. It's important the Dire's Curse learn what is to become of her father. Give her a chance to do the right thing..."

Chapter Four: The Apprentice

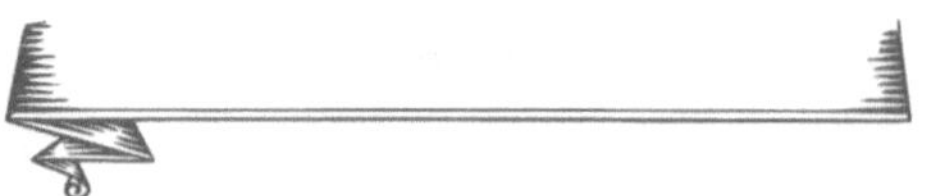

The Vaskan Forest…

"*Brace yourselves,*" Feran cried over the whistling wind as Saber hurtled through the trees and into a leaf-covered clearing.

The Dire Wolves flew from his back and rolled straight into the hard embrace of the surrounding trees. Saber's behind towered in the air, his tail tickling his nose, before he tilted forward and collapsed. He snorted at the leaves, exhausted.

Roeseph coughed and sat up stiffly. "Is everyone ok?"

Sova lay face down in the grass. "My ankle has a heartbeat," he mumbled.

Bones bruised and muscles aching, the Dire Wolves made camp in the clearing. The setting sun shone through the trees like a spotlight onto their unlit firepit, where Saber laid, curled in a ball. Feran reclined against his side, watching Kyce strike a stone against stone in an attempt to conjure a spark. With each fruitless strike, his face grew tenser.

"You need help there, friend?" Feran arched her brow.

"No—" Kyce grunted as he struck the stone again, "—thanks."

Elling shrugged, "Maybe the stones are wet."

"They're not wet," Kyce grumbled.

"Maybe you're not using the right type of stone," Roeseph interjected. "What stones are you using?"

"Rocks."

"Try striking harder," Feran advised.

"I'm striking as hard as I can."

Elling opened her mouth to interject, but before she could so much as mutter a syllable, Kyce threw the stones into the teepee of timber. Drawing a deep breath, he looked at the concerned expressions on his comrades' faces.

"I've had a long day," he began, "if you all could let me try to do this without any remarks or suggestions, that would be great."

Before Kyce could return to his work, Sova stole the stones from where they lay and, with a single strike, bore a spark that engulfed the timber in tremendous flames.

"Hey, I did it!" Sova cheered and looked to the side. Kyce glared at him with the eyes of a rabid wolf. "Uh oh."

Sova sprung from where he sat and ran around the clearing, Kyce at his heels like a bloodthirsty hound after a hare.

"Get back here, you Vaskan rat!"

Roeseph, Elling, and Feran watched from the fire as Kyce made his daily attempt to kill the Royal Traitor. Saber raised his head, his tongue lolling out smiling jaws. Sova facing terrible danger always brought a wag to his tail. Roeseph looked away from the pathetic scene to Elling, surprised to find her emerald-green eyes filled with sorrow.

"Elling?" he said softly. "Are you alright?"

Elling snapped out of her daze. "Mhmm," she nodded and looked back to the fire. "Just lost in thought."

She glanced back at him to find his gentle gaze still locked onto her.

"What?" she asked.

"You can tell me if something's bothering you. You know that, right?"

"I told you, I'm fine."

Feran threw her head back, a long, annoyed groan bursting forth from her gut.

"How about I save you both some time," she exhaled impatiently. "Elling, something's bothering you. I know this because Roeseph pointed it out, and he always knows when something is bothering you. So instead of denying his constant attempts to console you and driving me into madness, please, enlighten us with your troubles."

Sighing heavily, Elling looked back to their captain.

"I guess I'm a little ashamed of how I handled things in Seavale today."

"What are you talking about?" Roeseph questioned. "You didn't do anything wrong. If anything, it was Sova's fault."

"It was a lapse in judgment!" Sova screamed across the clearing.

Roeseph exhaled irritably while Elling held back a fond chuckle.

"That's not what I meant," she sighed, her grin fading. "When that Seavallian attacked us in the alley, I couldn't do anything. You all know how to hold your own in a fight, and I... I'm useless."

"You're not useless," Roeseph corrected sternly.

Sova rolled to Elling's side, trapped in Kyce's headlock, his face bluer than the Seavallian sea.

"Yeah, come on, El," Sova croaked. "You're actually the most dangerous one out of all of us. All we need is a Siren's Call, and you're good to go."

"Kyce," Roeseph snapped.

"On it," Kyce growled and rolled away with Sova. The Royal Traitor's frightened cry filled the dusk. Feran snorted beneath her hand while Roeseph turned to face Elling.

"Elling, you're not useless," he stated once more. "We all had to fight because that's what life demanded of us. But your fighting ability isn't what makes you essential."

"Then what does?" Elling tested.

Feran snorting, unable to help herself. "Your winning personality?"

"Feran," Roeseph scolded.

"Sorry," she bowed her head.

Elling pulled her knees to her chest. "I appreciate what you're saying, Roeseph," she smiled weakly. "But you have to admit. Knowing how to hold your own is pretty crucial to winning a war."

Roeseph tilted his head in thought.

"Fair enough," he agreed and rose to his feet, offering his hand to the young emerald-eyed woman. "Then I suppose I'll just have to teach you."

Elling looked from Roeseph's hand to his noble eyes.

"Are you sure?"

"Of course, I'm sure," Roeseph smiled. "Come on, Elling of the Mosharick Plains. Let's see what you're made of..."

Chapter Five: The Traveler

S*eavale...*
    Word of the Dire Wolves' presence in Seavale spread through the town so fast it was predicted to reach Vaska by nightfall. Throughout all the taverns, whore houses, and alleys, sightings of the Last Soldier, Royal Traitor, Eradite Exile, Dire's Curse, and Feral Shepherd were made known, and their names not given rest from the tongues of those who witnessed.

In the tavern where the Dire Wolves had visited, as many as a hundred men crammed inside the small space eager to hear the stories the bartender spilled.

"I swear to ye sailors," the bartender recited as he stroked his liquor-damp beard, "I was standing as close to the Royal Traitor as ye are standing to me now. He had hair as white as Lykos in winter and eyes as silver as a cloudy day."

"What about the Dire's Curse," a drunken sailor spewed. "Did you see her?"

"Aye. I saw them all."

The tavern door slammed into the wall, making everyone turn and grab their swords. A young woman dressed in a tattered black cloak stood in the doorway with hair as black as ebony, skin fair as ivory, and eyes black as coal. Her hook-shaped metal leg creaking, she stalked through the silent crowd and took a seat at the bar. She smiled, her callused hands drumming the countertop.

"Oh, don't stop on my account," she said. "Please, continue."

"And who might you be, stranger?" the bartender growled.

"Just a traveler passing through," the woman pulled back the hood of her cloak. "My name is Taige. Now, please, continue your story."

"Yes, well," the bartender cleared his throat and turned to his audience. "There I was, staring into the mighty face of the famed—"

"Pardon me," Taige interrupted. "Would you mind getting me a mug of Odin Slayer?"

A sneer in his lip, the bartender made the olive-colored poison and plopped the mug before Taige, splashing everywhere but on her.

"Thank you, sir," she smiled graciously and took the mug in both hands.

"Anyway," the bartender continued, "the Royal Traitor pulled back his hood to reveal the face of the infamous—"

"Is that him right there?" Taige pointed behind the bar at the wanted poster of the Royal Traitor. The bartender turned on the woman, the snarl etched in his lips lifting higher over his canine.

"Are you trying to get a rise out of me, wench?"

"Yes, but that's not what I asked you. May I see that wanted poster, please? The one of the Royal Traitor."

"Why you little—who are you to come into my tavern—"

"I told you, my name is Taige. Perhaps you knew my father. He was quite popular around these parts."

"I don't give a sharick fawn's tail about your—"

"He was called the Viper. The late leader of the Venom Tongues."

The bartender's face turned a ghostly white as the thugs around Taige took a fearful step back. She looked from side to side, pleased by their reaction.

"Apparently, you do," she smirked.

"You—You're a Venom Tongue?" the bartender asked shakily.

"Indeed," Taige replied as she lifted the Odin Slayer to her lips. Like a whale drinking in water, she downed the entire thing and wiped the olive-colored liquid from her lips.

"Now, I won't ask again," she warned and nodded to the image of Sova behind the bar. "Please give me the Royal Traitor's poster, please."

Frantically, the bartender handed Taige the crème-colored paper. Taige stared at the face of the Royal Traitor, her smirk growing broader.

"If—If I may ask, ma'am," the bartender stammered. "Why are the Venom Tongues so interested in the likes of the Royal Traitor? The bounty, perhaps?"

"Good guess, but no," Taige grumbled as she crinkled the wanted poster into her pocket. "This is about revenge. Now, if you could please point me in the direction of the Royal Traitor. He and I have some unfinished business..."

Chapter Six: The Bet

The Vaskan Forest...

Elling fell to the grass with a hard thud. Kyce, Sova, and Feran winced in unison as they watched, leaning against Saber's back with their bare feet exposed to the dying fire.

"Ouch," Sova cringed as he shoved a fistful of wild blueberries into his mouth. "That looked like it hurt."

Roeseph hovered over Elling, his sword in hand.

"Are you ok?" he asked.

"Yeah," Elling coughed.

"Because we can stop if you want—"

"No," Elling answered quickly and picked up her sword. "No, I can do this."

Sova leaned towards Kyce's ear, his voice in a hushed whisper. "I bet you five coins she goes down again."

"Come on, man," Kyce scolded. "She's trying her best."

Sova pulled away, his heart pricking with guilt. Kyce was right. He really shouldn't bet on the failures of his friends.

Feran then leaned to his ear and whispered, "Ten coins Roeseph asks if she's 'ok' the next time she goes down."

His shame vanishing, Sova hissed, "You're on."

Elling stalked circles around Roeseph, her borrowed sword quivering in her grip.

"Remember to stay on the balls of your feet," Roeseph reminded. "If your weight shifts to your heels, you'll—"

"I got it," Elling snapped. "Just. Start, please."

Roeseph hesitated.

"Are you going to ask her if she's ok?" Feran asked from the sidelines.

"She's fine," Sova assured. "She can take care of herself. Show no mercy, Roe!"

Kyce exhaled through a scowl, "You two have no shame."

Elling and Roeseph had been training since mid-day into dusk, and still, he had yet to fall. Bitterness and frustration falling like scales over Elling's eyes, she charged. Like a swift wind, Roeseph dodged every attack. Roaring in frustration, Elling dove forward, only for Roeseph to grab her by the wrist, making her drop her sword, and shoved her to the ground.

"Elling!" he gasped. "I'm sorry, I didn't mean to. Are you—"

"I'm fine!" Elling snapped.

Sova jumped upright, his silver eyes wide as saucers, "He didn't finish! He didn't finish that sentence. It doesn't count. I win the bet!"

"That so does count!" Feran argued, springing up beside him.

"Ha!" Sova laughed. "Show me one reason why I should think you won the bet."

"I can give you three," Feran seethed. "One—he clearly asked if she was ok. Two—this," Feran tapped the Blesser's medallion hanging from her neck. "And three—that." She pointed to Saber laying behind her, his snout tensed in a snarl.

Sova glared at Feran, and reaching into his pocket, slammed ten bronze coins into her hand.

"Sore loser," he growled.

Feran smirked, "It was a pleasure doing business with you."

"You guys were placing bets?" came the scolding voice of the Last Soldier. Sova and Feran flinched and looked at their captain glaring at them with fiery blue eyes.

"It was Sova's idea," Feran said, pointing to her coconspirator.

"Traitor," Sova snarled.

Kyce snickered. Shaking his head, Roeseph looked at Elling as she wiped the autumn dirt off her sleeves.

"Look, Elling," he sighed, "it's your first day. I say we run through a couple more drills and adjust your posture and—"

"It's fine," Elling exhaled. "Let's just... call it a day."

"Are you sure? But what about—"

Before Roeseph could finish, Elling stalked to the fire and sat. Sighing with lament, Roeseph too joined his comrades by the withered flame.

"What a day," Sova yawned through a stretch and looked up at the magenta sky fading to black.

Feran pouted her lip. "Awe," she mocked. "Is the sweepy pwince tired?"

"Yes. The sweepy pwince is tired," Sova grumbled as he rubbed his silver eyes. "We were chased by a Seavallian mob for Lykos' sake."

"You mean the mob you caused?" Kyce grumbled.

"Yeah, that one," Sova yawned as he reclined against Saber's soft fur. The White Angel growled.

"Ah—ah—ah—ah," Sova tutted as he shut his tired eyes. "Not now, Growls. Sleepy."

While the others basked in their contentment, Elling sunk deeper into dread. For eight months, she'd been a burden. The faulty wheel on the carriage. The sled dog with a limp. The weak link in a chain. Her comrades were skilled with a sword, blade, or medallion while she was just a shepherd without a flock.

Roeseph nudged his shoulder against hers. "Elling?" he whispered. "Are you ok?"

Elling gave an irritated sigh, "I'm the same as I was the last time you asked me ten minutes ago."

"Ooh," Sova taunted, "burn."

Feran smirked. "Tell us, our dear sweet Elling," she interjected, "what's got you down?"

Elling exhaled, annoyed. "You guys just can't learn to mind your own business?"

"As a matter of fact, we cannot," Sova said.

"Is it the fact that you can't fight?" Feran joked. "I'll bet it's because she can't fight."

"I can fight," Elling argued.

"Of course, you can," Kyce yawned, "your falling technique is flawless."

The exiles laughed, the fire cackling with them. Even Elling couldn't help but bear a smirk.

"I have been thinking, though," Feran sighed at the end of a laugh. "Elling's probably the most capable fighter out of all of us."

"Don't mock her, Feran," Roeseph warned sternly.

"I wasn't," Feran smirked.

Realizing he had accidentally insulted Elling, Roeseph gulped and stole a nervous glance at the Feral Shepherd. She glared at him, her eyes like two pieces of emerald coals.

Roeseph gulped and looked away. "Please, Feran," he cleared his throat. "Proceed. Please."

Feran snickered. "Anyway, as we all know, Elling is a Hyde Howler."

"Thank you for clarifying," Sova nodded.

"You're welcome. Anyway. Like all Hyde Howlers, when summoned by the Siren's Call, she can become an unstoppable force capable of mass destruction."

"You're heading into sensitive territory, Feran," Elling warned.

"Hold on, I have a point," Feran assured. "You are literally hypnotized to become a lethal weapon. A Hyde Howler doesn't hesitate. They're calculated. Almost impossible to catch off guard."

"Your point?" Kyce exhaled.

"My point is," Feran pulled out the Blesser's medallion, "maybe I can draw it out of her."

"No," Roeseph snapped. "Last time you tried to get rid of the Hyde Howler, you nearly split Elling's head down the middle. We're not doing that again."

"I'm not saying we try to get rid of it," Feran corrected. "I'm saying... maybe we try to bring it out of her."

Silence filled the fire-lit clearing. Not even the crickets dare share their gossip.

"Do you have a death wish or something?" Sova grumbled. "Did that encounter with the Seavallian mob awake something in you? Do we have to be worried about this from now on?"

"I'm not saying we turn her into a Hyde Howler," Feran hissed. "I'm saying we bring out her fighting instincts while she's still just Elling."

Elling sat up, her eyes twinkling with false hope. "So you're saying I'd be just as skilled a fighter as I was if I were a Hyde Howler?"

"Exactly," Feran nodded.

"Woah—Woah—Woah," Roeseph interjected. "We aren't actually considering this, right? This is dangerous."

Kyce shrugged, "I'm considering it.".

"You don't get a say Kyce," Roeseph snapped. "You love danger."

"Fair point."

Chuckling, Feran swung her father's medallion around her forearm. "Oh, come on, Roeseph. Have a little faith."

Before Roeseph could argue, Elling grabbed hold of his arm.

"Please, Roeseph," she pleaded, her Mosharick-green eyes were like puddles of jade, glimmering with desperate hope. "None of us will go through with it unless you give the order."

"Elling, come on—"

"Please?..."

"I STILL THINK THIS is a horrible idea," Roeseph grumbled. Elling sat with her back to him, a bright and cheery grin on her face, while Feran crouched before her.

"Oh, come on, Roeseph," Feran exhaled, her father's medallion in hand. "Don't you trust me?"

"No. And apparently, neither do those two," Roeseph motioned to Sova and Kyce standing a safe distance away with their swords drawn.

"I said I love danger, not death," Kyce snapped from afar.

Feran looked over her shoulder, a heavy exhale rolling from her throat.

"Et tu, Brute?" she called to the Royal Traitor.

"My name is Sova, not Brute—and I'm afraid!"

"Uncultured swine."

Elling tapped Feran on the shoulder.

"Come on," she pleaded, "let's get this over with."

"Ok—Ok—Ok, I'm doing it," Feran sighed. Unable to bear it, Roeseph looked away as the Dire's Curse wove the medallion back and forth. Elling's tense body softened, and her pupil expanded—consumed in the mind melder's enchantment.

"Daughter of Chemon," Feran began, "and child of the Mosharick Plains. I ask for the roar of the beast you keep hidden. I ask that the Hyde Howler's strength and cunning emerge from its host, but the monster remain dormant. Become the fiercest soldier among us, one that fights for justice and opposes oppression. Come forth..."

All was still, and all was quiet.

"Elling?" Roeseph whispered and shook her lightly. "Elling, are you ok?"

Elling was like a statue, frozen and unblinking. When she didn't awaken, Sova and Kyce sheathed their swords and hurried to Feran's side.

"Feran, what did you do?" Kyce snapped.

"I didn't do anything," Feran cried, her eyes alive with fear.

Roeseph jumped from behind Elling, making Feran step back, and grabbed Elling's shoulders. He stared into her emerald-green eyes.

"Elling?" he called. "Elling, can you hear me?" She didn't speak. "Elling," Roeseph said again, softer than before. "Elling, please..."

With a trembling hand, he hesitantly reached for Elling's face. Suddenly, Elling lashed forward as a monstrous cry tore from her throat.

Roeseph, Feran, Sova, and Kyce screamed and toppled into one another like dominos. They scrambled over one another in the middle of the clearing, trying to find their way out of the knot they'd become. Elling laughed, her eyes glittering with tears as she rocked back and forth. Kyce looked up, his fear-filled gaze growing dark with rage.

"Elling!" he roared. "What's wrong with you?"

Elling stopped, trying to speak through a giggle, "You should see the look on your faces."

Roeseph exhaled and relaxed against the grass, relieved she was ok.

"Did it work?" Sova asked as he untangled from his comrades and found his feet.

Elling shrugged, unsure, "Let's find out."

Stealing Sova's sword from his sheath, she turned her blade on Kyce.

"On guard Eradite," Elling challenged as she charged. Kyce poked the handle of his sword into her gut, making her gasp and drop to the grass.

"Apparently not," Feran said.

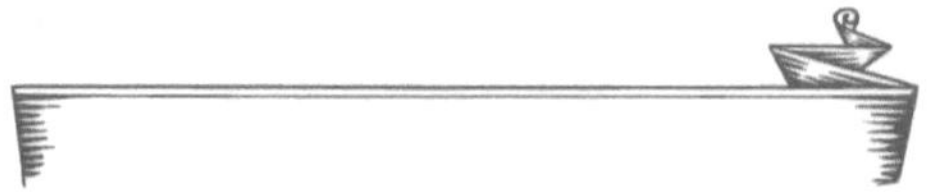

Chapter Seven: A Visitor

Under the midnight moon's watchful eye, the Dire Wolves huddled around the campfire, recalling their best stories and filling the air with their soft laughter.

Sova sat against Feran with Saver, at war with the heaviness of his eyes. He jolted between breaths, desperate to keep awake.

Feran was mid-sentence when she felt Sova collapse against her shoulder. She looked at him as he dozed, his cheek scrunching against her sleeve. Her initial reaction was to swat him on the head, but mercy took her by surprise, and she allowed him to sleep.

In slumber, he looked exactly like Saulder. Or at least what Feran assumed the dire would've looked like. She hadn't seen his face in well over a decade. Saulder and Sova looked the exact same as children, with only their height and hair length contrasting the other. But now, since they were grown, Feran was certain telling the two apart would be near impossible.

"Awe," Kyce pouted. "Is the poor sweet prince tuckered out?"

"Give him a break," Feran scolded. "It's rare he gets a good night's sleep these days."

"Oh yeah," Elling mumbled sympathetically. "His nightmares have gotten worse, haven't they?"

Feran sighed. "They're almost every night now. He's lucky if he can sleep through the night at all."

"What's the deal with his nightmares anyway?" Kyce grumbled as he reclined on his elbows. "Why is it only the dire he dreams about?"

"I'm not sure," Feran shrugged. "Sova talked about it once before. I think it has to do with some suppressed trauma revolving around his fight with his brother."

"Maybe," Roeseph said as he prodded a stick at the fire. "I know what the dire did to him really shook him up. The scar on his shoulder, for example—he can't even bring himself to look at it. Says he doesn't want to remember anything. I'm the only one who's ever seen it, and that's just because I was the one who tended to his bandages for the first few months."

"But he does his own bandages now," Elling shrugged. "How can he not see it?"

"He says he closes his eyes," Roeseph suppressed a laugh.

Feran exhaled, fighting to suppress the fondness in her voice. "He's like a toddler, I swear."

"He'll have to face what his brother did eventually," Roeseph added. "And when he does, we'll just have to be there for him."

Silence carried through the forest, leaving only the light cackle of the flames to battle the eerie quiet.

"So, what does it look like?" Kyce blurted. "Is it gross?"

"Disgusting," Roeseph grimaced as he traced a slit in the center of his pectoral. "It doesn't even look like an arrow shot him. He's got this long, curved scar right here. It looks like the dire may have jerked the arrow around a bunch before he pulled it out."

Feran's heart stooped lower and lower with the progression of Roeseph's description. She was usually so quick to mock Sova, but she hated what the dire did to him. She hated that he didn't know peace and that even in sleep, he couldn't escape what his brother did to him.

"Saulder will pay for what he did," she muttered. "The dire will pay for what he's done to all of us."

"Here—Here," Kyce agreed as he fell against the grass to stare at the sky.

"How?" Elling sighed. "We traveled all over the Mosharick Plains looking for soldiers. No one was brave enough to come forward with Oland and the Blind Seers still in prison. Seavale was our last chance."

"We could try Vaska," Roeseph shrugged. "Maybe there are some people there willing to fight."

"It's too high of a risk and too little of a reward," Feran grumbled. "Even if there were allies in Vaska, there wouldn't be enough to challenge the dire, and Vaska is too dangerous for us to enter."

"Well then, what do you suggest?" Kyce growled, sitting up.

Feran thought for a while in silence. Her chestnut eyes then widened as a morbid idea plagued her mind.

"Maybe we don't need volunteers," she said and drew her medallion. "Maybe all we need is this."

Roeseph glared at Feran and challenged, "What are you getting at?"

"The only reason Dire Zastar ever looked in the direction of that Seavallian witch, Lore, was because my father hypnotized him to fall in love with her," Feran recited. "That way he could marry the dire's betrothed, my mother. Zastar was so devoted to Lore that he overlooked all her flaws and would do anything for her. No matter how ludicrous. Now look at Saber," Feran said as she stroked her soaring wolf's fur. "The only thing keeping him from eating me and all of us alive is the trance I cast on him. He is purely devoted to me and does just as I instruct him."

"So?" Kyce hissed.

"So, what if we did the same to our potential soldiers? Find thieves, murderers, and criminals and make them our devoted subjects."

"No," Elling denied, her usual gentle tone sharp as blades.

Feran threw her head back and groaned, "Oh, come on, Elling."

"What you just suggested is no different than what the dire did to me. You'd be making your own Hyde Howlers."

"Not Hyde Howlers," Feran argued. "They'd be conscious. They'd still have their mind, they'd just feel the overwhelming need to obey and protect us."

Elling snapped to her feet.

"You'd be making slaves, Feran!"

Feran rolled her eyes. "I wouldn't be making slaves—or Hyde Howlers. You're taking this too personally. You're only so uptight about it because you're a Hyde Howler."

Roeseph stood with Elling, his dusk-blue eyes dark with warning.

"She's right, Feran," he said. "We can't fight the dire by bringing in people who are unwilling to fight. It makes us hypocrites."

"Are you guys serious?" Feran scoffed, her eyes wide with bewilderment. "We wouldn't be hypnotizing the innocent. We'd be taking on the worst of the worst. They'd deserve what they'd be getting."

"Monsters, thugs, and criminals or not," Kyce grumbled as he rose to stand beside Roeseph and Elling, "they're people, Feran. You can't just reach into someone's mind and make them do what you want. They deserve a chance to redeem themselves on their own."

"The last time I tried to let someone redeem themselves, I ended up with a knife to my throat. The Eradusks and Eradawns, while victorious, suffered unimaginable losses. And you. You, Kyce, lost Whisp. The only family that stuck by you in your exile. And you still think that we should allow the scum of Lykos to roam free without atoning for their sins?"

"We're not tyrants, Feran," Elling insisted. "If you go through with this, then you'd be no different than Dire Saul—"

"Don't you ever compare me to that monster!" Feran snapped to her feet, accidentally launching Sova off her shoulder. He lay face down on the grass snoring, undisturbed, while Kyce, Elling, and Roeseph scowled at Feran, unwilling to waver.

Her shoulders rising and falling rapidly, Feran looked away.

"Fine," she hissed through clenched teeth. "It was just an idea anyway."

Patting her leg, Feran summoned Saber to his paws.

"The fire's starting to go out," she grumbled as she pulled herself onto Saber's back. "I'm going to get some more timber."

"Feran," Kyce snapped, but Feran and Saber were already gone, lost to the dark forest.

Roeseph looked at Elling as she stared forlornly at the ground.

"Hey," he whispered and nudged her arm.

Elling looked up, revealing the twinkle of suppressed. She looked away and wiped her lashes. "Sorry. I'm ok."

"How about we take a walk?"

Giving a shallow nod, Elling and Roeseph started towards the shadows.

"What about me?" Kyce called.

"Babysit Sova," Roeseph ordered as he and Elling disappeared into the darkness.

Grumbling to himself, Kyce laid against the grass. As he stared at the sky, his heart began to ache as unbearable sadness filled his chest.

I hope you're flying, Whisp, he thought. *I really do.*

ELLING AND ROESEPH stalked through the dark wood, the moonbeams that bled through the trees lighting their uncharted path. Roeseph looked at Elling, sorrowed by the look on her face.

"You know she didn't mean anything by it, right?" he said. "She's just frustrated and angry. And scared... She really was just trying to do what's right."

Elling sighed, her voice heavy in her throat. "I know. I shouldn't have compared her to the dire. I know that probably really hurt her."

"She'll get over it. Nonetheless, she was out of line. We can't let our desire to overthrow Dire Saulder cloud our moral judgment. She knows it's wrong. She's just desperate to fix things. We all are."

"Do you think we'll ever be able to do it?" Elling gulped. "Defeat the dire, I mean? Inhumane solution or not, Feran was right about our lack of willing soldiers."

"We have to," Roeseph nodded. "My father is his prisoner. I promised myself I'd get him out. I have to get him out."

Elling stopped and took Roeseph by the hand. He stared at the ground, unable to look her in the eye, lest she see his weakness.

"Roeseph," she began softly, "will you please look at me?"

Roeseph gulped and looked to the Feral Shepherd, vanquished by the emerald-green oceans rippling in her magnificent eyes.

Elling cupped the sides of his face, making his gut flutter and flip.

"We'll get him out, Roeseph," she assured. "We'll figure it out. We always do."

Roeseph stared at the Feral Shepherd, laying his hand over hers.

"Elling," he began softly, his voice trailing off in a whisper.

Elling pulled away and averted her eyes. "We should, um—We—We should get back. Kyce might be worried about us."

His heart heavy as a stone, Roeseph watched as Elling retreated towards the clearing.

"...Yeah," Roeseph agreed. "Yeah, ok."

KYCE LAID ON HIS BACK staring at the sky, warmed by the fire flickering beside him. Feran, Roeseph, and Elling had been gone for a long while, and the quiet night had started to stir his restless soul.

From the silence came a soft sniveling, soft as moth wings. He sat up. Sova laid beside him, wincing in rapid repetition as sweat poured from his face and tears slipped through his lashes.

"Sova?" Kyce said.

Sova panted heavily, coiling into a ball as he quivered.

"Sova," Kyce said again, more urgently.

Sova gasped between breaths, his brows pressing hard into the center.

"Sova!"

Sova snapped upright and gasped.

"What—What happened?" he shuddered, frantically looking around. "Where is everyone? Where's Feran? Where is she?"

Kyce laid his hand on Sova's shoulder, making him flinch.

"Easy," Kyce ordered. "You're fine. Everything's ok. Feran went to get more firewood, and Elling and Roeseph went on a walk. Take a breath."

Sova sucked in a sharp breath, followed by a softer one. Then a softer one. And then a softer one. When his anxieties tamed, he laid against the grass and stared at the vast diamond-dappled sky.

Kyce eyed him up and down, smirking smugly.

"So," he began. "Worried about Feran, were you?"

Sova sighed and flipped his arm over his eyes.

"What are you talking about?"

"You woke up screaming 'Where's Feran,'"

"I said, 'where's everyone?'"

"So, you're just going to keep denying that you have feelings for her?"

"You should take a walk, Ky. I think the smoke's getting to you."

"Oh, come on, Sova. You act like you can't stand her, but you can't be apart from her for more than ten minutes."

"That because she's a crafty one," Sova argued, looking out from under his arm. "I have to keep an eye on her at all times, or she might jump me. Or her dog might eat me. I live in constant fear."

"Sure," Kyce sighed through a laugh. "Whatever you say."

They sat silently for a long while, listening to the quiet cackle of the flames.

"Besides," Sova sighed. "Even if I did feel that way, she'd never reciprocate anything."

"Why do you say that?" Kyce wondered. "She seems fond enough of you... In her own way, of course."

Sova scoffed through a lamented smirk. "You're forgetting something, Ky."

"And what's that?"

"I have the face of a monster... I can cut my hair the shortest I want, but it doesn't change the fact that I have Saulder's eyes. His hair. His face. There's just no escaping him. Not even in my dreams."

"Yeah..." Kyce sighed. "Feran said your nightmares have become more frequent. Do you know why that is?"

"Your guess is as good as mine," Sova shrugged. "I honestly don't even know why I have them... and I hate that I don't."

"Sounds like quite a predicament," a soft, unfamiliar voice said from the darkness.

Sova and Kyce jumped to their feet, their eyes wide and alert.

"Feran?" Sova called nervously. "Feran, is that you?" Only silence answered. "Cut it out. This isn't funny."

"She's not trying to be funny," Kyce snarled as he drew his sword. "And that's not Feran... Show yourself!"

The soft rustle of forest undergrow poured into camp as Sova and Kyce glance in every direction.

"I must say," came the voice, "your wanted poster doesn't do you justice, Royal Traitor. You're quite handsome."

"Oh yeah?" Sova gulped. "I appreciate the compliment. I bet you're just as beautiful too. How about you come out so we can see for ourselves?"

"That won't be necessary. After all, how could my face compare to that of a 'monster's.' Isn't that what you called it?"

Kyce's teeth gritted and he swung his blade into nothing.

"I command you!" he snarled. "Show yourself!"

"Feisty. I like it. You must be Seavallian."

"I'm an Eradite, you wench."

"Ah, the Eradite Exile then. I've heard a lot about you."

"I'm warning you," Kyce snarled. "Leave us be, or you'll be sorry. No bounty is worth the world of pain you're about to be in."

"Don't fret, my dear fellow. I'm not here for you... Just him."

Sova and Kyce pressed their backs together and looked around the dark clearing.

"I should warn you," Sova gulped. "My friend has a short temper and isn't one to go easy on his opponents."

"That's perfectly fine," came the voice again, closer than before.

Turning around fast, Sova and Kyce found a woman in a dark cloak with long, ebony hair and a metal hook-shaped leg standing before the flames.

She smirked, "I like a challenge."

Kyce roared forward. Before he was even a step within reach of his opponent, the cloaked woman kicked her metal leg into the fire, sending a hailstorm of splintered wood and embers hurtling toward Kyce. The Eradite Exile shouted and covered his face. When he looked up, the cloaked woman charged at him.

Sova slashed his blade at the cloaked attacker, only for her to intercept his sword with her own. She threw Sova, making him trip and flip over his head.

Kyce drew his sword and roared forward, only for the cloaked woman to duck to the side and plunge her metal leg into Kyce's ribs. He whipped against the grass, his lungs emptied from the fall.

"I must say I'm a little disappointed," the woman sighed over him. "I've heard legend of your fighting skill, Eradite. But you're just as weak as the rest of them."

Kyce rose onto his hands and knees and wheeled his fist back to strike the attacked. Catching him by the wrist, she slugged him in the jaw and fell again.

Sova groaned and rolled onto his side to see witness the brutal beating. The world still swaying around him, he rose and limped towards his friend.

"Hey," he coughed. "Leave him alone."

Just as he was upon the cloaked woman, she slipped behind him and trapped his arm against his back. A sharp needle dove between his jaw and neck, making him gasp. As his heart thundered, a dark haze condensed in his eyes, and numbness spread like wildfire from where the poison injected.

"Sova, no!" Kyce shouted through a split lip.

Sova's eyes rolled back, and he collapsed beside the Eradite Exile, still as a dead log.

"What have you done!" Kyce snapped at the cloaked woman.

"Relax," she sighed. "He's not dead. That was poppydil. The fastest working sedative from Seavale to Era. Don't worry about your friend. I'm taking him alive. Though, I don't know how long he'll last on the Adder's Isle."

The Adder's Isle, Kyce shuddered. "You're a Venom Tongue."

"Slow one, aren't you?" the woman snickered.

Slipping the hook of her metal leg under Kyce, she flipped him onto his back and pressed her foot on his chest. Kyce grappled her metal leg, unable to free himself.

"Who in Lykos are you?" he snarled.

"My friends call me Taige," the woman chuckled as she lowered. Kyce hesitated, taken aback by her stunning face. "Hope your head doesn't hurt too bad when you wake up."

"Don't you dare—"

Taige reeled her fist back. Everything hurt all at once. And then everything was black.

"KYCE?" A VOICE CALLED, distant and smothered as if it were under water. "Kyce? Kyce, can you hear me? Wake up!"

Kyce awoke to what felt like a million tiny hammers slamming into his skull. Roeseph loomed over him, his dusk-blue eyes wide and frantic.

"Oh, thank God," he exhaled. "I thought you were dead."

Eye pulsing and lip gushing, Kyce looked up to find Elling standing behind Roeseph, her hand clamped over her mouth in utter disgust.

"Do I look that bad?" he croaked.

Before the Feral Shepherd could give her heartfelt lie, Saber dashed into the clearing with Feran clinging to his back. While still mid-run, Feran leaped off the soaring wolf and landed before the fire.

"What happened to you?" she scoffed. "You look like you got run over by a horse."

"I feel like it."

"What happened here?" Roeseph gulped as he looked around. The remnants of the tossed firepit littered the clearing. Once burning timber faded to cold bones, and the living embers had died to ash.

"Where's Sova?" Feran asked, her eyes going wide.

All looked to Kyce as he bitterly wiped away the blood flowing from his lips.

"Gone," he muttered.

"Gone?" Feran snapped. "What do you mean, gone?"

"We were attacked by a Venom Tongue. She came at us and injected Sova with some sort of sedative. Poppydil, I think she called it."

"Venom tongues…" Feran hissed.

If there was ever a soul Feran hated more than Dire Saulder, it was the Venom Tongues. The gang who attacked the palace and crippled Dire Zastar. Who Killed her mother and stole her from home. She blamed them secondary to Dire Saulder for all the curses on Lykos.

And now they had wronged her again.

"Did she say where she was taking him?" Elling asked.

"Yeah," Kyce sniffled as dried blood clotted his nostrils. "The Adder's Isle."

Roeseph and Feran stiffened and looked worriedly to the other.

"The Adder's Isle?" Elling repeated. "What's the Adder's Isle?"

"It's the Venom Tongue hideout," Roeseph gulped. "It's been around as long as Lykos itself, but no one has been able to find it. They say it's a place everyone can go but never leave."

"Good. I've been in a mood to make history again," Feran sneered as she pulled herself onto Saber's back.

"What are you talking about, Feran?" Roeseph questioned.

"I mean, we're going to save Sova."

"How?" Roeseph blurted. "We don't even know where to begin looking."

"How about—the water?" Feran pointed south. "It's an island, isn't it? Besides, we've got an advantage in the sky. We'll spot them easier than any ship ever could."

"Then we need to get moving," Kyce coughed as he rose to his feet. "Whatever that Venom Tongue wanted him for, it wasn't for his bounty."

Chapter Eight: The Venom Voyage

Sova opened his eyes to find himself standing in the cold, black abyss of his nightmares, surrounded by endless nothing. He looked around, knowing full well who was about to greet him.

"You know this isn't the best time," he shouted through the echo-prone darkness. "I'm kind of in the middle of a crisis right now."

The demonic voice of the dire seethed through the abyss, summoning a mountain range of goosebumps up Sova's spine.

"Who are you?"

Groaning, Sova slumped around. The glimmering black armor of the dire stood a distance away, sword shining in hand.

"What do you want?" Sova grumbled. "Tell me what you want from me, and I'll do it! Just leave me alone!"

"Who are you?" the dire screamed again.

"I am tired of this. I've dealt with these nightmares for eight months now! You've given me no answers! What do you want from me, Saulder?"

"Who are you?" the dire roared towards Sova.

Roaring in frustration, Sova charged also. As he lunged, the dire thrust his sword upward, and Sova felt cold steal pierce his gut.

SOVA WOKE GASPING, his eyes so wide they nearly spilled out of his head. The night sky he fell asleep under had miraculously turned to a cloudless blue, and the grassy clearing was replaced with rolling waves. His back stiffened against a ship's mast, and thick, bristly ropes scraped his arms. A ship's deck lay before him, swaying gently in the ocean's playful tides.

What? Sova gulped as he looked around the strange ship. What's going on? Where am I?

"Oh, good," came a familiar voice. "You're awake."

Sova strained his neck to peer around the mast. A woman stood on the upper deck behind the wheel, the sun perching her shoulder as her ebony hair lashed in the wind beneath a blue rag. Leaving the tides to steer the ship, the sailor descended the rickety old steps on a metal leg, creaking with each step.

"You..." Sova growled, his eyes narrowing on the Venom Tongue.

"Did you get a good night's sleep?" Taige smiled. "First timers don't usually take to the sea so easily."

"Slept like a baby," Sova lied. "Do you mind telling me why I'm here?"

"Ah, yes," Taige nodded and leaned against the ship's railing. "I am taking you to the Adder's Isle. Ever heard of it?"

Sova's stomach sunk to the depths of the ship. He knew of the Adder's Isle:

The island you can go to but never leave.

"Doesn't ring a bell."

"Ah, that's too bad," Taige pouted. "It's a pretty nice place. Lived there most of my life."

"Uh huh... Can't relate. I've been living everywhere at the moment."

"You don't say? Sounds like quite an adventure. Coming to get you was my first time leaving the Island."

"Mhmm," Sova eyed Taige up and down. "You know, you're quite jolly for a kidnapper."

"Why, thank you," Taige shrugged bashfully. "You know, this is my first kidnapping."

"Ah, congratulations."

"Thanks."

The ship dipped ever so slightly in the rambunctious waves, making Sova's stomach roll, his tongue coil, and his cheeks implode—one badly timed wave away from giving up his dinner. Having taken notice of his nauseousness, Taige left and returned with a rusted bucket with a suspicious-looking off-white sludge outlining the bottom rim.

"You can throw up if you have to," she offered, holding the bucket below Sova's chin.

Sova gagged and hunched forward, his lungs flat against the ropes. Despite his ragged heaving, his stomach held its ground, and he pulled away.

"I'm ok," he gagged. "I'm ok."

"Well, ok," Taige nodded and placed the bucket beside him. "Just tell me when you need it again."

"If you don't mind me asking," Sova said, looking around, "where are the others? Are they here too?"

"Nope," Taige smiled and trotted across the ship, doing checks. "I left the Eradite Exile back in your camp. And I didn't run into the other Dire Wolves. Though I must say, the Eradite Exile is much more handsome than I would've thought."

"Don't make me laugh," Sova griped. "Why not take him too, though? Seems foolish that a Venom Tongue would take one of us when you could've had double the bounty."

"Oh, I'm not in it for the bounty," Taige skipped towards Sova. "I'm in it for revenge."

"Oh, good. You sound so giddy about it."

"Well, yeah. I've thought about nothing but for eleven years."

"Ah, I understand it now. Why you're so happy. It's because you're crazy."

"Or maybe I'm crazy because I'm happy," she sat next to Sova to tighten the springs and bolts on her metal leg. "Either way, I prefer to go about my day with a good attitude."

"You are full of surprises, Venom Tongue."

"How so, Royal Traitor?"

"For one, I didn't expect you to act so chipper. You might say I have a prejudice towards the likes of your people."

"That's fine. Most people do. After all, my father is the one who hurt your father."

Like the moon over the sun, Sova's playful eyes darkened, eclipsed with anger. For a moment, he looked exactly like Saulder—rage-filled and bloodthirsty.

"You're the Viper's daughter."

"Sure am," Taige sighed as she stretched out her metal leg, testing the kinks. "I take it that upsets you?"

"I guess I'm not entirely over when the Venom Tongues attacked my home, killed a beloved family friend, kidnapped my brother's betrothed, and crippled my father. But hey, maybe I'm just being sensitive."

"Maybe, but I don't blame you," Taige rose to her feet.

"So why come after me?" Sova growled. "I've done nothing to you."

"That is true. And please don't take this to heart. It's nothing personal," Taige rested against the ship's railing. "It's actually your brother I'm after.."

"Who isn't?"

"If I hold you captive, then he'll leave the safety of Vaska to come and save you."

"Not a bad idea. But you should know that my brother likes me just about as much as you do—"

"But I do like you. You're good company."

"Well, thanks—but my brother does not. He wants me dead."

"I disagree with you, Royal Traitor," Taige whisked out her curved sword, examining how it twinkled in the golden sun.

Sova gulped, his frightened expression reflecting perfectly in the blade.

"You see," Taige began, "family is quite complicated. The dire can say he hates you. Send armies after you. Challenge you to war. But despite all this, he'll always save you if given the chance. After all, you're his baby brother. He loves—"

"Bucket," Sova gagged.

"Pardon me?"

"Bucket. Now."

"Oh! Ok—I'm coming," Taige hurried to Sova's side and lifted the bucket to his lips. He heaved forward, once again, unable to expel the sickness in his gut.

"Don't force it if you can't," Taige scolded like an upset mother. "You'll get a headache."

Sova groaned and fell against the mast to stare at the sky. A massive black sail with a white cobra hissing on the front waved overhead. Past the sail, what looked like a white vulture hovered over the ship Sova smirked, recognizing the massive bat-like wings immediately. He knew then, all Hell was to break loose.

"So," Sova looked to Taige, "let's say I'm right and you're wrong, and my brother is praying for the day I die. What's plan B?"

"Well, I guess it would be the same as plan A. If the dire won't come to save you, he'd at least come to kill you. I'm fine with either as long as it's my blade that takes his life."

"Get in line, sister."

"Can I ask you something?" Taige poked the tip of her sword in Sova's gauze-wrapped shoulder. "Did the dire really do that to you?"

"That's what the Blesser told me," Sova sighed. "Why?"

"Nothing... I'm just sorry. The dire hurt me too," Taige glanced at her metal leg. "When the Hyde Howlers came for us, they did more than take the Viper from me."

Sova swallowed hard, and for a brief moment, he pitied his enemy.

"I lost my father too," he admitted.

"But your father still lives."

"No," Sova shook his head. "Not really, at least..." drawing a heavy breath, Sova forced himself to smile. "Well, I must say, miss Taige, I've actually had a decent time talking to you."

"Why thank you. I as well."

"But I'm afraid I must go."

Taige chuckled and crossed her arms. "Oh really?"

"Yeah. My ride's here."

Like an ivory comet, the White Angel cast from the sky and slammed onto the lower deck, causing the ship to dip into the waves as he roared into the wind. Taige spun around fast, coming face to face with the White Angel of legend—the very beast that had scarred the dreaded Dire of Vaska.

As Saber snarled and scratched the planks, Roeseph, Elling, Kyce, and Feran sprung from his back. Feran glared at the Venom Tongue, her father's medallion clutched tight in hand.

"Feran!" Sova exclaimed. "Long time no see. Have you met my friend, Taige?"

"No," Feran growled as she drew her medallion from her neck and twirled it at her side. "But I've met her father. We didn't get along."

Taige drew a deep breath. "I'm sorry, but I really must ask you to leave my ship."

"Sure," Roeseph said, his pearl-capped knuckles unsheathing over the handle of his sword. "Right after we take back what you stole from us."

"Awe, so you do care about me?" Sova swooned.

Taige stepped in front of her hostage, her cheery eyes turning dark. "I'm afraid I can't let you do that."

"Good," Kyce snarled. "I was hoping for a rematch."

Kyce sprung forward, his sword rearing back to strike the black-haired Venom Tongue. Taige smirked and brought her sword down on Kyce's, bringing him to his knees. He struggled under the force of her blade, the jagged edge inching closer and closer to his face.

Feran charged next, her medallion in hand. Taige threw Kyce into Feran, making her drop her medallion across the deck. As Taige raised her blade to strike them both, Roeseph intercepted her sword against his. He threw her back. Finding her feet, Feran glanced rapidly around the ship.

"I lost Casavore's medallion!" she cried.

"Find it quickly, please," Roeseph panted as he and Taige fought. While Feran and Saber slipped away to hunt the Blesser's medallion, Kyce sprung from the deck.

"I've had enough of this," he snarled.

Roeseph pushed Taige into the center of the deck. There, he and Kyce circled her. She smirked, unbothered, and bowed, "After you, good sirs."

Sova watched from the mast, his eyes wide as Roeseph and Kyce battled Taige. Even with two capable soldiers at her blade, she wouldn't falter.

"Sova," came a soft whisper, breaking the Royal Traitor's daze.

"Elling!" Sova exclaimed and turned to find the Feral Shepherd hiding behind the mast with a blade in hand. "How the heck have you been?"

"Shhh," she hissed as she cut the ropes. "Sova, what in the heck is going on?"

"Ah well—" Sova began, not pausing to take a breath, "my brother had little miss Venom Tongue's father killed for conspiracy against Vaska and the attempted assassination of Dire Zastar, so, of course, she intends to hold me hostage in hopes of bringing the dire out of Vaska so she can make him pay for everything he took from her. You know, the usual."

"These ropes won't cut," Elling whined.

"Don't worry," Sova sighed. "Take your time. I've got nowhere to be."

Roeseph and Kyce stumbled back from Taige to catch their breath, exhausted from the fight. Taige jammed her sword into the deck to rest against. She hadn't so much as broken a sweat, while Kyce and Roeseph were nearly drowning in perspiration.

"Had enough yet, boys?" she teased.

"You little—" Kyce charged.

Ducking to avoid his attack, Taige launched her metal leg into his back. He hurtled across the deck and into the railing. He laid over the planks, knocked out cold. Taige turned to Roeseph next. Jerking her sword from the deck, she cut his blade from his hand and sent it flying across the ship right into the mast where Sova sat, just an inch from his ear.

"Hey!" Sova snapped. "Watch it!"

Roeseph stared at his empty hand. Kicking high, Taige hooked her metal leg around his neck and sent him crashing to the deck.

"Roeseph!" Elling cried, and without thinking, charged the Venom Tongue.

"Elling, stop!" Sova shouted.

The Venom Tongue looked up from the man pinned under her metal leg and grabbed Elling by the throat, making her gasp and drop her blade.

"Leave her alone!" Roeseph shouted beneath the Venom Tongue. Taige pressed her metal leg harder on his chest, making his ribs groan like a tree branch on the verge of snapping. She looked at Elling.

"So, you're the Feral Shepherd?" she smirked. "I have to say, of all the Dire Wolves, I disliked you the most."

Elling choked, her emerald-green eyes reddening with fear and oxygen deprivation.

"Leave her alone!" Roeseph gasped, his ribs slowly caving. "She's innocent."

"She's a Hyde Howler," Taige said. "None of them are innocent. When I was thirteen, they dragged my father out of his own home. When I fought back, they cut through my leg so I couldn't follow... They forced my brethren and me onto that Lykos forsaken island to escape genocide... So, no, this one isn't innocent. She's just like all the others. A good-for-nothing monster."

A tear painted Elling's cheek as Taige drew her sword back. Before she could strike Elling, Feran leaped out from behind the Venom Tongue with the Blesser's medallion in hand.

Chapter Nine: Cupid's Curse

Numbness rippled through Taige. The fire in her eyes doused, and her limbs went limp at her sides—completely subdued by the power of the medallion.

Roeseph pulled himself out from under her metal leg and untangled her hand from Elling's throat. Hugging Elling close, he collapsed with her to the floorboards.

"You're ok," he gulped between breaths as he hugged her tighter. "You're ok."

With Roeseph and Elling distracted, Kyce just starting to regain consciousness, and Sova tied to the mast, Feran wove the medallion from side to side. It then occurred to her. She had a Venom Tongue at her mercy. She could do anything to her. Anything at all. Including getting revenge on the Venom Tongues and Saulder too.

She gritted her teeth, the wicked glint in her gaze making Sova eyes widen.

"Feran, don't!" he cried.

"Venom Tongue," Feran seethed. "Enemy of Vaska, murderer of Fala, and crippler of Zastar... hear my words and hear them well. When you awake, you will be bonded to the first soul you see. You will fall for them, whether it be by fellowship or romance. You will be quick to execute their order and place their life above your own. Hear me—you wretched serpent—for the price of my mother's life, you'll devote your own..."

Without warning, she slammed the medallion against into Taige's temple, making her gasp and fall to the floorboards. The Dire Wolves stared at Feran, their eyes wide and mortified.

"Feran..." Roeseph whispered. "What have you done? What did you do to her?"

"What she deserved," Feran growled as she stepped over Taige and knelt before Sova.

Shaking her head, Elling gasped between breaths, "You—You said you wouldn't. You said you wouldn't hypnotize—"

"I didn't say anything of the sort," Feran snarled as she untied Sova. "I did what needed to be done."

"You've enslaved a human being, Feran," Roeseph yelled.

Kyce scoffed. "Calling her a 'human being' is being a little too generous, don't you think?"

Sova stood from the mast and rubbed the red marks on his arms left by the ropes. He glared at Feran, his silver eyes blazing.

"What?" she fumed.

"You went too far, Feran," he growled.

Feran laughed. "Oh, don't act so high and mighty, Sova. You would've done the same. Did you forget it was her people that hurt your father? That killed my mother?"

"Have you forgotten that the hypnosis you just used is the one Casavore used on Zastar?" Sova snapped, an inch from Feran's face. "The trance that put Lore in power? The trance that gave her the authority to bring the Venom Tongues into the palace in the first place? That trance is the whole reason Lykos is damned! Nothing good can come from it!"

Growling in frustration, Feran stomped to the far side of the ship, Saber at her side, and stared at the waves.

"So, what do we do?" Elling asked, breaking the silence.

Roeseph sighed and rubbed his neck, "We go back to Lykos and keep trying to find allies."

"What about the girl?" Elling looked to the Venom Tongue laying on the floor, blood flowing down the side of her face where Feran hit her. "We can't just leave her here."

"Then let's stay," Feran said to the waves.

Roeseph exhaled, his patience depleting. "What are you talking about, Feran?"

Feran turned and stalked towards the others.

"This ship is heading to the Adder's Isle," she said. "The infamous hideout of the Venom Tongues. It's literally an entire island full of people that want the dire dead."

"We aren't going to let you hypnotize more people, Feran," Kyce snarled.

"I don't need to. That girl is the daughter of the late Venom Tongue leader. The Viper. You remember him, right, Sova?"

Sova looked away.

He knew the Viper. He knew him well. After all, he was the first man Saulder ever killed. The first man Sova ever watched him kill.

Shaking his head, Sova growled, "Your point, Feran."

"The girl is likely to still have influence among the Venom Tongues. If we play our cards right, we can use her to gain their aid. We could have an entire army—" Feran snapped her fingers, "—just like that."

Roeseph, Kyce, and Sova looked to one another. The glint in their eyes horrified Elling.

"You aren't actually considering this are you?" she cried.

"They're Venom Tongues, Elling," Kyce growled. "Who cares if they die?"

Feran turned to Roeseph, her brow drawn in an arch. "What say you, captain?"

Roeseph looked from his comrades to Elling.

After a moment's hesitation, he sighed, "Fine. We'll sail to the Adder's Isle and convince the Venom Tongues to join our cause. Hopefully, Taige can vouch for us."

A cruel smile crept across Feran's face. "Excellent."

"On one condition," Roeseph took a daring step towards Feran. "When this is all over. Once we have our army and the dire is defeated... you have to release that girl from your trance."

Her grin sinking, Feran replied in a sarcastic tone, "Aye—Aye, captain."

Sova drew a whistling breath through clenched teeth, his eyes wandering to the unconscious Venom Tongue at their feet..

"So..." he began awkwardly. "Who are we giving her to?"

"Giving her to?" Elling repeated scornfully.

"What's wrong with you, Sova?" Roeseph yelled.

"I don't know how to say it!" Sova cried. "Go back to yelling at Feran. She's the one who hypnotized her!"

"Yeah," Feran snapped back, "saving your sorry hide, your highness."

As the Dire Wolves argued, Kyce looked to the Venom Tongue lying motionless on the floor.

He scoffed, "Not so tough now."

Lifting Taige into his arms, Kyce carried her across the deck and propped her against the mast to tie her up. Taige slumped forward, her forehead falling on his shoulder and bloodying his sleeve.

"Yeesh, Feran," Kyce grumbled as he drew a rag from his pocket. "Did you have to hit her so hard?"

"I have no regrets," Feran hissed, then returned to arguing with the others.

The Dire Wolves rambling behind him, Kyce dabbed the cloth lightly on Taige's head. She flinched. Her obsidian eyes fluttering open, she looked up to see the face of a handsome man loom over her. His skin was a sun-kissed tawny. His hair, a deep, dark-brown. And his eyes, such a magnificent amber she nearly mistook them for pools of lava.

Kyce pulled away.

"Well, look who's awake," he growled bitterly.

At the sound of his voice, the Dire Wolves turned to their hostage.

"Uh oh," Feran mumbled.

Taige gawked at Kyce, her marble-black eyes somehow glittering with stars in the middle of day.

"What?" Kyce sneered. "Nothing to say?"

"It's you," Taige whispered.

Kyce eyed her up and down, annoyed by the dumbstruck look on her face. "Yeah, it's me. The guy you left for dead back in Lykos. Surprised?"

"Not in all my years on this earth have I met a soul so perfect and true."

"Pardon?" Kyce arched his brow.

"Truly, you must be the one I was made for. Who the God of this earth designed me to be with. To love and protect. I swear to you, Kyce of Eradawn and Eradusk, I am forever vowed to you. For no human being on earth has ever been made more strong, beautiful, or majestic than you."

Kyce froze, his face turning a ruby red as Sova laughed hysterically.

"Oh," Sova gasped and wiped a tear from his eye, "this is going to be fun... Pfft—she called him majestic."

Feran rolled her eyes and marched to the Eradite Exile.

"Kyce," she began coldly and touched his shoulder, "you wanted to say something to Taige, didn't you?"

Kyce looked back to Taige as she gazed at him with eyes that made a puppy's look cold and marauding. He sighed, already sick of the situation.

"Listen—"

"Taige," the Venom Tongue daughter said, smiling. "My name is Taige."

Kyce exhaled, and pinched the bridge of his nose. "Listen, Taige. I need to ask you a favor..."

THE SUN DOUSED OVER the horizon as the ship drifted south through a sea of stars.

The Dire Wolves sat around an empty oil barrel set ablaze, a makeshift campfire, while Feran and Saber stood on the upper deck in exile. Kyce shivered and pressed his palms close to the flame while Taige latched onto his arm snuggling against his shoulder while humming.

"Quite the snuggle bug you got there, huh, Kyce?" Sova taunted.

Kyce growled, "Watch it, Princey."

"I'm so glad you're finally starting to settle down," Sova crossed his arms. "I was worried you'd end up an old hermit."

Kyce glared at the white-haired prince, making him step back from the flames.

"Oh, come on, Kyce," Roeseph smirked. "There are worse things than to be doted on by a pretty lady."

"Easy for you to say," Kyce growled and wiggled his arm. Taige moved with it, like a cat clinging to a pant leg. "You don't have a whole person attached to you. And I didn't ask for this. This is all just a big accident."

"A happy accident," Sova added.

Taige looked at Kyce, her big and loving eyes flecked with sparks of worry. "Are you ok, Kyce? You seem upset. Did I do something wrong?"

"Yes," Kyce growled. "You kidnapped Sova and got me wrapped up in this mess."

Taige looked away shamefully, her grip tightening on his arm.

Elling glared at the Eradite Exile, her emerald eyes dark with warning. "Come on, Kyce, give her a break. She had just as little say in this as you did."

Kyce grumbled something fowl under his breath and looked to the fire.

"It's all Feran's fault anyway," he said finally and looked to the upper deck where Feran and Saber stared out to sea. "If you want to scold someone, scold her."

Sova glanced over his shoulder, the resentment he tried so hard to cling to slipping away at the sight of Feran standing all alone.

"I'll be right back," he said as he started towards the upper deck. "Roeseph, do me a favor. Keep grilling Kyce. Preferably until he tries to throw himself overboard."

"Where are you going?" Roeseph called, though Sova was already gone, halfway to the stairs.

Taige stared at Kyce, her lashes fluttering like black butterfly wings. "Kyce, your eyes are so angry. Like fire. Like two beautiful fires."

Roeseph and Elling held back a chuckle while Kyce closed his eyes and sighed.

SOVA SCALED THE WOODEN steps to the upper deck. Feran leaned over the railing, staring at the black sea while Saber laid next to her with his large head on the same railing. Sova stepped onto the deck, the planks groaning beneath his feet. Saber lifted his head and snarled, his ears flattening against his skull. Feran looked back, her eyes red and misty as a single tear painted the side of her face.

Sova stopped.

"Feran," he whispered, unable to hide the ache in his voice.

Feran turned back to the sea. "You need to go," she sniffled.

"I'm not here to yell at you," Sova said, daring to draw near. "And I'm not going to make fun of you either."

"Sova, please—"

"Just hold on a second," Sova laid his hand on her shoulder. "Look, I know I said some things that probably hurt, but it's just that I was surprised you would do something like that. Even if it was to a Venom Tongue. But I'm not ever going to stop being there for you if you're going through something. I know coming face to face with a Venom Tongue can bring up a lot of bad memories—"

"For Lykos sake, Sova!" Feran snapped. "I'm not crying I'm seasi—"

Cheeks imploding, she hunched over the ship's side and became sick.

"Oh, Lykos!" Sova lunged back, his silver eyes widening. "The bucket. We need the bucket! Taige!" he cried through cupped hands. "Where's the bucket?"

"Forget the bucket, Sova!" Feran shouted between gasps.

Cringing, Sova patted Feran awkwardly on the back.

"There—There," he tutted uncomfortably. "Just let it out."

Face pale as seafoam and red eyes glossed, Feran gulped at the end of her sickness and collapsed next to Saber, the soaring wolf whining as he laid his snout on her thigh.

Sova shook his head and scoffed as a taunting smile crossed his lips.

"So, you can fly a soaring wolf above the clouds at the speed of lightning, but you can't tolerate a little boat ride?"

"What are you doing here, Sova?" Feran gagged. "Or have you come to yell at me some more?"

"No," Sova slumped next to her. "I think God's punished you enough."

"I'll say," Feran raked her forearm over her lips.

Sova reached for her face, and she drew away quickly.

"What are you—"

"Would you hold still?" Sova scolded and pressed the back of his hand against her forehead and neck. She averted her gaze, her cheeks turning a subtle red. "You don't feel warm," Sova mumbled. "Have you been sick all night?"

"M—Most of it," Feran stammered and pulled away.

"You should come hang out with us around the fire. It might help distract you."

"No, I'm fine. Besides, I don't think my exile is quite over yet."

"They're upset, but they'll get over it. Come sit with us."

"It's ok, Sova," Feran said, her voice tattered. "I'm used to being a hermit, remember?"

Sova swallowed hard, the wound in his heart tearing into a gash. He looked to the stars.

"So um," he cleared his throat, "how are you feeling? I mean, are you ok with facing an island full of Venom Tongues?"

Choking down another wave of nausea, Feran inhaled. "How I feel doesn't matter, Sova. We need soldiers. And as long as we have that little Venom Tongue rat following Kyce around like a lovesick puppy, then we've got a shot. Then, once we've dethroned Saulder, I can set the little serpent free and be done with her."

"I know what they did to your mother is unforgivable. But Taige isn't responsible for any of that. You should try being a little kinder to her."

"Didn't she kidnap you?"

"Yes, but in her defense, you did too."

Feran snorted as a fond smirk broke across her pale face.

"I forgot about that," she sighed. "Things were simpler back then... Back then, I thought all it would take for Saulder to become good again was for him to see me, and everything would be all right. Back then, I believed stories like Saul of Tarsus could be real. That's why I can't trust this girl, Sova. People don't change."

"I'm not asking you to trust her," Sova shrugged. "Just... be kind to her. I mean, the scriptures say to guard your heart, but it also says to love your neighbor as yourself. And who knows, maybe it'll be Taige that walks that Damascus road you love so much."

Feran hummed tiredly. "Maybe. If God wants to make children from stones, He can do so as pleases. But I'm done talking to rocks."

"...That's what the Eradites used to think," Sova replied. "That the safest course of action was to alienate themselves from people who needed God most. Is that the way you want to be?"

"Of course not," Feran sighed. "Sometimes, it's just hard to keep faith."

Sova nudged Feran's shoulder. "What was that thing you said to me back on the Cliffs of Era? That you wanted to go out like Paul the Apostle? ... Throwing hard punches?"

Feran snorted softly. "Fighting a good fight."

"So, just stick to it, Feran. I know you can. Fight a good fight. Finish the race. Keep the faith..."

"I feel like you're taking that verse out of context."

"Probably."

THE KINGDOM OF VASKA...

Hidden in the highest tower of the Vaskan palace, in a secret passage, beneath a dark stairwell lay a lonely jail cell. Remnants of bones turned to dust, and busted chains littered the prison floor.

Blesser Casavore sat with his back to the wall, silence, his only company. When he was sure the dire was gone, and he was completely and indefinitely alone, he drew Feran's medallion and stared at the charred treasure. As if the pendant were a key to an archive of lost memories, visions of a smiling child, untarnished by the world flashed through his mind.

He sighed and reclined against the cold wall, holding the medallion close as he recalled a tender memory:

A candle burned at his bedside, warming his back. Feran sat on his knee, and his dear wife, Fala, rested her cheek against his shoulder. With the two women he loved most in the world in his embrace, he read his daughter's favorite story from the book of Acts.

He read of a man called Ananias, and how the Lord called on him in his sleep to go to the home of an enemy, and renew his sight which was taken from him.

"'Lord,' Casavore had read. "I have heard from many about this man, how much evil he has done to your saints at Jerusalem. And here he has authority from the chief priests to bind all who call on your name.' But the Lord said to him, 'Go, for he is a chosen instrument of mine to carry my name before the Gentiles and kings and the children of Israel. For I will show him how much he must suffer for the sake of my name.'"

And so Ananias went to Saul's home to lay hands on him, and when the scales finally fell from Saul's eyes, Saul saw.

Casavore opened his eyes to find himself still trapped in the dimly lit confinement of his cage. He exhaled and looked at his daughter's treasure, wishing so badly he could see her. Hold her. Tell her how much he missed her.

"God…" he called to the stone-covered sky. "Hear my prayer. Forgive me for what I have done to Zastar's son. If you have a punishment in store for me, let it be so. But spare Feran the fate I fear she may have inherited from your servant. Don't let my mistakes plague her as well. Free her from the curses I have cast. Forgive your servant. And free her from this wicked ruler…"

Come nine sunrises, Casavore would meet a fate much like Paul, the man from Feran's favorite story.

Chapter Ten: The Viper's Garden

The Sea of Lykos...

The sun rose out of the Seavallian sea, staining the ripples amber.

Kyce lay beside the ship's mast on a bed of tangled netting, his face warmed by the ocean air beating at the sail. He yawned and opened his eyes. His throat stinging, dried by the salty mist. As he turned on his side, he came face to face with Taige, staring at him with big, unblinking owl-like eyes.

"Great Lykos!" he cursed and tried to scramble away from his bright-eyed stalker, only to get wrapped up in the net he laid on.

"Good morning, Kyce!" Taige greeted in a merry tone.

"What in Lykos are you doing staring at me like that?"

"I couldn't sleep last night," Taige said, sitting up. "So I just stayed up watching the stars and waiting for you to wake up. Hey. Did you know you talk in your sleep? Who's Whisp?"

"None of your business," Kyce fought in the net he'd snared himself in, his frustrated attempts only worsening the tangle.

"Let me help you."

Grabbing hold of the net, Taige effortlessly unraveled the ropes. Kyce lay flat on his back, scowling at the sky as his mortally wounded pride bled out over the planks.

Suddenly, Sova's mocking laughter poured from above. The Dire Wolves and Saber stood on the upper deck, leaning over the railing as they smiled at their comrade.

"Good morning, love birds," Sova taunted. "Did you have a nice nap, Ky?"

"Oh yes," Taige answered for him. "He slept so peacefully. Sometimes he snores like a kitten."

"So sweet. Hear that, Ky?" Sova leaned over the railing. "A kitten."

Kyce snapped to his feet, his face twisted in a snarl.

"Watch yourself," he threatened. "I've had a rough couple of days and am this close," he pinched his fingers together, leaving barely enough space for a dust mite, "to throwing you overboard."

"Easy there, Eradite," Roeseph eased with a swinging voice. "You shouldn't talk like that in front of your lady."

"She's not my—" Kyce stopped and looked at Taige sitting on the floor. She smiled at him, her obsidian eyes clueless and doting. If she had a tail, Kyce was sure it would be wagging. "What are you looking at?"

"You," Taige said and popped upright, shifting from her heels to her toes. "I like to look at you."

"Well, stop it."

Taige stepped forward. "Why?" she tilted her head.

"Because I—"

Feran laughed from the upper deck. "Because he's bashful," she teased, her cheek scrunching over the fist she rested on.

"Shut up, Feran!" Kyce snarled. "You're the reason I'm stuck with this."

Elling pouted. "Awe, look how red he's getting."

"You too, Elling?" Kyce barked. "I thought you were against this?"

"Oh, I am," she nodded. "But I figured if I have to be part of this disgusting scheme, I might as well make fun of you."

Scowling, Kyce looked back at Taige.

"Don't watch me sleep anymore," he growled and marched up the rickety stairs to join his comrades.

"Okeydokey," Taige smiled, trotting after him.

"So, what's got all of you up so early?" Kyce stepped onto the upper deck. "Sova have another night terror?"

"This time—no," Sova answered. "See for yourself..."

Kyce looked to the ocean ahead of their ship. A massive emerald-green island with a dormant volcano settled on the horizon's edge, a gold belt of sand wrapping its waist.

"I present to you, the Adder's Isle," Roeseph said, opening his hand to the magnificent land.

"Great Lykos," Kyce mumbled, his eyes widening. "Venom Tongue hideout or not, it really takes your breath away, doesn't it?"

Feran scowled at the sin-stained sea.

"Yeah," she crossed her arms. "Almost makes you forget that a bunch of filthy, hell-bound, scummy, barnacle-infested, sea water-guzzling, snake kissing, bunch of crooks and thieves live there..."

The Dire Wolves stared at her, their lips pierced and eyes big with worry.

"What?" Feran shrugged.

Taige stepped onto the upper deck, her gleeful grin sinking at the sight of the isle.

"What is that?" she asked, her face paling to a shade whiter than seafoam.

"The Adder's Isle, what else?" Sova shrugged. "Don't tell me we went to the Copperhead's Landmass instead."

The Dire Wolves glared at him, unamused.

Sova glared back, "Oh come on, that was funny."

Taige stepped back, shaking her head as she gasped, "We weren't supposed to get here until late in the day."

"Is that a problem?" Roeseph asked.

"There's a reason all can go to the Adder's Isle, but none can leave," Taige snapped and ran to the wheel. Gripping the prongs, she lashed the ship to the side, knocking the Dire Wolves to the deck.

Kyce caught himself against the railing, his amber eyes burning into Taige as he snapped, "What in Lykos are you doing?"

"Trying to save your lives," Taige hissed back. "Because we arrived so early, I couldn't redirect us through the safe route."

Roeseph looked up. "Safe route? What safe route?"

"The safe route to the isle around the Viper's Garden—around the Destroyer of Ships. The entire island is surrounded by coral fields. And we're about to sail straight through it!"

The ship stalled suddenly, hurtling Taige into the wheel and the Dire Wolves back to the planks. The floor burst open, the upper deck divided by a rift.

"What in Lykos was that?" Roeseph cried and looked over the railing to find what looked like a massive stalagmite jutting into the ship's side.

Taige pushed herself from the wheel, long strands of black hair falling over her face. "We've impaled ourselves on a coral branch."

Violent waves thrust into the gash in the vessel's side, billowing rapidly through the rift in the floor as the boat slowly sunk.

"We're going down!" Sova shouted as he helped Elling to her feet.

"Everyone," Feran shouted, "get on Saber!"

As the Dire Wolves ran towards the soaring wolf, the brutal waves pushed the boat deeper onto the coral. As the floorboards cracked into splinters under their feet, Feran, Roeseph, Elling, Sova, and Taige lunged onto Saber's back. Just as Kyce was about to board, a support beam below deck thrust through the planks between him and the soaring wolf. Saber yelped and lunge into the air while the floorboards beneath Kyce snapped, and he fell through to the darkness below.

"Kyce!" Roeseph shouted, his eyes latched on the gaping hole Kyce had fallen through.

Without hesitation, Taige dove off Saber's back and into the ocean. For what seemed like hours disguised as seconds, the Dire Wolves hovered over the shipwreck, anxiously scanning the rabid waves. The ship groaned and lurched a little lower into the waves, an indicator time was running out.

"I don't see them," Roeseph yelled.

Elling gripped his arm, tears racing down her cheeks as she cried, "Where is he?"

Sova swung his legs over Saber's side. "I'm going after them."

Before he could jump, Feran grabbed the collar of his shirt and jerked him back.

"Don't you dare!" she snarled, her eyes more vicious than the waves below.

"We can't just leave Ky to drown!" Sova argued.

Roeseph grabbed him by the shoulder and lashed him around, the severity in his blue eyes making Sova gulp.

"If you go in there, you'll only make things worse. Taige'll get him. Have a little faith."

"Faith in her?" Feran snapped. "She's a Venom Tongue, Roeseph! For all we know, she swam back to the isle and left Kyce for dead."

Just then, Taige burst to the surface with Kyce floating unconsciously under her arm. Coughing her lungs raw, she waved at the soaring wolf in the sky.

"There," Elling pointed at the Viper's Heir. "I see them!"

Saber stooped to the waves as Sova and Roeseph plucked Kyce and Taige from the Viper's Garden. Sova looked back at the ship as they flew towards the island, watching as the whole thing ripped to shreds against the coral fields. He shuddered and looked away to the Adder's Isle growing uncomfortably close.

Just as Saber's paws breached the sand, the Dire Wolves threw themselves off his back and lowered Kyce to the ground. His eyes were locked shut and a line of water trickled out the corner of his mouth.

"Is he going to be alright?" Elling cried as they surrounded the Eradite Exile.

"Yes," Taige huffed, positioning her hands over his sternum to force breath into his lungs. "He has to be."

"Come on, Ky," Feran pleaded, her stomach sinking with each violent jolt of his body.

Taige continued to beat at Kyce's chest, mumbling something under her breath as he mocked her with his stillness.

"He isn't breathing," Sova shouted. "Why isn't he breathing?"

Roeseph grabbed Sova's shoulder.

"He's going to be ok," Roeseph said, unsure, as he watched the color drain from Kyce's skin.

"Then why isn't he breathing?"

Taige lowered to Kyce, her soaked, black locks masking his face as they traded breaths.

Suddenly, a geyser spewed from Kyce's lips, followed by a fit of coughs that shook his entire body. The Dire Wolves gave a collective sigh of relief.

"Oh thank God," Feran exhaled.

Chapter Eleven: The Adder's Isle

K*yce coughed at the unforgiving sun*, his back grating against the rough sand.

"Where am I?" he mumbled at the blurring world.

"Kyce?" came a distant voice, sweet and gentle. "Kyce, are you with me?"

Kyce blinked in an attempt to sharpen the world. Taige loomed overhead, her soaked, black locks dripping onto his face.

"Great..." he looked away with a scowl.

"You had us worried sick," Taige exhaled. "I thought I'd lost you."

"Would you please give me a little room to breathe?" Kyce sat up, making Taige shuffle back as he angrily wiped his face. "You're getting me all wet."

Roeseph glared at his comrade, the relief in his eyes turning to rage.

"She just saved your life, Kyce. Show a little gratitude."

Sova crouched beside Kyce and slapped his back hard.

"Yeah," he smiled. "Perk up, Ky. After all, you just had your first kiss."

Kyce glared over his shoulder. "Shut up, Sova."

"Aww," the Royal Traitor pouted. "He's shy."

Kyce lunged at Sova, only for Taige to grab his wrist, keeping him in place.

"Sit down," she begged. "You just nearly drowned. You shouldn't exert yourself."

Kyce bared his teeth in a snarl.

"Get off me!" he snapped and jerked away.

"That's enough!" Roeseph shouted.

Kyce sprung to his feet, getting all but an inch from his captain. Sova and Elling stepped between them, Sova walking Kyce back and Elling, Roeseph.

"Guys," Feran whispered, interrupting the battle. "Guys look."

The fighting ceased instantly as the Dire Wolves collectively looked up at the dense, dark jungle beyond the beach. The leaves and undergrowth shuffled, stirred by some unknown creature and creatures lurking in the darkness.

Feran drew a shuddering breath, frightened by the silence. The dark jungle before her was home to the Venom Tongues, the wicked gang who ten years ago invaded Vaska, crippled Zastar, and slaughtered her mother.

Sova stood next to her, his chest rising as he drew a tremendous breath.

"It's smaller than I thought it would be," he joked.

Feran stayed silent as Saber growled at her side.

Roeseph stepped ahead of his troops to stare at the dark jungle.

"Well, Dire Wolves," he sighed. "Welcome to the Adder's Isle."

With Roeseph leading the charge, the Dire Wolves marched off the golden coals and into the jungle where an unearthly heat hit them like a wall. Beads of sweat trickled down their temples, stinging their shoulders and necks.

Light streamed through the treetops, breaking and reforming with each shift of the leaves as Roeseph and Elling led the way hand and hand down a root covered path. Kyce walked behind them, Taige clinging to his shadow while Feran, Sova, and Saber lingered in back.

Sova whistled a happy little tune as he looked around, the obnoxious noise like acid in Feran's ear.

"Are you going to do that the entire time?" she growled over her shoulder.

"What?" Sova shrugged. "It's entertaining."

"It's annoying is what it is."

"Good," he continued to whistle.

"You'll attract the Venom Tongues doing that, you know."

Taige looked back, her brow drawn in an arch.

"They probably already know we're here," she admitted. "The Viper's Garden is meant to destroy ships, but it also serves as a warning bell."

"Oh good," Feran scowled. "Very elaborate system you have there. Destroying ships and leaving sailors to drown at sea."

"Well, for a while, the only ones to come here were the Vaskans and Hyde Howlers," Taige replied, her gaze falling on Sova. "Say what you will about your brother, he's persistent."

"Yeah," Sova agreed sarcastically. "Having your father crippled, the woman who practically raised you killed, and your betrothed kidnapped in one day might make you a little obsessive too."

Her lips piercing in a bitter grimace, Taige turned away. Her gaze then fell to Kyce walking ahead of her, sand speckling his broad shoulders. Overruled by her intrusive instincts, she brushed away the grains.

Kyce came to a stumbling stop and looked back.

"What are you doing?" he glared.

Taige shrugged, "You had sand on your shoulder."

"Well, leave it," he sneered. "I like it there."

"I'll be sure to leave it next time."

Grunting, Kyce continued down the path.

"Are you feeling well?" Taige asked. "That was a lot of water in your lungs. You might need to stop and rest—"

"I didn't ask for your help," Kyce protested. "I had everything handled before you came along."

Elling's head fell back in a derisive laugh. "Sure you did. You handled drowning perfectly."

"I would've come up eventually! Just got the wind knocked out of me, that's all."

Roeseph looked back, his blue eyes dark with warning.

"She saved your life, Kyce. You don't have to be her friend, but you will treat her with respect. That's an order."

"Ha," Sova laughed at Kyce. "You got yelled at."

Scowling, Kyce continued down the path. Taige followed, careful not to get too close, lest she upset him again, or get burned from the steam billowing out his ears.

"So, Tay-Tay," Sova began abruptly.

Feran arched her brow. "*Tay-Tay?*"

"Yeah, Tay-Tay," Sova smiled. "Everyone here has a nickname. Roe is Roe. Ky is Ky. El is El. And Tay-Tay is Tay-Tay."

Feran shrugged. "I still don't have a nickname. Why does she get one?"

"Ah," Sova nodded as he held up a finger, "That's because I still don't like you."

"You're a child, Sova."

"And you're jealous."

Taige looked to the sky. "Tay-Tay," she repeated under her breath. "I like it."

"See, she likes it," Sova said. "So, anyway, Tay-Tay, concerning the coral reef of death that surrounds this island—"

"The Viper's Garden," Taige corrected.

"Yeah, that one. How do we get out of here once you've convinced the Venom Tongues to join us?"

"Well," Taige began, "if the Venom Tongues ally themselves to you, you'll have a variety of our ships to choose from. Any one of them can get safely through the Viper's Garden. After all, the Viper's Garden is meant to prevent ships from getting *in*, not out."

"Perfect," Roeseph replied. "Once we discuss things with the Venom Tongue captain, we'll set sail for Lykos and continue our search for more allies. Maybe with greater numbers, people will be more obligated to join."

"Or it'll make things worse," Feran grumbled beneath her breath.

"Oh come on, Feran," Sova said carelessly. "Tay-Tay's got it handled. She'll schmooze those scurvy-infected bunch of murders and we'll have ourselves a formidable army, Saulder will be dethroned, and Lykos will finally be free. Easy-peasy."

"How do you know anyone will want to join us once the Venom Tongues are involved?" Feran challenged, clutching her medallion. "They're enemies of Vaska for a good reason. They've hurt people, Sova. A lot of people."

Sova looked at her, his heart weighing at the dread in her eyes.

"Hey," he began and gently nudged her shoulder. "Keep your head up, Fer. Everything will work itself out."

Feran grimaced. "Fer?"

"What? You wanted a nickname. I thought it would make you feel better."

"It doesn't."

"Welp, can't say I didn't try."

Feran stifled a laugh. Sova smirked.

"If it's any consolation, I'm kind of uneasy about being here too," he added.

Feran hesitated for a moment, then said, "You are?"

"Of course. The Venom Tongues hurt me too. Because of them, my father might never wake up. This is the last place I want to be. But," Sova drew a deep breath, "as long as it's for the greater good, I think I'll manage."

Feran sighed, wishing she could walk off her grief as easily as Sova. "Confronting the Eradites was hard, but..." she shook her head. "This is so much worse, Sova."

"Hey, if the Eradites taught us anything it's that forgiveness can build nations. Why not give it a try?"

"Easier said than done."

"It doesn't need to be done immediately. Baby steps, Feran. Baby steps."

Feran snorted, amused by her happy-go-lucky rival. "So, how would you go about your baby steps?"

Sova nodded to the Venom Tongue ahead of them. "Being nice to Tay-Tay for starters."

"Hard pass."

"Oh, come on, Feran," Sova groaned. "She's literally hypnotized to be stupid-in love with our beloved yet moody Eradite friend. You literally couldn't come across a more harmless Venom Tongue. She's a great place to start."

Saber stopped quick, the skin of his snout scrunching in waves as his amber eyes darted about the jungle. The Dire Wolves stopped, concerned by the soaring wolf's grievance.

"You ok, boy?" Feran asked, looking back.

Saber shifted, crouching lower and lower as his snarl rumbled on. As Feran went to inspect her winged companion, Taige looked down to see they were standing on a heap of conveniently placed leaves.

Her eyes widening, she pulled at Kyce's arm. "We have to move!"

Kyce jerked away, his face gnarled in a sneer.

"I said don't touch me!" he hissed and stumbled back into an unseen tripwire.

A large net sprung from under the leaves and swept the Dire Wolves into the trees with a screaming as Saber yelped and stumbled aside to safety.

The gang hovered over the ground, trapped in a massive tangle of legs and limbs.

Taige smushed against Kyce's chest, Roeseph lay pinned under Feran's arm, and Sova and Elling sat with their backs pressed tightly together. Taige pulled away from Kyce, grinning bashfully. He shoved her away and pressed himself to the far side of the net. Saber stalked in circles beneath them, whining worriedly.

"We're fine, Saber," Feran called to him. "Just a little cramped."

"Hey! Stop pinching me!" Sova shouted.

"Sorry—" Elling apologized.

"Ouch!" Roeseph shouted. "Taige, your leg is poking me!"

"What do you want me to do about it?" Taige fired back. "It's a metal leg."

"Kyce, scooch over," Feran snapped.

"I'm as far over as I can get. We're in a net, for Lykos sake!"

As the Dire Wolves griped, the forest stirred around Saber, drawing his amber gaze to the shadows. His wings coiling at his sides and a snarl rumbling in his throat, he stalked towards the sound.

"For the record," Sova grunted, "I blame Kyce for this."

"Me?" Kyce snapped. "What did I do? Taige was the one who knew it was a trap."

"I was trying to help you!" Taige argued back.

"I never wanted your help!"

Feran sighed impatiently. "I think it's safe to say bonding the Venom Tongue to Kyce was a bad idea."

"Take you that long to figure out, mind melder?" Kyce growled.

Elling jabbed her elbow into his shoulder. "It wouldn't kill you to act like a human being. It's not like she wanted this either!"

"You tell him, Elling!" Sova barked.

"Would you all stop bickering so we can figure this out?" Roeseph shouted and then sighed. "Maybe we can cut ourselves down. Does anyone have a blade on them?"

"I do," Taige said and reached into a secret compartment on her metal thigh, drawing out a silver blade. The others pressed to the far side of the net, frightened and in awe.

"You had that the whole time?" Kyce blubbered. "Just stashed in your leg?"

"Yep," Taige smiled proudly.

Sova eyed her up and down, impressed. "You're like a chipmunk. But instead of hiding nuts in your cheeks, you hide lethal weaponry in your limbs."

"Here you go, Roeseph," Taige laid the blade in Roeseph's hand.

He stared at the weapon for a moment, shocked, then, shaking away his daze, turned to the net.

"Hmm," he pondered.

Feran arched her brow, her arms crossed over her chest. "Forget how to use a knife, Roeseph?"

"No," he hissed back. "I just want to do this right, so none of us get hurt—"

"I go this," Sova exclaimed and snatched the knife from Roeseph.

"Wait! Sova, don't!" Roeseph cried as Sova cut the tether. Screaming, the six hurtled to the jungle floor. Saber yelped and spun away. Forgetting whatever sound had piqued his interest, he circled the Dire Wolves.

"Sova," Elling groaned, crawling away. "You are an imbecile."

Sova lay on his back, staring at the vast blue sky beyond the trees. "I know."

Taige found her feet first, and then turning to Kyce, offered her hand.

He swatted her hand away.

"Ah," Sova sighed, wiping dried mud from his elbow. "Young love."

Roeseph looked to the jungle, his eyes narrow.

"We should keep moving," he urged as he and the others rose. "Whoever set that trap could be back any second."

"Make that three seconds," Sova interjected.

Roeseph looked back. "What do you mean, Sova?"

"There—" Sova pointed to a shadow drifting in the darkness.

Suddenly, a cannonball-weighted net spiraled out of the jungle, lassoing Saber's paws. The beast fell to the jungle floor with a yelp.

"Saber!" Feran shouted and rushed to his aid, only for Sova to pull her back as a hoard of pirates sprung from the darkness, cawing like crows. Taige reached into a slit along her metal thigh and drew a curved, khopesh-style sword.

Sova gawked at the Viper's Heir, his jaw hanging, "I love that thing."

"Stop staring at the Venom Tongue's leg, Sova," Feran griped and drew her medallion.

As the Venom Tongues pressed inward, a single voice rose from the ranks, making them halt.

"At ease, you dogs," came a voice, scratchy and bitter like salt. A man emerged from the Venom Tongues. He was short and wide, with a jaw lurched forward like a bull dog's. His skin was white like seafoam, and he had a black eyepatch over his right eye.

"Pyter," Taige greeted half-heartedly. "Long time no see."

"Taige," the bulldog-looking man growled, "do you have any idea the trouble you've caused?"

She shrugged, "I take it Rayze didn't take my departure too well?"

"She had an entire ship's worth of men flogged from day into day out for three days."

"Sounds painful."

The bulldog-looking man, Pyter, looked to the Dire Wolves, his spite-filled eyes widening.

"By the great Valley of Lykos," he gawked. "You've brought us the Dire Wolves."

The Venom Tongues looked to one another, salivating at the thought of the bounty hanging over the exiles' heads.

"They're not for selling, Pyter," Taige sneered and grabbed Kyce's arm. This time, he didn't fight her. "They've come here to speak with Rayze."

"Are you insane, Taige?" Pyter scolded. "You're helping these do-gooders infiltrate our sanctuary? What's gotten into you?"

Feran stuffed her medallion down her shirt, looking away as she whistled guiltily.

"Subtle," Sova grumbled.

Taige glared at Pyter, her grip on both Kyce and her sword tightening.

"These exiles are guests in my home," she threatened. "Now you have a choice. Escorting us safely to Rayze and survive, or stand in my way, and bloody my sword."

The Dire Wolves looked to Taige, their lips pierced and eyes bright with fear.

"So violent," Sova whispered in Kyce's ear. "She's perfect for you."

Pyter looked from Taige to the Dire Wolves, his jaw swinging from side to side as he pondered. "Very well, Taige," he grimaced. "You'll have your way. But on one condition."

Roeseph stepped forward. "And what condition would that be?"

Pyter scoffed through a smirk. "You don't scream."

Suddenly, a cluster of weighted nets soared through the air and crushed the Dire Wolves to the ground.

"What?" Roeseph yelled as he struggled. "What is the meaning of this?"

"I said don't scream," Pyter reminded and snapped his fingers.

Within a moment, the Dire Wolves were covered in a burlap sheet and hauled onto the back of a mule-pulled wagon. Just as the six exiles managed to sit up, the wagon lurched forward, and they all fell into one another again.

Feran forced herself upright, her angry eyes covered in curtains of fallen hair.

"Just out of curiosity, Taige," she grumbled. "How do you think this is going?"

"Not well, Feran," Taige admitted. "Not well."

Chapter Twelve: The Captain

The cart jostled down the rickety jungle path, throwing the Dire Wolves against the sides of the cart and into one another.

Kyce kicked at the net.

"Forsake the valley!" he roared, frustration burning so hot within him that his comrades got second-hand burns. "I knew getting involved with a Venom Tongue was a bad idea!"

He jerked violently to the side, accidentally knocking Feran over.

"Move your butt!" she hissed at Sova as she struggled in the tangled heap.

"My butt's nowhere near you!" Sova hissed back.

"Then whose is it?"

Elling raised her hand. "Sorry."

Sova pointed at the mind melder. "See! My butt was nowhere near you."

"No," Roeseph growled beneath him. "But it is on me."

Sova looked down. "Is it everything you've dreamed it would be?"

"Get off!" Roeseph pushed him into Taige. He came down on her metal leg, the iron screeching beneath him.

"Sorry, Taige," he winced, "you ok?"

"No," Taige replied stoically and patted her metal leg. "We may have to amputate."

As the exiles argued, an overwhelming heat flooded through the burlap sack.

Elling coughed, startled by the warmth, "What is that?"

Taige swallowed hard. "The Venom Tongue's hideout," she uttered. "We're in the Serpent's Sanctuary."

Sova maneuvered in the burlap sack to line his eye to a hole at the bottom of the bag. A massive, dark mountain loomed overhead, black smoke billowing from its jagged peak.

"That's not good."

"What?" Roeseph grunted as he tried to sit up. "What is it?"

"Ok, so don't freak out," Sova gulped, "but I think we're about to be thrown into an active volcano."

Feran sighed irritably, "Fitting."

Taige sat up, her head pushing against the burlap.

"You'll all be fine as long as you do as I say. Don't speak unless spoken to. Don't look the captain in the eye. And please—for the love of Lykos—don't let Sova say a word. Not a word."

The wagon stalled, sending the Dire Wolves toppling into one another like a heap of dominos. Feran pushed herself off Sova, only to stumble right into Taige. She glared ahead, tuffs of chestnut hair falling over her dark, violent eyes.

"You guys know I love you," she said. "But if I'm not as far away from all of you as I can get in the next ten seconds, I'm gonna—"

Before she could finish, someone jerked the burlap sack off the wagon to the hard, hot floor. A blade cut through the burlap ceiling and red light to streamed in.

Blinking away the sting in their eyes, the Dire Wolves crawled through to find themselves at the bottom of a somewhat-dormant volcano, complete with a pool of lava boiling near the outer rim. A massive skylight loomed overhead, the cloudless sky eclipsed by heaps of black smoke. Slanted paths spiraled up the sides of the angry mountain, where thousands of Venom Tongues armed with swords watched the Dire Wolves like scurvy-infected vultures.

Stone grated against stone, making the band of exiles look back to see a massive boulder roll over their only exit. The volcano darkened, the only light, the red glow of the fiery lake. A hoard of Venom Tongues took them by the wrists, forcing them to their feet before tying each of their arms behind their backs.

"Would now be a bad time to say I have a nose itch?" Sova said, twirling his nose in a circle.

The group was silent. Dead ahead, a throne carved from lava rock stood before them on the edge of the neon river. There, a woman sat, beautiful and lethal as an oleander, with golden hair braided down her shoulder. Her skin was tan, and her eyes were dark as a starless night. She wore a blue bandana over her hair, a raggedy navy-blue shirt, and moth-eaten trousers. Jewels wrapped her fingers, and a gold-handled sword strapped her thigh, glittering in the light of the lava's glow.

She leaned on the arm of her throne; her chin rested on scar-bleached knuckles.

"Well—Well—Well, what have we here?" grinned the Venom Tongue captain. "The Dire Wolves, I presume? I am honored to be in the presence of such exalted fellow exiles."

Roeseph bowed as far as his restraints would allow him. "The pleasure is mine, captain. If it pleases you, my comrades and I would like to speak to you about—"

One of the Venom Tongue pirates behind Roeseph chucked him hard in the back and he fell flat on his face.

"Roeseph!" Elling wailed and lunged after him, only for one of the Venom Tongues to pull her back.

Sova winced and shook his head. "That had to hurt."

Taige shook her head at Roeseph, "I told you not to speak unless spoken to."

"Thanks for the tip," Roeseph grunted airlessly as he struggled upright.

The stone over the exit rolled away briefly as dozen mules struggled in, hauling behind them a massive soaring wolf tied down by weighted ropes. Saber snarled in muzzle, his pearly white fangs shining.

Feran gasped.

"Ah, the White Angel," the Venom Tongue captain smiled. "I've heard tales of the beast's power and ferocity. Who would've guessed it would be so easy to subdue."

Feran lunged at the Venom Tongue captain, only for two Venom Tongues to pull her back.

"Don't you dare touch him!"

"Ah, and let us not forget the monster's master," the captain greeted. "The infamous *Dire's Damsel.*"

"The Dire's Curse," Feran corrected. "I'm no more that tyrant's damsel than you."

"Hmm, yes," the captain rose and walked up to meet her. She lifted the medallion around Feran's neck, her brow drawn in a curious arch. "Pretty little thing. A gift from your father I presume?"

Feran stayed silent as the captain turned to Sova with a troublesome grin.

"And who is this handsome young man?"

Sova gulped, "I'm scared to answer, ma'am."

"That white hair... those silver eyes," she chuckled, her polished fingernails drumming her cheek. "You're the Royal Traitor, no doubt. Had your hair been longer, I would've mistaken you for the dire. It must be so hard having the face of a monster."

"You would know, wouldn't you," Feran sneered.

"Feran," Sova snapped out the side of his mouth.

The captain smirked.

"Bold one, are you?" she praised. "It seems you have something to say to me? Go ahead. Speak your mind, mind melder."

Feran glared at the captain, the flame in her eyes making the lava look like frozen brooks.

"I don't like having to ask again, Damsel," the captain warned and leaned in, just a mere inch from Feran's face. "If you have something to say... then say it."

"I have something I'd like to say to you," Taige intervened. "That is if you're done provoking my guests."

The gleam in the captain's eyes faded, eclipsed by anger.

"Taige," the captain growled as she drew her blade. The Dire wolves held their breath as the Venom Tongue captain lashed her sword down at Taige, straight through the ropes, cutting her free.

"Where in Lykos were you?" she demanded.

Taige rubbed the red imprints on her wrists, her obsidian eyes dark with resentment.

"Making new friends," she shrugged. "It got lonely here on this hell-hole."

"Do you have any idea what you put me through? How worried I was? You've never been beyond the shallows alone, let alone stepped foot in the Valley of Lykos. What is wrong with you—"

"Relax, Rayze," Taige rolled her eyes. "You're not my mother. You needn't act like her."

"Enough!" the captain, Rayze, snapped. "I've been with you since you were three. I raised you alongside the Viper. I am just as much your mother as that crone from that Seavallian whore house."

"Rayze, are you trying to say you care about me? Because I'm not quite there yet. You should know your boundaries."

Rayze scowled and looked away, her gaze falling to Kyce.

"Well—Well—Well. Look at this tall drink of poison," she tutted. "I take it you're that Eradite Mutt from the legends?"

Taige gritted her teeth, "Don't call him that."

"Oh, relax, Little Seal. I'm just having a little fun."

"I said don't call him that," Taige warned again, more threatening than before.

Rayze looked from Taige to Kyce, her gaze piercing through his soul like a freshly sharpened blade.

"Fond of this one, aren't you?"

"They've come for your help," Taige stated. "The Dire Wolves are looking to grow their army and defeat the dire once and for all. I promised I'd speak on their behalf."

The Venom Tongues roared with laughter, nearly awaking the volcano from its dormancy.

Rayze, however, was not so amused.

"Join their army?" she repeated. "First, you go to Lykos to kidnap the Royal Traitor. Now, you come here hoping to aid them. They must be real persuasive."

Taige crossed her arms. "I'm not looking to play games, Rayze. Will you help them or not?"

"Hmm," Captain Rayze pulled back, her fingers drumming the edge of her jaw. "I see you've also brought a Hyde Howler into our midst. The Feral Shepherd."

Every Venom Tongue looked to Elling, making her shrink to the size of a mustard seed as her shoulders rose to her ears. Roeseph stepped in front of her, his eyes darkening despite the lava's light.

"Elling is a soldier in my army. I won't tolerate you disrespecting her in my presence."

"A soldier, is she?" Rayze looked past Roeseph to the woman cowering in his shadow. "Even when she's like this? Or do you keep a bugle on hand?"

"My patience for you and this island is growing dangerously thin, Captain Rayze," Roeseph warned. "So before I lose my temper in front of my men, I'll ask you this once and then be on my way... Will you or will you not help us?"

Rayze looked from Roeseph to the Venom Tongues watching from above, their faces plagued with violent grins. She turned back to the Last Soldier.

"Brave one, just like your father," she smirked. "He's the Blind Hound, right?"

Roeseph clenched his jaw.

"Yes, the Blind Hound," she continued. "The kind son of a Mosharick medicine man, turned Hyde Howler. You and I are a lot alike, Roeseph. The dire destroyed my family too. Had my husband torture himself to death using the very medallion hanging from your mind melder's neck."

Feran gripped her father's medallion and stole a worried look at Roeseph as Rayze played with the collar of his shirt.

"They sent the Hyde Howlers into our tavern by the hundreds. Killed every Venom Tongue in sight. My Little Seal was just thirteen years old when those monsters sawed off her leg... all because she tried to protect her father. In one day, I saw my husband get dragged to his own execution, and the little girl I raised get butchered before my very eyes. For months we rotted on this isle, waiting for Dire Saulder's hell to pass. Every day Taige would ask me if her father was coming back, and every day I lied... And now, you bring a Hyde Howler—the very same beast that ruined our lives into my presence, and ask for my help?... This sort of disrespect won't be tolerated," she nodded to the lava boiling behind her throne. "Throw them in the lake. Once they've fried, we'll deliver their corpses to Lykos for the bounty."

"No!" Taige cried and lunged at Kyce, only for two Venom Tongues to grab her by the arms and force her to her knees as the Dire Wolves were herded towards the boiling river.

Saber roared from the wagon he laid tied down to, his cry drowned out in the Venom Tongue cheers.

"You're making a mistake!" Roeseph shouted as he and the others edged closer to the boiling sludge. "We might be your only chance to destroy the dire!"

"There is no destroying the dire, Soldier," Rayze called above the chanting. "There's only pacifying him. As long as my people stay in his good graces, we're safe."

"No, you're not!" Sova shouted, his heel skimming the river's edge. "You'll never be safe! Lore is the one that conspired with your husband to attack the palace! When all went south, she let the Venom Tongues take the fall! She's why your husband is dead! As long as a Venom Tongue lives, she won't stop until you're completely eradicated from the face of Lykos!"

The volcano stilled, and the chanting silenced. Rayze's eyes softened.

"Is this true?"

"Yes!" Sova cried. "She's why the Viper is dead. She's why you and the Venom Tongues have been banished to this cursed island. If you want a chance to free your people and go back to the way things were, you have to get rid of her!"

Rayze lifted her chin.

"...I remember your mother," she said in a soft but cold voice. "She was a daughter of one of the whore houses we owned. The Viper thought she would be of great use to us since she was married to the dire... but now you say she betrayed us?"

Roeseph stepped forward. "She betrayed all of us. But it's not too late to set things right. If we stand together, we can take she and Dire Saulder out of power for good."

Rayze shook her head. "No. The only hope is to wait out their rule. Maybe then there will be hope for my people again. But until then, I'll have to settle for destroying you in her stead."

Rayze snapped her fingers, and the Venom Tongues pressed their prisoners toward the lava. The Dire Wolves pushed against the wall of pirates, the skin of their heels roasting as they neared the boiling lake.

Taige twisted in her captor's grip, wailing, "Stop! Stop, Rayze! No!"

The Venom Tongue captain turned her back to the Viper's Heir.

"Throw them in the lake."

Taige stopped struggling, her eyes digging like daggers into her stepmother's back.

"If you kill them..." she huffed. "My blood will be on your hands as well!"

"Stop!" Rayze ordered and her goons froze.

The Dire Wolves stood on the edge of the river, their backs seared by the heat.

Rayze glared over her shoulder. "What did you say, girl?"

Taige panted against the ebony hair fallen over her eyes.

"I said," she said between breaths, "if you hurt Kyce or any of his friends, I'll die too. I'll present myself to the dire if I must. Confess to the sins of my father and my own, so I may be executed before Vaska. Touch one hair on their heads, and I will make it so."

Rayze turned to her stepdaughter. "Taige," she hissed, "I swear by Lykos—"

"I am telling you this as a warning," Taige gulped. "Without Kyce, there is no breath in me. What you decide next is up to you... Either way, I go where Kyce goes, whether it be into battle or into the Heavens."

Rayze' gaze narrowed as she searched for the bluff in her stepdaughter's gaze. To her horror, she found nothing.

"Release them," the captain uttered.

One of the Venom Tongues straightened at her order. "Pardon me, Captain?"

"What are you, deaf? I said, release them!"

The Venom Tongues cut the Dire Wolves free and allowed them away from the boiling river.

"Well," Sova coughed, hunched over with his hands on his knees. "That was intense."

Ripping herself from her captors, Taige hurtled into Kyce's chest.

"Kyce!" she croaked. "I was so scared. I thought they were going to..." Unable to finish her sentence, she buried her face in his chest.

Kyce stood awkwardly with his elbows elevated at his sides as he looked around, very aware of the Venom Tongue gazes searing into his soul.

"Uh... There—There," he said awkwardly as he patted her back.

Sova popped his lip out. "He's never held me like that."

Feran elbowed his side. "Don't make things weird, Sova,"

"But it's my *favorite* thing to do."

Rayze stalked to the Dire Wolves, eyeing Roeseph up and down.

"You wanted my answer, Blind Seer?" she said. "In short, I can't give you one. You've not only brought a Hyde Howler into my sanctuary but also the brother of the dire, and the Blesser's daughter. All whom I find untrustworthy. Nonetheless, I'll have my answer by the week's end. Make yourselves comfortable. As long as you're on the Adder's Isle, you have my protection."

Roeseph bowed. "Thank you, captain."

Feran arched her brow. "Really? You're going to bow? She just tried to burn us alive."

"Ease up on the attitude," Sova said through a clenched smile. "She could still change her mind and kill us."

Drawing her blade, Rayze lashed around to meet Sova, the silver tip pointed right at his chin.

"See," he said, almost proud he was right.

Rayze slid the edge of her blade along the bandages on Sova's shoulder, eyeing the concealed wound.

"I've heard legends of your scar," she said, her eyes dense with fascination. "The damning mark made by the dire himself. They say not even your own eyes have seen it."

Sova swallowed, his unseen scar burning beneath the gauze.

Rayze looked up, barely slipping the blade beneath one of the straps. "Might I?"

Feran grabbed the captain's wrist. "He'll pass," she sneered, pushing the blade away.

Rayze eyed the mind-melder up and down with a smirk.

"Interesting," she said, then turned back to Roeseph. "I'll put you in Taige's command for the remainder of your stay. Please refrain from causing trouble."

Rayze turned and started towards the exit, the boulder rolling out of her way and allowing light into the lava-lit cavern. When the Venom Tongue captain was out of sight, Feran hurried to Saber, held down by the rope and weights.

Drawing a blade from her belt, she cut him free. The white soaring wolf lunged to his paws and let out a mighty roar that shook the volcano. The Venom Tongues let out a collective shriek and raced down the ramps, out of the exit.

Saber shook his head angrily, his tail looping Feran's waist as he snorted a thick, angry mist from his nose.

Feran looked to his wing. It coiled at an awkward angle against his body, the white feathers frayed near the shoulder joint.

"Oh, poor baby. Here, let me see," she whispered, and reached for the wing. The beast coiled away with a whimper.

Feran's fingers coiled into her outstretched hand. "It looks like he's sprained a wing. Must've hurt it from being dragged over the hard ground by those mules. It doesn't look bad, but he won't be flying today or tomorrow," she let out an irritated sigh. "Guess we're stuck here."

Roeseph bowed to Taige, his dusk-blue eyes shining with gratitude. "Thank you, Taige. You saved our lives."

"Again, with the bowing," Feran griped.

"We are indebted to you," he thanked graciously as Taige clung to Kyce like a bur.

"There's no need to thank me, Roeseph," she said. "I was just looking out for my man. You're all his family, so that makes you my family."

Elling pouted her lip and looked to the Eradite Exile, "Awe. We're your family, Kyce?"

Kyce rolled his eyes. "Please," he growled and pulled away from Taige. Like a magnet drawn to steel, she flung back to his side.

"You can't escape me," she whispered beneath her breath.

Kyce sighed, shaking his head. "This is going to be a long week."

Chapter Thirteen: The Docks

The sky was red, and dappled with diamonds, the starlight staining the tides creeping up the sand. After setting up camp on the beach, the Dire Wolves followed Taige through the thick jungle, heading west. Though the sun was all but gone, the heat remained, extracting bead after bead of sweat from the exiles as they trudged after the endless ball of energy that was Taige.

"Hurry up, guys," she cheered as she ran ahead. "You're going to lose your minds when you see this."

"Where are we going?" Sova grumbled. The black bags under his eyes were like anchors, weighing his face to the ground. "And does it have a place to sleep?"

"There's no telling when Rayze is going to send all of you back to Lykos," Taige pushed through a cluster of rain polished leaves. "I want you guys to get the full Adder's Isle experience before we leave."

"We already got the full Adder's Isle experience," Feran griped. "We were almost thrown into a lake of lava, remember?"

"But I mean the *real* experience. The Adder's Isle is home to the best liquor in all of Lykos. We all need to have a drink together before our stay is up."

"*Our*," Kyce repeated with a huff. "There truly was no escaping her."

Roeseph grabbed his shoulder and gave him a hearty shake.

"Chin up, Kyce," he grinned. "She won't be with us forever. Just until Lykos is free."

"Yeah," Sova pepped as he walked by. "You should enjoy it while it lasts. I mean, who know when someone will love you again?"

Kyce glared at Sova as he strolled on, his hands itching to be around the prince's neck.

"We're here," Taige cheered and pushed through a wall of vines and branches to reveal a vast, blue bay.

Ships floated in the shallows, separated by rickety old docks lined with torches. The wind stirred the sand drunkenly, intoxicated on the liquor emanating from the barrels stacked on the shore. Venom Tongues gathered around the dock, drinking like parched whales as they laughed and cursed.

Elling grimaced and took a step back.

"You know," she gulped. "I really shouldn't be drinking. The last time all of us drank together, we had to fight for all of Era hungover."

"Oh, I remember that night," Sova recalled and nudged Feran. "Do you remember, Feran? It was the night before Saulder betrayed and humiliated you in front of all of Era and Vaska?"

"Yes, Sova," Feran grumbled, her brows sinking lower with each syllable. "Thank you."

"Just wanted to make sure you didn't forget."

Taige spun around.

"Oh, come on, guys," she pouted. "It's completely safe here. Everyone here loves me."

Kyce crossed his arms and scoffed, "I find that hard to believe."

"Well, in all honesty, they're horrified of me," she shrugged. "But in my opinion, that's better than being liked."

Taige reached for Kyce's arm, her obsidian eyes big and pleading.

"Please," she begged. "Drinking in the bay is a rite of passage for newcomers. We've got everything. Crimson Stars. Captain Byorgan. Seavallian whisky. Mosharick moonshine. Vaskan bourbon. Seavallian Odin Slayer. Vaskan rum—"

Sova flinched alert, like a dog hearing the word 'bone.'

"O—Odin Slayer?" he stammered past salivating lips. "You guys have Odin Slayer here?"

Roeseph shut his eyes tight. "Oh no."

"Of course," Taige pointed over her shoulder. "We make it here. It's one of our biggest exports."

Eyelashes batting and hands folded, Sova floated towards the docks like a giddy cloud.

"I am home..." he whispered.

"Hold on," Kyce snarled and jerked him back by his shirt. "Are you really just going to go marching into a bay full of Venom Tongues and risk your life for a drink?"

"Yes," Sova nodded.

"You're an idiot."

"Hey, I won't be in danger if we all go," Sova threw his arm over Taige's shoulder. "You don't want to disappoint this sweet face, do you?"

Kyce cocked his jaw and rolled his eyes. "The Venom Tongue's face has no effect on me."

"I was talking about mine, you brute."

Feran sighed.

"Well," she said, her hands slapping her sides. "If I'm going to be stuck on an island full of Venom Tongues, might as well forget the majority of it," she pushed herself out of the jungle and stood beside Sova.

"I've got Feran and Taige," Sova smiled. "Any other takers?"

Elling pulled at Roeseph's sleeve. "We might as well go with them. Sova might start a riot if left unattended."

Roeseph looked from Elling to Sova's stupidly eager face.

"Fine," he exhaled, his patience dead and buried in the sand. "Let's get this over with."

"Wonderful," Sova cheered and led the way toward the docks with Feran and Taige under his arms. "Come. We drink."

Kyce looked to Elling and Roeseph, his brow drawn in an arch. "Is giving Sova unlimited access to Odin Slayer a good idea?"

"Of course not," Elling insisted. "But the quicker we get him drunk, the quicker we can go to bed."

As the group neared the docks, the laughter coming from the Venom Tongues silenced. Some glared over the rims of their cups, others sharpened swords, and it was evident that not one—not one—of them was happy the exiles were there. Regardless, the Dire Wolves stepped onto the dock, the planks groaning beneath them.

Roeseph pulled Elling close as they passed, careful not to look them in the eye. The last thing he needed was to test Captain Rayze's limited hospitality by causing a fight.

Feran, however, scowled right back. A part of her wanted them to cross the line. Then she'd finally be able to lay hands on them for killing her mother.

Sova, ever unaware of the threat against his life, trotted to the edge of the dock where a stack of pungent barrels awaited. The Venom Tongues kept their distance, watching as he filled an abandoned mug with the jade liquid.

He held his drink to the red sky, foam spilling over his knuckles as he cheered, "To the Dire's end."

He downed the Seavallian poison in one gulp. The Dire Wolves stood behind him, shaking their heads in disapproval.

"Oh yeah," Sova rasped painfully at the end of a gulp. "That's the stuff."

"You're a disgrace to Lykos," Kyce jabbed.

"Here, Ky," Sova sniffled as he overpoured a second mug and handed it to the Eradite Exile. "Have some."

Kyce grimaced and raised his chin involuntarily from the (somewhat) edible acid.

"I'm good," he said pushing the mug away. "I've gone this long without drinking that poison. I'm not caving today."

Sova hand flung to his chest in a gasp. "You mean to tell me you lived in Seavale for eight years, and you've never had Odin Slayer?"

"Most Seavallians haven't, Sova. That's how horrible Odin Slayer is. I think I once saw a guy use it to burn barnacles off a ship."

"You fraud," Sova hurtled the remnants of his mostly empty mug at him. The jade droplets slipped down Kyce's tan face as he blinked in silent rage.

"What about you, Feran?" Sova said, turning to face her. "Are you man enough?"

Feran shrugged and stole the mug meant for Kyce. "Might as well. Anything to forget I'm here."

"I feel like that's a cry for help," Sova said as he threw down another mug. "But we'll cross that bridge at another time."

Feran lifted the cup to her lips and inhaled. She pulled back with a grimace, choked by the wretched stench of rotten meat, salt, and vinegar.

"That is rancid," she coughed, holding the mug a safe distance away.

"You're not supposed to smell—or think," Sova burped as he filled his mug. "Just drink."

Feran grimaced and brought the mug back to her lips, suspicious of the slow popping bubbles and the way the liquid moved as if it were alive.

"Elling, if I go, Saber's yours," Feran shuddered and took a cautious sip of the Seavallian drink.

As soon as the liquid touched her tongue, the taste of boiled blood, liquidized salt, and edible anguish coiled her tastebuds, and her throat swelled shut to save her stomach.

"Oh dear Lykos!" she gagged and clutched her neck. "That is the most disgusting thing I have ever tasted in my life!"

"Give me a mug," Kyce ordered and motioned for Sova to make him a drink.

"Oh," Taige smiled. "Me too."

Sova had two mugs of Odin Slayer in their hands in an instant.

"To the Adder's Isle," Taige cheered and raised her drink.

"To the Adder's Isle," Sova, Kyce, and Feran said half-heartedly. Roeseph and Elling watched from the sidelines as their comrades drank without conviction.

"Roeseph," Elling began nervously.

"Yeah, Elling?"

"This is going to go badly, isn't it?"

Roeseph drew a deep breath through the nose. "Yeah."

THE SKY GREW A LITTLE darker with each mug of Odin Slayer downed, the line between sky and sea ceasing. Kyce, Feran, Sova, and Taige sat arm and arm on the edge of the docks, laughing at the ripples beneath their toes.

"By the great lands of Lykos," Sova sighed as he swayed between Kyce and Feran. "Odin Slayer is a Godsend."

"More like Hell-sent," Feran heaved. "I've never had the displeasure of tasting anything more fowl in my life..." Feran looked back at Roeseph and Elling standing guard. "Captain, be a dear and fill me up another, would ya?"

Roeseph's shoulder's sunk in an annoyed breath. "No."

"B—But why?" Feran blubbered, her eyes wide with hurt.

"You're drunk, Feran."

"Yes, that was the goal."

"Feran—"

"Insolent fool!" Feran snapped and drew her medallion. "You'll fill my Odin Slayer whether you want to or not."

Roeseph pinched the bridge of his nose, and exhaled, "Put that down, Feran. The Blesser's medallion is not a toy."

"You're a toy!" Sova said over his shoulder, nearly falling backward.

"Everyone—Sova—shut up," Feran slurred, her eyelids blinking out of sync. "I need to concentrate."

"Oh—" Sova pushed his finger to his lips and hushed himself. "Oh sorry."

"It's alright. I just need to concentrate on my hypnosis—*is*—*sis*. So that I can get another drink."

Kyce raised his hand and burped, "Have him get me one too."

"Ok—Ok," Feran tutted as she began her drunken enchantment. "Roeseph. Pain in my side and all-around joy killer. I command thee to—Wait—Why—What are you doing?"

Roeseph stood with his hand clasped over his eyes. "Closing my eyes," he answered.

"You—You can't do that," Feran gasped. "That's cheating."

Elling exhaled and shook her head. "Feran, will you please stop trying to hypnotize, Roeseph?"

A fizzy grumble bubbled in Feran's throat, and she turned back to the sea.

"Fine," she muttered, placing her medallion around her neck. "But only because you asked nicely."

Roeseph dragged his hand down his tired face, exhausted.

"My father has been through a lot as captain of the Blind Seers. He's led men into battle. He's dealt with insubordination—desertion. Once, he even carried an injured brother for miles. I don't think he ever had to do this."

Elling shook her head, chuckling, "You better make your peace with them, captain. I think we're stuck with them."

Roeseph sighed and looked at Taige as she kicked giddily at the ripples.

"How are you holding in there, Taige?" he asked. "What drink are you on?"

Taige looked back with a shrug. "Seven, I think."

Elling tilted her head, confused by the Venom Tongue's clear eyes and perfect diction. "You seem to be oddly sober, Taige."

"Oh, yeah," Taige shrugged. "Everyone here's a pretty heavy drinker. I developed a tolerance to Odin Slayer by the time I was seventeen."

Sova fell back on the planks with a thump. He stared at the stars, the storms of a thousand seas sloshing within his gut.

"Tay-Tay," he burped. "You're my hero."

"Awe, thank you, Sova."

"You're welcome," Sova looked to Kyce. "Hey, Kyce. She's a keeper. You're a lucky, lucky man."

Kyce moaned and shook his head like a toddler on the verge of a tantrum. "No. No, I don't want her to be my girlfriend."

"Kyce," Elling warned.

Taige shrugged, not at all phased.

"That's ok, Kyce," she said, stroking some strayed hair out of his face. "I don't have to be your girlfriend. I just want to be with you. I can be anything you need me to be. A friend, an ally, a soldier. Whichever you wish, as long as I'm there."

Kyce looked Taige up and down. Had he not known she was under the influence of the Blesser's medallion, he might've believed her. He had to admit. It sounded nice that someone wanted him so dearly. After all, he'd never been truly wanted before.

"Sounds like something a girlfriend would say, to me," Feran mocked, suckling on the rim of her empty mug.

"Go drown in the sea," Kyce spat.

"I'm on my way," Feran coughed and shook the empty mug over her gaping mouth.

Chuckling, Sova struggled toward the barrels of Odin Slayer and filled his mug, unaware of the unkind eyes piercing into him.

"Look at 'em," a Venom Tongue growled to his buddy, "drinking our liquor like it's theirs."

"Keep to yourself, Fidi," his friend warned. "They're with Taige. Lay a hand on 'em, and you'll have an entire metal leg up your—"

"Don't you worry about me," the Venom Tongue, Fidi, smiled crookedly. "After all, what's the harm in some good old friendly conversation."

Followed by four other Venom Tongues, Fidi, stalked onto the dock and up to Sova. Had Sova been slightly soberer, he might've recognized the danger he was in. But instead, he gave them a lopsided smile and waved.

"Well, hi," he squeaked through a burp. "The Odin Slayer is fantastic. You've really outdone yourselves. You should feel proud."

A Venom Tongue grunted a hot breath in Sova's face, making him cough at the stench of spoiled liquor.

"Who are you to come on our island and steal our Odin Slayer?" Fidi growled, clasping the handle of his sword.

"Who am I?" Sova stopped and held up a finger as he held his breath, allowing a wave of nausea to pass before he spoke. "Of course, I haven't introduced myself. My name is drunk, and I'm a little Sova." His brows furrowed and he looked down. "That's not right."

Elling looked over her shoulder, her eyes widening when she saw the trouble Sova had gotten himself into.

"Roeseph," she whispered and pulled at his arm.

"Hmm?" the Last Soldier answered and looked back. "Oh no."

The Dire Wolves, the drunk and sober alike, sprung from the dock and stalked up to Sova, ready to defend their brother.

"—And so there I was," Sova burped, midstory, "face to face with Dire Saulder. I had fought a good fight, but that bloody tyrant got the best of me. Shot me through the shoulder he did. I don't remember much after that. In fact, I don't even remember getting shot. When I woke up, Casavore was looming over me, saying I needed to run. And now here I am." Raising his mug to his lips, Sova stumbled back, right into the arms of the Eradite Exile. "Ky," he beamed and patted Kyce's scowl. "There you are buddy. I missed you."

Kyce threw him to his feet. "Get a hold of yourself, Sova," he grunted.

Roeseph stepped in front of his comrades, eyes narrow with warning.

"What's going on here?"

"Nothing, captain," Fidi sneered and arched his brow. "Just having a nice conversation with the Royal Traitor there."

Roeseph looked back to see Sova chasing an ant in a circle and giggling. Elling grabbed hold of Roeseph's arm and stepped close.

"We'll be leaving now," she gulped. "We don't want any trouble."

"I'm sure you don't," Fidi chuckled and looked to Sova. "Better take care of that one. Gets in any worse shape, and he'll end up like that good for nothin' father of his."

Sova stopped. He looked up slowly, the drunkenness in his eyes disintegrating as he turned to face the Venom Tongues.

"You want to run that by me again, pirate?" he growled.

Roeseph grabbed Sova and pulled him back. "Easy," he hissed. "You're drunk, Sova. You don't want to do this."

"On the contrary, Roe. I think I do."

Fidi chuckled, his voice like acid in Sova's ears.

"You're Dire Zastar's boy, right? You must be. You have those same silver eyes. Folks around here that survived the Vaskan palace talk about those eyes of his. How big they got when that blade met his gut, and how he trembled with fear as he bled to the brink of death... Yes. You must be Zastar's; that crippled old dire, whose better off dead than alive."

Sova's fist met Fidi's jaw like a battering ram. The sound of bone cracked across the beach like war bells as the foolish Venom Tongue hit the water. Before Sova could regret what he'd done, the entire beach charged the Dire Wolves.

A man grabbed Elling, making her shriek, and brought her to her knees.

"Elling!" Roeseph shouted, only to be intercepted by another Venom Tongue. "Elling, hold on!"

Elling trembled in the shadow of her assailant, tears quivering in her emerald eyes as the Venom Tongue raised his blade to the moon.

"Lykos forsaken Hyde Howler," he snarled.

A blunt, metal object slammed into his ribs, making his bones cackle as he hit the deck. Taige stood over Elling, her face wrenched in a scowl.

"Enough," she shouted, and the battle stilled.

Sova lay curled up on the dock, his lip bleeding and his gut blackened by Venom Tongue boots. Roeseph stood sword to sword with another, a bruise patching his eye. Kyce knelt at the end of the dock, ducking someone's head into the sea. Feran huffed, her lungs ragged from the fight and her medallion swinging from cracked knuckles.

"Anyone who lays another hand on either of the Dire Wolves will have me to deal with," Taige snapped, her voice like a whip across Venom Tongue ears.

"Oh yeah?" Fidi, chuckled. He pulled himself out of the water and onto the deck, his soaked rags hanging like anchors on his ink-covered body. "And why should we listen to you? You have no power over us."

"You clearly haven't learned anything from the last time we fought," Taige arched her brow. "Have you, Fidi?"

Fidi's grin tensed into a scowl.

"You listen here, Little Seal," he snarled through gnarled teeth. "You think yourself this mighty sailor, but you're not. All you are is the damaged brat of the Viper, who I might add, is the whole reason we're hiding on this barnacle-bitten island in the first place. We used to be a proud people—unafraid of Vaska or anything else in Lykos. That was until your father got us involved with the dire. All you are is a crippled reminder of his failure. You're no more pathetic than these *Dire Pups*. All that's keeping you from our blades is that rabid witch of a woman, Rayze. Had that power-hungry wench had any sense, she would've drowned you in the sea and been done with her husband's defective orphan a long time ago."

The Venom Tongues looked up, their eyes filling with fear as a shadow fell over Fidi's back. Fidi's scowl softened, his greatest fear confirmed when he saw his comrades take a collective step back.

"What was that you were saying, Mr. Fidi?" came the smooth yet venomous voice of the Venom Tongue captain. "That I was a rabid... power-hungry... witch?"

Trembling, Fidi turned to meet the cold gaze of the Venom Tongue captain.

"I—I—I'm sorry, Captain," he bowed. "I'm drunk. I don't even know what I'm saying. Please. Please forgive me."

Rayze glowered down at the Venom Tongue, her fingers drumming the handle of her sword. "Hmm, you're forgiven, Fidi," she dismissed. "My pride is not so easily damaged."

"Oh, thank you," Fidi shook and kissed his captain's hand. "Thank you, captain."

Rayze smirked.

"However," she drew her sword, the silver hissing briefly before she drove it through the Venom Tongue's stomach. He turned over the blade, a choppy gasp escaping from his throat as she leaned to his ear. "I won't tolerate any disrespect towards my daughter."

She threw Fidi off the blade and into the waters, staining the tide a deep scarlet. The Dire Wolves looked away, unable to stomach the gruesome sight.

Taige glared at her stepmother, immune to the gore, "I had it handled."

"He was of no use to me anyway," Rayze said as she wiped the blood from her sword. "He was unable to stop you when you ran away, and he has no respect for his superiors. He had to go."

Roeseph hurried to Elling sitting on the dock, and helped her to stand.

"Are you ok," he whispered under his breath. Elling froze, her emerald eyes wide and latched on the floor. "Elling," he shook her slightly. "Answer me."

"I did nothing," she whispered. "He just grabbed me, and I didn't do anything."

Roeseph gulped and pulled Elling to his chest, hugging her tight. He looked up, he found Rayze glaring at him with dark, unforgiving eyes.

"I bring you into my home," she began sharply and stepped towards him. "I promise you safety. I let you help yourself to our resources. And I even give you the courtesy of considering an alliance. And you attack my men?"

"I'm sorry, Captain Rayze," Roeseph said and guided Elling behind him. "There was a misunderstanding, and—"

"You've disrespected me and all the Venom Tongues by taking advantage of my hospitality!" Rayze drew a deep breath, her expression turning calm by the end of it. "...No matter, all you've done is make up my mind."

"Captain, please—"

"The Venom Tongues won't join your battle. You are to leave this island come morning and never return. Since your mongrel is still injured, I will supply you with a ship, but that's all you'll ever get from me."

"Captain—"

"Don't test my patience, *Seer Pup*."

Roeseph gulped and looked to his soldiers' defeated faces. After all the trouble they'd gone through trying to reach the Adder's Isle, he had failed them.

Taige stomped up to her stepmother, fists clenched at her sides. "You can't do that," she hissed. "Fidi was the one out of line. They were just defending themselves—"

"That's enough, Little Seal," Rayze dismissed and looked to Roeseph. "Take your people, leave this bay, and don't return until morning."

Roeseph nodded and rounded his troops. Sova knelt on his hands and knees, coughing blood-flavored bile on the planks as the shadows of his comrades condensed around him. Feran hauled him to his feet, her eyes soft and sympathetic.

"You ok?" she asked.

"Oh yeah," Sova swallowed. "You should see the other guy."

"Let's get out of here."

Tails between their legs, the Dire Wolves stalked off the dock and toward the jungle.

"I'm sorry, Roe," Sova groaned, his head rolling back and forth. "I really messed everything up."

"It's not your fault, Sova," Roeseph assured. "You didn't do anything wrong."

As Rayze and the Venom Tongues watched the Dire Wolves disappear into the jungle, Taige stomped past her captain to join them.

"Hey," Rayze snapped and grabbed her by the wrist. "Where do you think you're going?"

Taige ripped her hand away. "You told us to leave. So, I'm leaving."

"Them. Not you. You're not one of them, Taige. Come to your senses. Don't you see they're using you? What I don't understand is why you'd allow them to."

"I've already told you. Where Kyce goes, I go. Whether that be to Heaven or the gates of Vaska, I'll always follow him. I'll see you in the morning when we come for our ship."

"Taige!" Rayze snapped, but her Little Seal didn't stop. All she could do was watch as the Viper's Heir disappeared into the shadows beyond the bay.

THE DIRE WOLVES STRUGGLED to move Sova through the jungle, his body like an anchor over Feran's shoulder.

"For Lykos sake, Sova," she grumbled. "Move your feet."

"It's no use," Sova whimpered. "Leave me behind. Save yourselves."

Feran shook her head, sighing. "Lykos—you're the worst."

Taige rushed up from behind and threw his other arm over her shoulder.

The Dire Wolves looked back at her, shocked to find she'd returned.

"Shall we?" Taige said as she nodded ahead.

Roeseph grinned fondly and led the way toward camp.

Chapter Fourteen: The Ally

The Dire Wolves emerged from the jungle onto the lonesome, cold, silver beach, where Saber waited by the campfire, his sprained wing wrapped in gauze. The soaring wolf spung to his paws, did a twirl, and then, yipping, hurried to greet his master. Feran sputtered as he licked away her frown, his scratchy tongue leaving red lashes up and down her smiling cheeks.

"Saber," she gasped, turning from side to side to evade his invasive greeting. "Saber—I missed you too. Down, boy. I know—I know. Down."

Sova smiled painfully at the cheerful mongrel, his eye bulging black and his lip oozing red.

"I missed you too, Saber."

Saber turned quick on Sova with a snarl.

Sova barely reacted, his face like stone. "What did I ever do to you?"

Under the midnight moon, the Dire Wolves fed the fire and settled around its warmth.

Resting against Saber, Feran unwound the gauze from her hand. Taige unwillingly stole a glance, surprised to find the imprint of a mind melder's medallion branded into her palm, traced by red flesh and callused blisters.

"Woah," she marveled, and pointed at Feran's hand. "Where did you get that?"

Feran didn't bother to look up as she answered, "Just a childhood injury."

"Well what happened?" Taige asked, unwilling to let the story die.

Feran looked up from reapplying the new gauze, her glare glowing red in the flames. "I got it trying to escape the Venom Tongues."

Sova and Elling traded a nervous glance while Roeseph raised his head to interject. "Feran—"

"After your people killed my mother, I was taken hostage," she continued. "They threw my medallion in the flames so I couldn't hurt them. They got what was coming to them though. Saber showed up not a second later and had himself a feast. I knew he'd come for me next, so I reached into the fire for my medallion. Hence the burn."

Taige nodded knowingly, ignorant to the spite in Feran's voice. "Hmm. I think I got you beat."

"Excuse me?" Feran challenged. "You think you have me beat? Your people killed my mother and stole me from my home. I have the scar," she held up her gauze-wrapped hand, "to remember it all."

Taige scoffed, her lip twitching with a competitive grin. "Um—your kingdom sent out Hyde Howlers to kill my father, forced my people into hiding, and—" she lifted and slammed her metal prosthetic onto the sand. "Leg..."

Silence overwhelmed the beach. Not even the fire dared cackle. From the strangling quiet, Feran choked on a repressed laugh and clamped her lips to keep from smiling. When she couldn't fight herself any longer, she fell against Saber, laughter bursting from her throat like cannonballs. Before Roeseph could scold her, Taige joined in as she and the mind melder laughed themselves breathless.

"Fair enough," Feran sighed.

"Hey," Sova raised his hand. "I have a scar too," he said and smacked his gauze-wrapped shoulder. "I got mine battling my brother for the freedom of Lykos. Got shot with a crossbow I did..."

Taige and Feran traded a look.

"Meh," Taige shrugged.

"Not impressed," Feran shook her head.

Roeseph, Elling, and Kyce laughed at Sova as his jaw dropped open.

"I survived an encounter with the Dire of Vaska," he blubbered. "My scar is of legend. No eye has seen it—not even mine!"

"I've seen in," Roeseph interjected as he prodded at the fire. "You made me do your bandages for almost a year because you were too scared to do them yourself."

"Shut up, Roe!" Sova looked back at the girls. "Come on, admit it. My scar's impressive."

Feran arched her brow and raised her gauze-wrapped hand. "I got my scar fighting off Venom Tongues and surviving a soaring wolf attack."

"And I lost my leg trying to save my father from Hyde Howlers," Taige added.

Sova glared at the two smug women, his arms crossed over his chest as he reclined from the fire, grumbling, "It's not a competition."

The Dire Wolves chuckled, their anguish burning in the warmth of fellowship and fire.

"You know, Taige, I got to ask," Sova began. "Why help us? I mean, I get that you're just *oh so in love* with Ky. But why us? You could've easily just protected him and left us for dead, but you didn't. Why help us out back there?"

Hugging one knee to her chest, Taige gave a shallow shrug. "I don't know. Well, I guess it's because Kyce loves you."

Kyce scoffed. "That's debatable."

"Lie all you want, Kyce," Taige elbowed his arm. "But I know how you feel. These people are your family. And well, if you see something in them worth defending, then so do I."

"Awe," Sova pouted and looked to Kyce. "She's way too good for you, man."

Kyce rolled his eyes.

Roeseph stretched and turned to the Viper's Heir. "Well, Taige. If you're willing to fight for us, we're willing to fight for you." He extended his hand. "Welcome to the Dire Wolves."

Taige gasped, her eyes glittering with the stars as she greedily took Roeseph's hand.

"Woah—Woah—Woah," Kyce stammered as he sat upright. "Don't you think we should discuss this?"

"I'm the captain, Kyce," Roeseph smirked. "What I say goes."

"Tyrant," Kyce sneered and looked to the Dire's Curse. "Surely you don't agree with this."

Feran raised her chin. "Who I do hate the Venom Tongues, I like this one. She's like a puppy."

Sova snorted and looked at Kyce. "Are you really such a monster that you'd hate a puppy, Ky?"

Kyce drew his fist back, making Sova yelp and scurry to Feran's side. Saber growled at his closeness.

"So it's official?" Taige asked. "I'm a Dire Wolf?"

"Until Feran withdraws that curse she set on you, I guess so," Kyce snarled and leaned towards the fire.

Taige tilted her head; her obsidian eyes clouded with confusion.

"What curse?" she asked innocently.

Kyce looked up, struck dumb by her aloof expression.

"What do you mean, *what curse*?" he glared. "Don't you remember anything from the voyage?"

Taige shrugged. "Bits and pieces. I don't remember much after Feran knocked me out after trying to hypnotize me."

"Trying?" Kyce repeated. The flame in his eyes dwindled. "Pirate, she *did* hypnotize you."

"No, she didn't," Taige laughed. "That's why she hit me. Because it didn't work. Then I woke up and saw you. And..." her shoulders fell with a smitten sigh, "I don't know. I just knew you were someone worth protecting."

Kyce swallowed and looked to Feran. The mind melder stared guiltily into the flames, her arms crossed over her knees. Looking around, Kyce saw the same look of shame on each of the Dire Wolves, not one of them able to look he or Taige in the eye.

"You really don't know what happened to you," he whispered, "do you?"

"What do you mean?" Taige shrugged. "Nothing happened. I'm fine."

Kyce stared at her for a long while, his disdain melting into remorse. He looked to the fire, desperate to distract himself from the guilt crushing down on his chest. Lucky for him, Sova wasn't one to tolerate silence for very long.

"So," the Vaskan prince clapped. "Taige, now that you're officially a Dire Wolf, what's the first thing you're going to do when we take back Vaska from Dire Saulder?"

Taige hummed thoughtfully and stroked her chin.

"Let me think," she wondered aloud. "I'd say once we break into the palace, I'll invade the treasury and claim it all in the name of the Venom Tongues, so we can rebuild our empire to what it was before we were forced into hiding. After that, I'll force the dire to kneel before me, and I'll kill him just as he killed my father."

"Woah—Woah—Woah," Sova interrupted. "Why do you get to kill the dire? I'm the one who he scarred for life. Look at my shoulder!"

"Look at my leg!"

Sova rolled his eyes as quiet laughter plagued the beach.

"Hey, if anything, I should be the one to take down, Saulder," Feran added. "We were betrothed, and he betrayed me in front of all of Era. Not to mention he took my father captive... Till death do us part, right?"

"That's not fair," Roeseph grumbled. "Two generations of dires have wronged my family. Zastar turned my father into a Hyde Howler, and Saulder imprisoned him. I should be the one to decide his fate."

"That's not nearly as bad as having a loved one killed, captain," Taige spat back.

Kyce straightened, his face twisted in determination. "Why shouldn't I be the one to kill him?"

"No way," Taige shook her head. "He killed my father."

"He killed my soaring wolf."

"He took my leg!"

"Are you going to bring that up every time?"

Laughter exploded into the night, making the fire cower against the timber. But Elling stayed quiet, her knees drawn close to her chest as she stared at the sand.

"None of you are qualified to kill Saulder," she said with a voice so emotionless and cold it nearly doused the flames. The camp went silent as all looked to the Feral Shepherd. "The dire came to my village on a night of celebration. He turned my own mind against me and used me to destroy my entire village. He used me to kill my mother. My Little brother. My father. I should be the one to kill him... And yet, I'm the least capable of us all."

Roeseph laid his hand on her back.

"You'll get there, Elling," he assured. "You just need to—"

"What? I need to what, Roeseph? Be patient? Practice? We've been on the run for almost a year, and I still have no idea to defend myself, let alone you guys. Every day someone else has to pick up my slack, and I'm sick of it. And yet—" she scoffed, her eyes starting to glitter. "I'm probably the most lethal one among us. I could probably storm Vaska alone and bring it to its knees. Only, I'd have to become a monster to do it..."

Elling exhaled and looked back to the sand. For a while, the only thing brave enough to make sound was the soft cackle of the fire's embers.

Taige shifted where she sat, her black eyes shining with innocence despite a lifetime of bloodshed.

"You're not a monster, Elling."

The shepherdess looked up, "With all due respect, Taige, you don't know what I'm capable of."

"You're not a monster," Taige repeated. "You're not a soldier either. You're a shepherd. Nothing has changed that. Not this war, or the Blesser's hypnosis."

Roeseph straightened, his dusk-blue eyes brightening with a grand idea. "That's it."

"What's it?" Elling mumbled.

Leaping to his feet, Roeseph grabbed Elling's hand.

"Come with me," he commanded, jerking her away from the fire.

"Wait—Wait—Wait," Elling stammered as he dragged her down the beach. "We can't just leave them here. They've all been drinking."

"Taige, you're in charge," Roeseph called as he and Elling disappeared into the night.

"Aye–Aye, Captain," Taige saluted.

Sova looked around the camp smiling like a fool. "Good news, guys. I think I'm starting to sober up. I now only see two of you instead of three."

Taige's salute drooped. Suddenly playing babysitter to a moody Eradite, a sarcastic mind melder, and an obnoxious prince didn't sound as fun anymore.

ROESEPH LED ELLING as far from the flames as they could get until the only light was the light of the moon. The wind surfed over the waves and tousled the silver sand, making figure-eights between the soldier and the shepherdess' feet as they ran up the shore.

"Roeseph," Elling huffed. "where are we going?"

Roeseph stopped and let go of her wrist, allowing her to catch her breath. With the excitement of a child playing war, he bolted off into the jungle and returned with a long branch as tall as him.

"Taige was right," he said and tossed Elling the stick. "I've been training you the way I was trained, like a soldier. But you've spent your entire life tending to sharick fawns and livestock."

"Yeah, so?"

"Point is," Roeseph pointed, "you already have a fighting style. And it's been going to waste."

"What are you talking about, Seer?

"Did you ever have to fend off predators from your flock?"

Elling paused, confused by the question. "Yes?"

"Did your father train you to deal with thieves that tried to wrangle your herds?"

"Yes."

"Every time you went to tend to the sharick fawns, did you go with the expectation that you might have to fight something bigger than you?"

"Yes, but—"

Roeseph snapped and pointed at Elling, the giddy gleam in his eyes enhanced in the moonlight. "Then you're already trained."

Without warning, Roeseph sprinted down the length of the beach.

"Where are you going?" Elling shouted above the roaring waves.

Roeseph turned, his smile still visible from the distance. "Get into your battle stance."

"Why?"

"Because we're going to fight," Roeseph said, drawing his sword.

Elling hugged her stick close. "Now?" she cried. "We're doing this now?"

"Get into your battle stance," Roeseph ordered again, bouncing eagerly on the balls of his feet.

Elling sighed, tired from the day's unwavering wrath, "Roeseph, come on—"

"You said you wanted to pull your own weight, right?"

"Yes."

"Then hold your staff the way you're supposed to and prepare yourself as if you were in an actual fight."

Elling swallowed hard, thrown off by the Last Soldier's authoritative tone. He was usually so soft-spoken with her. He never raised his voice or scolded her, even when she was sure her limitations frustrated him—or rather, should've frustrated him. But in that moment, he was stern, like a captain addressing his soldiers.

Her heart shined at the thought; *she was a soldier.*

Swallowing hard, she drew the staff from her body and held it at her side. Once, when she was fourteen years old, she once chased off a hoard of vultures from an injured sharick fawn. She remembered swinging low on offense and swinging high on defense. But that was the extent of her battle training.

"Ready?" Roeseph called.

"No."

"Great!"

He sprinted towards her, kicking up sandstorms in his wake. Elling looked to his sword glimmering in the moonlight, suddenly very afraid.

"Do you think we should be training with an actual blade—"

Roeseph lashed his sword at her, the blade hissing through the wind as Elling barreled to the side.

"Nice reflexes," he praised with a smirk.

"You nearly killed me!" she yelled.

"Just remember to stay on the balls of your feet."

Roeseph came at Elling again, only for her to deceive his advance once more. Coming up behind him, Elling slammed the staff in the small of his back, making him shout and spring forward. Elling cupped her mouth to hide her laughter.

"Ouch, Elling," he complained as he rubbed the bruise.

"Sorry," she laughed.

Roeseph suppressed a grin. "You're going to pay for that," he growled playfully.

Elling shrieked and ran across the beach, Roeseph tailing behind as their laughter ruined the somber night. Just as he was upon her, Elling lashed around and swung her staff low at his ankles, just as she did to the vultures. He fell to the ground in a puff of silver sand. He lay there, groaning at the stars above.

"Cheap move," he grunted.

Just as he was about to rise, Elling pointed her staff at his throat. She stared at him, panting through a smile.

"I did it," she managed through a giggle. "I beat you. You lost."

"No need to be a sore winner, Elling. I was taking it easy on you."

"I won," Elling repeated. "I beat you."

"Congratulations," Roeseph rolled his eyes. "Now, will you help me up?"

"Huh? Oh, yeah!" Elling offered the end of her staff for Roeseph to grab and pulled him upright.

He stumbled forward, eclipsing the moon as he loomed over the shepherdess. Elling gulped at his closeness, butterfly wings tearing through her gut like razors.

Roeseph loomed over her for a moment longer, still gripping the staff as he marveled her intoxicating green eyes. Truly, there was no one in Lykos, Era, or the Isle more beautiful than Elling—his dearest soldier. Elling cleared her throat and looked away.

Roeseph shook away his daze and stepped away, his cheeks pink with embarrassment.

"Sorry," he apologized and picked up his sword. "Got lost in thought. Ready to go again?"

Elling nodded bashfully, "Mhmm."

Chapter Fifteen: Nightmares

Sova opened his eyes with gasp, alarmed by the frigid air sinking into his skin and the endless black void that surrounded him.

No, he said to himself. *I must've fallen asleep. Stupid Odin Slayer...*

"Who are you?" came the hostile voice of the dreaded dire. Sova spun around. The ghostly tyrant stood on the other end of the void, dressed in black armor with his gloved hand clutching his holstered sword.

"Saulder, now's not the time," Sova growled.

The dire drew his blade, the weapon hissing against its sheath as he snarled, "Who are you?"

"*I* am tired of this," Sova rolled his eyes. "You know what, let's just get this over with."

He held out his arms and craned his head to the black sky, welcoming death.

"Who are you?" the dire shouted and charged.

Sova sighed, exhausted. "Same time tomorrow night?"

Just as the dire's sword plunged into his heart, Sova awoke with a jolt on a blanket of warm sand.

The fire was still young and wild, and the moon and stars reigned king over the Seavallian sea, indicating he had failed to sleep through the night yet again.

Please, God, Sova groaned to himself. *Just one night. One night is all I ask. One night of sleep.*

"Looks like the Odin Slayer finally got to him," came the low chuckle of the Eradite Exile.

Sova flinched. He'd forgotten he was in the company of Feran, Kyce, and Taige. They must've thought him asleep.

Feran lay against Saber, her gaze falling to her childhood foe lying with his back turned to her.

"Poor guy can't hold his liquor," she chuckled and patted his shoulder.

Say that to my face, hermit-wench, Sova growled to himself.

"So," Taige began as she prodded a stick into the fire, "is it true what they say about his scar? Did the dire really shoot him?"

One of Sova's eyes popped open.

Feran drew a long, deep breath, and answered, "About nine months ago, Sova and the Blind Seers attacked the Vaskan Palace in hopes of defeating the dire. Sova sought out his brother to finish him himself, but Saulder got the upper hand... He tried to kill him."

"Great Lykos," Taige mumbled. "I'm no stranger to the dire's wrath. But to try and kill his own brother... It's monstrous."

"Yeah, well," Feran inhaled and looked away. "Saulder has a tendency to betray those who loved him."

Sova stomach tightened at the remorse in her voice.

"Sova also said he's never seen his own scar," Taige wondered. "Is that true?"

"Yeah," Kyce answered, sitting up. "Roeseph's the only one." He smirked. "Says it's the ugliest thing he's ever seen."

Go drown in the ocean, Ky.

"It's not funny, Kyce," Feran growled, her defensive tone taking Sova by surprise.

"Oh, come on, Feran," Kyce rolled his eyes. "You mock Sova more than any of us."

"Yeah. And I'm the only one that gets to," she threatened, reclining deeper into Saber's fur. "There's a reason Sova forgot his altercation with the dire. It traumatized him to the extent that he literally has no recollection of the fight. Seeing the scar might awaken some bad memories."

"Traumatized is a little strong of a word, isn't it?" Kyce challenged.

"He has nightmares every night now, Kyce," Feran replied. "Sova makes jokes and acts like he's fine, but I know he's hurting..." Feran stared into the fire, her hand clutching in and out of a fist over her knee. After a while of not speaking, she said finally, "I don't want him to see that scar of his. I don't want him to remember what that Lykos-forsaken monster did to him." She looked to Sova lying with his back to her, his shoulders rising and falling with each gentle breath. Reaching forward, she stroked the gauze along his shoulder. "I don't want him to get hurt again. I don't know if he could take it."

Sova swallowed, his heart and stomach tingling at Feran's touch. Not in a thousand years did he think he'd hear the Dire's Curse say such things. Neither did Kyce or Taige.

Kyce cleared his throat. "I um," he stood from the flames. "I should go get some more firewood."

Taige stood with him, her marble-black eyes shining. "Can I come too?"

Kyce exhaled and slumped around to deny the Viper's Heir, but the desperate look in her blameless face truck him dumb.

He looked away, defeated. "Sure," he replied. "Yeah, sure, come on."

Smiling brightly, Taige skipped into the jungle after Kyce. Feran chuckled and looked back to the fire.

The camp lay quiet under the midnight sky. The waves that crashed along the shore sounded of timid thunder, and the dying fire cracked into a spit of embers. Saber's gentle snores filled the air, harmonizing with the restless crickets singing from the darkness. Feran sighed as she stared into the endless diamond sky, comforted by the hymns of a peaceful night.

"If I didn't know any better, I'd say Tay was growing on Ky," Sova blurted.

Feran cursed and jumped away.

"Sova!" she hissed lowly as not to wake Saber. "You nearly gave me a heart attack. How long have you been awake?"

Sova smirked and rolled onto his side to face her. "Only long enough to hear that you care about me."

"You're delusional."

"And you're a softie."

Feran grabbed hold of her medallion, making Sova flinch away laughing. When Feran calmed, Sova laid his head in her lap and stared at her with a boyish smile.

Feran arched her brow. "Do you have a death wish or something?"

"So hostile," Sova mocked. "You're starting to sound like Kyce."

Feran sighed and shook her head as she averted her gaze to the stars.

"Don't be embarrassed, Fer," Sova yawned. "I get scared for you sometimes too."

Feran's brow furrowed and she looked down. "You do?" she asked, her tone defensive.

"Mhmm," Sova nodded, his eyes closed. "I was scared for you all day. I have my own grievances with the Venom Tongues, but you—" he shook his head. "They killed Fala. They took you—a little girl—away from your father and home. I didn't want you to have to be here."

"Sova—"

"I'm scared to take you back to Vaska. I used to be so sure that if you showed yourself to Saulder, he'd magically become the person he used to be. I put you in terrible danger because of it. And now every time I think about the day we storm Vaska, I think..." Sova paused, his voice clotting in his throat. "...I think what if he tries to hurt you again?"

"Sova..." Feran whispered. "Is that why your nightmares are getting worse? Why you see the dire almost every night now?"

"Of course not. Not everything's about you, Feran."

"Sova."

The Royal Traitor shrugged.

"Honestly, Feran, I don't know. I started seeing the Dire in my dreams more frequently after the battle on Era, so maybe. I just..." he sighed. "I don't know why he won't leave me alone."

Before Sova could drift further into despair, Feran raked her fingertips through his hair, making his eyes pop open.

"What are you doing?" he snapped. "What is this? Are you going to rip my hair out our something?"

"Would you relax?" Feran scolded. "Try to get some sleep. God knows you don't get enough of it. If you start having nightmares, I'll wake you up."

Sova eyed Feran up and down, uncertain of her kindness. "I'm not sure I trust this," he grumbled as the numbing sensation of her nails riding over his scalp sent shudders down his spine.

"Fine," Feran shrugged and withdrew her hand, "if it makes you uncomfortable—"

"No!" Sova shouted and, grabbing her hand, placed her fingers back in his hair. "No takebacks."

Feran snorted and strummed her fingers through Sova's hair. His eyes drifted closed. As he lay at sleep's door, his head resting in Feran's lap, a fond warmth filled his chest—one hot enough to burn away any threat of nightmares.

"Good night, Sova," Feran whispered as she closed her eyes and reclined against Saber's fur.

"Night," Sova grumbled sleepily as he drifted further into Feran-induced slumber.

THE KINGDOM OF VASKA...

A dark staircase twisted down into a hidden chamber, where a single torchlight was dwindling close to the wick.

The Blesser of Vaska lay in an isolated cell, the echoes of shrieking quiet driving him to the brink of madness. He stared at the cobwebs across the ceiling, his back, flat against the cold, damp floor.

Seven more sunrises and he'd meet his end.

He'd never know freedom again. He'd never know if Oland and the other Blind Seers would make it out of Vaska. And Feran, his sweet daughter, he'd never see her again. That was what he feared the most, never seeing Fala's child again. Every time he tried to envision her, her face interchanged between the twelve-year-old he knew and the visage of his departed bride. She had already begun to resemble Fala as a child, but he knew nothing of what she looked like now. Did she look like her mother? Or was her face like his? Either way, she'd be beautiful. Just as he always knew she would be.

He blinked away a tear as he drew his daughter's charred medallion from his cloak and stroked his thumb along the rough edge.

"*Father,*" Casavore prayed as he clutched Feran's charred medallion, "*hear my prayer. I know I have betrayed my brother Zastar, and I have betrayed his children. But please—if I'm to be punished, let Feran go free. Don't let her pay for my mistakes. Please, Father, protect my daughter. Protect the Last Soldier. The Eradite Exile. And The Feral Shepherd. Those kind souls who care for my little girl. And Father, protect Zastar's son... And please, let him know I am so sorry for what I've done...*"

Chapter Sixteen: Seven Sunrises

The Adder's Isle...

A seagull's shrill cry and the sizzle of foam receding back into the sea awoke Sova from his dire-less dreams. He clenched his eyes shut, groaning painfully to himself as his skull throbbed, punishment for last night's ventures.

As he laid there in the Sova-shaped crater, he ran his fingers through his hair, remembering Feran, and how her fingers had done the same. He couldn't help but grin at the memory. He opened his eyes, expecting to find her in the same place, smiling down at him with kind eyes and a playful grin. Instead, he found a string of saliva dangling a mere inch above his eyes from a pair of pearly white jaws.

"Great Valley of Lykos!" He shouted and scrambled out from under the soaring wolf. "What is wrong with you?"

Saber growled, his ears and wings flattening. Sova growled right back. Laughter sounded behind him, and he turned to find the Dire Wolves huddled together.

"Morning sunshine," Feran mocked as she stroked her medallion. "Sleep well?"

"Feran," Sova said, not looking away from the hostile beast, "why does your dog hate me so?"

Feran shrugged. "Same reason everyone else despises you, I suppose."

"Which is?"

"I'm not sure. Just you know—" she pointed Sova up and down, "—all that."

Saber stalked up to Feran, his glare never leaving Sova as he rested his bared jaws on his master's shoulder.

"Sadistic mutt," Sova sneered.

Kyce chuckled as he stomped the campfire to ash. "Maybe the beast's upset because you got all close and personal with his master last night."

Sova felt his cheeks burn red with embarrassment.

Feran groaned. "You still won't let that go?"

Kyce shook his head, "Never."

Elling sighed through a laugh, quick to join in the fun, "You two looked so cute snuggled up together."

While Feran rolled her eyes, Sova looked to the sand and bit his lip to stop from smirking. Humiliating or not, he wouldn't change last night for all of Lykos.

"You all can tease Feran later," Roeseph said. "Rayze is expecting us at the docks. I have a feeling she doesn't take too kindly to folks keeping her waiting."

"She doesn't," Taige answered. "Once, a Seavallian steel dealer was late to a drop off, and she cut off his—"

"That's enough, Taige," Kyce interrupted hastily, "thank you."

"Let's try to be early if we can," Roeseph added. "Feran, is Saber strong enough to fly?"

Feran shrugged. "It's a short ways to the bay. He should be fine. Might be in for a rocky landing though."

"Let us be off then," Roeseph said and motioned to the soaring wolf. Sova walked stiffly with the others, still thinking of the man Rayze had maimed, while Elling stayed at Roeseph's side.

She looked up at their captain, her bright expression dimming when she saw the disappointment in his eyes.

"Hey," she touched his shoulder. "We'll find ourselves some allies soon enough."

Roeseph sighed. "It's been eight months, Elling. With an army like the Venom Tongues, we could've had ourselves a competent fighting force. Now we have nothing."

Feran raised her medallion from atop Saber's back. "There's still the Feran protocol."

"We're not hypnotizing more Venom Tongues, Feran," Elling scolded.

Taige laughed, her eyes soft and blameless.

"It's not like your plan would work, Feran. After all, your mind-melder tricks didn't work on me. Oh, Kyce!" she lashed out a bouquet of wildflowers out of thin air, sending petals flying everywhere. "I picked these for you this morning. They reminded me of you."

Kyce hesitantly took the flowers. "Yeah," he scowled at Feran. "Very ineffective, mind melder."

Roeseph squinted at the sun slowly rising out of the sea.

"We should get going," he said as he pulled himself onto Saber's back. One by one, the Dire Wolves mounted their steed, with Sova sitting in the far back, as usual, and Taige clinging to Kyce like a bur to cotton. Opening his powerful wings, Saber launched into the sky.

VENOM TONGUES CROWDED the drinking bay, hauling barrels of liquor and gunpowder off the ships and onto the beach.

Rayze watched from the dock, her arms crossed over her chest, as her fingers drummed against her bicep. She clenched her jaw, enslaved to her own troubling thoughts.

A tremendous howl struck the wind, and all looked to the sky as the White Angel of legend descended the bay. Landing with the grace of a comet, Saber skid across the beach, sending Sova sailing off his back and into the sand.

Feran pointed at her foe, and shouted, "Ha!"

"Nice landing," Sova said into the sand. Rising, he wiped the itchy grains from his arms and walked with the Dire Wolves to the docks where Captain Rayze waited.

"You're early," Rayze growled, looking Roeseph up and down.

Roeseph raised his chin, "We didn't want to keep you waiting."

Rayze turned to Taige next.

"I don't suppose you've changed your mind about leaving?" she asked, her voice stoic as stone.

Taige hugged Kyce's arm. "No," she replied, looking down then back up. "Have you?"

Rayze smirked and shook her head. "Such a brat," she muttered fondly.

Taige hugged Kyce tighter, prompting him to look down. For once, he pitied his lovestruck shadow. Hypnotized or not, it was no easy task leaving one's family behind.

"Where's our ship?" Feran growled impatiently, her voice like a blade, cutting through the sentimental moment. "The sooner we get off this Lykos-forsaken island the better."

Rayze glared at Feran. She turned to a massive ship, black against the rising sun, its cobra-stamped sail rippling in the wind. The Dire Wolves lost their breaths, in awe of the glorious sea drifter.

"Her name is Storm Walker," Rayze said. "She's the smallest of our ships, but she'll get you back to Lykos in one piece."

Sova cleared his throat, "It'll do I suppose."

Rayze looked back at Roeseph, her gaze turning from cold to searing hot. "You'll be facing a lot of danger in Lykos. If anything happens to my daughter—"

"We'll keep her safe," Roeseph assured. "We always watch after our own."

Rayze raised her chin, his eyes narrow with distrust. "Taige should be able to navigate out of the Viper's Garden. Try not to destroy this one."

"Yes, ma'am," Roeseph nodded, and led the way down the dock toward the ship.

On the beach, several Venom Tongues huddled close around an empty barrel, gossiping about what went on in the valley across the sea.

"They say the execution is in seven sunrises," one of them said lowly.

Feran stopped halfway across the dock, Saber with her.

"I can't believe it," another said. "I mean, I know the dire's wrath is unpredictable, but to kill him? He'd have to be a fool to slaughter his greatest weapon."

Feran lashed around and stomped towards the Venom Tongues, Saber close at her side.

Roeseph looked back.

"Feran!" he called. "Where are you going?"

Feran stopped short of the pirates, Saber's disgruntled snort hot on her back.

"What execution?" she demanded.

The Venom Tongues looked fearfully at one another, hesitant in the presence of the loathsome mind melder.

"The Blesser Casavore's execution," answered one of the bold. "Some sailors were talking about it in the Seavallian taverns last night."

Feran froze, her mouth trembling open as dread pierced her heart like a branding iron.

"Is everything ok over here?" Roeseph called as he and the Dire Wolves marched up to stand beside her.

Feran croaked, unable to speak, as tears glittered in her eyes.

"Feran?" Sova whispered, concerned by her silence. "Is everything ok?"

Feran's look of terror suddenly morphed into a sneer. Lashing out her medallion, she grabbed one of the Venom Tongues by his throat. The surrounding pirates drew their swords, as did the Dire Wolves.

Elling looked at Feran, her eyes full of panic. "What are you doing?" she shouted.

"Feran, stand down!" Roeseph ordered.

Feran ignored them both. Tears rising in her eyes, she began her trace. "Don't lie to me, Venom Tongue. Tell me what is to become of the Blesser Casavore!"

The Venom Tongue's eyes widened, and his horrified expression softened to numb.

"In seven sunrises," he began in an emotionless voice, "the Blesser will be presented to the people of Vaska and executed for his crimes against the dire. These are the things we have heard. Come seven sunrises, the Blesser will die."

A trembling gasp fell from Feran's lips. She clasped her medallion to her chest, withdrawing her hypnosis, and the Venom Tongue fell to the sand, unconscious.

"What is the meaning of this?" Rayze snarled as she shoved her way to the center of the crowd. "Are you so brainless as to attack my men in broad daylight, mind-melder?"

Feran stepped back into the protection of the Dire Wolves, her face paling to a shade so white she made snow look dark.

"He's going to kill, Casavore," she shuddered. "My Lykos. Dire Saulder is going to kill my father."

Sova lashed around to meet the Venom Tongues.

"Are you're certain of this?"

"Every tavern was talking about it," the Venom Tongues admitted. "The Blind Seers are to die as well."

Roeseph froze, his shoulders trembling as they rose.

"We need to break them out," he said quickly.

"How?" Elling asked.

"I don't know," he began to pace. "But we can't just leave them in Saulder's dungeon to die!"

"Maybe we can go through the sewers again?" Elling offered. "Maybe Saulder didn't seal off the entrance."

"How we get in doesn't matter," Kyce challenged. "Not when the entire palace is practically crawling with guards. Not to mention, what's stopping the dire from turning the Blind Hound or Elling into Hyde Howlers?"

"We can't go to Vaska," Sova said.

Feran looked up, her glistening eyes wide with shock, "What?"

"This is obviously a trap. It's to get us back in the dire's firing range. He knows we're trying to build an army against him. How else to get us back in Vaska if not by threatening to kill his Blesser?"

Elling shook her head, "You'd just have us leave them there for dead?"

Roeseph took an abrupt step toward Sova, his patient eyes construed with rage. "My father was imprisoned because of you, Sova. Because you said we could win!"

Sova lashed around to face his captain, getting an inch from his face. "So, you'd have us walk straight to our own deaths?"

"To save my father, yes!"

Taige shoved herself between the two and drew her blade, forcing them to step back.

"Trap or not," she spat, "the dire has never been one to bluff. Despite the Blind Seer's loss, they are still numerous. If we free them, we'll have ourselves an army. One maybe capable of destroying the dire."

Rayze marched up to her daughter, her face twisted in a scowl.

"You can't be serious, Taige! You don't think I'm actually going to let you storm the Vaskan palace?"

"You don't have a say in what I do."

"You'd suffer a fate like your father for the likes of these outcasts?"

"Yes!"

"Taige, I am your mother, and you do as I say!"

"You're not my mother," Taige shouted.

Silence plagued the bay. Kyce stared at Taige in disbelief. Never, in all his years in Era or exile, had another soul, other than Whisp, laid their life on the line the way Taige just had.

Roeseph stepped up to the Venom Tongue captain, his eyes dark with determination.

"I've already asked you to join my army, and you denied me. But if you care about Taige like you say you do, you'll join us. Help us deliver the Blesser and the Blind Seers from the dire, or leave us to fend for ourselves. The choice is yours, captain."

Rayze looked from Roeseph to the Venom Tongues, her lips pierced in a scowl. In any other instance, Roeseph and his comrades would've been killed on sight, their bodies thrown to the waves. However, with the Viper's Heir at their side, the Dire Wolves were near untouchable.

There was no other choice.

Rayze sighed, her eyes shut tight with regret, "How many men do you need?"

Chapter Seventeen: The War Meeting

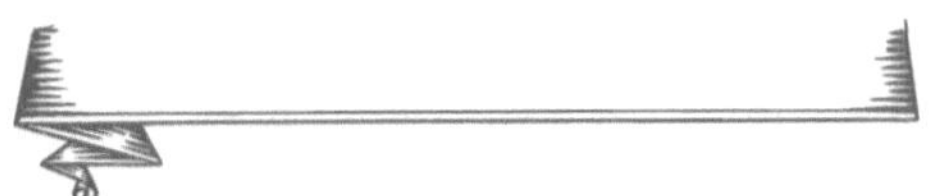

With swords in hand and bellies filled with rum, the Venom Tongues boarded three ships along the dock. The Dire Wolves, Saber, and Captain Rayze stood before a ramp leading onto one of the ships, engrossed in plots of war.

A great fight awaited them beyond the sea—one long-anticipated.

"Five hundred men will accompany you to Vaska," Rayze stated as golden strands of hair raked across her venomous eyes. "If you actually survive this fight, return to my isle when you plan to storm Vaska. The Adder's Isle will stand by you."

"Thank you, Captain," Roeseph nodded. "My troops and I are forever in your debt."

Feran sputtered. "Forever in her debt? Please," she taunted, her tone turning dangerous. "This is just evening the score."

Rayze smirked at the mind melder before turning to Roeseph. "My men will act only under Taige's orders. Though I have a feeling she'll be compliant with your demands."

"Thank you, captain," Roeseph dipped his head. "We'll have your daughter back home soon. You have my word."

"You're relieved," Rayze dismissed and stepped aside for the Dire Wolves to pass. As they ascended the ramp, Rayze grabbed Kyce by the arm. "Eradite. Stick around for a bit, would you?"

Taige looked back, a protective glint flashing in her eyes. "Kyce?"

Kyce looked at the captain and then to Taige, knowing full well what the mother pirate wanted to speak to him about.

"I'll be fine," he replied. "Go on ahead. I'm right behind you."

Taige glanced warningly at her stepmother, taking slow, hesitant steps up the ramp before disappearing onto the main deck with the others.

"She seems fond of you," Rayze mumbled. "I would hope you hold the same keenness for her as well."

Kyce clenched his jaw, hesitant to speak.

"I—" he stopped to clear his throat. "Taige is a capable soldier. She's deeply valued by all of us."

"Ah, yes," Rayze nodded as she circled him. "But her adoration isn't as genuine as it seems, is it?"

Kyce scowled. "I'm afraid I don't know what you're talking about."

"Don't play dumb with me, mutt. I'm aware of the mind melder's power. Taige is under the same trance Lore used to snag Dire Zastar, is she not?"

Kyce met Rayze's gaze. Though his eyes were hard, he could not hide the guilt stowed deep within them. And that was all the proof the pirate captain needed to know she was right.

"Know this, Eradite Mutt," she hissed, taking a step closer. "If you dare take advantage of my daughter's trance—"

"Stop it," Kyce snapped. "I would never do something so disgusting—not even to the likes of a Venom Tongue. Besides, once this whole thing is over, Feran will release Taige and we'll be done with her."

Rayze's shoulders relaxed a little, and she nodded, "Listen well, Mutt. I don't trust the Blesser's brat to release Taige from her curse. Lykos knows my daughter is far too skilled a fighter to give up, and Feran has too much history with my people to act mercifully."

"We'll have no desire for soldiers after the dire's fall. And I don't have the patience to babysit your pup for much longer. I assure you, she'll be pardoned of her curse and returned to you as soon as Lykos is free."

"Very well then," Rayze looked him up and down. "Taige's condition will stay between you and me. But beware, Mutt," she leaned to Kyce's ear. "Should she perish," she paused and chuckled darkly. "Well, let's just say there won't be anyone left to save you from me."

Rayze pulled away to take in Kyce's fearful expression, but he returned her gaze stoically.

"Taige will return to the Adder's Isle. I swear on the life of Whisp."

Rayze grimaced, unamused. "Get out of my sight."

Kyce stomped past her, his shoulder barely grazing hers as he made his way up the ramps.

"Hoist the anchors!" a voice rough as barnacles called from one of the ships.

The chains jostled as they hauled the anchors out of the sea and the sails fell with a snap. The wind burrowed in the sails, pushing the three out the bay and towards the horizon.

On the upper deck, Feran pressed herself to the railing and stared at the Adder's Isle, drifting further and further from view. She let out a pent of breath as Saber nuzzled her side, whining with concern.

"Good riddance," Sova snickered as he walked up beside her. "I have to say. I didn't think I'd ever meet people who hated us more than the Eradites." Saber growled at Sova's closeness. "Hello to you too, rat." Sova looked back at Feran. "Are you going to be ok to be traveling with a bunch of Venom Tongues?"

Feran drew a sharp, reluctant breath.

"If it helps us defeat Saulder, I'll go to war with the whole Adder's Isle."

"Look on the bright side," Sova chuckled and prodded her side. "We've been given complete authority to bully the Venom Tongues for the entire duration of this war."

Feran smirked up at Sova, her usual, irritated eyes turning soft.

"Thank you, Sova."

"It's no trouble," he shrugged. "I know how much you love to torture the meek and helpless—"

"Not that," Feran rolled her eyes. "Thank you. For... you know. Trying."

Sova smiled. "Of course. After all, if someone else makes you miserable then how am I special?"

"Hey, love birds!" An impatient voice called up from the main deck, making the pair look down to see Kyce standing below. "Roeseph's calling a meeting in the captains' quarters. So stop your needless flirting and get down here."

"Yeesh, what's with the attitude, Ky?" Sova smirked. "Did Captain Rayze give you a stern talking to?"

Kyce rolled his eyes as he started into the captain's quarters. "Just stop wasting time and get down here."

"Ooh, touchy," Feran teased. "I'm guessing mommy dearest didn't give you her blessing?"

Kyce slammed the door hard, making Sova and Feran laugh.

"Nice," Sova praised and high-fived her.

The door to the captain's quarters creaked open.

"I said get down here!"

Smiles fleeting, Feran and Sova hurtled down the stairs.

"Go—Go—Go—Go," Sova tutted, half nudging, half pushing Feran down the stairs.

"I'm going. I'm going!"

SABER LAID OUTSIDE the captain's quarters, whining with his nose pressed to the door. Inside, Roeseph gathered the Dire Wolves and crew around a crème-colored scroll rolled across a wooden table. The Dire Wolves stood close to one another as the Venom Tongue glared at them with all the loathing a human soul could muster.

Feran choked down a gag as the scent of marinated sweat and liquor-stained breath filling the close quarters. She would've had an easier time breathing with her head shoved underwater.

"It smells like something died in here," she grumbled, not bothering to lower her voice.

The murderous gazes intensified.

Sova chuckled through clenched teeth and elbowed her in the arm. "Something might die in here if you don't shut your trap."

Elling edged closer to Roeseph's side. The Venom Tongue's disdain for the Dire Wolves was apparent enough, but she was a Hyde Howler; an unwilling soldier to Vaska and a lethal weapon of the dire's making. Sensing her discomfort, Roeseph stepped in front of Elling to shield her from their gazes.

"Thank you all for being here," he began. "As you know, the Blesser and the Blind Seers are to be executed come the seventh sunrise. If we can rescue these men, we'll have a capable fighting force for when we challenge the dire in battle."

One of the Venom Tongues, a woman with a shaved head and a large silver ring in her nose, scoffed. "Is that what we're risking our hides over? A rescue mission? Wasted on that of a Hyde Howler and his loyal simpletons?"

The Dire Wolves glared at the Venom Tongue while Roeseph drew a deep breath to keep his anger in check. "This mission will dictate the victor of this war. Either the Blind Seers and the Blesser die, and the dire wins. Or, our army instantaneously grows by a thousand men. You and your brethren have a chance to come out of hiding—to leave the Adder's Isle behind."

The Venom Tongues went silent, their gazes still hot as a branding irons.

"So," Taige asked, "what's the plan, Captain?"

"The plan is to invade Vaska through the same sewage tunnel the Blind Seers had used. If we go through the tunnels, we should surface west of the gardens. We'll locate the dungeon and free the Blesser and the Blind Seers, then retreat into the Vaskan Forest."

"Hold on," barked another Venom Tongue. "You mean to tell us we're going to break into the Vaskan Palace just to save a couple of worthless prisoners? Why not attack the dire then and there?"

"The Blind Seers attacked the Vaskan Palace with plenty more soldiers than we have now and lost. We can't risk it. The plan is to get in and get out with as few causalities as possible."

"Causalities are going to happen, either way, Roeseph," Taige added sadly. "But if we challenge the dire now, we might save Lykos from a worse fate."

"Or we'll be sealing it."

Sova scoffed and shook his head. "I still think going in there is a bad idea."

Feran turned on him. "And what would you have us do, Sova? Leave Oland and my father to die?"

"No—Of course not. But," Sova paused and exhaled. "There has to be a safer way to do this. One that doesn't end in a massacre."

"How?" Kyce growled. "Ask nicely?"

Elling stepped forward, her emerald-green eyes big with revelation. "Yes."

Kyce's brows lowered, "I was being sarcastic."

"Sova's right," Elling continued. "It's too dangerous to send all our forces in at once. But what if we only needed one soldier? One that could go by unnoticed."

Taige eyed Elling up and down. "How would we do that? Your faces are known throughout all of Lykos. You'd be lambs walking into a lion's den."

Feran scoffed and looked at the Venom Tongues. "And it's not like we can send any of these guys in. The stench'll give 'em away."

"For the love of Lykos, Feran!" Sova scolded. "Do you have a death wish?"

"I said what I meant."

Elling shook her head. "No," she answered, "we wouldn't send in any of our own. We'd send in someone the Vaskans wouldn't suspect."

"Who?" Roeseph asked.

Elling looked at the Royal Traitor. "We'd send in Dire Saulder."

The Venom Tongues stared silently at the shepherdess, some turning to their neighbor in hopes they knew what she was talking about. Kyce looked from the baffled crowd to Elling, his jaw cocked to the side.

"Care to elaborate there, Elling?"

"Sova," Elling said up at the Vaskan prince. "Your resemblance to your brother is one of legend. You could slip right into the palace, and no one would suspect a thing."

"Send in Sova to pose as Saulder?" Feran scoffed. "What happens if he and the dire run into one another? There's no telling if Sova could actually defeat Saulder this time. He could die!"

Kyce smirked. "Then we'd finally be free."

Sova glared at Kyce. "What did I ever do to you?" he asked, more curious than offended.

"How much time you got?"

"Sova!" Elling snapped, making Sova turn. "You are the only man in Lykos outside of the palace to have seen the dire's face. If we sent you disguised as your brother, do you think you could you do it?"

Sova swallowed. He knew he had the face of a monster, but no one had ever been so bolt to point it out before.

"Sova?" Feran began softly. Sova looked down at his childhood foe, startled by the look of desperation in her eyes. "Could it work?"

He sighed and looked back to the Dire Wolves.

"If you can get me some halfway decent garments that could pass for royal robes and something to make my hair longer, I *might* be passable as Dire Saulder."

Roeseph shook his head. "No. It still won't work."

Elling turned to face him. "But it could," she argued. "Roeseph, we could save everyone without anyone getting hurt."

"Sova might be able to get into the dungeon, but it won't be as easy when he's herding a thousand men into the sewers like cattle."

"Roeseph, think about it for a moment."

"I have thought about it. It won't work."

Elling's gentle eyes hardened at his dismissal. "You're not even going to consider it?"

"Drop it, Elling."

"Is it because it's not your idea? Because only the great Last Soldier can come up with a halfway decent strategy?"

"You've been fighting for five days. I've been fighting for twenty-three years. I know how to do battle."

"Oh, so because I'm a measly shepherd, I couldn't offer anything to the fight?"

"You haven't yet, have you?"

Sova winced and hissed in a breath through clenched teeth. "That was not the right thing to say, my friend."

Elling stomped up to Roeseph, eyes blazing like green fire. "You are such a hypocrite. You act like you want to make me a capable soldier—but the moment I offer you something, you shut me down. What is it? You can't stand a challenger?"

Roeseph scoffed. "A challenger?"

Kyce grabbed his shoulder. "Maybe take a breath, man."

"No. No, Kyce, everything's fine. You're right, Elling. I am a hypocrite. I'm a hypocrite because I promised myself I'd never leave my father like my mother did, only to abandon him when he needed me most. So, I am sorry if my critique of your plan was a little harsh. Because my main concern is saving my father and winning this war, not appeasing you."

"Would you just—"

"Of course, there's also the fact that my father is a Hyde Howler, and if caught, could be unleashed on Sova and his own troops and bring everything we've—or sorry—Kyce, Feran, Sova, and I have built, crashing down. Did you think of that, Elling? Or were you just too caught up in playing soldier to actually consider that I might actually know what I'm talking about?"

Elling glared at Roeseph, her lip starting to bubble. The Last Soldier's anger slipped away like a passing shadow as he closed his eyes in regret.

"Elling, I—"

"Casavore," Elling said emotionlessly. "The Blesser Casavore can bring the Blind Hound out of his trance should he be summoned by the Siren's Call. And he can hypnotize the Vaskans to escort the prisoners out of Vaska, so no one gets suspicious. Not that they would with our fake dire leading them."

Roeseph's eyes narrowed as he thought on the plan, feeling for any cracks in the foundation. To his surprise, there were few.

"If that's all you need from me, I'd like to be excused, please," Elling said.

Roeseph hesitated and then, giving a shallow nod, stepped aside. Head raised high, Elling parted through the crowd of Venom Tongues, and slipped out the door, startling Saber out of the way.

"Smooth, Roeseph," Kyce taunted as he patted him on the back. "Real smooth."

Taige clapped, ushering everyone to look her way.

"So that's it then," she concluded. "Sova frees the Blesser and the Blesser frees the Blind Seers." She looked to the Royal Traitor last. "Sova?"

Sova looked up from staring at the floorboards, his arms crossed tightly over his chest. "Hmm?"

"Are you sure you'll be able to do this?"

Sova looked around the cabin, his eyes falling at last to Feran. She stared back at him with dark, pleading eyes that made his heart ache.

Sighing, he said "...Who would've guessed the monster's face would come in handy?"

Chapter Eighteen: The Serpents Passage

The sun melted over the orange horizon as all across the three ships, the Venom Tongues hauled out liquor barrels in hopes of forgetting the journey ahead. As the pirates drank and laughed, Kyce, Sova, Feran, and Saber watched from the upper deck with sullen expressions.

"That guy down there has a pair of queens," Sova mumbled as he pointed down at one of the pirates playing cards around a barrel.

"The guy next to him has a full house," Feran added.

Sova let out a long, exaugurated breath. "Ky," he whined at the Eradite Exile, "we're bored."

"What do you want me to do about it?" Kyce grumbled.

Feran yawned and scratched Saber behind the ears. "Can you go get Taige? She's a lot more fun than you."

"I thought you didn't like Venom Tongues?"

"She's the exception," Feran shrugged. "Look, I know I put you in an uncomfortable situation, Kyce—"

"Uncomfortable?"

"Shut up and listen, Eradite Grump," Feran scolded. "But Taige... she's a good person."

Kyce's jaw clenched and he looked back down into the crowd of Venom Tongues. Taige stood around a barrel, hustling a game of cards and laughing as she sipped on a mug overflowing with Odin Slayer. He'd never noticed it before, but when she smiled, her eyes glittered like stars—as if two pieces of the night sky had fallen into her gaze.

"I suppose I could've gotten stuck with worse," he admitted.

Taige looked up from her game to catch Kyce staring at her. She waved, her smile growing broader. Kyce barely lifted his hand in acknowledgment.

Sova and Feran traded a glance and then looked to Kyce, their brows drawn upward in intrigue.

"Ten gold coins he falls in love with her," Feran gambled.

"I would've bet fifty," Sova agreed.

Kyce turned quickly to the two, making them retreat to Saber's side. The beast leaned over the railing, snapping at the wind like a dog on a carriage ride.

Cursing something under his breath, Kyce looked down to see Roeseph ascend the stairs to the upper deck. His face was sunken, and he had a hopeless look in his eye that made the Venom Tongue passed out on the deck look lively.

"Ah, our fearless leader," Sova cheered. "Did you bring me any Odin Slayer?"

Roeseph glared at him. "If you want it, you can get it yourself."

"I can't," Sova pouted. "The Venom Tongues say mean things."

Roeseph rolled his eyes and looked down onto the main deck.

"Everything ok, cap?" Kyce asked.

Roeseph sighed, his head falling forward. "Not really. Have any of you guys seen Elling? I can't find her anywhere."

Sova shrugged, "Not since the war meeting."

Feran scoffed through a grin. "It's almost as if she's avoiding you."

Sova smirked at the mind-melders remark. "You have to admit, Roe," he said through a stretch, "Elling's plan wasn't all that bad."

"Yeah," Kyce joined in, "you should really check that temper of yours."

Roeseph scowled at Kyce. "You're right, Kyce. No woman deserves to be talked to the way I did to Elling. Not even the likes of a Venom Tongue."

Kyce's smug expression faded like a candle snuffed out by a violent wind.

Sova looked down at the floor, his shoulders rising and falling with restrained laughter that hissed through his teeth.

"Shut up, Sova," Kyce growled.

"Ok."

Before tensions could worsen, Roeseph's gaze fell to a beautiful shepherdess, who was sheepishly navigating through the outskirts of the crowded ship.

"Elling!" Roeseph called and hurtled himself down the stairs. Elling looked up, her usual, warm emerald-green eyes the coldest Roeseph had ever seen. "There you are," he huffed through a timid smile. "I've been looking all over for you."

"Can I help you with something, Roeseph?" Elling replied in a frigid voice.

The Last Soldier hesitated. "Yeah," he cleared his throat, "I wanted to tell you I'm sorry. Things got out of hand at the war meeting today, and you didn't deserve to be talked to like that. Y—You should never be talked to like that."

"There's no need to apologize," Elling shrugged. "Your father is currently imprisoned in Vaska under threat of execution. You were just thinking on his behalf. What matters is that we get him and the Blind Seers out."

"So—So we're ok?" Roeseph gulped. "You and I, we're good?"

"I don't see why that matters," Elling shrugged. "After all, there's no reason to worry about what I think. I don't offer much to fight anyway, remember?"

Mocking cackles and winces of sympathy bore down on Roeseph from above. His fiery gaze lashed up to the upper deck, just in time to see Kyce, Sova, and Feran duck behind the railing.

Roeseph scowled, shaking his head, then turned back to the Feral Shepherd.

"Elling, what I said, it wasn't—"

Before Roeseph could finish, a Venom Tongue gambling around a barrel looked up from his cards.

"Feral Shepherd!" he shouted drunkenly, prompting Roeseph to glare at him. "Why don't you get that Hyde Howler hide of yours over here and stop wasting time with that washed-up captain of yours?"

Roeseph stomped in front of Elling, his eyes blazing like blue fire. "You ought to know better than to talk to a lady like—"

"What are you playing?" Elling interrupted. Roeseph looked back at her, his eyes wide like two moons.

The Venom Tongue cackled. "An old Seavallian card game. Doesn't have a name. Folks like us just know how to play it."

"Grab me a mug of Odin Slayer, and I'll let you deal me in."

"Darling, for you, I'll get you a whole barrel."

As Elling stalked towards the Venom Tongues, Roeseph grabbed her wrist.

"What in Lykos are you doing?"

Elling looked him up and down. "What does it matter to you?"

"Oh come on, Elling," Roeseph groaned. "I said I was sorry. Don't do something stupid."

"The last stupid idea I had turned into our battle plan," Elling twisted her hand out of Roeseph's grip and walked up to the barrel.

Roeseph crossed his arms as he watched her go, his jaw clenching.

As if summoned by magic, Sova, Feran, and the soaring wolf appeared at Roeseph's side, gawking at Elling as she thumbed through her hand of cards.

"Oh sure," Sova grumbled. "They give her all the Odin Slayer she could want. But when I ask nicely, they threaten to throw me overboard and say horrible things about my mother."

"In their defense, Sova," Feran said, looking up, "your mother is Lore."

"Right."

WHILE THE OTHERS WATCHED Elling play her hand with the Venom Tongues, Kyce remained on the upper deck, leaning over the railing and staring at the vast black sky. As he stared, he thought of his dear soaring wolf, Whisp. He wondered if she flew again. If she could finally race the stars just as she had longed to do before her wings were taken.

He sighed, his heart like an anchor in his chest.

"Beautiful, isn't it?" came a soft voice.

Kyce looked over his shoulder to see Taige walk towards him. She leaned against the railing, the wind combing her ebony hair back from her face.

"On clear nights, when the waves are still, it looks like we're sailing through the stars," she said.

Kyce looked back to the ocean, fascinated to find she was right. The diamond-dappled sky shined perfectly in the black sea, looking as if their ship sailed on a tide of starlight.

"Why aren't you with your friends?" Taige asked, not looking away from the ocean.

Kyce shrugged. "Just needed a break. The white-haired one was getting on my nerves."

"Sova?" Taige smirked. "But he's so sweet and funny."

"Spend eight months with him. Then tell me how much of a little darling you think he is."

Taige snorted and nudged Kyce in the arm. "You love him, admit it."

"Love is a strong word. Tolerate is more fitting."

Taige sighed contently and looked back to the sea. "Well, he seems to *tolerate* you a great deal. They all do."

Kyce went silent, annoyed by the warming of his heart. He wished so dearly he could curse his obnoxious comrades and prove to Taige he cared nothing of them. But he couldn't.

"I um…" Kyce cleared his throat. "I wanted to thank you for what you did on the Adder's Isle. You know, for helping us recruit the Venom Tongues and all. Without you, we'd probably still be stranded on that beach."

"You'd actually probably be dead in the Viper's Garden."

Kyce rolled his eyes, and Taige laughed. To his surprise, he found himself grinning along with her.

"You don't have to thank me," Taige assured through her subsiding laughter. "I'm always going to have your back, regardless."

Kyce straightened, his brow drawn in an arch. "Regardless of what?" he asked.

"Regardless of whether you hate me or not."

Kyce froze and looked to Taige as she stared at the sea, seemingly unbothered.

"Taige, I don't hate you."

"You certainly don't like me. You've made that perfectly clear."

"Taige—" Kyce paused and drew in a deep breath. "I admit, I treated you in a way you didn't deserve to be treated. Unfortunately… I don't have an excuse as to why I acted that way."

"Is it because of the metal leg?"

"What?"

"It can be off-putting to some people."

"What—no—"

"Children often point."

"I'm not a child."

"That's debatable."

Kyce chuckled. He had to admit, Taige's company wasn't as agonizing as he once believed. In fact, she was almost enjoyable.

"But tell me," Taige continued, "why did you dislike me so?"

"As I said, I don't have an excuse."

"Make one."

Kyce drew in a deep breath, the salty air stinging his throat.

"When I was sixteen, I was cast from my home on Era. I don't know if you've heard, but I'm not exactly a pureblood."

"I've heard the legends."

"For a long time, it was just me and my soaring wolf, Whisp. She um," Kyce stopped to swallow the lump forming in his throat. "She stuck by me through it all. I was the reason she couldn't fly anymore, and she still stuck by me... Lykos—she even died for me."

"She was a loyal beast."

"No. That's the thing. She wasn't. Just like Saber, she was hypnotized to be loyal to her bond. Had she been given her freedom, she would've never lost her wings. She would've never gotten herself killed. That's something I regret most... that she gave her life for someone she didn't truly love."

"But you loved her?"

Kyce nodded, his eyes latched on the waves. "She was my bond, after all."

"Did she know that?"

"I believe so."

"Then she didn't die for nothing," Taige laid her hand on his shoulder. "She died for you. She loved you regardless of her trance. Your soaring wolf may have been hypnotized to devote herself to you—but what she felt was true."

"What she felt doesn't change anything," Kyce gripped the railing. "She died because her trance compelled her to protect me. She was more so a hostage than she was my bond."

Hostage, Kyce repeated within his head. *Hostage. That's what Whisp was.* She was a magnificent beast born with the gift of flight, and because of him, she was cursed to the earth. His stomach twisted at the thought. He looked away, fearful Taige might catch the glimmer of weakness in his eyes.

"Kyce?" Taige whispered, touching his hand.

"I'm fine," Kyce muttered and jerked his hand away.

Taige clutched her fist to her chest.

"I'm sorry," she apologized. "I'll admit, I can't begin to understand what Whisp felt. But I'm grateful for what she did." Taige brushed a tuff of dark hair out of Kyce's eye. "It's because of her I got to meet you."

Kyce flinched at her words.

You can't begin to understand? He thought. *You can. You do understand. You're just like her.*

Kyce cleared his throat and pulled away.

"But to answer your question. I guess I'm skeptical about having someone follow me so blindly. I hurt for a long time after I lost Whisp. I'm not looking for another servant to sacrifice. That's why I've acted so cruelly."

"I'm not a servant," Taige said and stepped closer. "I'm a Venom Tongue. And a pretty darn good one at that. And Kyce, no disrespect to Whisp, but I don't plan on dying any time soon. Nor do I plan on turning you away like the people of Era did... I won't leave you like everyone else."

I won't be left alone... Kyce gulped, horrified by the comfort he found in those words.

He looked away, desperate to escape Taige's enchantment. Growing bold, she took him by the hand. This time, he didn't pull away.

"Kyce," Taige began softly, the deep look in her eyes taking him captive.

Just as she went to speak, Feran hurtled up the stairs, out of breath. Kyce snapped his hand away from Taige and turned to face her, his face hot despite the cold.

"You guys—" Feran gasped between breaths. "You guys gotta... You guys gotta..."

"By Lykos, Feran, the stairs only have nine steps," Kyce scolded. "What's wrong with you?"

"Hey—" Feran snapped. "I don't need to run when I fly everywhere. But that's not the point. You guys gotta see this."

"What's going on?" Taige asked and pulled away. "Are the Venom Tongues causing any trouble?"

"No," Feran smiled. "But Elling is. You gotta see!"

Taige hurried to the stairs, smiling back at Kyce.

"Come on!" she called before disappearing down the stairs with Feran.

Kyce remained on the upper deck. He looked down at his hand, still tingling from Taige's touch.

"Hmm," he mumbled, making a fist. "This could be a problem."

KYCE WAS HALFWAY DOWN the stairs when the violent cheers of the Seavallian pirates nearly knocked him down. Every Venom Tongue sober enough to stand crowded around Elling as she played her hand. With each card she laid on the barrel-top, she took a long swig of her mug, mirroring the pirate across from her.

Kyce made his way through the drunken crowd to the Dire Wolves and stood by Taige.

"What in the name of Lykos is going on?" he grumbled, crossing his muscular arms over his chest.

"It's Elling," Sova gawked, shaking his head. "She—She's evolved!"

"She's drinking like a monster," Feran added.

Taige chuckled, amused. "Gut of a Seavallian that girl has."

Kyce looked at Roeseph. "Did you know she could drink like this?"

Roeseph scoffed as a smirk of admiration lifted one side of his lips. "Let's just say I'm no longer surprised when she surprises me."

Elling lifted another mug of Odin Slayer to her lips, downing it all in one gulp. At this point, the cards on the tabletop had been forgotten, and all was left was the drinking portion of the game. She slammed her empty mug down, provoking the crowd to roar.

Across the empty barrel, her opponent grabbed hold of the sides of the barrel to keep himself standing. His skin had paled to a greenish-blue, and his lips were glossy with bile. He swayed with the ship, filled to the brim with Odin Slayer.

"Who are you, shepherd girl?" he burped as he slowly dipped to the planks.

"You already know," Elling seethed before she threw her head back and downed another mug. She cringed at the burning taste. Then, wiping her lips, tossed the empty cup to the crowd. "I am the Feral Shepherd."

The drunken challenger fell against the barrel and pulled it down with him. The crowd roared out with glee.

"Long live the Feral Shepherd!" a pirate yelled, followed by another, and then another, until the whole ship filled the night with their praise.

Elling stumbled around to see the Dire Wolves watching her, their jaws hung and eyes wide with awe. She smiled, her lips glazed with Odin Slayer.

"Sova," she called and motioned for him to come. "C'mer. All of ya."

Sova looked from side to side before eagerly joining Elling, followed by the rest of the Dire Wolves. They lifted the fallen barrel back on its feet and gathered around to join Elling in the sinner's sport with the rest of the Venom Tongues. Within moments, each of them had a mug in hand—a peace offering from the pirates of Seavale.

Roeseph shook his head at the Feral Shepherd, completely and utterly in awe.

"What in the Great Valley of Lykos was that, Elling?" he managed to say through a spreading smile.

Sova, already half-drunk, raised his mug to the sails.

"Something beautiful," he said. "You're my hero, Elling."

Elling smiled through a slow blink. She swayed into Roeseph's shoulder, looking up at him with glazed-over eyes.

"Ah, captain," she giggled and shook her head against Roeseph's shoulder. "There are many things you have yet to learn about me."

Chapter Nineteen: Drunken Nothings

"I am the Feral Shepherd," Elling blubbered as she failed about in Roeseph's arms.

"I know, Elling," Roeseph chuckled as he prodded the door to the captain's quarters open with his foot. "I know."

He stepped into the cabin and shut the door, muffling the drunken cheers of the Venom Tongues outside.

Elling blinked slowly and looked around the captain's quarters. It was quite peaceful when it wasn't playing host to a war meeting. It reminded her of a place her father would've liked. The walls and floors were made of sanded mahogany, broken wheels and torn nets hung on the walls, and it had the distinct scent of fire and bourbon.

Nestling her face against Roeseph's chest, she sighed, "Roeseph."

"Mhmm?" Roeseph hummed as he carried her across the room.

"Your heart is beating too loud."

"I'll try to be quieter."

Roeseph stopped before a bench beneath a wide window overlooking the sea, and laid Elling on the red cushions. She burrowed against the soft bedding, groaning in regret of the many drinking games she'd partaken in.

"Roeseph," she whimpered. "I don't feel good."

"That's ok, Elling," Roeseph whispered as he sat on the floor, his back against the bench. "I'll be here if you get sick."

"Do you not feel sick?"

"No. I never finished my mug."

Elling snorted. "Stiff."

"You sound like Sova."

"Sova was a trooper tonight," Elling managed through a yawn.

"He drank three barrels of Odin Slayer. I'm worried for him."

"We've *been* worried for him."

Roeseph nodded, listening to waves as they clawed against the ship before receding back into the sea.

"You actually drank more than him, Elling," he said. "I have to admit. I'm surprised you lasted as long as you did."

"Impressed?" Elling yawned as she nestled deeper into the cushion.

Roeseph shook his head, smiling. "I guess impressed isn't quite the right word. More like frightened. Or intrigued. Where did you learn to drink like that, Elling? I think in the months I've known you, you've only drank once. And yet you somehow managed to outdrink a Seavallian pirate?"

Elling hesitated, and turned her face into the cushion.

"It was the only way to make me forget," she said finally.

Roeseph chuckled. "Forget what?"

"Make me forget what I did to my people."

Roeseph's smile faded, his heart sinking deeper than the ship's anchors could ever hope to dream.

Elling drew a deep breath. "After my Hyde Howler awoke, I ran away to Seavale. Lots of folks like me end up there, and Lykos knows it's not hard to get a drink around there. But... no matter how much I drank, it wasn't enough. It wouldn't let me forget."

"Elling—"

"I don't want to be a monster anymore, Roeseph," Elling said, her voice fading off as her eyes drooped shut. "I don't..."

The shepherdess went still as gentle snores filled the quarters. Roeseph brushed a strand of hair out of her face, watching her as she drifted deeper into blissful slumber.

"You never were one," he uttered.

MEANWHILE, ON THE UPPER deck, Feran kept vigil over a very drunk Sova.

"I told you, Sova," she warned, her arms crossed over her chest as she leaned against Saber's strong leg. "Don't touch it."

Sova stood at the far end of the deck, swaying with the sea and giggling like a child as he eyed the unattended steering wheel.

"I am the captain now."

"Sova, if you try to touch that wheel again, I'll do it, I swear."

"You won't be able to stop me," Sova hissed, licking away the excess Odin Slayer from his lips. "I am like lightning."

"Sova," Feran warned in a swinging tone. "Don't do it."

Giving a mighty battle cry, Sova half ran half stumbled toward the wheel of the ship. Feran snapped her fingers. Saber lunged in front of the wheel and roared in Sova's face. The prince fell flat on the planks. Had he been slightly soberer he might've feared the wrath of the White Angel. But he was not sober, so he just lay there, giggling at the stars.

"Great Lykos, he's scary," Sova said as he rolled from shoulder to shoulder. Saber snarled, annoyed by Sova's unbreakable stupor.

"I told you not to do it," Feran scolded as she walked up to Saber and scratched him behind the ears.

"I just want to steer the boat for a little bit," Sova whined. "It's not like I can get us shipwrecked. There's nothing but open sea for miles and miles."

"And yet somehow you'd find a way."

Sova giggled. "Thank you."

Feran sighed and pulled Sova to his feet, leaning him against her shoulder for support. Saber snarled at their closeness.

"Relax, Saber," Feran grunted as she whisked Sova to the far side of the upper deck, a safe distance away from the ship's wheel, and helped him to sit against the railing.

Sova smirked up at Feran, his head swiveling from side to side.

"Feran. Do you want to know a secret?"

"Not really," Feran sighed as she settled next to him.

"I like you," Sova slurred. He fell onto the floorboards, his head landing perfectly on Feran's thigh. "Now, do the thing to my hair that you did last night. The thing with the playing and—and the stroking."

"Get up, Sova," Feran shoved him upright.

Sova pouted. "I am hurt, Feran. Nonetheless, I still like you."

"I'm flattered," Feran exhaled and stared up at the sky. Saber lay beside Feran and rested the tip of his snout on her leg, staring up at her as she stroked his ears mindlessly.

Sova scowled at the beast, envious, "Thorn in my side."

Saber snarled.

"Don't provoke him," Feran warned coolly. "I swear, one of these days you're going to get yourself bit."

"I'd like to see him try," Sova grumbled and looked to Feran as she stared sadly at the sky. "So, what's with you?"

"Hmm?" Feran looked down.

"Your face is doing a thing," Sova gurgled through a liquor-flavored burp. "Why is it that every time we're on a boat, you get super depressed?"

"Sorry to inconvenience you," Feran raised her brow.

"So, what's got you down, sky wench?"

Feran grimaced. "*Sky wench*?" she muttered. Sova's capabilities of absurdity never failed to baffle her. "It's nothing," she shook her head. "Nothing worth talking about."

"Gha—" Sova roared and threw his arm around Feran's shoulders, "speak to me, ye emotional woman. I desire to hear of your head's quarrels."

"I have never wanted to feed you to Saber as dearly as I do right in this moment."

"Noted," Sova scooted away. "What's troubling you?"

Feran sighed and looked at Sova. He smiled at her with a smile so big and toothy, his face wrinkled at every corner.

Feran snorted. "What are you doing?" she shook her head.

"Comforting you," Sova said through the clenched smile. "Is it working?"

Feran laughed and looked back to the sky. For a while, only the waves spoke, their white claws raking down the sides of the ship.

"I'm scared, Sova," she admitted, her grin fading. "I'm scared for you, the others, my father...What we're about to try is bold. Not even bold. Stupid. We don't know if you'll be able to fool the Vaskans, and even if you do, what if my father can't hypnotize the Vaskans? What if you can't get them out of there?"

"Before you, Casavore was the most powerful mind melder in all of Lykos," Sova assured. "If anyone can get the Blind Seers out of there, he can."

"But what if he can't?" Feran turned to Sova with tear-speckled eyes. "Sova, what if I lose my father?"

Sova swallowed hard, agonized by the look of helplessness in the eyes of his childhood foe.

"You won't," he promised. "I'll get him out of there, Feran, you'll see."

"But what if Saulder—"

"Saulder won't touch him," Sova said more sternly and scooted closer to Feran, ignoring Saber when he growled. "I promise, Feran. I won't let him."

Feran stared at Sova, her eyes softening.

"And what about you? What if he comes for you?"

Sova grinned playfully and shrugged. "Well, then I suppose Kyce's prayers would finally be answered."

"That's not funny, Sova."

"Sure it is. I'm hilarious," Sova nudged his shoulder against Feran, desperate to pull her out of her dread. "Hey. Everything will be ok. You'll see."

"You promise?"

"I promise," Sova nodded. "And in the unlikely event, Saulder does take my life, you have my permission to let Saber kill me."

"You'd already be dead."

"Saber scares me enough that I'd come back to life just to get away from him."

Feran shook her head, smiling. Yawning through a stretch, Sova rested his head on Feran's shoulder.

"You'll see," he sighed tiredly. "Everything will be fine."

His smile softened and gentle snores slipped from his lips in calm repetition; proof he'd fallen into a deep slumber.

Feran smirked down at him, and snaked her arm around his shoulder so she could draw intricate symbols in his hair.

"You better keep that promise," she said. "Goodnight, Sova."

Chapter Twenty: Land Ho

The sun shone white behind a veil of clouds as the Seavallian ships raced north, through the grey sea.

The Dire Wolves gathered at the front of the vessel, searching for the coast hidden somewhere beyond the waves. Sova knelt before the railing, drumming his fingers rhythmically on the wooden surface while Elling glared at him with eyes anchored by thick black bags.

Sova looked up, his eyes big and innocent. "What?"

"Are you going to keep doing that the entire time?" she seethed.

Sova looked from left to right. "Doing what?"

"The drumming," the shepherdess hissed. "That incessant drumming, are you going to keep doing that?"

Feran chuckled. "Awe. Your head still hurting you, Elling?"

"Don't mock me, mind-melder," Elling growled as she rubbed her temples.

Feran looked to the sea sputtering. "You're nicer when you drink."

No one talked for a long while. The morning was quiet, except for the waves drumming against the sides of the ship and the *thwap* of the sails rippling in the wind. For a moment, Elling thought she might get her peace and silence.

That was until Sova wailed, "Are we there yet?"

Elling exhaled, this time not rubbing, but digging her fingers into her temples.

Roeseph answered, "What did I tell you two minutes ago, Sova?"

"Not yet."

"So, what do you think I'm going to say now?"

Sova rested his chin on his crossed arms with a pout as he stared at the clouds pregnant with rain; the future mothers to a storm.

"I'm bored out of my mind," he complained.

"Then go play with the Venom Tongues," Kyce seethed.

"No."

"Why not?"

"They're mean to me."

"I'm mean to you."

"You won't throw me overboard."

"Don't tempt me."

"Would you all please!" Elling snapped. Everyone stilled, frightened. Even Saber stepped away.

"Feran's right. You're way nicer when you're drinking," Taige admitted under her breath. When all was silent again, Elling drew in a deep breath to calm herself.

"Now, if we can all be quiet for just ten minutes," she stopped and inhaled, "... There. Isn't that nice?"

A bullhorn blared across the ocean as a Venom Tongue shouted from the crow's-nest, "Land ho!"

"Man, no!" Sova cried.

Elling drew in a deep breath, her face stoic, but her eyes blazing.

"Wonderful..." she exhaled.

"There it is," Feran pointed to a black line rising out of the sea. Slowly, the black line grew spikes and brightened to green. A gold beach emerged from the waves and the mountains of Era rose behind them.

"Finally," Sova sighed. "It's good to be home. I swear if I had to spend one more moment on that Lykos-forsaken island with those scurvy rats, I was gonna—" Sova paused and glanced at Taige. She glared at him, her fingers drumming on the railing. "Pssht—I wasn't talking about you, Tay-Tay. You're a very nice rat."

Taige rolled her eyes and turned to venture across the ship, barking orders and insulting her crewmates as she went.

"Do you think she heard me?" Sova grumbled.

"*No*," Kyce shook his head sarcastically.

Roeseph pressed himself closer to the railing, staring at the Valley of Lykos as it neared.

"Prepare yourselves, my friends," he said. "Our day of reckoning is coming..."

Chapter Twenty-One: Purple Garments

For two days, the Dire Wolves and the Venom Tongues traveled on foot toward Vaska, only stopping when they came to the Mosharick Plains. There, they pitched their tents in the forest shadows on the east side of the river.

The fourth sunrise before Casavore's execution bled through the curtain of Sova's tent, warming the bare skin of his back. He stood before a tall mirror in nothing but a kilt, with white sharick fawn beards intertwined in his hair to mimic Saulder's long locks. His stomach churned at his reflection.

Ironic, he thought as he traced the gauze wrapped around his shoulder. All it took was a few hair extensions to transform him into the monster who scarred him for life.

The tent's curtain lashed to the side, making Sova looked up into the mirror. Feran stood behind him, a purple robe hung over her arm. She froze, her eyes widening into saucers.

"Wow," she whispered.

Sova scowled and looked away from the mirror. "Paint a portrait. It'll last longer."

Feran shook away her daze.

"Sorry," she mumbled, and handed Sova the purple garments. "These were all the Venom Tongues could find in the Mosharick villages. But they'll pass for Vaskan robes."

"Great," Sova grumbled as he held the garments out to examine.

They looked nothing like the royal garments he wore back in Vaska. His robes were made of fine, violet silk woven by the best seamstresses in the kingdom, with silver twine needled around the neckline in crossing designs.

The robe before him looked more like a giant purple monster had thrown up onto a shepherd's garment.

He sighed, "It'll do."

Feran looked Sova up and down, her expression sinking. "You ok?"

"As ok as someone impersonating their murderous older brother can be," Sova replied, pulling at the loose gauze on his shoulder.

Feran watched as he fiddled. Her brow arched.

"How long has it been since you last changed those?"

"I don't know," Sova shrugged as he tossed the purple garments on a stool in the corner of the tent. "Eight days maybe. I was supposed to change them, but then I got kidnapped by little miss sunshine out there. You know, for a Venom Tongue, she's really quite chipper."

Feran was silent, lost somewhere in the depths of her thoughts. Then, without saying another word, she left.

"Good talk," Sova retorted.

Feran returned not a moment later with a wad of clean gauze.

"Hold still," she ordered as she approached.

Sova cowered back, clasping the scar hidden beneath his wraps. "Stop," he ordered sternly.

Feran exhaled, annoyed, "What's the problem?"

"I'm not letting you touch my scar."

"Why not?"

"Because. I don't want you to see it."

"Well, you don't want to see it either. So it's better if I do it."

"No, Feran," Sova jeered as he stumbled back, nearly knocking over the mirror.

Feran stared at him, her expression wavering between pity and frustration.

"How about this. You turn around so I won't see anything. Fair?"

Sova stared at her, hesitant to agree.

"Sova, we've got a kingdom to invade before sunup, and it's already dusk. Please make a decision."

"Fine," Sova groaned and turned his back to Feran. "Sons of Lykos, you're bossy."

"Hold still," Feran ordered. Sova shut his eyes tight. With each layer Feran peeled back, he grew more anxious, his heart like a fleeting rabbit set loose in his chest.

"Promise you won't look?" he asked.

"I said I wouldn't, didn't I?" Feran said as she applied the fresh gauze to Sova's shoulder. Her eyes drooped to the sharick fawn locks woven in Sova's hair. They didn't match his striking white color exactly, but it was enough to fool the Vaskan guards, especially under the cloak of night.

"Saulder really never cut his hair, huh?" she asked.

Sova turned his chin over his shoulder, his eyes still shut. "Yeah. Something about not wanting to lose his strength like Samuel."

Feran stopped. Sova cautiously pried one eye open to look back at her.

"What?" he asked.

"Nothing," Feran shook her head, continuing to wrap his shoulder. "It's just that... he was talking about Samson. His favorite Bible story. When we were little, Saulder thought that if he never cut his hair, he'd never be weak."

"Hmm," Sova nodded. "I was never a fan of Saulder's hair. Growing up, I'd have to listen to the maids gossip all day about Dire Saulder's beautiful hair. My hair's just as beautiful. I'm just not a heathen."

"Oh, for sure," Feran smirked. "You look so mighty with your mane of sharick fawn beards."

"Very few can pull it off."

Feran chuckled and tied the gauze tight. "Ok," she said, patting his shoulder. "You're done."

Sova threw on his purple garments and walked up to the mirror. His heart sunk at the sight of the monster staring back at him.

"You're all ready for your debut, Dire Saulder," Feran smirked, her grin sinking when she saw the distraught look on Sova's face. "Now what? Did I tie the gauze too tight or something?"

Sova didn't respond, the bulge in his throat bouncing as he stared at himself.

"Sova?" Feran came again, gentler than before.

Sova shook his head in disgust. "You just never really get used to it," he admitted. "Staring into the face of a monster."

Feran stepped between Sova in the mirror.

"I don't see the face of a monster," she assured as she brushed a lock of sharick fawn hair over his shoulder. "I just see you."

Sova stilled, snared in Feran's hypnotic gaze like a fish in a net. Words of longing he dare not speak sat on the edge of his lips, begging to be said.

"Feran, I—"

Before he could finish, Kyce pushed back the tent's curtain. Feran and Sova pulled back from the other.

"What is taking so long?" Kyce hissed. "The sun's going down. Sova should've left for the sewers a long time ago."

"Feran tried to seduce me," Sova tattled.

"Sova!" Feran snapped, her eyes like whips of fire lashing on him.

Kyce rolled his eyes. "Yeah, sure, and I'm a soaring wolf's uncle. Now hurry up and get out here."

Kyce retreated out of the tent, letting the tarp fall shut behind him.

Feran smacked Sova on the shoulder, making him flinch and rub his arm.

"Sova!" she sneered. "What in Lykos was that?"

"I'm sorry, I panicked."

ROESEPH, ELLING, AND Taige waited in the forest shadows outside camp, watching the Venom Tongues as they sharpened their swords outside their tents and around campfires under the magenta dusk.

"What's taking them so long?" Roeseph grumbled as he paced.

"Patience, young captain," Taige said as she reclined against the trunk of a tree. "They're coming."

"Maybe this is a bad idea," Roeseph shook his head. "Maybe we should call the rescue mission off."

Elling grabbed his hand, stopping him mid-pace.

"Everything will be fine, Roeseph," she assured. "Sova knows what he's doing."

Kyce stalked out from the camp, his eyes shining amber in the light of the setting sun.

Like a pup catching wind of its master's scent, Taige sprung up from her tree and hurtled toward him.

"Kyce!" she cried and threw her arms around his neck. "I missed you."

"You saw me ten minutes ago."

Roeseph stepped away from Elling, his dusk-blue eyes growing stormy. "Where's Sova?"

"He's coming," Kyce assured as he tried to untangle Taige from his neck with little success. "By Lykos, woman, let go."

"Never!" Taige roared as Kyce stumbled around.

Sova and Feran departed the camp last, accompanied by Saber. Sova stood before his comrades, dressed in purple garments, his long, white hair flowing in the breeze.

Elling's eyes widened.

"Woah," she whispered. "You look—"

"Like a grown man wearing a wig of goat hair," Sova finished.

"To be clear, its sharick fawn hair," Elling corrected.

"What does it matter?"

Roeseph walked up to Sova. "Are you sure you're up for this?" he asked, his eyes dense with worry.

"Of course," Sova smiled. "It's about time I visited Vaska. Don't get me wrong, I love you guys, but a guy can't help but feel a little home sick."

As Sova and Roeseph talked, Kyce charged by with Taige dangling from his neck. He stopped fast and Taige whipped over his head and onto the grass. She laughed up at him, her dark eyes sparkling like two pieces of night.

"That was fun. Let's do it again."

Kyce shook his head as a repressed smirk cracked his face. "Not a chance," he huffed. "You look small, but you weigh a ton."

"That's all the metal leg, love," Taige slapped her prosthetic. Kyce couldn't help but chuckle.

Roeseph cleared his throat. Kyce looked up, his smile flashing away in an instant when he found his comrades staring at him. Sova, whom of which, was smiling.

"What are you looking at, Vaskan?" Kyce sneered.

"Nothing," Sova shrugged. "It's just nice to see you finally starting to settle down."

Just as Kyce took a step towards Sova, Roeseph stepped between them.

"Listen, Sova," the Dire Wolf captain began. "Once you pass through the sewers, head immediately to the dungeons. Try not to be seen, and don't talk to anyone."

"Then how will I make friends?"

"Focus, Sova. Get the Blind Seers and the Blessers out. Tell Casavore to hypnotize a couple guards so they can safely escort you out of Vaska. Be sure that you're not being followed."

"Aye–Aye captain," Sova saluted as he turned to march toward Vaska.

"One last thing" Roeseph called and grabbed Sova by the shoulder. "Don't get yourself killed."

Sova smirked, his heart warmed by the genuine concern in his captain's voice. "I mean, I wasn't planning to."

Feran stepped up to Sova. "Before you go, I have something for you to give my father."

"I don't know Feran," Sova shrugged, his brow drawn in a mischievous arch. "I mean, it's sweet if *you* give Casavore a kiss on the cheek. But if *I* do it—"

"Don't kiss my father, Sova."

"Well now I wanna."

Feran rolled her eyes and drew the Blesser's medallion from her neck.

"I need you to give this to him."

Sova's smug expression dropped. "Feran," he whispered. "I can't take that from you."

"It was never mine to begin with." Feran grabbed hold of Sova's hand and placed the golden medallion in his palm. "Casavore asked you to protect it. You should be the one who returns it. Besides, if you don't take it, this whole mission goes up in flames. Casavore needs a medallion."

Sova swallowed hard and looked down at the Blesser's weapon shining in his hand.

"I'll bring him back, Feran," he dipped his head. "I'm bringing all of them back. I promise."

Sova turned and charged into the darkness. Feran watched as he went, clutching the place over her chest where her medallion used to be. Saber nuzzled the side of her cheek, whining at the stench of fear emanating off her.

"I'm ok, Saber," she assured. "Everything's going to be ok. You'll see... Sova's going to be ok."

Chapter Twenty-Two: The Traitor Returns

Sova raced through the Vaskan Forest, the stars lighting his path through the ever-shifting leaves. Finally he came to the walls of Vaska. They towered above him, standing so tall they seemed to curve against the sky.

Sova sighed, his heart weighing in his chest like an anchor. It had been so long since he'd been home.

He looked to the right. Sure enough, a large tunnel jutted out of the west wall where a bubbling brown brook leaked out into the woods. Sova hurried inside, standing ankle-deep in the warm sewage. The rancid stench of dung and swamp moss burrowed into the back of Sova's throat, making him gad.

"Great Lykos," he wretched and lunged into the darkness, splashing through the rotten waters until he came to a grate, which to his luck, was unlocked. He carried on.

At the end of the tunnel, a crescent-shaped spotlight bled overhead through a gap in a manhole cover. Sova pushed the lid away and pulled himself up.

He gasped at the clean air and emerged just outside the royal stables. A stallion poked its head out from its stall, staring at Sova as it chewed on a clump of hay. Sova nodded at the beast in greeting and looked around. Behind him, stood the palace of Vaska, its stalagmite-like towers piercing straight through the moon.

Sova stalked toward the west wall of the palace where he came upon a large black door with a wheel-like handle on the front. Sova pulled at the prongs, his teeth gritting in frustration as he tried to get it to budge.

"For Lykos sake," he growled through his teeth.

"Halt!" ordered a stern voice. Sova froze. "Stay where you are."

God of Lykos, help me, Sova mumbled and turned to face the Vaskan guard. He was a handsome man, with dark, fluffy hair, and eyes like two pieces of amethyst. Sova recognized him in an instant. He was the son of the previous general, General Hylan, and a close friend of Sova and Saulder's up until Zastar's injury that resulted in Hylan's banishment.

"Arison?" Sova whispered. "Arison, is that you?"

The Vaskan Guard straightened.

"Dire Saulder," he gasped and fell to his knee. "Forgive me, my dire. It's been so long since I've seen you without your armor that I didn't recognize you."

Sova cocked his head back. *This is going better than I expected.* "Ah yes, tis I," Sova began with a deep and pretentious voice that really didn't match Saulder's at all. "How dare you speak to your dire in such a way?..." he looked from left to right, unsure what to say next. "I am very upset."

"My apologies, my dire," Arison lowered his head. "Please—Please forgive me."

"Hmm," Sova pondered as he stroked his hair extensions. "Perhaps I can pardon you. If you do this one thing for me."

"Anything Dire Saulder. I am your loyal servant."

"Yes, indeed. So, you know how sometimes you can't open a pickle jar?"

"Yes?"

"Yeah—imma need you to open this door for me."

"Don't you have the key, sir?"

"You dare question the actions of the dire?" Sova bellowed.

Arison fumbled for the keys hanging on his belt and unlocked the door. It open with an eerie creek, revealing a stairwell leading down into darkness so deep it looked like it led straight into a black wall.

Sova gulped. "Lykos, it's dark down there."

"Would you like me to accompany you, my dire?" Arison dipped his head.

"No!" Sova snapped. "No. No, thank you, Sir Arison. I'll be fine on my own. But if you could, please guard the door. And don't let anyone pass through until I return."

Arison bowed, "Yes, sire."

Taking the keys from Arison, Sova descended the dreary staircase. The dungeon door creaked shut behind him, consuming Sova in complete darkness. When his eyes adjusted, and he came to the bottom of the stairs, he found a long hall with prison cells running on either side. The only light came from the torches, the wicks shortened to a measly red stub.

The prisoners inside the cells peered through the bars at Sova, their eyes shining with hate in the torches glow.

Sova stalked down the hall, scanning the cells. In his search for the Blesser, he came across another legend of Lykos.

Oland sat against the wall of his cell, his hazel eyes latched on the cracked ceiling overhead. His strong figure had withered slightly, and his glorious gut had shrunk. Gray stubble aligned his jaw, and his bald head glistened with sweat.

"*Psst,*" Sova hissed as he lowered himself before the bars. "Oland. Oland it's me."

Oland's head rolled to the side, his hazel eyes narrowing when on the Royal Traitor.

"You..." he seethed, hatred seeping out his lips with his spittle. "You're mighty bold to show up to me without a sword or your armor. If you're not careful, you might get hurt."

"*Shhh,*" Sova whispered and pressed close to the rusted bars. "I'm getting you out."

Oland lunged and grabbed Sova by the collar of his shirt, jerking him into the bars and making them chime.

"I don't care if they kill me," Oland snarled through clenched teeth. "I'll die a happy man with the dire's blood on my hands."

"Oland!" Sova gasped, his cheekbone scraping against the cold bar. "Oland, it's me, Sova. Roeseph sent me!"

Oland's snarl softened briefly, only to return ten times stronger. "You lying snake..."

"Really," Sova trembled and pulled out the Blesser's medallion for him to see. "We've got an army waiting for you outside Vaska. I'm here to help you escape."

The storms in Oland's eyes cleared, and he dropped Sova. The prince fell to the dungeon floor, sending a couple rats squealing into the darkness.

"Sova?" Oland whispered. "What are you—What are you doing here? Why are you dressed like that?"

"Believe me, it wasn't my choice of wardrobe either," Sova grumbled as he pulled himself to his feet. "But Roeseph said either I wore the disguise, or I didn't go at all."

"Roeseph? He's here?"

"Yes. He sent me to free you."

The prisoners gathered at the doors to their cells, murmuring to one another as they salivated at the idea of freedom. Sova looked at their faces, his heart sinking when he realized one vital figure wasn't among them.

"Where's Blesser Casavore?" he asked the Blind Hound.

Oland bowed his head against the cell bars. The sorrowed expression on his face made Sova's stomach drop.

"Oland, where's Casavore?" he asked more urgently and grabbed the bars to Oland's cell.

"Gone," Oland sighed. "The dire took him for questioning a few days ago. He's being held in another dungeon within the palace."

A secret dungeon? Sova thought to himself. *How come I lived here for twenty-one years and am just now hearing of a secret dungeon?*

"How do I find it?"

"It's hidden within the highest room of the north wing."

Sova shuddered. *The north wing... that's my father's chamber.* "Thank you, Oland," Sova dipped his head. "I'll be back for you once I find him."

As Sova dashed to the stairs, Oland called out to him. "Follow the portrait, Sova! Follow the portrait, and you'll find Casavore. Follow the portrait!"

SOVA ORDERED ARISON to guard the dungeon door and rushed into the palace. Somehow going unseen, he made his way to the north wing and trumpeted up the twisting staircase, only tripping on a step or two. He stopped cold when he came to a lonesome door at the top. He stared at the doorknob, his soul turning to ice under his skin.

He hadn't seen his father in so long; not since the day he betrayed his kingdom—his home.

Drawing in a deep breath, Sova unlocked the door with a shaken hand and stepped into Dire Zastar's chamber. The room hadn't changed since he'd last seen it. The canopy bed was still freshly made, without so much as a wrinkle in the violet sheets. The mirror over the dresser was freshly shined, and the cold light of the moon shone through an opened window.

Sova turned to the bed, his heart lurching.

Dire Zastar, laid beneath his many blankets in a death-like sleep. His copper skin had paled and his grey hair which was usually kept short had grown long and tangled.

Sova puzzled at his father. Ever since his injury, Casavore always made sure the old dire looked presentable, with his beard shaved and hair trimmed weekly. But since the Blesser's arrest, it seemed neither Dire Saulder nor Lore had bothered with Zastar's wellbeing. It made Sova hate them all the more.

His steps and heart heavy, Sova made his way to his father's bed. Zastar lay still, his chest rising with shallow, labored breaths. Sova tried to swallow, but his guilt choked him.

"Pa?" he whispered as he knelt by Zastar's bed. "It's me. Sova."

Zastar was silent. Sova swallowed hard. Even after eleven years he never got used to this version of his father—the quiet, still, practically lifeless version.

"I um... I'm here to get, Casavore," Sova continued. "I know the last time we spoke, it wasn't under the best circumstances. So... I suppose I should catch you up." He stopped to clear his throat. "I uh... Well, since getting banished, I made a new best friend, Roeseph. You know, the son of the Blind Hound. That guy you hate. Him. Uh, anyway, we were in hiding for a long while until we came across Kyce. He's my other best friend. He's an exiled Eradite with daddy-mommy issues. And then we met my other best friend, Elling. She's nice. Oh—and we also have a Venom Tongue as a pet now. It sound's weirder than it is. I um... I also found Feran. Came as quite a surprise to me that she's not dead. But I'm sure you've heard plenty about the Dire Wolves and me."

Zastar was silent, as far away from Sova's presence as he could get without being dead.

Sova clenched his jaw to stop it from trembling. "She's not as unbearable as she used to be. Feran. In fact, she's... kind of... kind of important."

Sova clutched his father's hand, his already broken heart shattering into dust. Tears welling in his yes, he looked up at the portrait over the bed.

The once-proud Dire Zastar stared back at Sova, immortalized in paint, corralled in a silver frame. He wore royal garments and fine jewelry. His hair and the thin beard tracing his jaw were black as ebony. His skin was a dark copper color, and his eyes were like two pieces of silver harvested from the Vaskan mines.

Sova stared at his father's memory, praying he might one day return.

In his mourning, his mind shifted to Lore and the hatred he had for her. She was the reason his father was hurt—why Saulder was evil, why General Hylan was banished, why Fala was dead, why everyone and everything he cared about was in shambles. Sova hated her. *He hated her.*

As he stared at his father's portrait, he noticed the eyes were focused on something. He followed them across the room, to the mirror and dresser opposite from the bed.

He remembered Oland's warning.

"Follow the portrait, Sova. Follow the portrait, and you'll find Casavore. Follow the portrait!"

Sova fled from his father's bedside and shoved the mirror and dresser aside, the legs scraping against the stone. Behind it, he find a secret door. He looked back at his father, his heart heavy with guilt.

"I'm sorry, Pa," he said sadly. "I'm going to make things right. You'll see."

Sova opened the chamber door to find yet another dreary staircase twirling down into darkness. Closing the door, he descended into the black, the light echo of his steps sending shivers up his spine.

A hoarse voice called from the void. "Have you not anything better to do than mock me, you vicious snake?"

Sova stopped, his eyes misting at the familiar voice.

"What?" Casavore came again. "Nothing to say, witch?"

Sova hurtled deeper into the secret chasm where he found at the bottom of the stairs, a small dungeon with a single jail cell. Ancient skeletons belonging to both rats and men littered the cell floor, the single torchlight casting long shadows across the stone.

A skinny man with tangled hair sat with his back to the bars, his humble garments falling off boney shoulders as he stared at the wall.

"Is it not enough you've sentenced me to death?" Casavore rasped. "Must you come and waste my time?"

Sova stood at the bottom of the stairs, speechless. For nearly a year, he'd gone without seeing the Blesser. And there he was—half-starved, denied of sunlight, and all.

"Well, speak up, won't you?" the Blesser growled.

Sova took a hesitant step forward, speaking quietly enough so his voice wouldn't echo. "C—Cas?"

The Blesser sat up.

"By the God of Lykos..." he mumbled before lashing around, tears appearing in his eyes as if by magic. "My boy, is that you?"

"Cas!" Sova fell to his knees before Casavore. "Cas, it's me."

"How can this be?" the Blesser shook his head. "Why—Why would you come back?"

"Roeseph sent me. I've come to rescue you."

"Roeseph sent you? Then is—is Feran—" Casavore gulped, his voice shaking when he went to speak again. "Is Feran—"

"She's alive," Sova smiled and pulled out the Blesser's medallion. "She wanted me to give you this."

Casavore stole his medallion out of Sova's hands, tears plipped onto the golden pendent.

"Feran..." he sniffled. "My sweet little girl..."

"She's waiting for you back at camp," Sova said and drew out the keys he acquired from Arison. "I need to get you out of here."

Casavore looked up at Sova, watching him as the door rejected each and every key.

"Come on," Sova growled frustratedly. "Why won't you open?"

"You need to leave, my son," Casavore pleaded. "Leave this place. Tell Feran I love her."

"No—I can do this," Sova grunted as he tossed the keys over his shoulder and pulled at the door.

"Your majesty, please," Casavore pleaded.

"No! I can get you out. I promised Feran I would."

"Lore has the key. There's no getting me out. Please. Please, go back to Feran."

"No! I'm not leaving you here. I won't let Saulder win!"

Casavore's face went pale, and his jaw hung. Sova looked down at Casavore, confused by the horrified look on his face.

"What?"

"What did you say?" Casavore whispered.

"T—That I'm not leaving you here..." Sova stammered as he looked the Blesser up and down. "That Saulder isn't going to win this time."

Casavore's jaw quivered, his eyes shining with tears.

"You don't know," he sobbed as he gripped the bars. "Oh Lykos, I am so sorry. I am so sorry, my boy."

"What—What are you talking about, Cas?"

"I am so sorry. I didn't mean for this to happen. I didn't know how else to save you."

"Cas, you're scaring me."

The Blesser lifted the old medallion, staring at his guilty reflection in its golden face.

"God forgive me," he whispered as he pressed the medallion to his brow.

"Cas," Sova said hastily. "Casavore, speak to me."

Casavore's eyes flashed open.

"Your nightmares..." he growled. "How frequently have they been happening?"

A heavy weight dropped into Sova's stomach, nearly taking him to the floor.

"How did you know about the nightmares?" he asked, stepping back.

"You're trying to remember," Casavore said. "But you refuse to answer him."

"A—Answer who?"

Casavore looked up at Sova, "I am sorry for what I've done to you, my boy. I didn't know how else to save you."

"Cas, what are you talking ab—"

Without warning, the Blesser lifted the medallion. Sova froze, captured in the clutches of Casavore's hypnosis. He tried to scream, but he couldn't. It was as if the mind-melder had stolen his voice.

Casavore, Sova screamed within himself. *What are you doing?*

The Blesser glared at Sova as a tear stroked his cheek.

"Son of Zastar," he began. "Blood of Vaska, you've repressed your purpose for far too long. You've forgotten your oath to your kingdom and to your people. For this, I will make you remember the day you raised your sword against your brother—"

No! Sova wailed silently. *Casavore, please, no! I don't want to remember, please!*

"—You will remember. You will remember what the dire has done…"

Chapter Twenty-Three: Forgotten Sins

The Royal Traitor woke up with a gasp. He looked around, shocked and horrified to find himself miraculously transported in the middle of Dire Saulder's bed chamber.

The sun was out, seeping through the balcony along with the faint cry of battle. The world around him had a sort of iridescent hue to it, as if he was looking at it through a glass window.

He tried to take a step, but found he couldn't lift his feet.

What's going on? he gasped. *How'd I get here?*

"Casavore?" he called, looking around. The Blesser was nowhere in sight. "Blesser Casavore, answer me!"

"You were a prince of Vaska," shouted a familiar voice.

The Royal Traitor contorted himself to look back. Dire Saulder stood across the chamber, wearing his nightmarish black armor with the sharp horn-like shoulder plates. His helmet was off, revealing a bloodied lip and vicious silver eyes.

"A respected and trusted royal to this kingdom!" Saulder continued. "And you just threw it all away!"

An exact and bloody replica of the Royal Traitor stood before the dire, a sword clutched in hand.

"Because I care for my kingdom," the clone fired back. "I won't let you hold my people hostage any longer."

No... The Royal Traitor shook his head, looking from the dire to his clone. *This is the day the Blind Seers attacked the palace. This is the day I fought Saulder.*

Saulder lunged at his brother with sword in hand, causing the clone to stumble back. The Royal Traitor looked frantically between the two, his heart sinking lower and lower as the battle waged on.

"I'm the one holding them hostage?" Saulder hissed. "You brought Vaska's greatest enemies into the palace. You're a traitor to your nation."

"No," the younger version of Sova shook his head. "I'm its savior!"

He punched Saulder in his injured shoulder. The dire roared out in pain and stumbled back. Saulder then caught his brother by the wrist, causing the prince to drop his sword, and punched him hard in the stomach.

The Royal Traitor winced as he watched himself hit the floor.

That had to hurt... and it did.

Saulder glared down at his brother through fallen strands of white hair with jaws bared. Then, he grabbed Sova by his foot and dragged him away.

Sova reached for his sword, grabbing just short of the handle as his brother dragged him away. Without warning, Saulder dropped Sova's leg and kicked him hard in the stomach.

"Stop!" the royal traitor called, but Saulder ignored him. It was then he realized, just as he couldn't move, he couldn't be heard.

"How could you turn your back on Vaska?" Saulder shouted between kicks.

The Royal Traitor watched his replica gasp in pain as tears welled up in both their eyes.

"How could you turn on your dire?" Saulder roared. "How could you betray our father? How could you betray me, your brother?"

"How could you?" the clone fired back. "Since Feran died, you've become a completely different person. You're a tyrant. And you've only gotten worse. Becoming the dire changed you. You used to be so kind, so merciful. I wanted to be just like you. Everyone was so proud of you and eagerly awaited the day you'd surpass our father. Instead, you've become a monster. What would Feran say if she saw you like this?"

Saulder roared out and kicked Sova square in the jaw. The Vaskan prince spun straight into the wall where he lay motionless.

Saulder stared at his brother, his sharp shoulder-plates falling with each, ragged breath.

"Feran isn't here," he grumbled.

The Royal Traitor gazed into the dire's eyes. They had a sort of hurt he hadn't noticed before—a deep mourning, harsher than any sword could hope to be. After all those years of Feran being gone, he was still in pain.

The Royal Traitor couldn't help but wonder, *If you loved her so much, why did you betray her?*

Dire Saulder turned away from his brother and marched to his bed.

Groaning on the floor, Sova looked up to see Saulder grab the crossbow.

"Enough is enough," Saulder muttered as he loaded an arrow. "The Blind Hound dies today."

"N—No," Sova grunted, his entire body trembling as he tried to force himself up onto his knees. Saulder stamped his heel down on Sova's spine, pinning him to the stone.

"Stay down," he growled.

Sova grimaced against the cold floor, glaring up at his brother with teeth bared in a snarl. Dire Saulder turned from his brother and marched onto his balcony. Standing against the railing, he raised his crossbow.

No. No! the Royal Traitor cried, his voice like a whisper in a thunderstorm.

Sova's replica rose shakily to his feet.

"Leave them alone!" the clone shouted. Picking up his sword, he charged the dire. Saulder looked back, his eyes going widening just as Casavore burst through the chamber doors.

"No!" the Blesser shouted.

Sova's lashed his sword through Saulder's brow. As the dire roared, he accidentally turned the crossbow away from its target and fired.

Sova gasped and stumbled back, as Saulder's enraged expression softened with horror.

"...Sova," the tyrant whispered.

The Royal Traitor watched as his replica turned to face Casavore in the doorway. The Royal Traitor gasped at what he saw.

No. he said to himself. *It can't be. This isn't what happened.*

His clone looked to the arrow lodged in his abdomen and then to the Blesser, his jaw trembling.

"Cas?" he uttered and collapsed to the floor. Casavore caught him at the very last second, hugging him close as tears speckled both their eyes.

"Sova. Sova," the Blesser stammered, his voice quivering like an autumn leaf. "No. Oh no. G—God, please no."

Sova looked up, sniffling. "Casavore. I saved him."

"What—What are you talking about?"

"I saved Oland. We can win now," Sova's said through a shaking smile. "We can be free."

"Sova," Casavore brushed back the prince's hair. "Sova, why would you do this?"

"We need to save everyone, Cas," Sova coughed, his lips framed in scarlet. "You need to stop him."

Saulder's shadow cast over them, making the Blesser look up. Sova followed his gaze, his face tensing in a sneer when he saw his brother.

"You're enjoying this, aren't you?" the clone wretched, blood spilling over his chin.

Saulder glared at his brother, his eyes sparkling with tears.

"Why?" he snarled. "Why would you sacrifice yourself? What good comes of this battle if its beacon dies?"

The Royal Traitor watched from the sidelines, tears painting the sides of his cheeks as an unbearable knot twisted his gut.

No. No, this isn't right, he thought. *This isn't what happened. I—I was shot in the shoulder. I wasn't hurt this badly...*

The clone chuckled up at Saulder.

"You don't get it, do you?" he mocked. "This whole battle. This rebellion... It's because these people would rather die than suffer through your reign another day. Me among them."

Saulder drew in a sharp breath, the tears he refused to let fall trembling in his eyes.

"I guess Feran's the lucky one of us all," Sova said. "She's the one who managed to get away from you."

Rage flashed in Saulder's eyes, and he grabbed the arrow in Sova's gut.

"Saulder! No!" Casavore screamed, and reached to stop him.

Saulder ripped out the arrow, making Sova's eyes bulge and a geyser of blood splurge from his lips.

The Royal Traitor stumbled to his knees, watching as his replica bled out over the stone. Saulder stood over his Blesser and brother, bloodied arrow clutched in hand.

"Sova!" Casavore cried as he pressed his hand down on the weeping wound. "Sova, stay with me!"

Sova trembled, his silver eyes melting into tears. Casavore looked up to the dire.

"Saulder!" he cried desperately. "Saulder go get the physician."

Saulder gripped the bloody arrow tighter, making the wood creak.

"No..." he growled.

"Saulder!"

"I said no," the dire shouted. "I want to watch the royal traitor bleed."

The Royal Traitor shook his head. *This doesn't make any sense. This is all wrong. This can't be how it happened.*

The injured clone looked up at Casavore, his eyes misty and helpless, like a child's.

"Cas," he whispered. "Cas, I'm scared."

"Don't be," Casavore sniffled, holding the prince's head to his chest. "You're going to be fine."

"What if He doesn't want me?" the Vaskan prince sniveled, tears racing the blood that flowed from his lips. "What if I didn't do enough?"

"...Do you believe in your heart that Jesus is the Christ and the son of the living God?"

Sova choked before managing to squeak out a, "Mhmm."

"Now confess with your mouth."

"Jesus is the Christ," Sova shuddered, his copper cheeks paling to the color of snow. "The son of the living God."

Casavore swallowed. "Sova, my boy," he said through gritted teeth. "You needn't be scared anymore."

The prince smiled. The muscles in his face relaxed, and his pupil swelled as he sunk a little in Casavore's arms. He was still. So very still.

"Sova?" Casavore sniveled and gave the prince a light shake. "Sova?"

The Royal Traitor's heart stopped midbeat as he watched.

I don't understand. This—This isn't right. I'm supposed to wake up. I have to wake up.

"You killed him," Casavore uttered as he lifted his tear-filled eyes to the dire. Saulder glared down at his brother's corpse, blood painting the side of his stoic face from the slit in his brow.

"He brought this on himself," he said and tossed the bloody arrow onto the body.

"You—You killed Sova," Casavore repeated, his voice growing louder with each syllable. "You killed your brother!"

Saulder smacked Casavore across the face, nearly making the Blesser drop the corpse. The Royal Traitor lunged forward, only for a supernatural force to pull him back.

Saulder snarled down at the Blesser, "No. You did this, Casavore. It's because of your alliance with the Blind Hound that my brother betrayed his people. It's because of you that Vaska is under siege. It's because of you that Zastar's son is dead!"

Casavore hugged Sova tighter as he sobbed.

"I'll deal with you later," Saulder growled as he started toward the balcony.

"I never betrayed you, Saulder," Casavore sniveled, making the dire stop. "In all my years, I never sought out Oland or the Blind Seers. I couldn't do that to you. I... I just wanted you to go back to the way you were. The man that my daughter was supposed to marry."

"Your daughter is dead," Saulder roared. "And so is the boy who loved her... And now... so is Sova."

Saulder stomped past the Blesser and the royal corpse, his cape painting his brother's blood across the stone.

"I'm sorry, my boy," Casavore sobbed and kissed the prince's forehead. "I should've been here. I should've saved you..."

The Blesser picked up the corpse and laid him on the dire's bed. He straightened, his tear glistening face suddenly void of emotion.

"Do you think it's a good idea to go back out there, my dire?" he asked.

The dire stopped short of the doors and glared back at his Blesser.

"You've suffered a devastating loss today," Casavore continued as he stalked into the center of the room. "Traitor or not, Sova was your brother. You can pretend you're unbothered, but I know you, Saulder."

"You don't know a thing about me," Saulder seethed and marched up to the Blesser, getting just an inch from his face.

"I beg to differ," the Blesser challenged.

The Royal Traitor looked from the corpse on the bed to Casavore, deeply and utterly confused.

What are you doing, Cas? He wondered.

"Whether you claim to love your brother or not, the prince's betrayal is sure to have shaken you," the Blesser stated. "You'll be distracted if you go into battle. You could very well lose your life. But I can fix that."

Dire Saulder looked from his brother to his Blesser. "How?" he growled. "Mind melding can't take away emotions. You can only manipulate the ones you've cursed the person with."

"Yes, but I can make you forget. I can make you forget this whole confrontation. And when the battle is done, and the threat is abolished, I'll return your memories to you so you can grieve in peace."

I don't understand this, The Royal Traitor said to himself as he looked from his corpse to the Blesser. *Why haven't I woken up yet? Why don't they know I'm alive?*

Saulder raised his chin, intrigued. "I'd forget everything?"

"Everything," Casavore assured. "Until you're ready to face it."

"Very well then. Get this over with quickly. I have a Hyde Howler to kill."

Casavore lifted his medallion, weaving it from side to side.

"*Dire Saulder,*" he began, "*Hear my trance...*" The Blesser paused, his jaw clenched tight in regret. "*Become paralyzed. Forget your strength. Forget your power. Fall to the floor so that I may tower.*"

"What—" Saulder hissed just as his legs to give out from under him. He fell to the floor, his head slamming against the stone. He growled through gritted teeth, his eyes blazing like fire up at the Blesser. "Casavore, what is the meaning of this?"

Casavore stared down at the dire, his eyes misty with tears. "I'm sorry, Saulder. You've given me no choice."

As Saulder's frustrated screams echoed through the palace, Casavore hurried to the bed where the dead prince lay and wrapped him in the sheets. Concealed in a coffin of silk, Casavore shoved the corpse under the bed, streaking blood across the floor before he returned to the dire.

"You'll pay for this, Casavore," Saulder shouted. "I swear to you, you'll pay with your life!"

Casavore stripped Saulder of his armor until he was laying just in his gambeson.

"Don't touch my armor!" Saulder shouted as Casavore stowed it with the body beneath the bed. "That's my father's armor!"

Casavore knelt by the dire's side, tears pouring down his scowl.

"If you're going to kill me, just get it over with," Saulder sneered. "Better you than that Lykos forsaken Rogue Eradite that attacked me."

"I'm not going to hurt you, Saulder," Casavore said. "I love you. Just as I loved your father and your brother. Sova lost hope that you could change, but my faith is not so easily wavered." The Blesser gulped down a quivering breath. "I've run out of ideas on how to help you, Saulder... So, I hope you'll forgive me for this."

"You can't help me!" Saulder roared. "Sova realized that! At least he had the decency to die a noble death instead of ambushing his dire like a coward."

"Yes..." Casavore nodded. "Sova. He had wished you healing more than any of us... I hope you find yourself again someday soon, Saulder. Until then..."

Casavore lifted his medallion.

"No!" the dire shouted as he writhed on the floor. "No, get away from me!"

The Royal Traitor watched from afar, his jaw hanging in shock as Casavore continued his trance.

"Dire Saulder, you have let evil rule your heart for far too long. You have given the wrong master your grief and expected healing in return. So, Dire Saulder, I will give you a chance at restoration. A chance to return to your true self. The one my daughter loved—"

"Casavore!"

"Sleep..."

Saulder's writhing stilled, and his eyes fluttered closed.

Casavore, the Royal Traitor called. *Casavore, what are you doing?*

"*Dire Saulder,*" the Blesser continued, "*listen to me and listen to me well. I don't know how to grant you peace without releasing you completely from your pain... So, I have realized the only way to free you from yourself is to make you forget it all... Dire Saulder, I command you, take on Sova's memories. Believe you are the brother you killed and forget the arrow that took his life. Forget your atrocities as if it was another who committed them. Forget who you are until your broken heart has healed. And when you are ready to accept your sins and embrace the new creation you have become, I give you the authority to recall it all. When you awake, you will be Sova, prince of Vaska. The brother you have lost..."*

Casavore dropped his medallion to the stone and hunched forward, sobbing over Saulder.

No... the Royal Traitor thought as he shook his head. *No, this isn't real...*

Sniveling, Casavore drew Dire Saulder's blade, and with one swift swoop, cut the tyrant's long white hair so it became short, like Sova's.

No. No. This is all wrong.

Casavore cut away the bandages around Saulder's shoulder, revealing a deep, crescent-shaped scar above his left pectoral; a perfect outline of Saber's bottom jaw. Tossing away the old wraps, Casavore reapplied new bandages.

Stop it, the Royal Traitor begged. *Stop. This isn't what happened. I'm alive. I'm right here. I'm Sova!*

Casavore sat there for a second, staring at the imposter he had made. Choking down a sob, he shook Saulder by the shoulders.

"S—Sova? Sova?" he called, nearly calling the dire by his given name. "Sova, can you hear me? Sova? Sova!"

Saulder woke with a gasp, his chest leaping off the floor.

"Sova?" The Blesser said again. "Sova, can you hear me?"

"Yeah," Saulder groaned through a wince. "I can hear you. Could you lower your voice, please?"

The Royal Traitor shook his head, his eyes lining with tears. *No. No, God, please no.*

"Do you remember what happened?" Casavore asked.

"Not really," Saulder grumbled. He lightly touched the cut in his brow, drawing his fingertips away to see they were coated in scarlet. "Actually, everything's kind of scattered. When's my birthday again?"

"You—You hit your head when you were fighting S—Saulder," Casavore stammered, nearly saying the wrong name again. "You might've forgotten a few things, but it should all come back."

"Saulder..." the dire's eyes widened. "Where—Where is he? Where's the dire?"

"Gone. After—After you went down, he left. He ordered me to keep an eye on you."

"What happened there?" Saulder asked, pointing to the gauze around his shoulder.

"Saulder shot you."

"He what?" Saulder squeaked. "Why—Why don't I feel anything?"

The Royal Traitor shook his head, watching as his enemy played out his own memories word for word as *him.*

No. No, that's not me! I'm—I'm asleep under the bed. C—Casavore, wake me up! I'm alive! I'm right here!

"I hypnotized you so that the pain wasn't too unbearable," Casavore lied.

"Well, thanks," Saulder said as he struggled to his feet. Casavore stood with him, taking him by the arm to keep him steady.

"Try not to push yourself, son."

"I—I need to find, Saulder. I need to end this."

"Sova, you can't. You can't beat him."

"I can. Now we're both injured. I've evened the playing field."

"Sova. Saulder is probably in the protection of his guards by now. You won't get near him."

Stop calling him 'Sova!' The Royal Traitor shouted. *That's not me! That's the dire!*

"So now the dire hides from a fight," Saulder scoffed. "Coward."

You're the coward! The Royal Traitor roared. *You're the monster!*

"Sova..." Casavore gulped. "...I hereby banish you from the Kingdom of Vaska."

"Pardon?" Saulder said, arching his brow.

No, the Royal Traitor pulled at his hair. *No. This isn't happening.*

"You attacked the dire," Casavore said. "Mutiny won't be tolerated in Vaska."

"Playing favorites, are we, Cas?" Saulder grumbled. "Still upset I read your private letters?"

"I'm trying to help you, Sova," Casavore said. "Saulder may be your brother, but he won't forgive what you've done. You'd be lucky to live the rest of your days in the dungeon, but—"

"He's going to have me executed, isn't he?" Saulder asked, his eyes dense with sorrow.

"He told me himself," the Blesser sniffled. "'*I want to watch the royal traitor bleed.*'"

The Royal Traitor held back a gasp, remembering what the dire had said when he stood over the dying clone.

"*Royal Traitor*," Saulder smirked at the floor. "Has a nice ring to it."

"You need to run, Sova. I can't save you this time."

"I'm not going to run from him—"

"You will, or I'll make you," Casavore clutched his medallion. Saulder took a nervous step back.

"C—Cas," he whispered in a voice like a terrified child's.

"Please, Sova. I've lost..." Casavore paused, his jaw trembling through a restrained sob. "I've lost *everyone*. Let me save you."

Everyone... The Royal Traitor repeated to himself. *No. No— Casavore, I'm alive! You put me under the bed! I'm there! I'm alive! I'm not the dire! I'm there. Please just look!*

"I—" Saulder paused and looked from the Blesser to the door. "Where will I go?"

"Go to the forest and stay there. I'll come for you when all is safe."

"C—Can't you just come with me?"

"I can't."

Saulder shook his head and scoffed. "After all he's done, you still remain at that monster's side. After all the people he's killed—after he tried to kill me!"

Casavore grabbed Saulder by his head, forcing his eyes to meet his.

"I'm doing this to save you, Sova!" the Blesser sneered as tears drenched his beard. "There's something I need to take care of. Otherwise, you'll never be safe. Now please... go."

Casavore snapped Saulder into his arms, hugging him tightly.

"Why would you do it?..." he whispered through clenched teeth. "How could you?"

The Royal Traitor's heart dropped to the bloody floor.

No. No. No! No! Casavore! Look at me! Tell me this isn't real!

Pulling away, Casavore took his medallion off his neck and handed it to Saulder.

"Take this," he ordered. "I'll come back for it and you when all is safe."

"Cas, I can't take this."

"Please. It isn't safe here with the dire."

Saulder looked from the medallion in his hand to the beloved Blesser. "You have to promise you'll come back for it."

"I will," Casavore nodded as he wrapped his cloak around the Royal Traitor. "Now go."

Saulder charged toward the chamber door.

"Sova, wait!" the Blesser called, reaching out.

Saulder stopped midway out the door and looked back.

"The scar on your shoulder..." Casavore gulped. "Never show it to anyone. Lest they figure out who you are. You'll be an enemy to Vaska come morning."

The Royal traitor shook his head in disbelief as the world around him started to crumble.

No. God, please no.

"I won't, Cas," Saulder promised and fled out the chamber.

No! the Royal Traitor shouted, his throat-ripping at the force of his screams. *No! This isn't real! That's not me! That didn't happen! This is all wrong! It's a lie! Casavore! Casavore, tell me it's wrong!*

"Saulder, wake up!"

Chapter Twenty-Four: The Mind Melder's Crime

Sova awoke falling to the cold prison floor. He crawled backward, ramming into the wall on the far side of the room. His chest lunged forward, each breath, a blade in his lungs.

Casavore stared at him through the bars of his cell, his medallion swinging in hand, his eyes full of shame.

"What—" Sova gulped as tears built up in his eyes, "—What was that? What did you just show me?"

Casavore drew a deep breath. "I showed you the memory I made you forget."

"No," Sova shook his head. "That—That wasn't a memory. That was a nightmare."

"Son—"

"No!" Sova leaped to his feet. "No! I'm not him! I'm not that monster! You left me under the bed! I am a prince of Vaska! I am Sova!"

"Sova is dead!" Casavore shouted, the horrible confession echoing through the prison. "He's been dead for some time now..."

"That's impossible," Sova whispered. "I—We—We saw Saulder on Era. He tried to kill Feran."

"The one who wears Zastar's armor is not the dire. It is your mother, Lore."

"Lore?" Sova repeated in disbelief.

"After I sent you away, I burned your brother's body so no one would know what you'd done. But after Lore had me arrested, she happened upon his corpse. But by then, the fire had made him unrecognizable, so she believed it was the dire who was dead. She stole the dire's identity so she could rule Vaska. It wasn't until she saw you on Era that she realized what I'd done. You are the only thing keeping her from the right to the throne."

"You're a liar," Sova whimpered, his voice turning violent. "You're a liar!"

"The dreams you have aren't dreams at all. When I hypnotized you to take on Sova's memories, I crafted it so you had authority over your own trance. The dire you see in your nightmares is your identity trying to seep through. Saulder, you have to accept who you are—"

"No!" Sova shouted. "No, I'm not the dire. My name is Sova!"

Casavore paused, his eyes rippling with tears. "No, you're not," he said gently. "You never were. I gave you Sova's memories so you could let yourself heal, but you are and have always been Saulder. The only thing you have of Sova's is his past."

"A person's past is what makes them!" Sova rebuked. "The killings, the kidnappings, the torturing—that was Saulder's past. Saulder's past was turning Elling into a monster. Taking Taige's leg—killing her father. Forcing Roeseph and Oland into hiding! Naming Feran a wanted criminal! Kyce wasn't directly affected by him—but he hates everyone anyway. This is Saulder's past, not mine. I'm not him!"

Casavore hung his head. "Your shoulder," he mumbled, his eyes turning dark when he looked up.

Sova's heart dropped. "My what?"

"Your shoulder, your majesty," Casavore repeated. "I told you, you were scarred by the dire's arrow. But the truth is, it's the mark of a soaring wolf. The soaring wolf that attacked Dire Saulder that night in the Mosharick Village."

The night Elling became a Hyde Howler. Sova shook his head. "You're lying."

Before Casavore could reply, the chamber door at the top of the staircase creaked open, and the sound of heavy metal boots descended the steps.

"It's her," Casavore hissed as a torch light grew brighter along the stairwell walls. "Hide, your majesty. Hide."

Sova hurried into a cranny behind the stairwell. His back pressed to the cold stone, he cautiously peeked out from behind the wall. The Dire of Vaska stood before Casavore's cell, his ghastly black armor glittering in light of the torches.

Saulder, Sova growled to himself. *It has to be Saulder. Casavore was lying. He's lying. I know he is.*

"Ah, my dear Blesser," said the dire, their voice masked by the metallic echo of the helmet. "How are you this fine evening? Three more sunrises until the big day. Excited?"

Casavore was silent, his blue eyes burning with hate.

"What?" the dire shrugged. "Nothing to say?"

"We're alone, Lore," Casavore snarled. "There's no need to wear that Lykos forsaken armor."

Sova's heart jolted at the mention of his mother's name.

The dire snickered behind his mask. "Did you miss my face that much, dear friend?"

The dire removed his helmet, revealing a tan face, sea-blue eyes, and hair as long and white as willow branches. Sova gripped his mouth to keep from screaming.

"Why are you here, Lore?" Casavore glared.

"To talk," the ex-queen of Vaska shrugged. "I figured you might be lonely." Casavore spit at Lore's boot. She grimaced. "Classy, Casavore. Real classy."

"I have nothing to say to you, witch."

"Very well, I just thought I'd let you know that it seems our children have seemed to have vanished into thin air."

"Is that so?"

"Yes. Last I heard, they caused a riot in Seavale. Haven't been seen since. Rare for them. Perhaps I was wrong to think they'd come for you."

"I told you they wouldn't. Feran is far too smart to fall into your trap."

"And what of Saulder?" Lore smirked. "He's an impulsive one, is he not. But, then again, he killed his baby brother, so maybe losing you doesn't trouble him much at all."

Sova nearly collapsed to the floor.

"I'm sorry to disappoint you, Lore," Casavore continued. "Your plan to capture the Dire Wolves has ended in vain."

"We'll see, Casavore," Lore arched her brow. "There are still three sunrises left after all. Even if I don't slaughter those *Dire Rats*, I'll still have the pleasure of killing you."

Smirking slyly, Lore placed the dire's helmet over her head.

"Have a good night, Casavore," she said, her voice once again masked by the metallic ring. "Not very many more left after all."

She scaled the staircase, her footsteps growing fainter and fainter before the chamber door slammed shut.

Casavore waited a while before he spoke, his eyes not leaving the stairs.

"Your majesty?" he whispered. "Your majesty, are you there?"

Sova stepped out from his hiding place. His eyes weighed to the floor as he rested his hand against the wall to keep himself standing.

"I..." he shuddered, his breathing shallow and quick between gulps. "I—I'm not Saulder... Cas, please. Please tell me I'm not Saulder."

"Son—"

"Please, Cas," Sova fell to his knees. "Please, Casavore. Please tell me I'm not him."

Casavore paused, his eyes full of regret and tears.

He answered, "...You are Saulder—"

Sova shook his head, "No."

"—The son of Zastar and Lore. Brother to the late Prince Sova. And reigning Dire of Vaska."

"No," Sova snarled. "No. You're lying. I don't care what you say! I *am* Sova!"

"Believe what you will, your majesty," Casavore sighed. "But until you make peace with what you've done, the dire will continue to ravage your nightmares. The only way to be free is to accept yourself as a new creation."

While Sova struggled to his feet, Casavore reached into his cloak and pulled out a medallion that was charred on the side.

"Where did you get that?" Sova rasped. "You've had that thing this whole time, and you didn't try to escape?"

"I did try. After the war on Era, Lore showed me my daughter's medallion. I tried to use it against her, but she bested me. Arison returned it to me out of kindness, and I was far too selfish to rebel again. I just—I just wanted to keep this one thing. One thing to remember my daughter... But you must take it now."

"What?"

"The medallions," Casavore said as he handed both his and Feran's medallion to Sova. "Take them both. Tell Feran, I've thought of her every day she's been gone."

"Cas, I can't just leave you here—"

"Take the medallions to Feran. Get she and Roeseph as far away from here as you can. Oland and I are willing to die if our children get to live. Please, Saulder."

Sova's blood turned to ice in his veins.

"I—I'm—" Sova gulped, suddenly mortified of the skin he lived in. "I'm—I'm not—"

"Go!" Casavore shouted.

Like a dear frightened by a lion's roar, Sova stumbled into a run and sprinted up the stairs. He tried to open the door, only to find it didn't open much more than inch. Lore must've moved the dresser back in place. He rammed down the door with his shoulder, tipping the dresser over, and shattering the mirror. Sova looked down into the broken glass, horrified by the reflection staring back at him, and fled out his father's chamber.

MEANWHILE, CASAVORE remained in his secret dungeon, his eyes misty with tears.

"You'll understand one day, Saulder," he whispered. "You just need time to adjust to the light."

SOVA TORE OUT OF THE palace unseen, and back into the sewer tunnel. He sprinted through the murky water, his eyes wide and darting from side to side.

"He's lying," he gasped. "He's lying. Casavore's wrong. I'm not him. I'm not him. I survived that fight. I'm Sova. I'm not the dire!"

As Sova argued with reality, his foot caught a stone hidden in the murky water, and he fell with a splash. He sputtered, his soaked sharick-fawn locks hanging heavily on his scalp.

"It's not true," he whispered between gasps. "It's not true."

Sova looked down at his reflection rippling in the sewage. The resemblance was uncanny. His hair, his eyes, his face all belonged to Saulder. The urge to vomit clawed up his throat as Sova's eyes dropped to the gauze around his shoulder.

What Casavore had said about the scar on his shoulder echoed in his head, about how the scar wasn't made from an arrow, but the jaws of a soaring wolf.

"The scar..." Sova muttered. Drawing a blade strapped to his thigh, Sova slashed carelessly at his straps. He didn't care if he cut himself. He just needed to know Casavore was wrong.

He lied, Sova told himself. *He's wrong. Saulder shot me, but I lived. I lived. He woke me up after Saulder left. Lore was only wearing the armor because she's a power-hungry witch. I'm not him. I'm not him. I'm not—*

Sova froze. He saw it in the water, the crescent shaped scar taking up about half of his left pectoral; a scar carved from the jaws of a soaring wolf, not a misfired arrow. The scar belonging to the Dire of Vaska. The scar belonging to Dire Saulder.

"No..." Sova whispered, his tears corrupting his reflection into ripples. "No. No—No—No."

Sova punched at the water.

"No! No! Please, no!" he cried. His punches slowed, and the water stilled as his quiet sobs filled the tunnel. "No," he wept. "No..."

Teeth clenched, he lunged down the tunnel.

Chapter Twenty-Five: Snapdragons

"Well, he's sure taking his sweet time," Kyce grumbled impatiently as he sat against the trunk of a tree.

In the shadows beyond the Venom Tongue camp waited the Dire Wolves, their eyes sworn to the starry east where Sova had disappeared earlier that evening.

Roeseph leaned against a tree, scraping a stone down the length of his sword and making the silver hiss.

"I'm sure he's fine," he said, not looking up. "You know Sova. He likes to sightsee."

Elling stood between he and Kyce, swinging her staff at the pillars of light that pierced through the leaves, immersed in an imaginary battle.

"Yeah, give him some grace," she huffed. "Sova hasn't been home in almost a year. Besides, it can't be easy helping an entire army escape the Vaskan palace."

Kyce scoffed, his jaw swinging to the side. "Give him grace? The fact that I haven't broken that obnoxious royal's face yet is grace enough."

"You don't have to pretend with us, Kyce," Elling smirked as she laid her staff across her shoulders. "We know you have a soft spot for him."

"Ha!" Kyce laughed. "You're delusional. There's no room to be soft in this forsaken valley, least of all for that prince. Here, you're either strong, or you're dead."

Taige skipped out from the woods, holding a single red and yellow snapdragon to her chest.

"Kyce," she smiled and fell at his side. "Look at this flower I found. It's just like you! Red for Eradawn and yellow for Eradusk." She tucked the snapdragon into Kyce's pocket, helping to fan out the petals. "Do you like it?"

Kyce's jaw clenched as he met the Venom Tongue's eyes; her big, seal-like, eyes.

"It'll suffice," he grumbled.

"Awe," Elling pouted, prompting Kyce to throw a pebble at her. She deflected it with her staff, sending the small stone bouncing off a nearby tree.

While Roeseph and Elling teased the Eradite Exile, Feran stood a short distance away, leaning against a tree as she watched the forest, Saber laying at her feet. An owl hooted in the darkness, and something small scurried in the undergrow. Saber yawned, completely unbothered, while his master clutched the place over her chest where her medallion used to hang.

"Where are you, Sova?" she whispered.

Roeseph looked up from sharpening his sword.

"Hey," he called, making Feran look over her shoulder. "Worrying won't make him come any faster."

"He should be back by now," Feran replied. "If he's making us wait for him just to worry us, I'm going to kill him."

Kyce scoffed through a snide smirk. "The only one worried about your boyfriend here is you."

"He is not my boyfriend."

"Oh yeah?" Kyce arched his brow. "You two looked pretty cozy earlier."

Feran glared at the Eradite Exile, his cheeks burning red with embarrassment.

"You don't know what you're talking about, *Mutt*."

"Ooh, using insults now, are we?" Kyce chuckled. "Why so sensitive all of a sudden? Unless... you actually have feelings for our dear prince."

Taige nuzzled his shoulder as she watched Feran. "I think you might be onto something, love," she said, all too eager to join in. "Look at her. All flushed."

Feran rolled her eyes as her comrades snickered and teased, unaware of the shadow approaching in the east. Saber snapped up from where he lay, his snout twisting in a snarl.

Feran turned fast. "Saber," she called. "What's wrong?"

Saber's snarl rolled on. Troubled by the soaring wolf's burst of aggression, Feran hurried to his side and reached for her medallion, only to find it wasn't there. Her stomach sunk.

"Maybe giving Sova your medallion wasn't the greatest idea, no?" Kyce sneered as he stood and drew his blade.

The Dire Wolves gathered close, weapons drawn and ready for a fight.

The undergrowth shifted in the distance. A stick snapped.

"Show yourself!" Roeseph shouted.

Out from the shadows stumbled a man in soaked, purple garments. He fell to his knees, pulling out fistfuls of hair.

"Sova?" Feran said beneath her breath.

Sova pulled out another fistful, screaming in anguish down at the grass.

"Sova!" Feran yelled, leading the charge.

Sova ripped out another lock of the sharick-fawn extensions, completely oblivious to his comrades growing near.

"*Get them out,*" he muttered between sobs. "*Get them out.*"

"Stop it, Sova!" Kyce shouted, and grabbed him by the wrist before he could yank out the last lock of hair. "Get a hold of yourself!"

"Get away from me!" Sova shrieked and jerked his robe over his chest to hide his gauze-wrapped shoulder.

The Venom Tongues in the camp jumped up at the sound, and, grabbing their weapons, rushed toward the commotion.

Taige looked up to see the wave of Seavallian thugs hurtle their way. She, ran at them, holding up her hands and stopping the stampede.

"Get him down before he hurts himself!" Elling shouted.

Roeseph and Kyce shoved Sova to his chest. He writhed beneath them, his wrists pinned in the center of his back.

"Sova!" Roeseph bellowed. "Sova, what's wrong with you?"

"Get them out!" Sova shouted. He lurched upright, slamming his head right into Kyce's jaw. The Eradite Exile whipped back onto the grass, clutching his bleeding mouth.

"Kyce!" Taige shouted and hurtled to his side.

"Sova, what's gotten into you?" Roeseph shouted.

"Get off of me!" Sova cried and opened his hand to strike him. "I need to get it out!"

Feran grabbed Sova by the wrist. "Sova," she rasped. "Why are you acting like this?"

"Let me go!" Sova jerked away from her.

Saber's pupil shrunk—a predator's gaze locking in on its prey. He lunged in defense of his master, sending the Dire Wolves falling back. Sova froze, consumed in the shadow of the soaring wolf as it snarled down at him.

He understood it then, why Saber hated him so. As talented a mind melder as Casavore was, he couldn't trick a soaring wolf's nose.

"Woah—Woah—Woah," Feran tutted and threw her hands in front of Saber. The soaring wolf paced from side to side, trying to get around her as his yellow eyes pierced Sova's soul. "It's ok," Feran eased. "It's ok, boy. Everything's fine. It's just Sova. It's just Sova."

Sova's heart tore down the middle.

"No," he choked, his bottom lip pressing against his teeth. "No. No. No..."

He fell over the grass, crunched in a ball and bawling. His comrades traded frightened glances, unsure what had caused the prince of Vaska's outburst.

Feran turned from Saber and fell at Sova's side. "Sova?" she whispered and touched his shoulder.

Sova slammed his hand over the exposed scar beneath his purple garments.

"Sova, what happened?" Feran asked again.

Sova's eyes closed tighter as he gripped the grass, parts of his skull stinging from where he'd ripped out his own hair. "I want it out," he whimpered between sobs. "I want it out."

Feran's eyes fell to the last lock of sharick fawn hair woven into his scalp.

"Ok," she said, reaching for it. "Ok, I'll get it out."

With gentle hands, Feran unwove the extension from Sova's hair.

"There," Feran whispered, drawing out the blond lock.

Sova's shoulders trembled with his breath. "It's gone?"

"Yeah," Feran nodded, rubbing her hand up and down his back. "It's gone."

Sova shook his head. It didn't matter. His hair could be cut all the way down to his scalp, but it wouldn't change anything. There was no escaping what he was; what Casavore had revealed him to be.

Roeseph knelt beside Feran, his blue eyes dense with concern.

"Sova?" he whispered gently. "Sova, what happened?"

Sova wheezed, smothered by his own sobs.

"Sova?" Roeseph asked again, but the prince still couldn't speak.

"Sova, you're scaring us," Feran joined in.

Sova looked up at the Dire's Curse, his silver eyes trapped behind a pane of tears. Swallowing a breath, he managed to say through the lump in his throat, "It's a trap. Casavore refused to come with me. He wants us to leave."

"Leave?" Roeseph spat, making Sova flinch. "He told you to leave?"

Feran's eyes fell to the grass. "He didn't get out..." she whispered.

"I'm sorry, Feran," Sova sniveled. He reached into his garment, careful not to reveal the dire's scar, and withdrew both Feran and the Blesser's medallion. "I tried. I swear I tried."

Feran clutched the medallions to her chest, a tear nearly seeping through her lashes as she squeezed her eyes shut.

"That can't be it," Roeseph shook his head. "What else did he tell you, Sova?"

Sova's quivering intensified, and he lowered to the grass again.

Roeseph clenched his fists in frustration, his knuckles cracking.

"Fine," he growled and rose to his feet. "If the Blesser won't help the Blind Seers escape, we'll figure it out ourselves. Kyce—"

Kyce looked up, his hand bloodied from the lip Sova had split.

"—Help me get Sova to his tent. We'll try talking to him again once he's calmed down."

His hand still clasped over his scar, Sova was grabbed under his arms and hoisted to his feet.

Kyce strung Sova's free arm over his shoulders.

"We got you, buddy," he whispered as he and Roeseph escorted him through the crowd toward camp.

Feran stood, still clutching the medallions to her chest as Taige and Elling took their place at her side, Elling hugging her around the shoulders.

"What was that all about?" Taige panted.

"I don't know," Elling answered. "It's like he'd seen a ghost..."

Chapter Twenty-Six: The Sunrise Sentence

The third sunrise before Casavore's execution rose over the tree line, chasing away the cursed night and covering the Venom Tongue camp in an amber glow.

Since his encounter with the Blesser, Sova hadn't left his tent. He laid on a cot, scrunched in a tight ball under a sharick-skin blanket, with his back turned to the entrance. Gauze wrapped the dire's scar, hiding it from the eyes of the world as it burned his skin like a branding iron.

The tarp entrance whipped to the side, and a shadow slipped across his back.

"Hey," came Roeseph's gentle voice. Sova stared at the wall, seemingly ignorant to his captain's presence. "The war meeting's about to start. If you're feeling any better, you're welcome to come."

Sova didn't answer. He just pulled the sharick fawn blanket further over his shoulder.

Roeseph looked to the floor. "Alright. Get some rest, bud. I'll check on you after."

Roeseph pushed away the tarp and stepped into the golden morning. Thin, wispy clouds raked across the sky like white serpent tracks, escaping over the sharp green peaks of the evergreen trees.

The Dire Wolves and Saber sat outside the tent, springing to their feet when they saw Roeseph.

"Well?" Feran asked eagerly, clutching the two medallions hanging from her neck in one hand.

Roeseph shook his head. "He's not up for it."

The Dire Wolves gave a collective sigh.

"I haven't known him to be so quiet," Taige mumbled, crossing her arms. "What do you suppose happened in that palace to shake him up so bad?"

"It's my fault," Elling hung her head. "I was the one that insisted we invade the palace. Whatever happened to Sova is because of me."

"No," Roeseph interjected. "None of this is your fault, Elling. None of us could have expected this."

"So, what do we do now?" Kyce asked through a scabbed lip.

"We find a different way to free the Blind Seers," Roeseph answered. "And the Blesser too. Taige. Are the Venom Tongue's ready?"

Taige dipped her head. "They're waiting in the main tent."

"What about Sova?" Elling whispered, stepping close to Roeseph's side.

"He'll be ok on his own for now," Roeseph said. "I said I'd check on him later."

Kyce scoffed. "Better yet, send me in," he batted his fist in and out of his hand. "That Vaskan jerk has to pay for giving me a split lip."

The Dire Wolves left in pursuit of the war meeting, careful not to step over the empty bottles of Odin Slayer in their path. The camp was eerily quiet, as all had gathered in the main tent; the only sound was the gurgle of the river just a little ways away from camp, and the chirp of morning birds.

Feran stopped about halfway through camp. She looked back at Sova's tent, catching a glimpse of him through the gap in the tarp as it blew to the side. She stood there a long time, just watching him.

"Feran," Roeseph called. Feran looked ahead to see her comrades waiting for her. "You coming?"

"Uh," Feran hesitated, looking rapidly between the tent and the others. "You guys go on without me. I'll stay here in case he needs someone."

"Are you sure?" Roeseph asked.

"Yeah," Feran nodded through a false smile. "Just fill me in after."

Roeseph hesitated for a moment before leading Kyce, Elling, and Taige toward a large tent in the center of the camp. Inside, the Venom Tongues gathered around a splintered table, snapping at one another like rabid dogs over the last bone. The musk of sea water and stale bourbon filled the place, making the air near-unbreathable as Roeseph and the others made their way to the table.

A chair flew across the room, and they ducked. Roeseph rose uncertainly and cleared his throat.

"Excuse me," he called over the chaos, growing irritated when it didn't cease. "Excuse me. Excuse—"

Impatience getting the best of him, Roeseph slammed his fist on the table. The Venom Tongues froze and looked his way.

"I'm sure many of you have grievances concerning last night's failed mission," the Blind Seer projected. "And while I am willing to hear your concerns, I can assure you, our journey had not ended. Blesser Casavore has refused to negotiate out fear for his daughter's safety. But we are not so easily deterred. So, we'll go with our original plan, and take back the Blind Seers by ambush."

"And how would you have us do that?" a Venom Tongue called out.

"Sova was able to access the palace through the same sewers the Blind Seers used, which gives us reason to believe Dire Saulder still isn't aware of the entry point. If we send in a troop of Venom Tongues, we'll be able to break out the Blind Seers and evacuate into the Vaskan Forest."

"And the Blesser?"

"The Blesser's execution will serve as our diversion. He is to be executed first, so it's likely the Blind Seers will remain in the dungeon. The Dire detests the Blesser the most, so he'll want all of Vaska to witness his fall."

Elling stepped forward. "So we're just going to let Casavore die while we escape?" she challenged. "What about Feran?"

"Casavore's not going to die," Roeseph assured. "The Dire only intends to use the Blesser to draw us in. So, we'll give Dire Saulder exactly what he wants. Taige and Kyce will lead a squadron through the sewers and release the Blind Seers. While they escape back into the tunnels, Sova, Feran, Elling, and I will hide in the crowd at the Blesser's execution. We'll cause a diversion and escape with Casavore. As long as we keep the focus on the plaza and not the dungeon, everything should go smoothly."

Elling clung to herself, her eyes wide like saucers. "You want me with you in the plaza?" she asked. "Is that a good idea? What if—"

"Cursed as a Hyde Howler or not," Roeseph interrupted, not looking away from the Venom Tongues, "you're a capable soldier, and we need as many in this fight as possible. Besides, Dire Saulder may be cynical, but even he wouldn't unleash a Hyde Howler on a plaza full of Vaskan citizens."

"But Roeseph, even if there's no Siren's Call, I'm no fighter. I've never been able to hold my own in—"

"Elling," Roeseph looked down, his eyes hard yet pleading. "I need you to do this for me. I need you at my side."

Elling stared at Roeseph, forgetting her apprehensions in a second.

"What about Sova?" Kyce interrupted. "Man can't even get out of bed. Is he going to be able to do this?"

Roeseph paused, his jaw clenching.

. "We'll cross that bridge when we come to it," he answered. "Until then, we only have three days to prepare for the Blesser's execution. I suggest you all prepare yourselves for battle..."

WHILE ROESEPH OVERSAW the war meeting, Sova laid in his tent, sinking deep into a reluctant sleep.

He opened his eyes and gasped, overcome by a frigid sensation that stabbed into his skin like needles. He looked around to find himself in the middle of an endless, black void; the place of his nightmares.

"No," he whispered as he gripped the roots of his hair, fighting to steady his breath.. "No—No—No—No—No—this can't be happening. No, I don't want to be here!"

As Sova panicked, a shrill, demonic voice called out from the black.

"Who are you?"

Sova spun around to find the dire's black armor standing across the void. For many moons, Sova had believed the dire's reoccurring presence to be only a nightmare. But now he knew the truth.

"No," Sova growled. "No. Go away! I'm not like you!"

"Who are you!" the dire snarled and drew his sword.

"I'm Sova! Prince of Vaska! A traitor to the dire's crown!"

The dire sprinted at Sova, roaring "Who are you!"

Sova cried violently and charged.

I'll kill him, he told himself. *I'll kill him! I can't become that monster if he's dead!*

Leaping into the air, Sova drove his sword down at the dire. The blade barely made a scratch in the armor. Grabbing Sova by the throat, the dire threw him to the ground. Before Sova could so much as gasp for breath, the dire raised his sword.

"*Sova!*" a voice cried in the darkness as the cold silver plunged into the Royal Traitor's chest. "*Sova, wake up!*"

Sova woke with a gasp, shivering from a cold sweat that frosted his ever inch. His eyes lashed about, only to find himself facing the burlap wall. His jaw hurt from clenching his teeth so tight, his throat burned with tears, and his heart thundered so vigorously he thought it might shoot right out of his chest.

I can't beat him... he thought. *He'll never let me go unless I... No. No.* He gripped his blanket in his fists. *I'll never be him. I'll never be Saulder. I'll never be the dire.*

"Sova?" came a soft voice.

Sova flinched and looked over his shoulder.

Feran sat at his bedside, her worried eyes shining in the sunrise bleeding through the tarp entrance. She clutched two medallions, one charred and one clean, hanging from her neck, curtained behind curly dark hair.

Sova marveled at her. Even frightened, she was remarkably beautiful. But then again, he was seeing her through Saulder's eyes.

Perhaps that's where this feeling comes from.

"Feran?" he whispered. "What are you doing here?"

"I heard you having a nightmare, so I let myself in," she dipped her head, her father's medallion slipping out from behind her hair. "Are you ok? It sounded like a bad one."

Sova hesitated, unsure how to reply. He sought to change the topic.

"W—Why—" he gulped down a dry swallow, "Why aren't you at the war meeting with the others?"

"They'll fill me in when it's over," Feran shrugged. "I'm more worried about you. We're all worried about you."

"Really?" Sova scoffed. "Even Kyce?"

"Especially Kyce. But he's still sore about you giving him a split lip last night," Feran smirked. "Taige fixed him up ok, though. I don't think he'll ever admit it, but he's starting to like the gal."

Sova looked down, guilt weighing him down to the cot.

"I'm sorry," he whispered as he clutched the blanket in his fists.

"I'm not the one you have to apologize to," Feran joked. "But you should know, Kyce will be expecting a blubbering apology when he gets back."

"I'm sorry I failed," Sova murmured, his eyes shutting to stop the tears. "I told you I'd get Casavore out, but I..." he stopped to swallow a lump in his throat. "But I—"

"You didn't fail me, Sova," Feran said sternly. "If Casavore wasn't willing to cooperate, there's nothing you could've done to make him leave. The fact that you were able to bring these back to me is enough," Feran motioned to the two medallions hanging from her neck. "You found him... He just wasn't willing to risk us getting hurt. I guess that's a father's weakness. But we'll show him. We'll see him and the Blind Seers free soon enough."

Free... Sova shivered. *What happens when Casavore is freed? Will he tell the others of my curse—my true identity? What will they think of me once they find out? They'd hate me. I'm their greatest enemy. The murderer of their families. They would hate me... Feran... Feran would hate me...*

"Yeah," Sova nodded as he turned his back to Feran. "Yeah, that's great."

Feran's smirk sunk, concern clouding her eyes.

"Hey," she began and laid her hand his gauze-wrapped shoulder.

He flinched again, horrifically aware of how close her hand was to the dire's scar.

"What happened last night?" she asked. "You scared us all half to death."

"Nothing," Sova said quickly as he pulled the blanket over his shoulder. "The forest just spooked me. That's all."

"I've never seen you cry like that. Not even when we were kids. I mean—once you got teary-eyed because Saber stepped on your foot, but it was nothing compared to last night."

"Ok, one—" Sova held one finger up, "that flying rat of yours did it on purpose. And two—it's nothing worth mentioning. Like I said, I just got spooked..."

Feran went silent, the only sound, the gentle snap of the tarp-entrance rippling in the breeze.

"Something happened with Casavore, didn't it?"

Sova flinched and looked back. Feran stared at him, her magnificent brown eyes glistening with restrained tears.

"Is he," Feran gulped through a quivering breath, "is he—"

Sova turned around quickly. "Casavore is fine," he replied, clutching Feran's hand. "I told you that last night. I found him in a hidden dungeon in Zastar's chamber. He was fine when I left him... But—"

"But?"

Sova looked away.

Memories of gore flashed through his mind like a lightning storm:

The one of the Vaskan prince lying dead in the Blesser's arms. Casavore's tears. The way the dire had stood over them both without an inkling of remorse. It was horrible. All of it was so horrible.

"Sova?" Feran began again.

"He made me remember," he admitted, unable to meet Feran's gaze.

"He made you remember what?"

Sova's lips pierced tightly. "That day," he whispered. "The day the Blind Seers invaded the palace. He showed me the fight I had with my brother."

Feran's lips parted with a gasp. "Sova..." she whispered. "Why would he show you that? What good could come from that?"

"Nothing," Sova hissed, clutching the blanket. "Nothing good could come from it.... I guess he just wanted me to know."

"If that's what's bothering you, I think I can help," Feran reached for one of the medallions around her neck. "I can make you forget—"

"No," Sova snapped and grabbed Feran's hand. He held it close to his chest, staring at her with intense, silver eyes. "No more medallions. No more trances."

Feran swallowed, her stomach twisting into knots. "O—Ok," she stammered. "Ok, no more medallions. I promise."

Sova exhaled and dropped her hand. He fell back on the bed, his arm falling across his eyes like a mask.

"Is there anything else I can do to help?" Feran asked gently.

Sova sighed and grabbed Feran's hand. "Just stay here with me. Like that night on the beach. Talk to me. Make crude jokes. Tell me stories. Anything to keep me awake."

Feran scooted closer to the cot.

"Of course," she said and ran her fingertips through Sova's hair.

Sova sighed, his wounded heart soothed by the rhythmic stroking of her fingertips along his scalp.

"So," Feran began. "While you were gone, Taige started reciting poetry to Kyce. It was the funniest thing you'd ever heard. Worst part was I think he liked it..."

Unbeknownst to the pair, Saber loomed outside the tent, his yellow eyes burning through the slit in the tarp. A quiet growl rolled out his jaws, his tongue lashing over lethal fangs.

Feran might've been oblivious to the kind of danger she was in, but Saber knew better. After all, he could never forget that night in the Mosharick Plain village, nor the taste of that monster's flesh in his teeth.

Chapter Twenty-Seven: Two Days Later

The final sunrise rose on the kingdom of Vaska, its light seeping over the rooftops and making its way toward the Vaskan palace at the highest point in the kingdom.

Casavore lay in his cell, his back grating against the cold floor as he waited for the guards to take him away. Blanketed by the shadows of the cell bars twitching in the torch-light, he stared at the cob-webbed corners of the ceiling,

Two nights had passed since the Royal Traitor's visit, and since then, the Blesser hadn't known rest.

Every time he closed his eyes, he saw the boy's horrified expression—the wide eyes, the tears on paling cheeks. He hated what he had done to Zastar's son, but the boy needed to know. *Saulder* needed to know if anything was to get better. They all did.

As Casavore stared at the stone-covered sky, wondering if it was cloudy or clear, he recited scripture:

"They will turn their ears away from the truth and turn aside to myths. But you, keep your head in all situations, endure hardship, do the work of an evangelist, discharge all the duties of your ministry. For I am already being poured out like a drink offering, and the time for my departure is near..."

The door at the top of the stairs creaked open, and two shadows ventured down into the dungeon.

The good guard, Arison, and another Vaskan guard stood before the Blesser's cell, dressed in silver armor with swords holstered.

Arison cleared his throat. "Blesser Casavore. The dire has called for you."

Casavore sighed, annoyed. "Of course *it* has. Come in boys. I'll behave."

Arison unlocked the cell door, the hinges creaking as it swung open. He and the other guard stepped into the jail cell. They grabbed Casavore under the arms, hoisting him to his feet, and cuffed his hands behind his back in tight, metal chains that cut into his skin. Casavore didn't even bother to flinch. They walked him to the stairs, each of them gripping a bony arm in their gloves.

"Do you boys mind if I finish the scripture?" Casavore asked.

Arison nodded, his amethyst eyes that belonged to a general the Blesser once knew, full of respect and regret. "Of course, Blesser Casavore."

Walking up the stairs toward death, Casavore finished his final declaration of faithfulness; Feran's favorite verse since she was a little girl.

"I have fought the good fight... I have finished the race... I have kept the faith..."

THE VASKAN FOREST...

The Dire Wolves, Saber, and their Venom Tongue forces gathered outside the sewage tunnel leading into Vaska, the dense, green forest to their backs.

Roeseph stared up at the daunting walls of Vaska. The precipice seemed to curve over him, like a wave of stone just about to crash down on him. The soldier clenched his jaw and turned to face his army.

"Listen up," he demanded, "This is a rescue mission, not an assault. Our goal is to get in and get out—*unseen*. Kyce and Taige will lead you to the dungeon and back to camp. Casavore's execution should bring in the majority of the palace's defense to the plaza, so you shouldn't run into any guards. And if you do... well, Kyce and Taige will handle it."

Kyce drew his sword.

"Yeah, we will," he hissed through a clenched smile. Taige hugged his arm.

Feran scratched Saber behind the ear, grimacing.

"Their keenness for violence worries me," she grumbled to Sova.

The prince was silent.

Feran looked up at her white-haired comrade. He stared at the ground, his silver eyes more grey than silver. His mind was elsewhere. They were mere moments from battle, and his mind was *elsewhere.*

"Sova?" she whispered and laid her hand on his shoulder.

He jolted and looked down at her.

"Are you going to be able to do this?" she asked. "You were pretty shaken up after what happened with the Bless—"

"I'm fine," Sova interrupted with a weak grin that wasn't convincing anyone. "I can do this."

Before Feran could press him further, Roeseph's authoritative voice rose over the crowd.

"Venom Tongues," he shouted. "Stay with Taige and Kyce. They'll get you out of there in one piece. Feran, Elling, Sova, and I will scout the plaza for Casavore. Try not to cause a scene. The less Vaska knows of our presence the better."

The Venom Tongues nodded in approval and gathered near the sewer tunnel. As Kyce and Taige walked up to join their troops, Elling grabbed the Eradite Exile by the wrist.

"You get out of there safely, you hear me?" she ordered. Kyce cocked his head, taken aback by the desperate look in her emerald-green eyes.

He scoffed through a smirk. "Elling. Come on. Have you ever known me to lose a fight?"

Elling remained silent, her eyes still deathly serious. Kyce arrogant smirk softened, and he patted her on the shoulder.

"Don't worry about me, shepherdess. I am strong... And so is the Venom Tongue assassin that's obsessed with me."

Taige stepped up to Kyce, smiling. "It's me. I'm the Venom Tongue assassin that's obsessed with him."

Kyce chuckled and wrapped his arm around her shoulders.

"Be safe, soldier," Roeseph ordered, and extended his hand to the Eradite. "And get out of there fast."

"Aye—Aye, cap," Kyce nodded and walked off into the sewers with Taige under his arm. As they disappeared into the murky blackness, the Dire Wolves heard Kyce gag and sputter.

Roeseph, Elling, Feran, and Sova turned to board Saber, who waited patiently in the shadows, his feathers twitching with anticipation.

"You think they'll be ok?" Elling asked as she reached up to Feran and Roeseph, who had already mounted the soaring wolf.

"Oh yeah," Feran nodded as she stroked the fur on Saber's neck. "Kyce has been fighting since he was sixteen. He's got it handled. And as for Taige... You know what, Taige could singlehandedly take down all of Lykos. The lad is in good hands."

"Everything will be fine, Elling," Roeseph assured as he pulled Elling up. "We'll be in and out. This is a rescue mission. Not a battle."

"Someone should tell Kyce that," Elling grumbled.

Sova approached the soaring wolf last. Saber's amber eyes lashed at him and he snapped just short of Sova's nose.

"Saber!" Feran scolded as Saber snarled at his enemy. "For the love of Lykos. I can't figure out what you possibly could've done to make him hate you so much."

Sova returned the beast's gaze with a cold, dead stare.

"It's fine," he replied blankly and walked around to crawl up the monster's back. Elling pulled him up the rest of the way.

"Are you going to be able to do this, Sova?" she asked worriedly.

"I'm the one that got Casavore into this mess. I'm the one that needs to get him out. So if someone could please get this flying flea-bag in the air, I would be forever grateful."

"As you wish, your majesty," Feran grinned, her fists tightening in the fur on Saber's neck.

The soaring wolf launched into the sky, breaking through the treetops and scattering twigs and leaves everywhere.

SPLASHING BOOTS ECHOED through the darkness as the Venom Tongues ran down the sewage tunnel with torches in hand. Kyce and Taige led the pack, sweat and sewage weighing heavily in their clothes.

"How long does this tunnel go for?" Taige panted.

Kyce replied, "Who knows."

Not a second later, they came to the tunnel's end where a crescent spotlight shone down through the rim of a pothole overhead.

Kyce smirked, "There you are."

SABER FLEW OVER THE Vaskan wall undetected and landed in a dark alley between two cobblestone buildings, scattering the rats under his wings. The Dire Wolves slipped off the soaring wolf's back and drew their hoods.

Roeseph looked wearily from side to side, and turned to his comrades.

"Kyce and Taige should've infiltrated the palace by now. Feran, you and Saber will scout from the rooftops while Elling, Sova, and I head to the plaza. After we grab Casavore, I'll give you the signal, and you swoop in and get us out of there."

Feran nodded and pulled herself onto Saber's back.

"Try not to get killed, will you?"

"We'll try our best," Roeseph shrugged.

Saber shot up onto the rooftops, shingles breaking off under his heavy paws and hurtling down toward Sova's head. The prince stepped away just as the clay rectangle shattered to bits. He glared up at Saber just in time to see the top of his tail disappear over the precipice.

"Homicidal beast," he growled, his stomach sinking the further Feran ventured. He wished she would've just stayed with them.

Roeseph slapped him on the back.

"She'll be ok," he assured. "Just focus on your job so we can get out of here in one piece."

Sova nodded unsurely, and pulled his hood further over his face.

"Right," he breathed.

Roeseph leading the way, the three stalked out of the alley and into the steady stream of civilians heading towards the plaza.

MEANWHILE, AT THE PALACE, Kyce, Taige, and the Venom Tongues pressed close to the walls of the royal stables, the stench of the sewers still wafting around them. The nicker and neigh of ornery horses shook the stables, making Kyce flinch with each noise they made.

He looked in through the window at the royal steeds, his eyes narrow and fire filled.

"Lykos-forsaken donkeys," he growled.

Taige popped up beside him, her lips curled in a mischievous grin.

"We should steal them."

"What part of discrete don't you understand?" Kyce hissed in her ear.

"I can't help it," Taige whined. "Thievery is part of my culture."

Kyce exhaled and shook his head, secretly humored. "If you can keep your hands to yourself, I'll steal you a horse or two the day we come back to fight Vaska."

"Really?" Taige squeaked.

"Yes, fine, whatever."

"I want the black and white one," Taige pointed to a white horse that looked as if a painter had thwacked black paint across its hide. "Her name shall be Patsy."

"Focus, pirate," Kyce growled and peeked around the edge of the stables.

A massive iron door stood against the wall of a palace, guarded by a Vaskan soldier. The guard wrinkled his nose at the stench of sewage but thought nothing of it. For all he knew, the horses had a lousy lunch.

"That looks like the door Sova described," Kyce whispered. "That must be the dungeon."

Taige peeked out from behind him.

"Wonderful," she smiled. "Let's go."

Kyce threw his arm out to stop her. "Now, hold on. I love picking a fight as much as the next guy, but Roeseph says we can't cause a ruckus."

"Ruckus? What are you, an old man?"

"His words, not mine. We need to find a way to get the guard away from the door without alerting the others."

As Kyce rambled on about tactics, Taige's eyes fell to the dirt, where she spied a shiny black rock.

"Pretty," Taige whispered as she picked it up.

"—Our best chance of getting him away from the door is a diversion of sorts," Kyce said, stroking his chin. "Maybe if I released a horse or two, that would be enough to get him to leave. Taige, are you even listening?"

"Nope," Taige admitted as she wheeled her arm back and threw her newly acquired rock at full force. The rock hit the guard square in the head and threw him against the iron door before he fell, face down on the grass.

Kyce stared at the unconscious guard for a while, stone-faced though he was in immeasurable awe.

"Yep, that'll do," he nodded.

Quick as fleeting shadows, he and Taige led the Venom Tongues to the iron door. They didn't bother to move the body, rather, they just let the door shove the man aside as they ventured down into rat-infested darkness.

"It's dark down here," Taige whispered, clinging to Kyce's arm as he led the way. They came to the bottom of the stairs to a hall, lit by torches already half-way out. Jail cells stood on all sides, holding within them Vaska's greatest threats and foes, starved to skin and bones.

Kyce looked back at his army of pirates, his amber eyes glowing in the torch flame.

"Release as many prisoners as you can," he ordered. "Blind Seers or not. If they're down here, they're no ally to the dire, which means they're an ally to us. There should be a set of keys on the walls or something like it. If not, I can search the guard we knocked out."

"There's no need for that, darling," Taige sighed and pulled a blade from a hidden compartment in her leg. "We're Seavallian, remember?"

Kyce's eyes widened. "What are you going to pull out next, a rabbit?"

"Maybe someday," Taige winked and walked up to the first cell with her blade.

After a few short seconds of jiggling the tip of her knife in the lock, the cell door clicked and squeaked open. A prisoner slept inside, a skeleton with a beard as long as a river running across the floor.

The Venom Tongues ran down the hall, opening cell after cell as the dire's enemies pressed themselves to the bars, waving at them and pleading to be rescued.

Kyce ran down the hall in search of Oland. Each miserable face he came across didn't match Roeseph's description. He exhaled in frustration as he looked around the dark, depressing prison.

"Where are you, Blind Hound?" he muttered.

A bony hand grabbed hold of the hem of Kyce's shirt, making him yell and fall against the cell across the hall. A woman stared through the bars of her cell. Her eyes were withered, her hair was thin at the part, and her skin curved under her cheekbones.

"Please," she croaked as she reached for him. "Help me."

"O—Oh," Kyce stammered and nodded. "Yeah—Yeah, I'm coming."

Kyce stuck the tip of his blade into the lock and jiggled it around. He did so for a long time without success, frustration burning in his chest like fire.

"For the good grace of Lykos," he cursed. "Open you forsaken—"

A gentle hand laid over his, and he looked up to see Taige standing beside him.

"Would you like some help?" she raised her brow.

Kyce scoffed. "I've got everything under c—"

"Yes!" the prisoner interrupted. "Yes—Please get me out of here!"

Taige took the blade from Kyce, smirking. "Seavallian, remember?"

"Don't get cocky, thief," Kyce grumbled.

Taige picked at the lock, her tongue lodging in the corner of her mouth.

"This one's a little tricky because of the rust, but I should have you out in a moment. What's your name?"

"Serifath," the prisoner answered.

"So, what's a pretty lass like you doing in a place like this?"

Kyce roll his eyes.

"My brethren and I broke into the Vaskan palace a couple months back," the woman answered.

Kyce jumped. "You're a Blind Seer?" he asked. "Did you serve under the Blind Hound?"

"I was one of his lieutenants."

"Do you know where he is? I was sent by his son to free him."

Grief washed over the woman's face as her gaze fell to the ground. Taige stopped picking the lock.

Kyce swallowed. "Serifath," he began. "Where is the Blind Hound?"

"I'm sorry," she whispered, her knuckles unsheathing as she gripped the cell bars. "You're too late…"

IN THE NORTHERN SECTOR of the kingdom, the people of Vaska gathered in the plaza, packed together like cattle, gawking at the empty stage with two pillars on top of it.

Unbeknownst to the people, Saber leaped from building to building. Crouching low to the roof shingles as to not be seen. He stalked to the edge to peer down into the plaza. He growled, his teeth twinkling in the cloud-covered light of day.

"Easy, Saber," Feran whispered as she slipped from his back and crouched down beside him. She scanned the fussing crowd in search of her father's face. "Where are you, Pa?"

As Feran searched from the roof, Roeseph, Sova, and Elling made their way through the crowd toward the stage, the shadows of the two pillars falling directly over them.

Elling froze where she stood, making Roeseph stop in his stride.

"Elling?" he said, looking back. She just stared at the pillars, tears glittering in her eyes. "Elling," Roeseph called again as he walked up to her.

Elling pulled her cloak tighter around her body.

"This is a mistake," she whispered as she looked frantically at the surrounding crowd. "What if the dire… What if he tries to—"

"He won't," Roeseph promised and placed his hands on her shoulders. "Dire Saulder may be a monster, but he's not cruel enough to summon the Siren's Call while all these people are here."

Sova looked away. His captain was right. *Saulder*, while a monster, wouldn't be so desperate as to sacrifice his own people just to capture a handful of rebels. Maybe one or two, but not a whole plaza. He'd lose the people's loyalty.

Lore, however, thought only of power. As far as she was concerned, the people were hers to dispose. If it meant getting her way, she'd turn oceans red. Which meant, Roeseph's assurance wasn't as sound as he believed.

"Uh, Roeseph," Sova began nervously.

Roeseph looked back at him. "Yes, Sova?"

Sova stopped, his voice curling up in his throat.

What do I say? he thought. *Hey Roeseph, so turns out Lore's been pretending to be the dire this whole time. Crazy right?*

And then Roeseph would reply with; *How do you know that?*

Then Sova would say; *Oh, you know how I was unable to get Casavore out of the palace? Well, turns out I am actually Saulder, and the real Sova is dead.*

Sova could see it now. He'd be whisked off to be burned at the stake, survive, then get his head chopped off, survive, then be fed to Saber. And if he survived that, then each of the Dire Wolves would each get a turn at torturing him in the most unbelievable way they could imagine. What Kyce could think up scared him the most.

No. He couldn't tell Roeseph. He couldn't tell anyone.

"Sova?" Roeseph said, breaking Sova from his daze. "Did you need something?"

"I, um..." Sova's fists tightened at his side, his heart twisting with both guilt and fear. "I—"

Trumpets blared over the plaza, making everyone look east where seven Vaskan soldiers stood with silver trumpets in hand. One of the guards stepped forward, her shoulders reeling back as she raised her chin.

"Presenting the ruler and defender of Vaska, your Dire Saulder."

Cheers broke out all around, drowning the Dire Wolves in a sea of jubilation. They watched as the black-armored dire walked out from behind her guards and ventured into the crowd who bowed at her coming. The Dire Wolves bowed with them, cursing themselves as they did so.

Feran glared down from the roof, whatever love she once had for her childhood friend and betrothed, gone.

Saber growled lowly and took a step forward, only for Feran to pull him back by his fur. "Not yet, boy," she said. "Don't you worry. Our time is coming."

The dire cut through the crowd, her cape rolling over the hands of those who bowed. Sova looked up to see the dire make her way towards him. His heart raced into the cobblestone floor.

Why is she coming this way? Did she see me? Does she know who I am? She'll tell everyone who I am. No. I have to stop her.

Just as Sova was just about to consider unsheathing his sword, the imposter strolled past him, her cape caressing his clenched fists. Sova let out a breath of relief.

The dire rose onto the executioner's platform and turned to meet her bowing audience.

"Rise brothers and sisters of Vaska," she ordered, her voice disguised by the metal echo of her helmet. "Rise."

The crowd rose as instructed.

"Today, we put to death a man who I trusted with my whole being. A man who tarnished his God given gifts, and betrayed the kingdom he was designed to serve. For these crimes, Vaska will see the Blesser fall."

Half the crowd burst into cheers of agreement, while others kept their silence; the closest they could get to rebelling without getting their heads chopped off.

Sova looked to the roofs where Feran and Saber hid, trying to catch a glimpse of her beyond the shingles. Though he couldn't see her, he knew she was terrified. Even so, it was unlikely she looked it. Fear is very easily masked by blood-lust. And Feran had plenty of it.

Roeseph's hand came down on Sova's shoulder, making him jump.

"Keep your head down and follow me," he ordered, and led Elling and Sova closer to the stage as the dire scanned the crowd in search of her prey.

"Nine months ago, on this very day, the Blesser Casavore conspired with the Blind Hound," she sneered. "The captain of the Blind Seers, and Vaska's greatest enemy since the Venom Tongues."

Sova stopped, his stomach and heart racing the other to the ground.

"The Blesser..." the dire continued, "even went as far as to turn my own brother against me. The Royal Traitor of Vaska, who sought to kill me in my own chamber with his own sword."

Sova's stomach began to churn as the cobblestone street beneath him blurred with tears.

Stop it...

"I fought him off," the dire lied. "By then, my brother was too far gone to bring back to the light. And now, he and his band of exiles haunt our lands, thirsty for blood. So, brothers and sisters of Vaska, if we are to save

Lykos from their treachery, we must first send them a message. A message that shows what happens to those who threaten the dire's reign."

Half the crowd burst into the cheers, spittle flying from their jaws.

Sova stared at the ground, the contents of his stomach rising to the brim of his throat, threatening to spill over. Before he could become sick with guilt, Elling touched his shoulder.

"Sova," she began gently, "are you alright?"

Sova gulped down hard. "Yeah," he coughed.

"You're really pale," Elling pressed the back of her hand to his forehead. "And you're burning up."

"I'm fine, Elling," Sova assured and lowered her hand. "Let's just get this over with so we can leave."

Elling nodded, though the concern in her emerald eyes never wavered, as she and Sova took their place at Roeseph's side. The stage stood a couple feet away, surrounded by Vaskan guards.

"How do we get through?" Sova mumbled.

Roeseph glared at his enemies, his eyes narrow with determination.

"With sheer force," he answered.

Sova turned to his captain. "That's it?" he hissed beneath his breath. "That's your master plan?"

"I'm making it up as you go along."

"You are a horrible—horrible strategist. I hereby appoint Elling as our honorary battle planner."

"You can't do that."

Elling shrugged. "I accept."

"Might I remind you, your plan didn't work to save Casavore either," Roeseph stated. "If it had, we wouldn't be here."

"Hey," Elling snapped, "my plan would've worked if Sova had fallen through."

"Guys, I did my best," Sova grumbled. 1

Before the three could argue further, the dire's voice fell upon the crowd like a whip, ripping away their voices like flesh off bone.

"However, what is the use killing one traitor if he has not learned his lesson?"

The Dire Wolves glared at the dire.

"What in Lykos is he talking about," Roeseph growled.

"The Blesser Casavore is a traitor to his people," the dire continued. "And has proven himself to be an ally to the Blind Seers. How are we, as the proud people of Vaska, expected to overcome our adversaries if we don't reveal the consequences of their betrayal?"

"What's he getting at?" Elling whispered.

"And so, I have decided it will not be I who executes the Blesser. But rather, one of his most trusted allies."

She wouldn't, Sova thought, his eyes wide with fear.

The dire turned to and beckoned to someone in the crowd. Two prisoners bound in chains were led toward the stage, a guard on each side. Many cursed and spat in their faces, while others reached out to them weeping.

Roeseph looked over the people's heads, trying to catch a glimpse.

"Please," Roeseph begged, "please don't let it be him."

The dire opened her hand to the approaching prisoners. "I present to you, Blesser Casavore, and the Blind Hound."

Oland and Casavore ascended the stage with their heads hanging low and reluctantly stalked up to the pillars where they were bound with thick, heavy ropes.

"No," Roeseph gasped beneath his breath. "No. He's supposed to be in the dungeon."

The guard tending to Olan jerked hard on the rope, burning his skin red. Oland gritted his teeth and uttered a vulgar insult, prompting the Vaskan to strike him across the face. Oland hardly turned his head as he glared at the guard with eyes like a rabid hound's. The Vaskan stumbled back, frightened.

"That's enough, Oland," Casavore said as he stared somberly at the silver sky.

The Blind Hound chuckled. "Oh, come now, Casavore. Have a little fun. So, how do you think they'll take us out? Swords? Firing squad? Perhaps this is a beheading?"

"You almost sound eager."

"A legend is only as good as the way he goes out."

Casavore drew in a deep breath. "I'm sorry I got you into this mess, old friend. I should've burned that Lykos forsaken letter the day you gave it to me."

"Ah—don't beat yourself up," Oland scoffed. "I would've ended up like this anyway. Besides, had none of this happened, those Dire Wolves of ours would've never come together. Our God has a tendency to make curses out of blessings, does he not?"

"Either way," Casavore looked to his ally, "I am sorry, Oland. Truly. I am."

"Don't be sorry. Be sorry if when word gets out about this, they only mention you. Even in the grave, I'll be sore about it."

Casavore gave a tired smirk. "I'm grateful to have met you, Oland. You truly have made my imprisonment that much more bearable."

"Of course. What are friends for?"

Feran crawled toward the edge of the roof, her eyes glistening with tears of relief.

"Papa..." she whispered.

He looked different then the last time she saw him. His blue eyes didn't shine the way they used to. His beard had grown mangled and was infested with the grey. His garments, while normally plain, were ragged and torn. And he had no medallion. There was not a day Feran saw her father without his medallion. She clutched the two pendants hanging from her neck.

"Don't worry, Pa," she uttered. "I'm coming."

The dire stood at the front of the stage, her venomous blue eyes burning the Vaskans crowding beneath her.

"I ask you, Vaska," she called. "How is a traitor to face justice, if not to be betrayed himself? This day, the Blesser will die by the sword of the Blind Hound."

Oland jerked forward against his restraints.

"You bloody—" he spat at the dire's metal boots. "Release me now, you tyrant!"

"Oh, I intend to, beast," the dire hissed over her shoulder. Slowly, she reached under her violet cape and withdrew a curved bugle horn; a weapon Elling knew all too well.

Elling made a small shrieking sound and took a fearful step back.

"He's going to summon the Siren's Call," she stammered.

Tears streaming down her face, Elling placed her hands over her ears in a last effort to prevent the dormant monster from awakening. Roeseph joined in, cupping his hands over her own. Should she turn into a Hyde Howler, their chances of surviving, let alone escaping with Casavore and Oland, would cease to exist.

Oland kicked and thrashed in his binds, desperate to escape. When he failed, he hunched over, panting breathlessly, and looked to Casavore with tear-speckled eyes.

"I don't want this."

"It's ok, my friend," Casavore said gently. "I don't blame you..."

Sova looked rapidly across the crowd in search of an exit.

"We need to get Elling out of here," he insisted.

Roeseph looked from Elling to his father.

"They're right there," he whispered. "We can still save them."

"We can't if Elling turns this entire plaza into a battlefield!"

Roeseph swallowed hard, and looked down at Elling. She stared up at him, trembling, her big, beautiful, green eyes bright with fear.

"Roeseph!" Sova snapped, making his captain look up. "What do we do?"

The crowd grew silent as the dire tipped the bugle-horn beneath the chin of her helmet. Roeseph, Elling, and Sova froze.

They were too late.

"Long live the Blesser," the dire whispered and drew in a deep breath.

An unearthly roar shook the surrounding buildings, sending loose roof shingles raining down onto the frightened people below.

The dire lowered the bugle-horn and looked up.

"Perfect timing," she said.

Roeseph, Sova, and Elling looked to the building tops. Standing on the edge of a tavern roof was the beast of legend, the White Angel, with the sun burning through its spread wings. Its jaws opened wide, letting out another roar so tremendous the very earth seemed to quake. Feran sat on his back, concealed behind his wings, with her chestnut locks flowing in the gentle wind.

Casavore stared up at his daughter, his jaw trembling open as a tear stroked his cheek.

"Feran…"

Saber flew down to the executioner's platform and landed before the dire, causing the planks to groan beneath his weight as the crowd shrieked with fear.

"My—my—my," the dire tutted. "Look at you, Feran. It's been too long."

"Not long enough," Feran growled and slipped down Saber's side to stand before the false dire.

"Mhmm," the dire nodded. She looked down to see two medallions hanging from Feran's neck. One belonged to the Blesser, and the other, she had stolen from Feran during the battle on Era many months ago. "Care to tell me how you managed to procure that pretty thing?"

"You took something from me, so I took something from you," Feran sneered over Saber's snarl.

"Funny. I didn't take you as a thief, Feran."

"If I'm a thief, it's only because you made me one."

The dire's shoulders jolted with a restrained laugh. "I should warn you, my sweet damsel—"

"I'm not called that anymore."

"Ah yes. You go by the *Dire's Curse*, now," the false dire chuckled. "Little brooding for my taste? I feel I should warn you. If you intend to fight me, it won't end well for you."

"I don't plan to fight," Feran growled and withdrew the two medallions from her neck. "I'm here to make a trade."

She tossed the medallions to the crowd, causing the people to scurry away as if they were plague ridden. The two golden pendants landed before Sova, who hastily swept the medallions under his cloak.

"What is she doing?" Elling whimpered. "This isn't part of the plan."

"No, it isn't," Roeseph agreed. "Follow me."

As the Dire Wolves snuck closer to the executioner's platform, Feran stared down the Vaskan tyrant, her eyes narrow and hands coiled into fists.

"Feran!" Casavore shouted and threw himself against his restraints. "Feran, what are you doing? Go! Get out of here!"

Feran marched toward the dire, Saber letting out a low, threatening snarl as she neared.

"It's ok, Saber," Feran assured and lowered her hand in his direction. "I'll be ok."

Saber scratched at the wooden planks and snorted. When she was sure the soaring wolf wasn't going to retaliate, Feran turned and stopped before the dire.

"So, my dear," the imposter chuckled. "What would you have me trade?"

"My life for Blesser Casavore's and the captain of the Blind Seers."

"Oh. Quite the bargain, huh? Do you hold yourself to such high regard?"

"You've spent nine months of your life trying to kill me. I figure this to be a generous offer."

"Kill you?" the dire snickered. "My dear Feran, who said I wanted to kill you?"

"You made that pretty clear on Era."

"Fair point. But that was before you showed me how truly special you really are," the dire reached forward to brush a lock of hair out of Feran's face. Feran grabbed the dire's wrist, squeezing so hard the metal creaked.

"Touch me, and I'll feed you to the soaring wolf," she warned and tossed away the dire's hand. Saber lowered his head, his tongue lashing over his fangs.

"Still quite the fiery one, are you?" the dire laughed. "You should be relieved to know that I no longer wish you dead. It would be a waste. Instead, I intend to make you my Blesser."

Feran raised her chin and scoffed, "Execution would be more appealing."

Casavore lurched forward again. "Feran, listen to me. You need to run. I've lived my life. I've made a lot of mistakes. I deserve this fate. You don't. Please—"

"Papa, the dire and I are talking," Feran dismissed.

Casavore collapsed back against the pillar in defeat.

Oland scoffed. "She's Fala's alright."

"How sweet," the dire pouted. "You'd give up your freedom for the life of your father and a monster?"

"Oh, I'm not doing this for them," Feran admitted.

"Then who would you do this for? It's not for the sake of our betrothal, is it my dear?"

"Oh, Lykos no," Feran laughed, her eyes blazing with spite. "No. No, I'm just stalling."

Chapter Twenty-Eight: The Blesser's Battle

A violent war cry swept across the plaza as Venom Tongues and Blind Seers alike rode through the streets on stolen horses toward the plaza. Leading them were Kyce and Taige, Kyce upon a brown stallion, and Taige upon a black and white mare. The Vaskan civilians cried out in peril and raced out of the plaza while their soldiers rushed to the streets, creating a parricide made of shields and swords.

Oland and Casavore gawked at the oncoming army, their eyes wide with disbelief.

"By the Great Valley of Lykos," Oland growled through a grin. "Well done, my boy."

Like two tidal waves crashing into one another, the Venom Tongue and Blind Seer army clashed with the Vaskans.

The dire froze where she stood. "No..."

Feran lunged to grab the bugle from the dire's glove, only for the dire to wrestle it away, and shove her to the planks.

"Why you little—"

Just as the dire rose her hand against Feran, Saber leaped in front of his master and snarled. The dire cried out and fell off the platform, devoured by the chaos like a pebble thrown into rapids. Feran crawled to the edge of the stage, trying to spot the dire in the blur of swords and armor. She saw nothing. Her teeth clenching in frustration, she slammed her fist down on the wooden floor.

Roeseph, Elling, and Sova pressed close together as the war enclosed around them.

"What's going on?" Elling cried.

"Well, it appears Kyce can't stick to a plan to save his life," Roeseph grumbled and drew his sword. "Sova! Get the medallions back to Feran and help her free my father. Go, now!"

Nodding, Sova disappeared toward the platform with medallions in hand.

Kyce rode out from the blur of blood and silver, his stallion rearing up on its hind legs before Elling and Roeseph.

"Did I miss anything?" he asked through a smirk as he slid off the horse's back.

Roeseph scowled at him. "I asked you to do two things," he sneered. "Don't cause a commotion, and get out quietly. This is a very loud commotion, Kyce!"

"Aren't you glad I didn't listen, though?"

"Kyce!"

"The Blind Seers said Oland was taken with Casavore. I knew you were going to need backup. So..." Kyce opened his arms to the battle around them. "I brought back up."

Before Roeseph could scold Kyce further, a warrior's cry rose above the rest.

"It's the Dire Wolves!"

Kyce, Roeseph, and Elling lashed around to see a hoard of Vaskan soldiers charge at them, swords in hand.

"Roeseph!" Elling said nervously as she clutched her staff.

"Stand your ground!" Roeseph ordered. "We'll take them together."

A shrill whinny cut through the battle, making the incoming soldiers stop and look to the side just as Taige trampled them with her black and white steed. Elling and Roeseph cringed at the sound of crunching metal and snapped bones while Kyce stared at the Viper's Heir in utter awe.

Whipping her hair out of her face, Taige rode up to the Dire Wolves.

"You alright, love?" she asked, her blood-thirsty eyes softening when they descended the Eradite Exile.

Kyce stood there with his jaw hanging open. "You're extraordinary."

Taige hopped down from her steed, landing a mere inch from Kyce.

"Took you long enough," she teased, scooping his chin with her finger. "Want to go fight some Vaskans with me?"

Kyce sighed in ecstasy. "Finally. Somebody gets me."

Taige and Kyce ran into the heat of battle screaming like Vikings while Roeseph and Elling stared after them, stricken dumb.

"That uh," Elling looked up at Roeseph, "that's going to become a problem, isn't it?"

"Probably," Roeseph concluded and turned to the battle. "We need to hold off the Vaskans for as long as we can until Feran can free my father and Casavore. You think you're ready, soldier?"

Elling twirled her staff at her side before jamming it hard into the ground. "Oh, most defiantly not."

"Perfect," Roeseph said, taking her by the hand before shooting off into the battle.

FERAN STOOD ON THE edge of the stage with Saber, searching for the dire in an unruly sea of swords and shields. When she saw no sign of the tyrant, she drew back and hurried to Oland and Casavore bound to the two pillars.

"Feran," Casavore sneered. "Feran, what are you doing here? I told Sova that you needed to leave. Why didn't you bloody list—"

Feran threw her arms around the Blesser's neck, silencing his scolds in an instant. She stood there for a long while, soaking his robe with her tears before she finally pulled away.

"It's you," she croaked. "By Lykos, it's you."

Casavore swallowed hard, his eyes glistening with awe.

"I thought you were dead. The Venom Tongues—they took you. How did you escape them?"

"Saber."

"Who's Saber?"

The White Angel walked up from behind Feran, his tail swishing from side to side. With no sense of restraint, he raked his tongue across Casavore's face, causing several strands of tangled hair to stand on end.

"Ah," Casavore nodded as he sputtered out the slobber making its way into his mouth. "Saber."

The soaring wolf panted gleefully while Feran hurried to the other side of pillar to untie her father. She dug into the knot, her nails nearly prying off her fingers.

"Feran," Casavore pled, "you need to get out of here. If they catch you, all of this was for nothing."

"I'm trying to focus here, Pa," Feran grunted. "These Lykos Forsaken ropes won't budge. Wait—I have an idea. Saber! Saber, come here, boy."

Saber snapped down on the ropes and pulled, making Casavore gasp when they dug into his gut. And yet still, the ropes wouldn't give.

Feran sneered, "What in Lykos are these things made of?"

"Please, Feran," Casavore begged. "Get out of here—"

"Will you stop saying that! I came here to free you. It would be a lot easier if you'd shut up and let me work."

Oland cackled beside Casavore. "Oh yeah," he sighed, shaking his head at the sky. "She's Fala's alright."

Feran roared in frustration and slammed her fists on the knot. "For the sake of Lykos, why won't it untie? Do either of you have a blade on you by chance?"

Before either Casavore or Oland could answer, a sarcastic voice rose from the battle.

"Yes, Feran. Before the dire brought them here to be executed—he thought he'd give them each a knife. Just to have."

Feran turned around to find Sova struggling to pull himself over the edge of the platform. He flopped onto the floorboards, his chest leaping at the sky.

"Great Lykos, that was scary," he panted. "So many Vaskans. So many Venom Tongues. Taige has horse. This is the stuff of nightmares."

"Sova!" Feran cried and ran to the Royal Traitor.

Before Sova had a moment to catch his breath, Feran jerked him to his feet.

"Thank Lykos, you're ok," she exhaled, her eyes big with relief.

"Of course, I'm ok," Sova shrugged. "You didn't think I'd be ok?"

"Well, Kyce and I have a bet going that you'll be the first of us to die."

"What?" Sova squeaked. "Why am I the first one to die."

"Well—"

"I am a skilled fighter. I've been training since I was seven."

"Uh, Sova, now might not be a great time—"

"If anyone's going to die first, it's Elling."

"She's a Hyde Howler."

"She fights with a stick!"

"Sova!" Feran snapped, frightening Sova silent. "Are you going to help me or not?"

"Right. Bur first..." Sova withdrew two medallions, one charred and one smooth. "Figured you might want these."

"Indeed I do," Feran nodded and slipped the two medallions over her head. "Come on. We don't have much time."

As they hurried back to the two pillars, Sova looked up to see the Blesser staring straight at him. He froze, his heart anchoring him to the floorboards.

"Cas..." he whispered fearfully.

Casavore swallowed, his eyes dark with conviction.

"Your majesty..." the Blesser hesitated for a moment, his silence causing Sova's blood to frost.

He's going to rat me out, Sova thought. *He's going to tell Feran.*

"...Sova," the Blesser said finally, giving into the deception. "I'm relieved that you're alright. I was worried that you hadn't gotten out of the palace."

Sova's chest fell with a breath of relief. The Blesser would keep his secret after all.

"See, Sova," Feran teased as she jerked at the ropes tying Casavore to the mast. "Even my Pa knows you're a dead man walking."

Sova and Casavore cringed at the poor choice of words. Feran jerked at the ropes again, her face contorting into a fierce snarl.

"For Lykos sake!" she cursed and punched the mast, provoking Saber to hurry to her side.

"Here," Sova said as he drew a blade from his cloak. "Let me try."

"No," Casavore ordered. "Cut Oland free first. He'll be able to hold his own in the fight."

Feran exhaled, frustrated. "Fine—Fine—Just get it over with, Sova."

Sova rushed to Oland's mast and began cutting the ropes.

"Hello, Oland," he nodded. "Long time no see."

Oland looked him up and down, his brow arched high with suspicion.

"Prince Sova," he greeted uncertainly. "I didn't recognize you for a second."

Sova flinched and stole a nervous glance at Casavore.

"There's something different about you," Olan continued. "You've changed since the last we met."

Sova laughed nervously. "Ha—Ha, yeah. I lost a little weight. Living in exile will do that to you."

"No..." Oland grumbled. "That's not it..."

Sova gulped and looked back to the ropes. He grimaced at their resilience. Cutting through the restraints was like trying to cut through a sequoia with a Seavallian toenail.

"What the heck are these things made of?" he whined.

"I don't know," Feran sneered. "But at this point, I might just chew my way through them."

Sova snickered at Casavore. "Saulder must really not want to let you go, huh, Cas?"

Casavore's eyes turned dark. "Vaska's tyrant knows what'll become of his rule should I be set free..."

Feran looked to the battle. All around the stage, rebel soldiers fell at the blade of a Vaskan. For every silver-armored foe they took down, two Venom Tongues and three Blind Seers fell also.

They were losing—and they were losing fast.

"Saber," she spat at her soaring wolf. He jolted upright, ready to take orders. "Help them."

Saber sprung into the sky and descended the army like a comet, sending Vaskans flying into the air. Roaring his mighty roar, he tore into the enemy forces like a fire through dry brush. Within just a few mere moments, the tide began to turn in the rebel army's favor.

Sova looked from Saber to Feran, for once, very nervous about the soaring wolf's absence. "Was that a good idea? Getting rid of him?"

"If there's no army, there's no fight," Feran grunted as she struggled to cut the ropes. "We need to prevent as many fatalities as possible."

"Just saying. The giant flying wolf might have come in handy."

"Just shut up and cut!"

Giving one last heave, Sova cut through the last of Oland's restraints. Oland sighed in relief and stepped away from the mast, rubbing at the red line in his wrists.

"Lykos, that feels good," he exhaled. "Where is the dire anyway? I want to repay him for his hospitality."

"I lost him in the crowd," Feran answered. "I figure he would've retreated to the palace by now."

"The coward," Oland seethed.

Sova looked to his gauze-wrapped shoulder. Beneath it, his scar burned in his skin like hot oil, growing hotter and hotter. Should Feran or any of the others find out who he truly was, he'd be fed to the White Angel without a second thought. They'd hate him. They'd fully, and utterly hate him.

"Sova!" Feran snapped. "Knife, please."

Sova blinked away his daze. "Huh? Oh. Yeah," he placed the blade in Feran's hand.

While she cut at Casavore's ropes, Oland and Sova pulled at the restraints, trying to speed the process along.

"Come on," Feran pleaded with the blade. "Cut faster..."

ROESEPH AND ELLING fought side by side, Elling with her staff and Roeseph with his sword. His face wrenched in a sneer, Roeseph shoved away a Vaskan soldier, and turned to check on Elling. She stood over an unconscious Vaskan, her shoulders and staff trembling as she glared down at her victim. Roeseph raised his brows, impressed, and a little frightened.

Elling looked up at him, stammering, "How—How am I doing?"

"With what?" Roeseph asked.

"The war. How am I doing?"

"Oh. Good. You are doing war very good, Elling."

"Oh," Elling nodded, her lips spreading in a stressed grin. "Oh, good. I'm doing good then... I feel like I'm going to be sick. How does Kyce enjoy this?"

"Kyce is a rare breed," Roeseph said, looking around the battle. "Speaking of which, where are Kyce and Taige anyway?"

Elling pointed across the plaza. Taige and Kyce rode through the battle on a black and white mare, cutting down every Vaskan in their path. Clinging to Kyce's back, Taige launched her prosthetic leg into the helmet of a poor unsuspecting Vaskan. Both of them laughed as they watched him fall.

Roeseph cringed.

"Barbaric," he uttered.

"They're good for each other," Elling shrugged.

Roeseph grabbed Elling's hand. "Come on," he ordered, as he led her away. "We need to make a path for everyone to escape once Feran and Sova free the Blesser."

SOVA AND OLAND CROWDED around Feran. Despite her efforts, she hadn't even managed to cut halfway through the ropes.

"Taking your sweet time, are you, Feran?" Sova mocked as he looked to the battle beyond the platform.

Feran spat back, "Would you rather do it?"

"Yes. I would've had him out by now."

"Oh, please, be my guest!"

As Feran and Sova bickered, Oland looked to Casavore.

"Quite the pair, huh?" he exhaled, annoyed.

Casavore smirked, his blue eyes dense with fondness. "They've been that way since they were little."

"What, at each other's throats?"

Casavore shook his head. "No," he answered.

Feran dug her blade deeper into the rope, nearly halfway through.

"I'm almost there," she said, daring to smile.

A low, eerie sound like a distant howl oozed across the plaza. Oland straightened, his eyes widening with terror as Sova, Feran, and Casavore stared at him.

The fear in the Blind Hound's eyes dissipated, and every sign of humanity with it.

"Oland, no..." Casavore whispered.

Chapter Twenty-Nine: The Siren's Call

Roeseph jerked Elling through the crowd, desperate to clear a path for their army to escape.

"We're almost there!" he cried. "We just need to secure the roads to the west gate, or else no one's gonna—"

Elling froze in her sprint as the eerie howl that struck Oland sept into her ears. She gasped, her green eyes vivid with fear. Then, like a candle doused by a flood, the emotion in her face melted away, and her expression became stone-like.

Roeseph looked back.

"El—Elling?" he called, perplexed by her stoic expression. "Elling, what's wrong?"

Elling stood deathly still in the middle of the chaos, like a boulder stuck in the middle of a raging river.

Across the battle, Kyce and Taige looked up from their fight.

"What's she doing?" Taige cried over the blood-curdling screams of the vanquished.

Roeseph's gaze lifted from Elling to the dire standing in the center of the battle, a bugle horn pressed to her lips. Roeseph's eyes widened. Taige trapped a gasp under her hand. Kyce's face wrenched into a snarl.

On the executioner's platform, Sova, Feran, and Casavore looked past Oland to the dire.

"He didn't..." Sova whispered.

Feran answered, "He did."

"He summoned the Siren's Call."

Casavore, Sova, and Feran looked up at Oland. His face was blank, and his eyes soulless.

"Oland?" Casavore whispered past a gulp. "Oland, listen to me. This isn't you. You need to fight this, my friend."

Oland turned from Casavore and marched to the edge of the platform. He grabbed a Vaskan right out of the chaos, ripping his sword out of the man's hand, before he tossed him back into the battle.

Sova gulped down a hard swallow. It was only a matter of time until the Hyde Howlers ravaged the place.

"Faster," he ordered in Feran's ear. "Cut faster!"

"I'm trying!" Feran shrieked.

Elling turned from Roeseph and started toward the dire.

Roeseph grabbed her wrist, and cried out in pleading, "Elling, snap out of it!"

Elling spun around and struck him in the side of the head with her staff. He fell to the cobblestone, gritting his teeth in pain as Elling turned and continued toward her dark master.

Roeseph struggled onto his hands and knees, his skull ringing like a gong. Before he could comprehend what had happened, Kyce had him under the arms and pulled him to his feet.

"Roeseph? Roeseph, are you ok?" he called through the ringing.

Taige ran up to join them, her obsidian eyes wide and frantic. Roeseph groaned and pressed his hand to his forehead, flinching at the pain. He looked up to see Elling parting through the battle, growing closer to the dire.

"No," Roeseph whispered. "He turned her... That monster turned Elling into a Hyde Howler."

THE DIRE CHUCKLED AS Elling walked up to meet her.

"Quite a beauty, aren't you," she seethed as she scooped Elling's chin with her finger. "Too bad Saulder had to go and turn you into a beast. Don't worry, dear. It'll all be over soon."

The dire looked to Oland on the platform, the rebel captain staring at her with the same blank expression as Elling. Two Hyde Howlers didn't seem like much, but one alone could've brought the entire plaza to its knees.

"Hyde Howlers," the false dire shouted. "My purest soldiers. I command you— slaughter the Blesser and destroy anyone who stands in your way!"

Sova sighed, his shoulders drooping forward.

"Lykos," he cursed under his breath. "She is just the worst."

Elling turned her gaze to Casavore, making the Blesser straighten against the mast. Slowly, she passed through the crowd and pulled herself onto the platform beside Oland.

Oland drew his sword and Elling her staff, their eyes void of soul. Feran and Sova shuddered, suddenly, very afraid.

The dire chuckled. "Let the fun begin."

Sova stepped in front of Casavore and Feran, and drew his sword, the metal hissing against its sheath.

"Sova," Feran hissed. "What are you doing?"

"Not sure," Sova admitted out the corner of his mouth and turned to the Hyde Howlers. "... Oland, Elling," he bowed in formal greeting. "First off, I want to say, love the new look. Soulless killer really suits you both. Now, before things can get out of hand, how about we all lay down our weapons and talk this out over a couple barrels of Odin Slayer? Aye?"

Oland and Elling stepped towards the Royal Traitor, their gazes blank and bloodthirsty.

Sova laughed nervously. "Wow, there is absolutely nothing behind those eyes right now. Just—Just a pure lust for death."

Casavore peeled around the mast to look back at his daughter. "Feran, get out of here!" he snapped. "Take Sova. Get to the forest, and don't come back!"

"Please don't distract me, Papa," Feran grunted as she sliced through another millimeter of rope.

Sova took a nervous step back as the Hyde Howlers neared. "How are those ropes coming along, Feran?"

"Not well!"

"Oh, good."

"I just need a little more time."

"Oh sure, take all the time you need," Sova grumbled. "Still think sending Saber away was a good idea? Because I think a giant biting machine would come in mighty handy right about now."

Oland charged and swung his sword down at Sova. Sova caught the blade against his own just a mere inch from his nose. He stared at his reflection in the Hyde Howler's sword, disgusted by the monster staring back. Oland shoved Sova away, making him stumble into Casavore bound to the mast. He looked back with an awkward smile.

"Hey, Cas," Sova greeted.

"Hello, Sova," Casavore replied, unamused.

Oland's heavy shadow fell over them, bringing their eyes to meet his lifeless gaze. Just as Oland raised his sword, Sova lunged and shoved him out of reach of Casavore.

Elling and Oland surrounded Sova, like two lions hunting a gazelle. Elling swung her staff at Sova, accidentally striking Oland across the face when he ducked. Sova popped back up, his eyes shining with mischief.

"Ha!" he exclaimed. "Missed me—"

Elling struck him on the back of the knee, making him fall. He clutched his leg to his chest, the tendon along his thigh vibrating painfully, like a strummed cord.

"Cheap shot," he croaked.

Oland and Elling enclosed around him, their faces void of regret or reluctance.

Oland raised his sword, piercing the sun veiled behind the overcast. Sova crunched into a ball and shielded his head.

"Oland, no!" Casavore cried.

"Sova!" Feran shrieked.

Just before Oland could descend the blade, Roeseph leaped out of the battle and dove in front of Sova, catching his father's sword against his own. His teeth gritted in determination, he shoved Oland back.

Elling stepped forward to challenge Roeseph, only for Kyce to appear out of nowhere and shove her to the ground.

"Sorry, Elling," Kyce huffed as he twirled his sword at his side. "Nothing personal."

Sova coughed and rose to his feet, surprised to find Roeseph, Kyce, and Taige around him.

"Quite the beating you took there," Taige teased. "I thought we wouldn't get to you in time."

"I had them just where I wanted them," Sova lied through the pain.

Feran called from behind the mast. "You were going to die."

"All a part of my plan."

Saber landed before the Dire Wolves, the entire stage trembling beneath him. His snout and chest was red, soaked with Vaskan blood.

"Oh, now you decide to show up?" Sova sneered.

Saber growled in response and Sova growled right back.

"We're not done yet," Roeseph uttered and nodded to the two Hyde Howlers on the edge of the platform. "Sova, Taige, you and I will defend Feran and the Blesser. Kyce, you ride Saber into the battle and try to cut down as many Vaskans as you can. Even if we get Casavore free, it'll be all for nothing if our troops don't survive."

Kyce leaped onto Saber's back, his sword drawn and eager for blood.

"Why?" Sova griped, his shoulders hunching forward. "Why do we keep sending the soaring wolf away? Maybe it's just me, but I feel like he'd do a pretty good job of keeping us from getting killed."

Before Kyce could take off, Taige grabbed him by the wrist, keeping him grounded.

"Send those Lykos forsaken dog-kissers running for the hills," she ordered.

Kyce grinned, his jaw cocking to the side as he said, "Don't get yourself killed."

"Oh please, Love," she snickered, her sword rested against her shoulder. "You couldn't get rid of me if you tried."

Kyce pulled away and plunged his heel into Saber's side. Saber roared and catapulted into the sky.

"Dire Wolves," Roeseph roared, so Taige and Sova dropped into their battle stances. "Protect the Blesser at all costs. And by no means should any harm come to my father of Elling!"

"Easier said than done, Captain," Taige exhaled.

"They're in there," Roeseph assured as he stared into Elling's soulless eyes. "We just need to get them out..."

Giving a mighty roar, the Dire Wolves collided with Oland and Elling.

Roeseph and Sova took on Oland, while Taige challenged the Feral Shepherd. Casavore watched helplessly from the mast, flinching at every blade that edged too close to those fighting.

"They're losing, Feran," Casavore yelled back at his daughter. "You can help them. Leave me here!"

"I'm not leaving you," Feran shouted as she sliced frantically at the rope.

"It's no use fighting them! Only a mind melder can release Hyde Howlers from their curse. Take my medallion, Feran. Free them!"

"I'm almost there!" Feran lied. "I can do this!"

Oland hurtled his sword down at Roeseph and Sova, who caught his blade against their own. They fell to their knees under the brute strength of the Hyde Howler, the sword trembling closer and closer to their faces.

"Father!" Roeseph shouted up. "Father, it's me! Roeseph!"

"A little louder," Sova snapped. "Maybe he didn't hear you!"

Oland kicked Sova away, sending him rolling across the stage, and swung his blade down at Roeseph. Roeseph barreled behind Oland and chucked his foot into the back of his knee, so he fell.

"Are you ok, Sova?" Taige called as she and Elling went sword to sword.

Sova pinched his thumb and pointer finger together in an 'ok' motion before he lifted his head. Through the blur of swords and blood, he spotted the dire's dark armor passing through the battle.

There you are... Sova growled, his eyes dark with a predator's intent.

As if the dire could feel Sova's gaze piercing through her, she looked back at him. Sova couldn't see her face, but he knew she was smiling. The false dire turned away and marched toward the buildings around the plaza.

Sova leaped to his feet and shouted, "I see the dire!"

"Then go get him!" Roeseph ordered as he danced around his father's sword.

"What about you guys?"

Taige grunted as she caught Elling's staff against her sword.

"Don't worry about us!" she yelled. "We'll be fine. Go! Bring me back that tyrant's head!"

Sova looked to Feran. She gasped through a restrained sob, her hands and blade trembling as she tried to saw through the ropes keeping her father to the mast. Sova felt his heart plummet.

"Everything's going to be ok, Feran!" he called above the roar of battle.

Feran raised her teary eyes to meet the Royal Traitor.

"You'll see," Sova assured as he doubled back. "I promise. Everything's going to be ok!"

Sova leaped off the stage and into chaos, struggling through the blur of swords and steel after the dire, who flashed in and out of view like beams of light through a forest canopy.

You're not getting away from me. Sova promised. *Not this time.*

The dire looked over her shoulder to see Sova pursuing, and hurried to one of the alleyways. Sova at her heels, she fled up a rickety lattice and onto the rooftop.

She stood at the edge of the roof, staring down at the battle thrashing below like a violent river. Hoping to evade capture, she turned to hurry back from which she came, only to meet a fist.

As the dire fell to the shingles, her helmet flew off and clanked down the roof before it finally settled on the gutter.

Sova glared down at his victim, his shoulders rising and falling with fiery breath. A woman with copper skin and flowy white hair stared up at him, her perfect red lips speckled with blood and curled in a malicious smile.

"Hello, dear," Lore greeted. "Expecting someone else?"

"No," Sova hissed. "I've known who resides in the dire's armor for a couple days now."

"Ah," Lore nodded as she suckled the blood dripping from her lip. "So it was you who was in your father's chamber. I thought I smelled a traitor."

Sova held the edge of his sword to his mother's chin.

"I'm no traitor," he hissed. "*You're* the traitor."

"Oh? Is that so?" Lore chuckled. "I'd have to disagree with you there, Saulder."

Sova pressed his sword into the dip of his mother's chin, making her hiss through clenched teeth and lean further from the roof's edge.

"Don't call me that," he growled. "My name... is Sova."

"Still under the Blesser's trance, I see. Tell me, did the mind-melder not tell you of what truly became of the poor young prince of Vaska?"

"Casavore lied."

"Oh, come on, Saulder. You're smarter than that. You know Casavore is no liar."

Sova gulped. "I'm not him," he growled, his statement coming out as a plea. "I'm not him. I'm not."

"Who are you trying to convince? You or me? Because I've already made up my mind on the matter. After all, the smell of my son's burning flesh still lingers in the dire's chambers."

Sova's eyes started to blur with tears as his sword quivered.

"I mean, for a long time I thought it was Sova who killed you," Lore shrugged. "It wasn't until I came to Era that I realized what Casavore had done. You can cut your hair as short as you like, but a mother knows the face of her children."

"Silence!" Sova lowered his sword to his mother's throat. "I'm not your son. You're not my mother. You never were. And this kingdom isn't yours. Come sunset, Vaska will be free from your rule."

"Are you sure you want that, Saulder?" Lore challenged. "If you and your little band of misfits succeed in taking Vaska, they will want to see me dead."

"I don't have a problem with that."

"Yes, you do. If they realize it's me walking around in the dire's armor and not Saulder, they'll start asking questions. And I, of course, will have no choice but to tell them the truth."

"Then I'll just bring you to them as a corpse."

"It won't be enough. Even dead, the question of the dire's identity will remain. And the fact that you wear his scar on your shoulder might raise suspicions. Tell me, how long do you think it would take before your friends to turn on you?"

"Then I guess I'll have to make you unrecognizable," Sova threatened. His voice was dark, as if his very tongue had blackened. Clenching his teeth, he raised his sword to take the life of the tyrant.

"Yes, kill another one of your family," Lore taunted. "After all, it's not out of character for you, my dear Dire Saulder."

Sova froze, guilt melting over his enraged expression like a mask. Lore smirked, pleased with herself.

"Poor sweet Sova," she sighed. "He loved you so dearly. Wanted to be just like you. Walk like you. Talk like you... Everything that he was, it was because you were it first. Or, rather, what he thought you were. But you and I know better, right? We both know Dire Saulder is a merciless, soulless monster incapable of human emotion. Oh, but that was what made you so great. What made you so powerful."

Sova felt his knees begin to quake.

"I will admit. Sova did a pretty good job of holding onto Casavore's delusions, but he had to accept reality eventually, right? So he rose against you... and you took his life. I have to know, what did it look like? The look in your sweet-sweet baby brother's eyes as he stared up at his hero... What did he look like, as you took his life."

Sova panted through the panic.

His memories, his very life, were based around the delusion of Sova's past. As far as he was concerned, conscious wise, he was Sova; Prince of Vaska. It was confusing to mourn one's own self. But at the same time, he lived in the flesh of Dire Saulder. A monster who was heartless enough to take the life of his own brother.

A tear traced Sova's cheek. *What have I done?*

Her opponent distracted, Lore drew her sword and lashed it at Sova. He pulled back, barely escaping her blade. She slid down the roof shingles and grabbed her helmet, looking back at Sova with a malicious smirk.

"Lykos forsaken snake," Sova growled.

"Ah, well, Casavore did say that was my biggest flaw," Lore shrugged as she slid the dire's helmet over her head. "I can't help but taunt."

Determined to take the life of the other, Sova and Lore lunged.

ROESEPH ROLLED ACROSS the stage, the floorboards painting bruises up and down his skin. He laid at the edge, one leg hanging limply over the side.

Coughing, he looked up to see the merciless eyes of the Hyde Howler taking refuge in his father's body.

"Father," Roeseph rasped. "Father, it's me."

Taige stood on the other side of the stage, sword to sword with Elling.

"Hold on, Roeseph!" she called. "I'm coming."

Taige tried to barrel around the Feral Shepherd, only for her opponent's staff to sever each path she took.

"Would you stop doing that?" Taige screamed. The Hyde Howler swung her staff at the Viper's Heir, making her duck. "You were a lot less annoying before the Siren's Call."

Casavore pulled at his restraints, his teeth clenched in agony as the ropes twisted into his flesh.

"Feran!" he cried.

"I'm almost there!" Feran shouted.

Casavore's head lashed to the side, horrified to find the Blind Hound standing over Roeseph.

"Oland!" Casavore shouted. "Don't do this! You're a good man! Fight this! Please wake up! Wake up!"

"He can't hear you," Feran grunted. "As long as the trance is on him, he'll never wake up. Not even for his own kid."

Feran's words echoed in Casavore's head like a gong.

As long as the trance is on him, he'll never wake up. Not even for his own kid...

"That's it," Casavore whispered, his eyes widening. "That's how we win this."

As the Blesser sunk into his revelation, Oland raised his blade to slay Roeseph.

"Roeseph, no!" Feran shrieked.

Roeseph hooked his leg around Oland's knee and grabbed hold of his shirt. Pulling back, he flipped Oland's massive body over his head and threw him into the chaos beyond the stage.

Casavore exhaled with relief.

Roeseph stood and limped toward the edge of the platform, unable to spot his father in the blur of soldiers.

"I'm sorry, Captain," he huffed. Turning on his heel, Roeseph rushed across the platform to Taige's aid as she battled with Elling.

"How's everything going?" Roeseph called.

"Not good," Taige panted as Elling pushed her back by her sword. "I have to say, I wasn't expecting this level of skill from your sweet-little shepherdess."

"Oh, come on," Roeseph said smugly. "She can't be harder to beat than my father. I'll admit Elling is advancing quickly in her training. But she can't defeat her own mentor."

Elling twirled her staff at her side, sending a wind that smacked Roeseph and Taige across the face. The staff still spinning at incredible speeds, she held it over her head, at her sides, and in front, then stopped it sharply beside her. Roeseph and Taige stared at her, wide-eyed.

"I didn't teach her that," Roeseph admitted.

Taige nodded, "You're going to learn that you didn't teach her a lot of things."

WHILE ROESEPH AND TAIGE battled the Feral Shepherd, Sova fought with Lore on the rooftops.

Sova dove at his mother, only for her to effortlessly evaded his attack. He huffed out a heavy breath, his lungs ragged with exhaustion.

"Fight me, you coward," Sova sneered, sweat searing his face.

"You would fight your own mother?" Lore gasped. "What would Zastar have to say?"

"If my father wasn't under the Blesser's trance, he would've had you killed a long time ago."

Lore chuckled. "I have to say, Saulder, I missed your sense of humor. You became so stoic after Casavore's brat disappeared."

"Stop calling me that!" Sova shouted and rushed his mother. Just as Sova's blade was upon her, she swatted his sword out of his hand, and rammed her shoulder into his chest. He fell face down on the edge of the roof, one of his arms swinging over the battle below.

He turned onto his back to find the dire standing over him, the mist-covered sun perching her shoulder.

"I have to say, I'm disappointed, Saulder," she sighed. "All that time Zastar spent training you, and you can't even defeat your own mother. Don't be too hard on yourself. After all, I was raised in Seavale."

"How could you do this?" Sova growled. "How could you hurt all these people? How could you hurt your own family?"

"Ironic," Lore laughed. "I was going to ask you the same thing. You act like I'm this horrific beast, but you and I are no different. After all, I'm not the one who killed my brother in cold blood."

Sova swallowed hard as the sins of another scorched his soul.

"You're wrong," Sova trembled. "I'm not him. I'm not a monster."

"Keep telling yourself that, son. Personally, I don't care what you believe. It doesn't matter."

Lore pressed the tip of her blade to Sova's throat, making him shudder. It was cold. As if someone was pressing an icicle to his neck.

"I once promised myself that one day I wouldn't have to listen to either you or Prince Sova," Lore recited. "Today... is that day."

Before Lore could strike the final blow, a chilling roar swept through the plaza.

"Sova!" Kyce cried, making Sova and Lore look up to see the Eradite Exile flying toward them atop Saber. Without thinking, Sova rolled off the rooftop to the plaza below. Before he could splatter the ground, Kyce snatched him out of the air.

"Are you ok?" Kyce called against the thundering wind.

Sova nodded as they soared over the plaza. "We—We need to go back. I can finish this."

"We can't."

"No! I need to kill him. I need to kill him now!"

"We can't, Sova! The others, they're in trouble."

ROESEPH AND TAIGE CAME at Elling on both sides. She thwarted their every advance. Taige stumbled back, her raven hair falling over her eyes.

"I'm going to be honest, Elling," she grumbled. "You're really starting to get on my nerves."

"Don't hurt her, Taige!" Roeseph ordered. "She can't help what she's doing."

"Well, we're running out of options, Captain!"

While Roeseph and Taige tried and failed to pacify the Feral Shepherd, Feran continued to cut at the Blesser's ropes.

"Are we almost there?" Casavore called back at his daughter as he pushed against the restraints.

"Almost," Feran said.

Elling struck Taige's metal leg, causing a gear to jam and a metal bar to jut out the side. The Venom Tongue clutched her leg, gasping up at Elling as the Hyde Howler raised her staff to deliver a fatal blow. Roeseph leaped between them, catching Elling's weapon against his own as she brought it down.

"Elling," Roeseph shouted as he tried to jerk his sword free. "Elling, you need to wake up—"

Elling pulled back her staff, Roeseph's sword with it, and smacked him across the jaw. He spiraled across the stage, stopping just an inch short of the ledge.

"Roeseph!" Taige shouted as she struggled upright, only for her busted metal leg to give out beneath her. "Roeseph, run!"

Roeseph groaned and looked up to see Elling stand over him. Her gentle eyes which were once filled with warmth were now void of life, as if she were a dead woman walking. The very sight caused his eyes to fill with tears.

"Elling..." he began in a broken voice. "When you come out of this, people might tell you that you did something bad to me... But I want you to try and remember what I'm about to say. What happened to me wasn't your fault. I don't blame you. I'm not mad at you. I could never be mad at you, Elling... I love you. I'm sorry I couldn't help you."

Chapter Thirty: Reunited

The magic words known for breaking so many fairytale curses went over Elling's head like a passing bird. Without a speck of remorse in her eyes, she raised her staff to strike her captain and friend.

A hand grabbed her wrist and she lashed to the side. She froze, ensnared by the power of the gold medallion swaying gently before her eyes.

"*Elling, of the Mosharick Plains,*" Feran began as she wove her father's medallion. "*Feral Shepherd of the Dire Wolves, hear my command... Awake from your state. Remember your kindness taken from you by the Siren's Call by which your heart was caged. Become the good soul that you once bore. Awake from this curse and remember no more...*"

Elling's eyes fluttered closed as her knees giving out beneath her. She fell into Roeseph's arms.

"El—Elling?" he stammered, holding her close. "Elling, can you hear me?"

"She's ok," Feran assured, placing her father's medallion around her neck before she hurried to help Taige. "She'll come to any second now!" Feran laid Taige's arm across her shoulders, helping her to walk to the mast where Oland had previously been bound.

"You couldn't have done that earlier?" the pirate griped, leaning against the mast as she adjusted the cogs in her leg.

"I was busy," Feran shrugged and returned to her father.

"*I was busy,*" Taige mimicked in a nasally voice.

Roeseph clung to Elling, his eyes misty with worry. "Wake up," he said beneath a quivering breath. "Come on, Elling, why won't you wake up?"

Elling groaned, her lashes fluttering open to reveal warm, emerald-green eyes.

"Roeseph?" she croaked.

Roeseph hung his head as every bit of air he'd been too scared to breathe out fled from his lips. "Lykos, Elling. You scared me half to death."

"I'm sorry..." Elling whispered as she looked around the execution's platform. "How did I get here?"

"There was a Siren's Call."

Elling snapped upright, her eyes alive with fear.

"What? Did I—Did I hurt anyone? Is everyone ok?"

Roeseph hugged her tighter. "Everyone is fine," he assured and pulled away to examine her face. "You didn't hurt anyone. Feran was able to release you before anything could happen."

Elling swallowed hard. "I didn't hurt anyone?"

"No, Elling, you didn't."

A tear traced Elling's cheek. "Oh, thank Lykos," she gasped and collapsed against Roeseph's chest. "I didn't—I didn't hurt anyone... I didn't do it again..."

Roeseph hugged her close. "And you never will," he swore. "I promise. I'll never let that happen to you again."

Saber descended onto the executioner's stage, the planks groaning beneath his impressive weight. Kyce and Sova hopped down from his back and hurried to Roeseph's side.

Sova grimaced at their public embrace. "Yeesh, get a tavern."

Roeseph looked up. "Are you both ok?" he asked, helping Elling to her feet.

"Yeah," Kyce answered as an amused grin spread his lips. "Saber and I were able to chase off a good amount of Vaskans. But we had to cut our little escapade short to save Sova."

"I had everything under control," Sova griped.

"You were held at sword-point on the edge of a roof."

"It was strategic."

Taige hobbled up to meet the group, her metal leg bending awkwardly beneath her. "So you didn't kill the dire, Sova?"

Sova looked away. "No. No, I didn't."

Elling's eyes widened, shocked by the state of Taige's metal prosthetic. "Great Lykos, Taige, what happened to your leg?"

"A Hyde Howler chopped it off."

Kyce choked down a snort.

"The newer one," Elling growled, glaring daggers at the Viper's Heir.

"Oh, you hit me in the leg with your staff," Taige said. "Quite an arm you got there."

"I did what? Taige, I'm so sorry—"

"Ah, Don't worry about it. I'll get you back. When you least expect it."

"What?"

"What?"

Casavore cleared his throat, making the Dire Wolves look up to find the old Blesser still tied to the pillar.

"Excuse me," he said, dipping his head. "I don't mean to interrupt. But Feran has been trying to cut through these ropes for a while now. Would any of you be so kind as to give her a hand?"

"Oh. Yes, of course, Blesser Casavore," Roeseph said as he, Sova, and Elling hurried to assist the Blesser. Kyce stayed behind to help Taige, placing her arm over his strong shoulders as they walked.

"I'm going to be totally honest," Taige whispered in Kyce's ear. "I totally forgot he was here."

The Dire Wolves and Saber gathered around the mast with Feran. After wasting nearly an entire battle trying to break the ropes, the restrains finally gave way at the slash of a sword combined with the snap of a soaring wolf's jaws.

Casavore exhaled as the ropes fell from his chest, finally allowing his lungs to expand. He stumbled forward and looked himself up and down. There were no shackles to bind him. No bar cells to trap him. No guards to belittle him. He looked to the sky, mesmerized by the silver haze. He had wished the sky to be blue. But the sky was still the sky, and he was finally free. At long last, he was free.

"Papa?" came a soft voice.

Casavore turned to find his daughter behind him. She clutched her medallion, tears filling in her eyes. Had he not personally buried Fala, he would've mistaken Feran for her ghost. She was her mother's exact replica, all except for the shape of her eyes, which were his own.

Casavore whispered through a trembling smile. "Feran..."

Feran rushed her father and hugged him around his neck. She hung there for a long moment, her tears drenching his robe as quiet, sob-soaked hiccups jumped from her lips. Saber walked up to his master, his tail drooping low as he licked the salt from her cheeks.

Casavore rocked back and forth with Feran, cradling the back of her head in his callused hand.

"I can't believe it's you," he croaked. "I thought... For so long, I thought—" Casavore hugged her tighter. "My sweet girl. You're alive. By Lykos, you're alive."

Elling clung to Roeseph's arm as she watched the reunion. She hid her face against his sleeve, hiding the tears of joy and envy that slipped down her cheeks. Roeseph grabbed her hand holding onto him, keeping her close.

"It's alright," he whispered, his voice barely a sound.

Sova watched as Feran and the Blesser embraced, hating himself for the unease that stirred inside him.

Now that Casavore was free, it was only a matter of time until he told everyone the truth—only a matter of time before they all hated him.

Feran pulled away from her father, her face shining with tears and glee. "Come on," she said, taking his hand. "I want to introduce you to my friends."

Casavore chuckled fondly as Feran dragged him towards her fellow exiles.

Elling pulled away from Roeseph as they approached, quickly wiping the tears from her eyes.

"Papa," Feran began. "This is Roeseph. Our captain."

Casavore shook the young captain's hand as Roeseph stared at him in awe. All through his childhood, Oland had told him stories of the infamous Blesser of Vaska, and all the battles he'd won because of his power. Roeseph never dreamed he'd stand so close to him.

Roeseph placed his fist over his heart and bowed. "It's an honor to meet you, sire."

"The Last Soldier," Casavore smiled. "Long before Lykos was calling you that, I just knew you as Oland's boy. We were both very proud to hear of all you and my daughter have accomplished in exile. Surely, it was God's will that brought you together."

Sova scoffed under his breath. "Actually, it was a bunch of thugs, but whatever."

Casavore looked down at Elling, who straightened at his gaze.

"You must be Elling, the brave shepherdess," the Blesser greeted, his eyes beginning to fill with regret. "I am so truly sorry for all the pain my curses have caused you. If I could remove it, I would."

"I don't blame you, sire," Elling bowed. "It's the dire who I blame."

Feran stepped in front of her father, her brown eyes big and eager. "It's all going to be ok," she said. "Come the day we take back Vaska, we'll force Saulder to free her and all the Hyde Howlers of Lykos."

Casavore stole a worried glance at Sova. The prince looked away.

Just as the Hyde Howler curse could be controlled by the dire, it could also be lifted using a secret phrase known only by him. The only reason Lore was able to control Elling and Oland, was because as far as they were concerned, it was Saulder in the dire's armor, not her.

"I see," Casavore mumbled. "Well, I hope the day comes when you know that relief soon, m'lady."

"Thank you, sire," Elling nodded as Casavore and Feran made their way down the line.

"Papa, this is Kyce," Feran said as she led the Blesser to the infamous Eradite fighter.

"The Eradite Exile," Casavore chuckled and shook Kyce's hand. "It's an honor to meet Lykos' greatest warrior."

Kyce nodded. "Thank you, Blesser Casavore. It's an honor to meet another brother of Eradusk."

Casavore nodded and followed Feran to the next person.

"Papa," Feran began, "this is—"

"Taige of Seavale," Taige exclaimed and grabbed Casavore by the hand, shaking it vigorously. "Thief extraordinaire. Pleasure to meet you."

Casavore pulled away as an amused smirk spread beneath his beard.

"Seavale, did you say? May I ask, do you hail from a gang?"

Taige's eyes, once bright and gleeful, darkened with fear. Her father was the Viper, the infamous captain of the Venom Tongues. And even though she loved him dearly, she could not deny his atrocities; how he had struck down Dire Zastar and murdered the Mosharick maiden, Fala, in cold blood.

"I um..." Taige began.

Kyce stepped in front of the pirate, acting as a shield.

"She's a Venom Tongue, sire," he interrupted. "She is the daughter of the Viper and an apprentice under the Venom Tongue captain, Rayze. Furthermore, she is a Dire Wolf and one of the most capable soldiers I have ever come across in my time in Lykos. She is also under my protection as long as she walks this valley, as well as your daughter's, and every other noble fighter you see before you."

The Dire Wolves stared at Kyce, eyes wide, jaws dropped. Had that interaction taken place a couple days earlier, Kyce would've thrown Taige under the carriage without any regrets. But in that moment, he acted as her defender, as if he truly cared about her the way she cared for him. Only difference was, Taige's feelings were born of a trance. Kyce was foolish enough to endanger his heart for real.

Casavore raised his chin, provoking Taige to grab hold of Kyce's arm.

"A Venom Tongue, you say?"

Taige nodded, her cheek scraping up and down Kyce's arm she clung to.

"Well," Casavore continued, "you must truly be something for the Eradite Exile to attest to your skill." Casavore extended his hand. "It's a true honor to meet you, Taige of Seavale."

Taige stared at the Blesser, in complete and utter awe.

In Seavale, she was taught to keep her guard up, to read an opponent's eyes and recognize hate when she saw it. Even the most harmless-looking souls could turn feral in an instant. But in the Blesser's eyes, she saw only kindness.

Taige threw herself at the Blesser, making his cheeks implode when she embraced him tight.

"Pleasure is all mine, sire," she replied and drew back.

Casavore walked up to the last Dire Wolf.

"Your majesty," Casavore dipped his head to Sova. "Or should I be calling you the Royal Traitor?"

Saber loomed behind Casavore, his snout tensing in a snarl. It was peculiar how the only two people to know Sova's secret could feel so opposite about him.

On the plus side, Sova thought. *Only one of them can speak. Downside—that one wants to eat me.*

"I'm proud of you, son," Casavore whispered. "I always prayed you'd find your way back to each other... Back to Feran."

Sova's heart sunk through the planks. He knew full well that the Blesser wasn't talking about him and Feran, but rather she and Saulder. Sova drew in a deep breath, his heart twisting in his chest like a rag.

"Cas," he began. "Look, I um..."

As Sova struggled to find the words, Casavore's eyes rose to what lingered beyond the prince's shoulder. His eyes bursting wide, he shouted. "Look out!" and shoved Sova aside just as Oland hurtled by.

A sword hissed through the air as the Dire Wolves' lunged and grabbed Oland by the wrists. He dropped his sword to the floorboards, painted red by another's blood. Kyce kicked Oland in the back of the leg, forcing him to his knees, while Taige pinched and lifted his jaw to meet Feran's medallion.

"*Oland,*" the mind-melder began in a hostile tone, "*leader of the Blind Seers. Father of Roeseph. Hear my words and know your*—oh forsake Lykos. *Wake up!*"

Oland's shrunken pupil swelled, and his tense face seemed to sink. Then, all at once, he collapsed back into the arms of Kyce and Roeseph, his impeccable weight nearly crippling them to the floor. Feran placed the Blesser's medallion around her neck, her chest crashing with a heavy breath.

Roeseph exhaled in relief.

"Is everyone ok?" he called.

Sova looked back, his heart sinking like an anchor.

"Cas?" he whispered, his voice barely detectable against the wind.

Feran looked up at Sova, horrified by the shock in his eyes. She turned around fast. Casavore stood before her, his hand and robe stained red from a gaping wound in his abdomen. He looked up, his blue eyes that were once full of freedom now dim with defeat.

"Feran..." he whispered and collapsed to his knees.

"No!" Feran shrieked and leaped to her father's side. Sova caught Casavore as he fell and laid him gently on the floorboards.

Elling gasped behind her hand while Roeseph stared at the wounded Blesser, his eyes wide with horror.

"Papa," Feran sniveled as she stroked her father's face. "Papa, stay with me!"

Casavore began to tremble. His face paled rapidly to ashen, and his deep blue eyes dimmed like a candle's flame.

"Feran," Casavore whispered and cupped his bloodied hand against his daughter's cheek.

"I'm here, Papa," Feran sniffled as she trapped her father's hand against her face. "I'm here."

Saber whimpered as he herded the three, overwhelmed by the stench of blood and grief. Sova placed his hand over the gash in Casavore's gut, desperate to stop the bleeding.

A tear painted Casavore's cheek as he stared up at his daughter.

"You look just like your mother," he sniffled. "Just like her."

Feran's lips peeled back in a pained grimace, allowing salty tears to seep through her clenched teeth.

"You're going to be ok, Papa. We're going to get you out of here. That's what we came here to do. We're going to get you out!"

"It's ok, my child," Casavore sighed. "I miss my wife. And my prayers were never to escape death. It was to see you... one last time... And God was merciful."

"Don't say that," Feran sobbed. "I'm going to get you out of here. I am. I can't do this without you."

"I am not the beacon of this war. You. Your friends. You are the fire in this fight. The very blood of the rebellion. The ones who will free Vaska and all of Lykos from this tyranny."

"Papa—"

"It's ok, sweetheart," Casavore whispered and turned his head stiffly to look at Sova. "You majesty?... Your majesty, are you there?"

"I'm here, Cas," Sova whimpered, his voice breaking into shards.

Casavore took his hand, pulling it away from his wound, allowing it to weep.

"You—You..." Casavore gasped through blood-framed lips. "You need to release the dire."

Sova's blood ran cold.

"You need to release the dire," Casavore choked. "It's the only way to win the war. You need to release the dire. It's the only way—"

Casavore made a slight croaking noise. The light in his eyes faded, like a cloud over the sun. Sinking ever so slightly in Sova's arms, the Blesser drew his last breath.

"P—Papa?" Feran whispered and shook her father lightly by the shoulders. "Papa?"

All was silent, as even the sound of battle seemed to fade into distant thunder.

"Papa?" Feran called again, her voice escalating from a whisper to a wail. "Papa? Papa! Papa!"

Sova grabbed Feran and pulled her away from her father's corpse.

"No!" she shrieked, digger her nails into his arms. "No! Let me go! Let me go, you brainless—you stupid—! Papa! Papa!"

Sova hugged her tighter, ignoring the searing pain in his arm as waterfalls streamed down his twisted face.

"Papa!" Feran cried again, her voice depleting into a sob. "Papa, please...."

She collapsed into Sova's arms, wailing so fiercely the battle stilled at her cries.

Taige hugged Elling close as they both wept. Kyce looked away, his teeth gritted in agony, while Roeseph knelt beside his unconscious father.

Oland shifted and gave a low groan.

"Ah, my head," he mumbled, sitting up.

Roeseph looked down at him, his eyes glossy with tears.

"What happened?" Oland said groggily as he rubbed his temple. He looked down to find his sword laying a couple feet away, red all the way to the handle. "Roeseph, what happened?" he asked again, more urgently than before.

Roeseph swallowed. "There was a Siren's Call."

Feran's cries of anguish struck Oland like an arrow through the heart. He looked up to find Sova holding her in his arms a few feet away, both sobbing—Feran loudly, Sova silently.

"No..." Oland whispered and looked to the side to find a corpse laying in a pool of blood. "Casavore..." he whispered and began to crawl towards the Blesser.

"Father, no!" Roeseph shouted and grabbed the Blind Hound.

"Let go of me!" Oland shouted as he fought to get to the Blesser.

Sova looked up from comforting Feran, his eyes red with tears. Hugging her tighter, he shouted, "Keep him back!"

Kyce snapped from his daze and rushed to help Roeseph. They forced Oland his knees, stopping him in his pursuit.

"Casavore!" Oland shouted, his voice turning ragged. "Casavore, wake up!"

"Father, stop!" Roeseph begged. "Please."

"Wake up, you dire-worshipping dog!" Oland raged through the tears. "Wake up! Wake up, please!"

Realizing what had become of his dear friend, Oland collapsed. He screamed into the floorboards, so loudly those battling in the plaza looked up.

"I'm so sorry," Oland sobbed as Roeseph knelt by his side. "I'm so sorry, Casavore."

Sova looked up to the rooftops. The dire's shadow stood against the grey sky, glowering down at him.

Returning the dire's glare, Sova helped Feran to stand.

"We need to get out of here," he said, and looked to Roeseph. "Before we lose anyone else."

Roeseph rose, wiping the tears from his eyes.

"We'll get our forces out of Vaska. You and Feran take Saber."

Nodding, Sova ushed Feran to the soaring wolf, who didn't bother to growl this time, while Roeseph and the others led Oland off the platform.

Roeseph rose onto an overturned carriage and shouted at his army. "Retreat! Retreat!"

The Venom Tongues and Blind Seers fled after Roeseph and the Dire Wolves leading them into the streets, the Vaskan army hot on their heels.

Sova helped Feran onto Saber's back and then returned to collect Casavore.

Feran looked away, unable to watch as Sova slung her father's limp body across the soaring wolf's back like a slaughtered boar in a hunter's carriage. Sova pulled himself up behind Feran and pulled her back to his chest. She clung to him, her entire body trembling against his.

Saber burst into the sky and over the Vaskan wall, unaware of the monster watching them from the rooftops.

"Run while you can, little girl," Lore chuckled coldly. "You can't hide forever..."

Chapter Thirty-One: The Beacon's Vow

The sun wilted in the west, turning the rolling hills of the Mosharick Plains a somber golden. A gentle breeze flattened the grass, slithering all the way up a knoll to where two gravestones stood. Feran knelt before the graves, her hair falling over her sullen face like the branches of a willow, while Saber lay at her side.

In the distance, five shadows emerged over a neighboring hill, watching the mind melder as she mourned.

"She's still there," Kyce mumbled sadly.

"It's been three days," Taige whispered. "Do you think she's had anything to eat or drink?"

Elling drew in a deep breath. "It's doubtful," she answered. "No one has seen her in camp since we buried him."

Sova took an abrupt step forward, leading the Dire Wolves toward the Blesser's grave.

Feran knelt alone on the knoll, clutching two medallions in her lap. She sniffled, but no tears came. Saber's head snapped up from the dew coated grass, sensing someone was near. He snarled, his ears flat against his head. Feran didn't so much as look up.

Five shadows crept across her shoulders, shielding her from the cold breeze cascading over the hills.

"My mother always said she wanted to be buried in the Mosharick Plains," Feran said down at the two graves. "My father did right by her in bringing her here. The least I could do for him was let him rest with her."

Sova swallowed hard and knelt beside Feran, ignoring the warning snarls of her soaring wolf.

"Feran," he began softly. "It's time to go."

"Go? Go where?" Feran replied stoically.

"Back to camp. We need to start planning our next move."

"Our next move, huh?" Feran nodded, her tongue sliding along the inside of her cheek.

Sova looked down, his heart aching with guilt.

"I'm sorry, Feran," he mustered to say through a shaken voice. "I promised you I'd bring him back. I failed you."

"You didn't fail me. It wasn't your job to save my father. It was mine..."

Feran looked down at the two medallions in her hand, one charred and one smooth.

She grinned sadly. "You know he made this for me, right? When my father married my mother, he swore he'd train his children in the way of the mind melders. He always felt bad for the way mine turned out. He told my mother he didn't think it could ever compare to Eradusk's craftsmanship. I thought he was crazy. It's the most beautiful thing I'll ever own."

Feran squeezed her medallion tightly. Shutting her eyes, she kissed her medallion and buried it in the soil over her father's grave.

"So that you have something to remember me by," she said as she placed the Blesser's medallion over her head. "Just like I have something to remember you..."

She rose to her feet, Saber with her.

"I'll make this right, Papa," she promised.

Roeseph stepped forward, his head hanging in respect for the deceased. "Is there anything we can do, Feran?"

"Yeah," Feran nodded. "Take me back to camp. I have unfinished business with the Blind Hound."

Roeseph looked up with a start. Before he could ask her to elaborate, Feran spun around and started west. The Dire Wolves followed, leaving Sova alone to stare at the Blesser's grave.

Casavore, he said to himself. *I don't think I can do this alone.*

"Sova!" Kyce called, making Sova look over his shoulder. "You coming?"

Sova looked back to the grave. Running his hand over the stone, he turned, and ran after his comrades.

THE SUN KISSED THE horizon, turning the sky a burnt-red. A couple miles west of the gravesite, a humble camp lay in a shallow ditch, wedged between two hills. Nearly a thousand tents circled the remains of a mostly-dead bonfire, the timber scabbed with embers. Grief-stricken Venom Tongues and Blind Seers alike sat on logs or gathered around barrels of liquor, none able to speak or look the other in the eye.

Oland sat alone on a log before the fire, staring silently into the coals. Gauze wrapped his head and ears, making him partially deaf to the world around him. As long as he could help it, he'd never allow a Siren's Call to reach him again. Never again.

His face falling into his hands, he prayed, "God forgive me."

"They're back," cried one of the Venom Tongues as the Dire Wolves and Saber emerged over the hills and descended into camp.

Oland drew a nervous breath and rose to his feet..

Roeseph led the way, his Dire Wolves trailing close behind him as they approached the fire where Oland waited. Feran parted from the others and walked up to meet the Blind Hound, Saber at her side. Roeseph took a step after her, only for Elling to catch him by the arm and pull him back.

"Let her go," she said softly.

Roeseph looked rapidly from his father to Elling. "It wasn't his fault," he whispered. "He didn't want this—"

"She knows that," Elling said, hugging Roeseph's arm. "Just leave her be. She needs this."

Roeseph drew a reluctant breath as he and his comrades watched Feran stop before the Blind Hound. Oland bowed his head, his tears already flowing.

"Feran—" he whispered, unable to form a solid word.

He fell to his knees, forced to the earth under the weight of his guilt.

"Daughter of Lykos and Era," he sobbed. "I am so sorry. I am so sorry for what I've done. Your father was a good man. A great man. The finest I've ever come across. I am so sorry for the pain I've caused. I would sooner die than hurt Casavore. I am so—so..."

Feran was still, not so much as a tear shimmered in her eyes.

"Stand up, Captain," she ordered.

Oland rose hesitantly to his feet, his hazel eyes red from tears.

"I don't blame you, Oland," she said calmly. "And neither should you. What happened to Casavore... that was not your doing." Feran turned to face the crowd gathering around. "No one is to blame but Dire Saulder."

Sova tensed, his soul freezing inside him.

"A Hyde Howler is no more responsible than I am for the sword in my opponent's hand," Feran continued, slowly growing more passionate. "It was the dire who cursed our people. Not just the Hyde Howlers, but all of Lykos, with his tyranny. And he will continue to do so as long as there is breath in his lungs. But by God's will, our rebellion has caught fire, and we are burning brighter than any flame."

The crowd stirred ever so slightly as murmurs of agreement rose into the wind. Kyce stepped forward, his lip twitching up in a grin.

"Will you, the destined soldiers of this rebellion, allow this demon to ravage our nations?" Feran challenged.

The soldiers' murmuring grew louder, their spirits catching fire from the spark in Feran's voice.

"Or will you join us, and fight for the freedom of Lykos? Fight for the end of the Dire!"

The crowd burst into roars of agreement and held their swords to the sky. Taige leaped to Feran's side, her dark eyes alive with a lust for vengeance.

"Venom Tongues," she shouted. "Will you be the ones to take the life of Vaska's beast?"

The Venom Tongues bellowed in agreement.

Roeseph joined Feran and Taige.

"Blind Seers!" he thundered. "Are you the ones that will free Lykos from this curse?"

The Blind Seers roared against the Venom Tongues, their voices of rebellion merging into one unified cry. Kyce joined his companions, holding his sword high to the sky.

"You foolish heathens of Lykos," he insulted through a rabid smile. "It will be my sword that takes the life of that armored demon!"

The crowd thrashed and roared like the waves of a stormy sea, every one of them hungering for the opportunity to take the dire's life.

Elling smiled from ear to ear and ran at Roeseph. He swung her into his chest, holding her tightly as he and his comrades cheered.

Sova stood on the outskirts of the celebration, his silver eyes wide with terror.

The crowd grew silent as Feran stepped forward to address the army again.

"In his last words, the Blesser of Vaska told me that my friends and I are the beacons of this war. And as your beacons, we will light your path to Vaska... With his dying breath, my father told us the only way to win this war was to release the dire. And so... we will release him. Let us release him of his crown. Let us release him back to where he came from. Let us release him to Hell!"

The entire rebel army gave a great battle cry. They dispersed in all directions in search of a mead and a feast, already drunk on the spirit of war. The Dire Wolves huddled close, smiling at the idea that the dire's final day was coming soon.

Sova watched from afar, placing a trembling hand over the gauze that hid his scar.

"*Release the Dire,*" the Blesser's voice echoed in his head. "*You need to release the Dire. It's the only way to win the war. You need to release the dire. It's the only way...*"

Sova shivered, his blood turning to streams of ice in his veins.

You're wrong, Casavore, he thought as he watched his friends. *I can never release the Dire... They can never know...*

Chapter Thirty-Two: The Visit

While the rebel army rejoiced in the Mosharick Plains, the Vaskan palace was sick with quiet.

In the tallest tower, the previous dire, Zastar, laid in his bed, crippled by a battle long passed. His chamber door creaked open, and a dark shadow slipped across his bed.

An imposter in monstrous black armor strolled across the chamber. She removed her helmet, and sat it down on the dresser. Long, white locks spilled down her shoulders as she lifted her sea-blue eyes to the mirror.

"Did you sleep well, my dear?" Lore asked with a scarlet smile as she sat at Zastar's bedside.

The old dire remained silent.

Lore pouted and ran her finger down his chest.

"Poor baby. Sorry I haven't come to see you the last few nights. I've been busy. I have good news though. Our little boy finally learned the truth. Your Blesser told him everything. It's a pity. I would've loved to tell Saulder myself that he killed his baby brother. Can you imagine the look on his face when he heard what he did?"

Lore looked down at her husband. Though his state amused her, she wished he could show at least some aspects of emotion. It would've been entertaining to see him cry.

"I suppose I should be on my way. You need your rest," Lore said as she stood. "Oh, I thought you should know, your Blesser is dead. Has been for three days now."

Lore looked down at her husband, hoping he'd at least flinch at her confession. Still, he did nothing.

"You'd be pleased to know he was able to say goodbye to his daughter. But he died nonetheless," Lore smirked at the memory. "I used the Sirens Call to turn the Blind Hound into a Hyde Howler. Did you know he and Casavore were close? Of course, not as close as he was with you. But they loved one another like brothers nonetheless... Which was why it was all so tragic when Oland thrust his blade through the mind melder's stomach. I suppose it's also your fault, isn't it? Because you commanded your Blesser to make that Mosharick brute a Hyde Howler in the first place?"

Lore's head tipped back as she chuckled, her ivory hair spilling down her shoulders.

"Ah, so beautifully ironic. I better get going. I have a son to kill and a Blesser to acquire. Feran should make a marvelous replacement for Casavore, don't you think?"

Lore kissed Zastar on the forehead, leaving a crimson stain on his skin. "Goodnight, my sweet," she taunted. "Next time I see you, I'll have Saulder's heart in my hand and his bride in my other."

Lore slammed the door behind her.

A single tear snuck out between Zastar's lashes and fell down his cheek.

What comes next?...
The Blesser
And the Prodigal Prince

More of The Blesser...

1. The Blesser... And the Charred Medallion
2. The Blesser... And the Curse of Damascus
3. The Blesser... And the Prodigal Prince

MORE TO COME...